Between Blood and Desire

by Faye Larkspur

Table of Contents

For every reader who dares to love deeply, dream wildly, and
believe in the impossible.

Chapter One

Aayla stood at the heart of the dimly lit bridge, gripping the edge of the console as the spaceship shuddered violently beneath her. The relentless barrage of enemy fire echoed through the vessel, drowning out the wailing alarms that screamed like death knells. The ship's shields were failing—she could feel it in every tremor.

Panic clawed at her throat, threatening to shatter her resolve, but she refused to let it show. Not here. Not now.

Her gaze darted to Talyn. He worked frantically beside her, his vibrant forest-green wings rustling with tension. The burst of golden hues at the base shimmered and gradually faded along the length of his wings, catching the dim light as if crushed diamonds had been sprinkled across them, a sharp contrast to the storm of determination and fear etched into his face. His every movement was precise and deliberate as he wrestled with the controls. Even in this chaos, Aayla couldn't help but admire him. Talyn was a fighter, a protector, and a force of nature.

And the man she secretly loved.

Guilt coiled in her stomach like a living thing, sharp and unrelenting. Her reckless decision led them into this deadly trap, and now Talyn might pay the ultimate price. The thought of losing him was a dagger to her heart, the pain nearly unbearable. But her own survival carried a different weight, one just as crushing. If she fell here, her people would lose a

Unix—the rarest and most revered among them. The weight of that loss loomed like a shadow over her, pressing against her shoulders with unbearable force.

She'd been raised with the knowledge that her bloodline was both a gift and a burden. It wasn't just a legacy, it was a destiny. One that demanded everything of her. Every decision she made carried the power to ripple through her people's lives, shaping futures yet unseen. Now, standing at the precipice of disaster, the crushing weight of that responsibility felt heavier than ever before.

"Shields are barely holding!" she shouted over the chaos, her voice strained with urgency. "We can't take much more of this."

Talyn smirked, a mischievous glint flashing through the storm of fear in his eyes. "Relax. We've got at least... five more minutes before the ship implodes."

Despite herself, Aayla's lips twitched upward. "Fantastic. I don't know why I was worried."

Another blast rocked the bridge, sparks raining down around them. "Talyn, this isn't sustainable! We need a plan."

"I have one!" he called back, punching a sequence into the control panel.

"Oh, really," she said, raising a brow. "Should I be worried?"

Talyn glanced at her with a lopsided grin. "I've got moves you haven't even seen yet."

"Is that a threat or a promise?" she teased, smirking despite the situation.

"Depends," he said, glancing at her sideways. "Are you impressed yet?"

Aayla rolled her eyes, though the hint of humour in his voice lightened the crushing weight in her chest. But her gaze lingered as he worked, and she saw the deep worry etched into Talyn's devastatingly handsome face, his wings pressed tightly against his back. She often admired his wings, longing to reach out and caress their exquisite form.

Talyn's light brown hair gleamed under the console's flickering lights, soft and tousled from exertion. His strong, sculpted arms moved with precision as he typed furiously, sending out a distress signal they both knew wouldn't be answered. The last plasma blast had torn through the ship's shield, destroying the comms port and one of the engines. A hull breach of that magnitude was catastrophic.

Yet, despite the severity of the situation, Talyn still fought on. For her.

As her Guardian, her dedicated bodyguard, his sworn duty was to protect her, even at the cost of his own life. And as his Charge, she was expected to accept that without question. But she couldn't. She wouldn't. The very thought of it ignited a fierce resolve within her. No matter the danger, she refused to stand by and let Talyn sacrifice himself for her. If it came to it, she would risk everything to protect him, even if it meant putting her own life on the line.

"Talyn..." she said, her voice barely audible over the alarms blaring around them. "I'm sorry."

Talyn shot her a quick grin, the corner of his lips tilting upward with practised ease. "Sorry? With you, Aayla, it's certainly never boring. If we make it out of this, I'll start charging for these thrill rides."

Aayla couldn't stop the soft laugh that escaped her, even as the chaos around them raged. His humour, as maddening as it was endearing, always managed to find her.

His deep green eyes flicked to hers for a brief moment, holding her gaze with a reassurance so steady it made her chest ache. Then he turned back to the controls, hands flying over the console. She watched him, savouring every detail as if she were etching his image into her mind for eternity. The faint gold accents in his wings, the way his emerald top clung to his broad shoulders, and the sharp lines of his jaw as he worked. She felt an urgent need to remember this moment as if it might be her last opportunity.

He wore the signature warrior attire of the Aldredth males, a soft, lightweight long-sleeve top and fitted pants. The attire was designed for functionality and style, allowing him to move with fluidity and precision in battle. The sleek material hugged his muscular frame, accentuating his powerful build in a way that was both striking and undeniably attractive. Though the design was standard for all Aldredth warriors, Talyn's choice of emerald green made him stand out effortlessly, its rich hue enhancing his commanding presence and undeniable allure. Aayla couldn't help but admire how the colour seemed to amplify his strength, drawing her gaze with every movement.

In contrast, Aayla wore a long-sleeved top and a lightweight, short skirt, which was a standard design for Aldredth females. She often chose pale violet hues, drawn to their softness and the calm they evoked. The clothing contoured across her body but was soft and flexible enough to ensure unimpeded movement. It was a far cry from the ornate, jewel-encrusted garments of their past, reflecting the Aldredth's new role as peacemakers throughout the universe. Over time, their attire had become more lightweight and battle-appropriate, crafted from a fabric interlaced with Aldredth minerals. Nearly indestructible, the fabric could be effortlessly rewoven if torn, restoring its original strength and ensuring the wearer remained agile in any situation.

Aayla's fingers absentmindedly traced the gold-embroidered Aldredth crest over her heart, a symbol of her lineage. Each crest featured an animal indigenous to their home world, representing one of the six Aldredth bloodlines, each imbued with unique magical abilities. Her name was stitched beneath it, but beside it lay an empty space—a void where her mate's name would eventually be sewn. The absence of that name ached deep within her, an unbearable emptiness that threatened to engulf her.

As a member of the Unix bloodline, Aayla bore the rare ability to heal. It was an ability that made her both treasured and targeted. Talyn, belonging to the Vajjer bloodline, possessed extraordinary fighting skills, the strongest of all the bloodlines. The other bloodlines each had their unique powers. The Vorax bloodline, who were markedly gifted in their control over the elements, the Aurra bloodline, who were especially gifted with the power of second sight and premonition, the Emba bloodline, who were the weakest and gentlest of all the Aldredth but were gifted scientists and medics, and the Lazuil bloodline, who were of the royal blood. The Lazuil governed the Aldredth and made all significant decisions, except when a Unix was present. With their rare and unrivalled power, the Unix could cast a decisive vote that overruled even the Lazuil. However, with so few Unix in existence, the Lazuils ruled in their absence, their authority nearly absolute in the absence of the elusive bloodline.

Unix were exceedingly rare because their bloodline emerged at random rather than being hereditary like the others. With only eight Unix's existing in the entire universe, they were the most treasured of the Aldredth and, consequently, the highest-value target.

Aayla leaned closer to the viewport. "Earth? Are you taking us to a Class 2A planet? Are you insane?"

"Possibly," Talyn admitted. "But this ship wasn't designed for battle, and I'd rather deal with humans than Vhurls."

She exhaled hard. "This is ridiculous. Even for you."

"Ridiculous is my specialty," he replied, flashing a lopsided grin that didn't quite reach his eyes.

Aayla gazed out the viewport at Earth, catching her reflection in the glass. Light golden-brown hair framed her small face, and her azure blue eyes flickered with worry. Her pure white wings, tipped with gold, shimmered even in the absence of light. Her wings were a pristine white, each feather soft and immaculate. A delicate trim of gold glistened along the edges, catching the light with a subtle sparkle. Yet, as she stared at her reflection, all she saw was the sadness etched into her features, and she felt the weight of their grim reality, that the odds of survival dwindled with each passing moment.

Lurking beneath that sadness was a soul-crushing fear that she could lose Talyn forever. Someone she loved with every fibre of her being, as if he were woven into the very essence of her soul. They were forbidden feelings that Aayla would never speak of, for it would result in the death of Talyn. She pushed those feelings deep down, focusing instead on the task at hand—surviving the fight raging outside and the turmoil within her.

Talyn, ever the fighter, worked relentlessly to regain control of the ship despite the overwhelming damage, his brow furrowed in concentration.

"The ship is lost," Aayla said, her voice cutting through the alarms and chaos. "Commence emergency landing procedures."

Talyn's jaw tightened, and he shot her a troubled glance, his hands never leaving the controls. "I've lost almost total control of direction, so I don't have much choice on where we land."

Aayla took a deep breath, pushing the flicker of fear down. "Then we improvise." She steadied herself, meeting his eyes. "You've pulled off worse miracles, Talyn. You can do it again."

He let out a dry chuckle, shaking his head. "If by 'worse,' you mean near-suicidal manoeuvres, sure. This might top the list, though."

She flashed him a brief grin. "Good thing I like a challenge."

Aayla turned back to the window, eyes drawn again to the planet below. Earth was classified as a Class 2A hostile planet. It appeared as a world of stark contradictions, where beauty and destruction intertwine in an intricate dance. She had been briefed on Earth as a child, as all Aldredth were, but since it wasn't a planet they had made contact with, the discussion had only briefly covered the basics of the planet. Earth contained breathtaking landscapes and vibrant ecosystems, with lush forests and pristine waters that teem with life and biodiversity. She was also aware of humans' devastating impact on their environment through deforestation, pollution, and habitat destruction. The once-thriving ecosystems were now threatened by the relentless march of industrialisation and urbanisation, leaving behind a trail of environmental degradation and loss.

As a child, she had learned of the profound disparities of wealth and power on Earth, the injustices faced by marginalised communities, and the pervasive influence of greed and exploitation. Earth's Class 2 hostile rating, the second-highest danger level, reflected its significant threat, primarily stemming from the capacity for human violence. War, oppression, and discrimination plague many parts of the planet, leaving behind a trail of suffering and devastation. Despite its inherent beauty, Earth's harsh realities were impossible to ignore. When she studied Earth as a child, she was filled with sadness and concern for the planet and its inhabitants, recognising the urgent need for change and collective action to heal the planet's wounds and create a more equitable and sustainable future.

The Class A rating denoted that Earth had never been contacted by an outside civilisation. Due to its high hostile rating, it was deemed too dangerous to approach. Only if the rating dropped to Class 3 would the Aldredth consider making first contact. The last thing they needed was another hostile planet spreading pain and suffering across the galaxy, so they used their power and went to great lengths to keep Earth hidden from other civilisations.

To make contact with Earth while its hostile rating was so high was to invite danger. And yet, here they were.

"Get ready to land," Talyn called over the noise of the alarms.

"Land? You mean crash?"

"Semantics," Talyn shot back with a grin, gripping the controls tightly as the ship hurtled into Earth's atmosphere.

As the ship descended rapidly, they had no time to learn Earth's languages or customs. Instead, they quickly reviewed essential information including weapons capabilities.

A loud boom rocked the ship as a proton blast from the pursuing Vhurl vessel struck the damaged rear of their ship. Aayla was thrown forward, but Talyn reacted instantly, darting forward to catch her in his arms just before she hit the floor.

"Are you okay?" Talyn asked as his eyes searched her face and body for any signs of injury.

A warm blush spread across her cheeks. "Yes," she nodded, her gaze lowering in embarrassment, yet she savoured the feel of Talyn's arms around her, pressed against the sensitive underside of her wings. "But we need to land before our ship is torn apart."

Talyn held her a moment longer than necessary, but as Aayla shifted in his arms to meet his gaze, he looked away and released her, returning to the console.

She watched out the window as their ship descended rapidly through the thick clouds, swerving wildly through the sky to avoid more hits. Buildings grew from the ground, and a glance at her Lumina, a handheld communicator, told her they were approaching a highly populated city called New York.

It was just her luck that she had to land in a heavily populated area.

As they neared the ground, she could make out the humans below them. They covered the ground, and Aayla was monetarily taken aback by the sheer number of them. Most of the humans were staring up into the sky at the ship, or maybe they were staring at the flames and black smoke trailing behind the ship.

Aayla spotted a large patch of grass off to the side. "Talyn, aim for the grass to your right if you can."

"On it," he responded, adjusting the coordinates. The ship turned sharply, and Aayla swayed on her feet, throwing her hands out to regain balance.

"Hold onto me. This will be a rough landing," Talyn warned, enveloping her in his arms and wrapping his wings tightly around them.

Talyn drew energy from within himself and created a shield around them. It was a type of forcefield created out of his life essence. It could withstand almost any attack but was only as strong as Talyn himself. If he were exhausted from battle, the shield would falter, barely able to stop a blade. Any attacks on the shield would also act to weaken Talyn and drain his energy, so a shield was a last-resort option.

The ship slammed into the ground hard, but they remained protected within Talyn's shield. Alarms blared around them, and Aayla glanced up at Talyn, concerned for his safety. Her thoughts scattered when she noticed their faces were mere centimetres apart. She could feel his warm breath against her skin, the press of his hard body against her own, and his strong arms enveloping her in a tight embrace as he wrapped his wings tighter around her. Talyn's lips parted slightly as he breathed deeply, his eyes lost in her gaze.

The building smoke made Aayla blink, and Talyn shook his head as if to clear his thoughts before he folded his wings away and grabbed her arm, pulling her up to her feet.

"We need to move," Talyn shouted above the noise. "Stay behind me. The humans might react unpredictably. Their fear could make them even more dangerous than the Vhurls."

First contact with a new race was typically a meticulously planned event to minimise stress on the inhabitants and ensure the safety of the Aldredth. Approaching a Class 2 hostile planet without any preparation was unprecedented and perilous. The planet's inhabitants had no forewarning of their arrival, and Aayla and Talyn had no real time to learn about the planet. Aayla almost laughed at the insanity of the situation they found themselves in. She was accustomed to attracting trouble, but this was a whole new level.

They quickly checked that their swords were safely sheathed on their backs, the familiar weight of their weapons a comforting presence before moving through the smoke-filled cabin. Aldredth swords were typically sheathed on their backs, or sometimes on their hips, and often concealed with a layer of glamour to hide their presence. The sword was not only deadly sharp, but it also acted as an amplifier for their magic. Aldredth wielded the power to control natural forces, enabling them to move objects with their minds and influence the elements. They could also communicate telepathically with other Aldredth and read the thoughts of different species. While most telepathic conversations required eye contact, mates and a few exceptionally powerful Aldredth could project their thoughts over long distances, though it demanded significant energy.

Talyn pried the damaged ship doors open, and they flew down onto the soft grass. He positioned himself in front of her, shielding her from danger as he had been born and raised to do. She turned and saw the undamaged sections of their ship shimmering like a smooth mirror on the grass. Beyond it, the Vhurl ship was closing fast. It was the polar opposite of the Aldredth ship. The Vhurl vessel, dark and colossal, radiated an aura of violence and terror.

Talyn grasped Aayla's hand and urged her forward. "Hurry, this way."

With a single powerful beat of their wings, they shot into the air and flew towards a cluster of trees on a small hill. They made it just in time to see the Vhurl ship deliver a final blow to the Aldredth ship. The force of the explosion whipped Aayla's hair across her face, and Talyn shielded her with his body, wings wrapping them as the ground rocked under their feet. Glass windows lining the buildings around them had shattered, and car alarms wailed.

As Aayla turned to look back at the wreckage of their ship, she saw only a smouldering ruin in a blackened crater. The Vhurl ship landed beside it with a slow, ominous thud. They knew they had Aayla trapped on this planet that didn't exist on their maps.

She turned and watched the humans, their mouths hanging open in surprise. Some fled in panic, others approached for a closer look, and a few stood frozen in shock. Their eyes stared at Aayla and Talyn in surprised awe, but as the Vhurls emerged, terror quickly overtook the awe, and most of those who had been stationary fled in haste. Talyn stepped protectively in front of Aayla, shielding her with his body, his stance unwavering.

The few remaining humans stared at the Vhurls, their faces etched with a mixture of dread and disbelief. Drawing a deep, steadying breath, she braced herself for what would come. But as she turned, her breath caught in her throat.

The sight before her was overwhelming. A vast, formidable enemy army stretched endlessly across in front of them. Among them, one figure in the distance caught her attention, drawing her gaze with an intensity she couldn't ignore.

She swallowed hard, her voice barely above a whisper, "Is that... Xiaas?"

CHAPTER TWO

Talyn's breath left him in a rush as he watched two entire battalions take their positions on the grass before them. He immediately recognised their leader, Xiaas, from Aldredth reports. He was a known, ruthless, and cunning warrior. Behind Xiaas, rows of Vhurls loomed like living mountains. Their matte black, stone-like skin exuded an aura of impenetrable strength, and they wielded enormous steel blades as thick as their massive forearms. Despite their colossal size, the Vhurls moved with surprising agility, their brute strength making them formidable adversaries in close combat.

In stark contrast, Aldredth bore an uncanny resemblance to winged humans. Male Aldredth possessed powerful, muscular builds and stood roughly as tall as the average tall human, exuding strength and confidence. In contrast, female Aldredth were gracefully slender, and their statuesque forms were slightly shorter than those of their male counterparts, embodying elegance and poise. Their perfectly proportioned faces, flawless symmetry, and innate beauty would have struck any human as breathtaking.

Talyn glanced over his shoulder, his wings pressed tightly against his back, meeting Aayla's worried gaze. The sight of her anxious expression made his chest ache. As her Guardian, his sworn duty was to protect her at all costs. Yet, his feelings for her had long since crossed the line of duty.

He harboured a deep, forbidden love, a fact that gnawed at his soul. The shame of it burned deep, for he coveted something that could never be his. Aldredth bonded only once in a lifetime, so even entertaining such thoughts dishonoured Aayla, her future, and the Lazuil she was destined to mate.

Aldredth believe they are born incomplete, as if only half of a person. But when they meet their true mate, it's as though they've found the missing part of their soul. In that moment, they feel whole and complete. Their bond is so powerful that their life forces entwine, creating an unbreakable connection. If one of them dies, the other cannot survive without them, their body refusing to go on. However, Talyn thought it was the grief that truly shattered an Aldredth. The agonising pain of losing the other half of your soul, the feeling that your very essence was torn apart. Aldredth feel their mate's pain as if it were their own, an unrelenting ache that consumes them. They cannot bear to live without their mate, and without the will to live, they fade away, drawn to their mate in the next life, where their souls are forever reunited.

An Aldredth knew instantly when they met their mate, the bond forming the moment their eyes met. The connection was immediate, often sparked by intimacy or powerful emotional moments. As Aldredth could not identify their mate through pictures or videos, from childhood they journeyed across various settlements, meeting other Aldredth of similar age who might be their potential match. This ritual was known as the Connexion or First Introduction. Finding one's mate was the most sacred and anticipated event in an Aldredth's life. It was the discovery of their soul's counterpart. Their reason for being. The celebrations that followed lasted for days, filled with joy and elation. It was a time of overwhelming happiness as the Aldredth embraced the unbreakable bond that would define their very existence.

As Aayla's Guardian, Talyn's sole purpose was to protect her and keep her safe until she found her Lazuil mate. Unix, like Aayla, could only bond with Lazuils. A Vajjer like Talyn was forbidden even to think of a Unix in such a way. Worse, as her Guardian, he wasn't allowed to feel anything beyond duty and respect for his Charge.

Yet no rule, no vow, no logic could stop the way his heart raced when she was near.

Nor could it stop the shiver that raced across his skin at her touch, the hitch in his breath when she smiled, or the way he drowned in the endless depths of her eyes. There were desires—deep, consuming—that stirred within him, longing to feel the warmth of her skin against his just one more time.

Aayla glanced at him, and he lost himself in her stunning crystal blue eyes that were as pure and luminous as a glacial lake beneath a clear sky. Their radiance was so intense that they seemed to shimmer like finely cut gemstones, capturing the light in a way that made them gleam with an almost ethereal brilliance, making Talyn's heart skip a beat. He dragged his eyes away from her, forcing himself to focus on the enemy.

Xiaas pushed his way through his battalion, shoving aside anyone too slow to move. When he reached the centre of the clearing, a predatory grin spread across his face, revealing rows of razor-sharp teeth.

A wave of red-hot fury surged through Talyn. He ground his teeth and tightened his grip on his sword, resisting the urge to break Xiaas's jaw.

"Surrender," Xiaas roared, his voice dripping with mockery, "and I promise not to torture you too badly. Maybe."

Talyn's rage flared at the veiled threat, especially at the idea of anyone laying a finger on Aayla. He clenched his sword tighter in his hand and planted himself firmly in front of

Aayla, shielding her with his body. Behind him, Aayla leaned slightly to the side, her piercing gaze locking onto Xiaas.

"Leave this planet immediately," she countered, her voice calm but laced with authority, "and I won't kill every single one of you."

Xiaas let out a harsh laugh, echoed by the rumbling chuckles of the Vhurls behind him. The soldiers didn't dare speak without permission. Their every move was governed by a brutal regime.

"One way or another," Xiaas said, his tone dropping into a dangerous growl, "you're leaving this planet. Willingly with me or in pieces. Choose quickly because I'm fast losing my patience."

Talyn growled low in his chest, a sound of pure defiance, but Aayla's hand lightly touched his arm, steadying him. That simple gesture ignited a storm within him, a potent mix of resolve and anguish. The impossible situation they faced was a knife to his heart.

"What do you want with me?" Aayla called out calmly.

Talyn had a sickening feeling that he already knew the answer, but it couldn't hurt to confirm it. The Vhurls were at least honest. Mostly.

"A Unix," Xiaas drawled, dragging out the word as if savouring it, "is a rare prize. The money you'll fetch is too good to pass up, especially if you're foolish enough to travel unprotected."

Talyn clenched his jaw, his rage palpable. He warned Aayla that this trip was too dangerous, but her stubborn determination won. Their small craft, meant only for short-distance journeys between allied planets, had been diverted when word came of an injured Aldredth in a distant colony.

Returning to a planet with a sizable Aldredth fleet would have taken too long, so Aayla persuaded Talyn to divert their course immediately. It was pure chance that they happened to pass the Vhurl ship on their way.

Soft movement behind his back told Talyn that Aayla was adjusting her stance, ready to fight. As much as Talyn wanted to look upon her, to drink in the sight of her, he dared not to take his eyes on the Vhurl in front of him.

"You know the rules," Aayla yelled, anger seeping into her words. "Harm us, and you'll be hunted down and executed."

Xiaas laughed again, a cold, dismissive sound. "I care nothing for your rules. Besides, that would require your people to catch us first. And no one would dare harm us while we hold you hostage."

The urge became too strong, and Tayln dared a glance behind him. Her delicate white wings, tipped with shimmering gold, caught the bright light. Her face was set with determination, but he could see the shadow of worry in her eyes. She was trying not to show it, but Talyn knew her too well. That tiny flicker of vulnerability made his resolve even stronger.

Aayla drew in a steadying breath. "And what of Tayln? What are your plans for him?"

"Your Guardian?" Xiaas mused, seeming genuinely surprised. "He's dead. It's a shame to kill such a valuable commodity, but we can't have him trying to rescue you, now, can we?"

Talyn let out a low, menacing growl. His teeth bared in a display of raw defiance. His stance shifted subtly, his body lowering into a fighting stance. He could feel Aayla's gaze on him, steady and intense, but before he could utter a word, her voice rang out, sharp and unwavering.

"What if I offer you a deal?" Aayla proposed loudly. "I'll go willingly, but only if you leave Talyn alive and unharmed."

"No!" both Talyn and Xiaas roared in unison.

Talyn whipped his head toward Aayla, his eyes locking with hers. His expression made it clear that he would fight to his last breath before allowing her to surrender.

Xiaas sneered in disgust. "Do you take me for a fool? There is no deal you can make where I leave him alive."

I'm so sorry, Aayla whispered telepathically in Talyn's mind, the regret in her tone slicing through him. He knew that this conversation had reached a close.

Talyn tensed, ready for the inevitable clash.

"Well then," Aayla said, her tone cold and resolute, "it's time to dance."

With swords drawn, they launched themselves at the Vhurls, their movements a blur of speed and precision. Their agility gave them an initial advantage, darting and weaving to deny the Vhurls any chance to coordinate their attacks. To the human eye, they were streaks of motion, too fast to follow, their blades flashing like lightning as the battle began.

The first strike was swift and brutal, a Vhurl lunging forward with a thunderous roar. Talyn met the onslaught head-on, his sword weaving through the air with calculated precision. With a deft twist of his wrist, he parried the blow, the clash of metal ringing out.

Another Vhurl lunged at him, blade flashing toward his chest. Without hesitation, he twisted his body and drove his sword forward with lightning speed, piercing its side. The

Vhurl staggered, eyes wide with shock, before collapsing to the ground in a heap.

Around him, the battle raged with relentless fury. Another assailant charged, swinging a heavy blade, but Talyn sidestepped with fluid grace, slashing a clean arc across its forearm. The cry of pain was swallowed by the chaos as Talyn moved onward, every step and strike seamless. His sword flashed left, then right, deflecting blows and cutting down Vhurls before they could regroup.

Beside him, Aayla moved across the grass with deadly grace, her movements a fluid symphony of lethal strikes and calculated evasions. A Vhurl tried to catch her off guard, swinging wildly, but Aayla ducked low, then spun, driving her sword through its back with a swift, merciless strike.

The Vhurls confidence cracked as their numbers thinned, chaos creeping into their ranks.

Talyn leapt back, unfurling his wings with a powerful thrust that lifted him from the fray. The wind roared past him, carrying the exhilarating freedom only flight could bring. Aayla rose up beside him, her movements graceful, her wingtips so close they nearly brushed his.

Talyn folded his wings tightly against his sides and plunged downward like a streak of lightning. His sword flashed before the Vhurls could even react, the sharp sound of steel cutting through flesh ringing in his ears as another Vhurl collapsed beneath his strike. In an instant, he spread his wings wide, soaring upward as the rush of wind whipped past him, narrowly evading a desperate swing aimed at his position. Beside him, Aayla moved with flawless precision, their movements perfectly synchronised.

The Vhurls quickly adapted to their aerial attacks, passing around several plasma blasters, crude but effective weapons that fired searing bolts of energy. A direct hit to an Aldredth's body would leave a painful burn, but a strike to their wings could prove catastrophic, shredding the delicate feathers and rendering them unable to fly.

For an Aldredth, wings were not merely tools of flight but essential for balance and precision in combat. Losing them would mean losing the fight. Worse still, the wings were the only part of an Aldredth's body that even a Unix could not heal. Aldredth protected their wings fiercely, knowing they were their strength and greatest vulnerability.

Talyn's sharp eyes caught the flash of a plasma blaster aimed at Aayla, but he was too far to reach her in time.

"Aayla, on your left!" he shouted, panic lacing his voice.

A bolt whipped past his ear at the same moment, forcing him to bank hard to avoid it. Aayla twisted gracefully in midair, narrowly dodging two blasts aimed at her. Her white and gold wings glistened in the sunlight, and the force of the wind pressed her clothes against her body, highlighting her delicate figure and full, rounded breasts. Tayln's eyes ran over the length of her, and it made him ache in a way he quickly shut down and pushed to the back of his mind.

With a powerful beat of his wings, Talyn flew up beside her. *That was too close. It's time to take this fight to the ground*, he said telepathically, his voice laced with urgency. Aayla nodded in silent agreement.

Suddenly, a plasma blast he hadn't seen streaked toward him, aimed directly at his wings.

CHAPTER THREE

Aayla watched as Tayln's shoulder muscles rippled beneath his clothes, flexing and contracting with every powerful beat of his wings as he expertly dodged a plasma blast that came dangerously close to striking him.

When they landed side by side, their wingtips were mere inches apart, igniting a deep desire. She longed to feel the soft caress of his wings against hers, to have the tenderness of his fingers trace the sensitive curve at the base of her neck where her wings emerged.

Her breath hitched as she admired the breathtaking array of green and gold hues on Talyn's wings. Each feather was a work of art. The greens shifted from deep emerald to bright jade, seamlessly blending with shimmering gold accents that caught the light with every movement. The colours seemed to dance with life. Yet, she knew that touching another Aldredth's wings was forbidden unless you were bonded as mates. Aldredth wings were extremely sensitive, and any touch felt sensual. The sensation of wings meeting was an intimate caress, a dance of feathers that spoke a shared language of trust and intimacy.

Aayla's heart skipped a beat at the thought, but she quickly buried the feeling because she would never feel Talyn's touch except in my deepest, darkest, forbidden dreams.

A large group of Vhurls surged towards them, spreading out to encircle and attack from every angle. When it was time to strike, Aayla folded her wings tight against her back, minimising resistance as she lunged forward, weapon in hand.

She sidestepped a vicious strike, countering with a precise, fluid thrust. Spinning on her heel, her sharp gaze caught a Vhurl breaking from the fray, sprinting toward a large cluster of humans gathered in the shadow of a nearby building.

The humans stood frozen, their wide eyes betraying their shock as they watched the battle unfold. Though slower than an Aldredth, the Vhurl moved lightning fast—far too fast for a human to escape. The humans screamed and scattered while a child shrieked with fear as the Vhurl dragged her into the battle, holding her up in the air by her throat as her small legs kicked wildly.

"Drop the swords, or I will kill this thing," the Vhurl hissed, its voice a venomous snarl.

Aayla's breath caught in her throat as she locked eyes with Talyn. This was clearly a trap, and the Vhurl had no intention of letting the child go, no matter what they did.

Vhurls thrived on chaos and revelled in cruelty, their twisted satisfaction rooted in the pain of others. This one would kill without hesitation, not out of necessity but simply because it could.

"Okay, spare the human!" Aayla shouted, slowly lowering her sword to the ground, aiming to divert his attention.

Talyn surged forward from the flank, deftly severing the arm that clutched the child. With a swift, fluid motion, Talyn gently swept the child into his arms and rolled to safety. He shielded the child with his body as he darted through the storm of combat in a blur of speed, his steps carrying them to the edge of the fray.

"Go," he commanded firmly in Aldredth, setting the child down a few meters away from the others. The child's tear-streaked face tilted up to him, eyes wide with fear, but there was no time for Talyn to comfort her. He turned back toward the battle, focusing on the swirling maelstrom of enemies.

With a sharp intake of breath, Aayla's gaze snapped to a small, metallic object rolling along the ground—a Vhurl explosive, its ominous glow growing brighter as it neared the terrified child.

"Talyn!" she shouted, her voice taut with urgency. But he was too far away to help.

Without a second thought, she sprang into action. Wings unfurling in a powerful burst, she flew in front of the child and threw a protective shield around them, the shimmering barrier forming just in time.

Pulling the child into a tight embrace, she wrapped her wings around them to absorb the impact and shield them from the debris. The ground shook violently beneath them as a deafening roar erupted, heat and light engulfing the air around them. Aayla clenched her teeth, her ears ringing from the blast, but when the dust settled, she and the child remained unharmed.

Panting, she glanced down to find the child clutching her tightly, tears streaking its tiny face. She nudged the child toward the huddled cluster of humans. "Go!" she urged, her tone firm but encouraging.

As the child quickly moved to safety, Aayla spun on her heel and lunged at the nearest Vhurl. If she could keep the Vhurls focused on her, they would forget all about the few humans still scattered around. Aayla knew they would never win this fight if the Vhurls kept using the humans as living shields.

Beside her, Talyn fought with a ferocity that mirrored her own, his blade a blur of silver and blood. He fought with terrifying control, each strike deliberate, every movement sharpened by instinct and honed through years of training. Together, they were a storm, a blur of metal and motion. She matched his rhythm without thinking, her body responding to his presence the way fire responds to wind—amplified, unstoppable.

She slid beneath a heavy swing, came up fast, and drove her sword into the exposed flank of a Vhurl. Its snarl turned to a wet gasp as it crumpled, but she had already moved on, twisting to avoid a second strike and countering with a clean slice across its throat. The blood sprayed hot against her arm, but she barely registered it before she twisted to counter the next strike.

Talyn was at her side again, stepping in front of her just in time to block a blow aimed at her wings. His blade deflected the attack with a metallic screech, and in the next heartbeat, he retaliated, severing its hand at the wrist. The Vhurl screamed, but Talyn silenced it with a brutal downswing, cleaving clean through the creature's collarbone.

The fighting was fierce and unrelenting, Vhurls falling by the dozens under their blades, but Xiaas was nowhere to be seen. A chill crept down Aayla's spine like a premonition, trying to warn her of something. She had no time to dwell on it, though, as the fight demanded her entire focus.

Another Vhurl came at her with his blade thrusting wildly. She sidestepped, catching the blade with her sword and using the force to spin into its blind side. Her sword sliced through the side of its neck. It staggered, choking on its own blood, and she shoved it aside without a second glance. All around her, the Vhurls were faltering, their formation collapsing under the relentless onslaught.

Talyn pressed forward, a force of fury and precision. Aayla watched him move, blood streaking his clothes, his expression carved from stone. He lunged into a knot of Vhurls, ducking low to evade a strike, then sweeping upward in a brutal arc that split its chest open. Another Vhurl rushed him—too slow. Talyn pivoted and brought his sword down in a savage diagonal, cutting through shoulder and chest in a single blow.

To his left, Aayla dispatched two more Vhurls in rapid succession, ducking a blade before stabbing upward through its chest. She twisted her sword free, spun, and slashed the next across the stomach, her movements fluid, unstoppable.

A Vhurl broke from the line in a desperate charge, blade raised in a reckless arc. Aayla surged forward to meet it, her wings sweeping back to give her momentum. She feinted left, ducked low, and drove her sword deep into its abdomen. It let out a strangled gasp, but before it could fall, Talyn stepped in and ended it with a clean, merciful strike through the heart.

The Vhurl numbers had dwindled, and the remaining began faltering, driven back by the sheer precision and strength of their joint assault.

Then, finally, after what felt like an eternity, it was over.

Aayla stood in the centre of the battlefield, chest heaving, heart pounding so loud it filled her ears. Her fingers clenched around her blood-slicked hilt. Around her, broken bodies lay strewn across the grass, weapons discarded, the earth stained black. Talyn stood only a few steps away, his breath just as ragged, his gaze sweeping the field. The silence that followed was thick and unsettling.

Her gaze lifted to the sky, searching the horizon. Still no sign of Xiaas. Her grip tightened.

Is that it? Aayla's voice echoed in Talyn's mind, a mixture of relief and lingering tension threading her words.

That was too easy, Talyn replied, a deep frown furrowing his brow. *Something is not right. And where did Xiaas go?*

Before Aayla could respond, Talyn surged forward, positioning himself protectively in front of her. A low, feral growl rumbled from his throat, his body tense. Aayla spun in the direction of his gaze, her eyes locking on Xiaas, who stood motionless in the distance.

A smile stretched across Xiaas's face as he stared at them, watching them, his stillness unnerving. Silence hung in the air for a moment, broken only by the faint rustle of leaves. Then, from the shadows of the forest behind him, an entire Vhurl battalion emerged, their figures cutting a menacing line as they stepped into view.

It was a trap, Talyn hissed, the realisation hitting him hard. *They were wearing us down, and we fell for it!*

Xiaas's laughter pierced the silence. "What's wrong?" he sneered, his tone dripping with malice. "You're looking a little... tired."

Aayla's face twisted in horror. "You sacrificed your own people? Did you hide and listen while they died?"

"They died to serve a greater purpose," Xiaas scoffed, his voice dripping with disdain.

Black Vhurl blood dripped from Tayln's sword, pooling on the grass beneath his feet. Aayla's gaze flicked to the vast number of Vhurl bodies scattered across the battlefield. "And what purpose is that?" she queried, glancing back up to lock eyes with Xiaas.

Xiaas's lips curled into a deadly snarl. "Keeping me safe. Besides, there are plenty more where they came from."

He prowled closer to Aayla, and Talyn's body instantly shifted into a fighting stance, every trace of exhaustion from the brutal battle masked by sheer determination.

"Now," Xiaas spat, his expression darkening, "last chance to surrender, and I promise to kill your Guardian quickly and relatively painlessly. I'll also promise not to hurt you too badly for. Pissing. Me. Off."

"No deal," Aayla shouted, launching herself at Xiaas's throat. But by the time she reached him, he had vanished.

The Vhurls charged forward, and Aayla and Talyn fought desperately, taking down as many as possible until only about a few hundred remained. However, the exhaustion from the relentless battle was taking its toll. Their movements grew sluggish, each strike lacking the power of the last, and their coordination began to falter.

A Vhurl lunged at Aayla, its blade arcing toward her. She ducked low, the weapon slicing harmlessly above her, and in one fluid motion, her blade flashed, severing its neck with precision. Before she could steady herself, a sudden force slammed into her back as she was tackled from behind. Her sword was knocked from her grasp, and a stone-like arm wrapped across her chest, squeezing the breath from her lungs.

The cold, sharp edge of a blade pressed against her throat, freezing her in place.

CHAPTER FOUR

The sharp blade started to pierce Aayla's skin, sending a jolt of pain through her body. She summoned every ounce of her strength, but couldn't budge the arms of steel holding her.

"Drop the weapon, or she dies," the Vhurl snarled, the blade pressing deeper into Aayla's throat.

She managed to twist her head just enough to see Talyn freeze mid-strike. His eyes flicked over the hold the Vhurl had her in, assessing the situation instantly. Without hesitation, he immediately dropped his sword, the weapon thumping heavily onto the grass beneath him.

Slowly, Talyn raised his hands in surrender, the tension in his posture unmistakable.

"Kill him," Xiaas ordered with a sneer.

Two Vhurls standing behind him raised their blades, preparing to deliver a fatal strike, while a third swiftly kicked his sword out of reach. "Goodbye, Guardian," it sneered.

"No, wait!" Aayla screamed, the movement causing the blade to dig deep into her neck. "He's my mate!"

"Stop!" bellowed Xiaas.

Everyone froze, including the two Vhurls with their blades poised inches from Talyn's neck. The sight of his willingness to sacrifice himself to protect her twisted painfully in Aayla's chest.

Xiaas stalked over and grabbed Aayla's chin, twisting her head up painfully, forcing her to meet his gaze.

"What did you say?" Xiaas drawled, his voice dripping with suspicion.

Her heart pounded so violently it nearly drowned out his words. "He's my... m... mate," she whispered, the words faltering and awkward as they tumbled from her lips.

Aldredth were notoriously poor liars. Their infrequent attempts at deceit came across as awkward and unconvincing. Fortunately, the Vhurl lacked keen perceptiveness, so they were unlikely to detect the hesitation in her voice. Additionally, her statement wasn't entirely false. Aayla had spent countless nights awake in the darkness, questioning whether Talyn could be her mate as her body, mind, and soul yearned for him with an intensity she couldn't ignore.

Xiaas's eyes narrowed as he scrutinised the crest on her chest, then snapped back to her face. "Lies," he declared with a smirk. "You don't bear his name, so he can't be your mate." His tone was dripping with smug satisfaction, as though he revelled in having exposed her deception.

"We've only j—just mated," she stuttered, trying to keep her voice steady while hoping the Vhurl holding her couldn't sense her trembling. "That's why we were travelling alone. We were heading to the nearest colony to announce our... bond... and have it formalised. If you kill him, you will be killing me, and then it was all for nothing. You can kiss that payday goodbye."

The Vhurl were not known for their intelligence, but even they understood that the Aldredth formed unbreakable, lifelong bonds and could not survive without their mates.

Xiaas gnashed his razor-sharp teeth and squeezed her jaw tighter until the bones threatened to crack. "Well, let's find out the fun way, shall we?" he growled, his breath hot and foul against her face. "On her back!" he barked.

Strong hands slammed Aayla onto the ground. She tried to twist her way out of their grasp, but several more pairs of hands pressed her into the cold grass. Talyn had started to move towards her, but several more Vhurls grabbed him and pressed his face down into the grass, his head turned towards her.

Aayla, don't you dare do anything stupid trying to save me. Save yourself. Please! Talyn begged.

She wanted to reassure him, but she couldn't lie to him. *I would rather die.*

Xiaas circled like a hunter stalking his prey. He finally stepped over her and slowly sat down on top of her. While Aldredth and Vhurl weren't sexually compatible species, it didn't mean that Xiaas wasn't smart enough to know that specific touching would give a larger rise out of her mate. He leant forward, bracing his hands on either side of her face.

"Now, tell me if you like this," Xiaas whispered as his black tongue flicked out and licked across Aayla's lips, leaving a trail of black oily slime behind.

Aayla's eyes blazed with fury as she spat in his face. Xiaas responded with a dry laugh before hitting her hard enough to draw the taste of blood to her lips. Slowly, he extended his hand, brushing his fingers along the outer feathers of her right wing.

She thrashed beneath him, a deep growl rumbling from her core as her body screamed at the violation of his touch. Her growl grew louder in warning, but even she was momentarily stunned by the ear-splitting growl that erupted from Talyn. The sound sent a shiver down her spine and promised a painful death to all those touching her. It was taking six Vhurls to hold Talyn down on the grass.

Xiaas glanced in Talyn's direction, the displeasure evident on his face.

The expression on Xiaas's face made her smirk. "Sorry for ruining your perfectly laid plans," she replied dryly, even as her heart continued to race.

Xiaas pretended to laugh before striking her hard enough across the face that the metallic tang of blood filled her mouth again. He drew his blade, pressing it against her cheek. "Interesting. Let's try something more fun, shall we?" Xiaas chuckled, followed by all the Vhurls around them.

"Cover his eyes," Xiaas sneered, and Aayla realised they would use pain to test the mating bond. She could use telepathy to tell Talyn exactly where she was hurt, but the delay might reveal the deception. There was a stark difference between conveying information and feeling the pain firsthand.

Aayla tried to move again, but couldn't budge the hands against her.

Xiaas slowly trailed the blade across her throat, down her chest, and paused above her stomach before plunging it deep inside of her. She muffled a cry of pain so they didn't get to enjoy her suffering.

Stomach, Aayla tried to convey to Talyn, but the pain was so overwhelming that she couldn't be sure if her thoughts had reached him.

Talyn arched off the ground, gripping his stomach in the same place Aayla had been stabbed, as another snarl ripped from him. "I'm going to make it hurt before I kill you," he roared as the blindfold was torn away, his gaze snapping onto Xiaas with searing intensity.

Xiaas appeared momentarily stunned into silence while Aayla let out a silent sigh of relief. Xiaas quickly turned his gaze back to Aayla and slid his hand up her arm, his grip firm and deliberate as he paused on her forearm.

"Are you telling the truth?" His voice was eerily calm. "Will you die if I kill him?"

Aayla's chest tightened. The thought of losing him was unbearable, something beyond pain, something she doubted she could survive.

In truth, she wasn't sure she'd want to.

Next to her, Talyn growled low and menacing, his body straining against the Vhurl who held him down, his eyes burning with barely contained fury.

Her eyes locked onto Xiaas's, unwavering, fierce. "Yes." The lie slipped out so easily, so close to the truth, that she couldn't be sure it wasn't real.

Xiaas raised an eyebrow, a thoughtful hum escaping him before he pressed down hard without warning. The bone in her forearm snapped with a sharp crack.

Aayla bit down on the scream threatening to escape, her teeth grinding together, muscles tense against the agony.

Talyn's growls deepened, his muscles tensing as he fought against the Vhurl's grip, eyes fixed on her in a mixture of fear and rage.

Xiaas's hand moved with slow precision, crawling up to her upper arm. "Will you die if I kill him?" he repeated, his tone chillingly casual.

"Yes," Aayla said calmly, her voice steady despite the pain.

With brutal force, Xiaas crushed her upper arm, the sickening sound of bone breaking filling the air. A small groan tore from her throat, but she locked eyes with him, rage burning in her gaze, refusing to show weakness.

Talyn's growls deepened into savage snarls, his muscles straining as he fought with renewed, desperate fury. He thrashed violently, forcing several more Vhurl to join in, pressing down harder into the grass to keep him pinned.

Xiaas's hand shifted, this time landing on her thigh, his grip heavy with the promise of more pain. "Will you die if I kill him?"

"Yes!" she spat, her voice sharp with defiance, even as her body braced for the inevitable. His hand came down with brutal force, crushing her thigh with ease.

She bit back another groan, her voice low and venomous. "Fuck you," she hissed through the pain. "The answer won't change, no matter how many bones you break."

Talyn let out a furious roar, the rage in his voice unmistakable, muscles straining against the weight of the Vhurl holding him down. A dozen Vhurl were now restraining him as he thrashed, his desperation palpable.

Xiaas chuckled darkly, amusement flickering in his cold eyes. "Maybe. Maybe not." His gaze drifted, then settled with chilling intent. Slowly, almost tenderly, his hand slid to the edge of her wing.

Aayla's blood ran cold. Panic surged through her, and her eyes widened with terror as his fingers settled on the fragile bones. "Will you die if I kill him?" His voice dropped to a whisper, quiet and menacing.

Her voice trembled, barely audible. "Yes."

With a cruel smile, Xiaas tightened his grip and shattered the delicate bones of her wing. Aayla's scream tore through the air, her body convulsing in pain as she trembled beneath his gaze.

Without warning, Talyn unleashed a deafening, primal roar, his fury erupting into a violent rage. Several more Vhurl surged onto him, straining to keep him pinned to the ground as he thrashed violently, his eyes burning with lethal intensity.

As Talyn's deafening roar echoed through the air, a rush of conflicting emotions surged within Aayla. The raw power of his voice sent a chill down her spine, igniting a flicker of fear deep in her gut. It was a sound filled with primal rage, a reminder of the danger surrounding them and the lengths he would go to protect her.

Yet, amidst the fear, a wave of warmth enveloped her heart. His roar spoke volumes of his devotion, a fierce declaration that he would not allow any harm to come to her. In that moment, she felt cherished, as if his love wrapped around her like a warm blanket that stirred things deep inside her.

Her gaze locked onto Xiaas, eyes blazing. "Yes, always!" she screamed through ragged, agonised breaths, her voice barely heard above the sound of Talyn's fury.

Xiaas remained motionless, uncertainty flickering in his eyes. Aayla's head was still spinning when, without warning, he leaned forward and struck her across the face. "Bind him, and let's move out," he ordered, rising to his feet and striding away without a backward glance.

As the Vhurls began to lift Aayla off the ground, she saw her opportunity and took it. As her hand passed the nearest Vhurls blade, she snatched it mid-motion. With a swift spin, she severed the hand gripping her and threw the blade into the eye of the Vhurl hovering over Talyn. The Vhurl fell backwards onto the others, clutching its eye in agony, giving Talyn the opening he needed.

Talyn lunged forward, snatching the blade with his free hand, and slashed his way free. He spun to the left, summoning his sword back into his hand with a burst of telekinesis just as Aayla drew her sword into her grasp.

Aayla swung her sword to the left in a clean, brutal arc, slicing through the nearest Vhurl's neck. It crumpled before it even registered the movement, but she didn't pause. Another Vhurl was already charging, but before she could react, Talyn was at her side, his sword intercepting the blow mid-swing. The clash of metal rang out between them as he shoved the Vhurl back with sheer force.

Their momentum merged instantly, movements syncing in a deadly rhythm that forced the Vhurl line to stumble. Step by step, they pushed forward—Aayla ducking low, Talyn striking high—clearing a narrow circle of space around them. Blood splattered across her body as she twisted and stabbed, and beside her, Talyn's sword cut a merciless path through the Vhurls. The ground beneath them was thick with blood, but they held firm, forcing the Vhurls to retreat just far enough to buy a breath of space.

Then, without warning, Talyn pivoted to her, his body still angled protectively between her and the next wave. His gaze dropped to her side, where bright red blood darkened the fabric near her ribs, and his expression turned sharp with concern.

Heal yourself while I hold them off, he commanded, voice low but edged with steel. *And don't you dare argue with me.*

His eyes locked onto hers with unshakable intensity, daring her to protest. Behind him, the Vhurl began to regroup, their growls rising, but Talyn didn't flinch. He planted his feet and raised his sword, every inch of him ready to protect her, no matter the cost.

As much as Aayla loathed the idea of Talyn facing them all alone, he was right. Her injuries were draining her strength with every passing second. If she didn't act quickly, the stomach wound would become too severe, and her fading strength would render healing impossible. The unwavering authority in Talyn's voice left no room for argument.

Okay, she relented, nodding as she dropped to her knees. Placing a trembling hand over her stomach, she closed her eyes and focused. Healing was a complex process that required her full concentration, leaving her vulnerable to attack.

Aayla focused her powers inward, accelerating her body's natural healing process. The pain was intense, nearly unbearable, as her powers worked to mend the torn flesh. Though she couldn't heal her wing, the injury was thankfully minor and could wait. After a minute, she opened her eyes, her breathing steady but shallow.

Before her, Talyn stood like an unyielding fortress as a shimmering barrier made of his energy encased them. The barrier absorbed every assault the Vhurl threw at it, but Aayla could see the toll it took on him. Each impact chipped away at his strength, the strain evident in the tightness of his posture and the sweat glistening on his brow.

I'm good, she conveyed to Talyn telepathically. However, as she stepped forward, she swayed slightly. The healing process had drained her energy, leaving her profoundly exhausted.

Talyn's eyes narrowed as he noticed the faint sway in her stance.

She drew a deep breath, steadying herself and masking her exhaustion. Any sign of weakness could give the Vhurl an opening they wouldn't hesitate to exploit.

With a swift motion, Talyn dropped his shield, and the battle resumed. Aayla and Talyn fought side by side, their movements synchronised to ensure their backs remained protected. Talyn began to subtly manoeuvre the fight towards the Vhurl ship, pressing their advantage with every calculated step.

Catching her gaze amidst the chaos, Talyn's voice cut through her mind. *If we can disable their ship, they won't be able to take you off this planet.*

But then we'd all be stranded here together.

Yes, Talyn conceded, his calm unwavering even in the heat of battle, *but we can hide and continue this fight later if we get too weak. We just need to survive long enough for backup to arrive.*

He was right. Talyn was known for his exceptional strategic thinking, and the sheer numbers against them made a direct victory impossible. They needed to start thinking of plan B.

Okay, Aayla agreed, determination steeling her voice. *Get us close enough, and I'll place a blastshell on their ship.*

Talyn gave a curt nod, a flicker of approval in his eyes.

Chapter Five

As the battle raged on, they forced the fight to the Vhurl ship. The ground was littered with Vhurl bodies, and the grass was soaked in thick, black blood.

Talyn's eyes locked on Aayla briefly, an unspoken understanding passing between them. Without hesitation, he lifted his sword sharply, summoning a fierce gale that roared to life across the battlefield. The winds screamed through the chaos, throwing Vhurls across the field and whipping up dust, leaves, and scattered debris into a blinding tempest. The Vhurls staggered, shielding their eyes against the relentless assault, their formation breaking apart as the storm tore through their ranks. The howling wind flung them aside like ragdolls, carving a path of disarray and confusion—the perfect distraction.

Seizing the opportunity, Aayla slipped through the chaos with fluid grace, her movements swift and precise as she darted beneath the ship. Her heart hammered as she planted the blastshell exactly where it would do the most damage, setting the deadly charge with practised efficiency. Before the Vhurls could recover, she was already retreating, racing back to Talyn's side. His strong hand found her arm, gripping firmly, pulling her to safety in one smooth motion.

Once at a safe distance, Talyn immediately enfolded Aayla in the protective embrace of his wings, shielding her from the impending blast. A deafening explosion ripped through the air as the blastshell detonated, engulfing the ship in a towering inferno of fire and smoke. The roar of the blast echoed across the battlefield, sending tremors through the earth beneath their feet. Flames licked the sky as the wreckage smouldered, a fierce beacon of their victory amid the chaos.

Safely cocooned in Talyn's wings, Aayla breathed in his intoxicating scent, a potent allure that sent a shiver down her spine and made her insides tighten.

When the smoke began to clear, her eyes shifted to the battlefield. The remaining Vhurls stood frozen, their faces twisted with shock and disbelief as they stared at the fiery wreckage of their once-imposing ship.

Aayla felt a grim sense of satisfaction bubbling within her. Her lips curled into a faint, defiant smirk as she savoured the short-lived look of defeat etched into their expressions.

Unfortunately, the explosion ignited a surge of renewed energy among the Vhurls.

The first wave hit them with a ferocity that threatened to overwhelm them. Aayla's heart pounded in her chest as she moved, her sword slicing through the air in swift, precise arcs. A Vhurl lunged from the shadows, blade held high, but she sidestepped just in time, her sword flashing out to sever its wrist in one fluid motion. Another Vhurl came from behind, but Talyn was there, spinning to intercept with a slash that left the Vhurl staggering.

Despite their skill and determination, the relentless onslaught pressed on, a tide of darkness that refused to break. Exhaustion weighed heavily on Aayla's limbs, each swing of her sword a battle against the growing fatigue. Her arms burned, her vision wavered, and the metallic scent of blood thickened the air. Still, she pressed forward, fuelled by desperation and the fierce need to protect the one she loved.

As the fight dragged on, the chaos condensed into a deadly rhythm. Her mind blurred, giving way to the muscle memory forged through years of training. Her body moved on autopilot—each strike calculated, each pivot exact. Aayla ducked beneath a wild blade swing and retaliated with a vicious upward slash that cut deep into its side. Talyn matched her every move, his blade a blur of lethal intent and unwavering control.

The Vhurls pressed harder, their snarls growing louder as they surged forward. Aayla's breath came ragged, her body trembling with exhaustion. A Vhurl aimed a desperate blow at her temple, but she twisted away, her sword slicing clean through its neck before it could recover.

Beside her, Talyn's strikes were flawless, each one landing with deadly intent even as fatigue gnawed at them both.

Time blurred into a relentless beat of breath and steel. Aayla deflected a slash from her left, spinning to face a Vhurl closing in from the right. The Vhurl's eyes widened in shock just before her sword found its mark, slicing through its chest with a chilling finality. The world narrowed to that moment— the clash of steel, the rush of blood, and the fierce, unbreakable will to survive.

As Aayla's blade descended towards another Vhurl, the urgent rhythm of approaching footsteps pierced through the din of battle. With swift precision, she landed a fatal strike, then pivoted with wings tight to her back just in time to see Talyn leap in front of her, shielding her with his own body.

Time seemed to slow, and she watched in horror as their blades struck simultaneously, each piercing the other's chest.

"Talyn!"

The cry tore from her throat, raw and filled with a depth of anguish she hadn't thought possible.

Talyn withdrew his sword from the Vhurls chest and watched it crumple to the ground. His knees gave way, and he sank to the earth, his breath ragged and shallow as crimson spread across his chest.

As he collapsed, his majestic forest-green and gold wings unfurled behind him like a fallen banner, their brilliance dimmed by the blood pooling around him. Aayla was at his side instantly, dropping to her knees as her trembling hands reached for him. She pulled out the Vhurl blade before she pressed down hard on his wound, trying in vain to stem the flow of bright red blood.

Gritting her teeth, she drew on her dwindling reserves of strength to erect a shimmering protective shield around them with one hand.

"I'm sorry," Talyn rasped, his voice barely audible as a weak, bloody smile tugged at his lips.

"Shut up so I can heal you already," Aayla snapped, her voice sharp with fear, tears blurring her vision.

"No," he croaked, his trembling hand cupped her cheek. "It's too dangerous... you'll be vulnerable."

"I will not watch you die!" she shouted, her voice cracking with desperation, but his eyes fluttered shut before her.

Her hands trembled as she pressed them harder against his blood-soaked chest, her focus narrowing to the faint, unsteady beat of his heart. Closing her eyes, she plunged into the intricate healing process, channelling her energy into the wound. Her power sparked to life, warm and golden, but it burned through her reserves like wildfire, each passing moment pushing her closer to the brink.

Outside her shield, the relentless onslaught of the Vhurls continued, their strikes hammering against the barrier. Each impact resonated inside her mind, sharp and jarring, as if the attacks were tearing at the fabric of her thoughts. Yet she refused to falter, her determination unyielding as she poured every ounce of herself into saving him.

Minutes stretched into what felt like hours, each second an eternity. A white haze began to creep at the edges of her vision, the telltale sign that her body was reaching its limits. Finally, with one last desperate surge of energy, she felt the wound beneath her hands close, and the flow of blood stemmed.

Her strength spent, Aayla collapsed onto Talyn's chest, her breath ragged and shallow as the shield around them flickered precariously. She pressed her ear against him, relief washing over her as she heard the steady, rhythmic thrum of his heartbeat.

He was alive.

She let herself linger there for a moment, her body too weak to move, her mind too frayed to process the battle still raging around them. But then, without warning, Talyn's body tensed beneath her. With a sharp intake of breath, he sat upright, a fresh determination burning in his eyes. His wings flared slightly behind him as he extended his hand, reinforcing her protective shield with one of his own.

"You should have let me die," he snapped, his voice low and ragged, raw with pain and fury. Blood coated his lips, and his eyes—normally sharp and steady—were glassy with exhaustion and something darker.

Despite his near exhaustion, Talyn paused to run his hands gently over Aayla to check for injuries. As he shifted, his wing brushed softly against her, the fleeting touch sending an involuntary shiver down her spine. His unwavering concern sent her heart fluttering, a tender ache that twisted into guilt, sharp and unrelenting. He was always the shield, always the one bleeding for her, and every bruise he bore felt like a weight she couldn't carry. A sacrifice she could never repay.

Are you okay?

I am now, Aayla reassured him, trembling as she gently cupped his cheek.

But Talyn wasn't convinced. The deepening frown between his brows said it all. He saw the truth—the shadows beneath her eyes, the subtle sway in her stance, and her shallow, uneven breaths. There was no hiding her exhaustion from him.

Silently, Talyn held out the Pixx, his expression grim and urgent. *Open up.*

Without hesitation, Aayla parted her lips, and he carefully placed a few of the shimmering tablets on her tongue. The sweet taste barely registered—her body already responding to the surge of restorative energy that followed. As she swallowed, warmth spread through her chest, pushing back the bone-deep fatigue and sharpening her senses.

Talyn tossed several tablets into his own mouth and swallowed them, blinking as the familiar tingle spread beneath his skin. Within seconds, the worst of the ache in their limbs began to dull, the tightness in their lungs easing as strength pulsed back into their weary muscles. The exhaustion that had been dragging them down began to lift, replaced by a tingling focus and clarity that cut through the haze of pain and adrenaline.

Their eyes met briefly—a flicker of understanding and renewed resolve passing between them. Aayla gave a small, firm nod, her breathing steadier now, the fire in her gaze reignited. Talyn mirrored the motion, rolling his shoulders back and drawing his sword up once more.

Then, without a word, they launched themselves back into the fray, swords flashing as they rejoined the battle with renewed ferocity. The Vhurls didn't see it coming—didn't expect the sudden speed, the precision, the unrelenting force that now surged from them.

Aayla's sword deflected a Vhurl blade with a resounding clash, the sharp ring of steel reverberating across the field. Besides her, Talyn's wings unfurled slightly with each powerful strike, allowing him to weave through the Vhurl assault.

The clearing thrummed with tension, every swing of their blades slicing through the thick air. The sound of laboured breaths and the clash of metal echoed against the weathered stone buildings encircling them. In the centre of the battlefield, Aayla stood momentarily still, her blade steady in her grip, eyes blazing as she stared down the encroaching horde. They circled like wolves, eyes gleaming with predatory intent.

Each parry and thrust was executed with ruthless precision. Aayla spun to the right, narrowly evading a blade aimed at her wings, and rolled forward with fluid precision, her sword slicing cleanly through the Vhurl in her path. Thick, black blood oozed from the blade, dripping onto the stained earth.

To her left, Talyn pressed on with unyielding energy, his strikes swift and devastating. Despite the gruelling pace, he showed little sign of fatigue. As a male, his natural strength outmatched hers, but his Vajjer heritage gave him an unparalleled mastery of combat. Each move was a testament to his superior skill, felling twice as many Vhurl as she could manage.

Like all Unix, she was a healer, not a warrior. Combat was not her calling, yet she fought with a determination born of necessity and raw strength.

Her sharp eyes scanned the battlefield, noting the enemy's dwindling ranks. A flicker of hope ignited within her for the first time that they might actually survive this.

Suddenly, a deafening explosion tore through the air, its force hurling her backward. She hit the ground hard, the impact rattling through her bones as she tumbled across the grass. Blinking through the haze, she realised that the Vhurl had detonated a small explosive in the middle of the battle, killing several of their own in the process.

The only sound she could hear was the high-pitched ringing in her ears until the chaotic noise of the battle gradually returned. Disoriented, Aayla stretched her arm to the side, searching blindly for Talyn, but her fingers met only the cold grass.

A sharp, searing pain flared in her side, drawing a hiss of breath through her gritted teeth. Ignoring it, she rolled over and spotted Talyn several feet away. He was struggling to his feet, clearly disoriented by the blast, but otherwise seemed uninjured. Relief washed through her as she shifted her focus inward, assessing her injuries.

She was bleeding internally. With urgency, she began to heal herself, knowing she didn't have the time or energy for a full recovery. She patched up the most significant tear in her liver, planning to complete the healing later when it was safe.

Pushing herself upright with a groan, Aayla barely had time to react before five Vhurl warriors closed in, surrounding her in a tight formation and separating her from Talyn.

She shifted her stance, every muscle tensed, when an unnatural sound sliced through the din. A sharp, rhythmic clicking followed by a low, ominous hum.

The air behind her thickened, charged with an otherworldly energy that made her blood run cold. She angled her body slightly to see a portal materialising behind her.

Vhurls possessed the technology to open portals, allowing them to travel instantaneously between two points. These portals, however, came at a steep cost. Each one was a single-use technology reserved for only the most dire or strategic moments. The portal materialising before Aayla crackled with dark energy, its swirling surface reflecting an ominous, shifting light.

Her mind raced. This portal likely led to one of their nearest strongholds, a fortress teeming with thousands of Vhurls. They had learned from their previous encounter, abandoning their usual taunts and delaying tactics. Instead, they intended to bypass the fight altogether and drag her straight to their base. If they succeeded, there would be no escape. Once through, she would be entirely at their mercy—mercy the Vhurls didn't possess.

Panic flared in her chest as another thought struck her. If the portal swallowed her, the Aldredth—who she prayed had received their distress call and were en route—wouldn't be able to track her. The Vhurls' portal technology cloaked its destination, severing all ties to the outside world. Aayla would be alone, cut off, and defenceless in enemy territory.

She tensed, her focus darting back to the circle of Vhurls closing in. Clawed hands grabbed her from every direction, pulling her toward the portal's opening. She struggled, twisting and kicking with all her strength, but their grip was ironclad.

The hum of the portal grew louder, the pull of its energy almost palpable as she was dragged closer.

A burst of movement shattered the circle. Talyn barrelled in with fierce precision, his blade a silver blur. In three swift, devastating strikes, he cut down the Vhurls holding her, their bodies collapsing to the ground.

"Go!" he bellowed, his voice cutting through the chaos.

Aayla didn't hesitate. She scrambled to her feet and ran, heart pounding as she bolted from the portal. She weaved between the Vhurls, slipping past them with swift, practised agility. One swiped at her, its blade grazing her shoulder, but she twisted away and kept moving. Behind her, the clash of battle raged on, but she didn't look back. She just ran, putting as much distance as possible between her and the chaos.

Breathless, she turned around, expecting to see Talyn right behind her. Instead, the space where he should have been was empty.

Her chest tightened with panic as she scanned the battlefield, her gaze darting desperately in every direction. Finally, she spotted him near the portal, locked in a fierce struggle with Xiaas. The clash of their blades rang out sharply, cutting through the chaos around them.

A gasp escaped her lips as she started to run back, her instincts screaming to reach him.

Aayla's heart leapt into her throat as she saw Xiaas swing his weapon towards Talyn's neck. Talyn deflected the blow swiftly, his blade catching Xiaas's strike just in time. He used the momentum to drive Xiaas backward, forcing him closer to the portal's churning, ominous void. With a final, powerful shove, Talyn sent Xiaas hurtling through the glowing threshold.

For a fleeting moment, relief surged through her, a fragile sense of victory washing over her as she slowed her steps. But that relief evaporated in an instant, replaced by pure terror.

Talyn's footing faltered, the force of his movement throwing him off balance. He teetered at the portal's edge, his arms outstretched as if trying to regain stability, but there was nothing to hold onto.

"Talyn!" Aayla's scream tore through the air as her body instinctively surged forward, though she knew she could never reach him in time.

Time seemed to stretch unbearably. Their eyes met, locking together in a single, heart-wrenching moment.

And then, he was gone, swallowed by the portal's swirling void.

Chapter Six

As Talyn vanished through the portal, a chilling wave of fear seized Aayla's heart, freezing her in place for a fraction of a second.

"No!" she screamed, the word tearing from her throat as her legs propelled her forward before her mind could catch up. There was no place Talyn could go that she wouldn't follow him.

"Explosive!" someone shouted, but the warning was drowned out by a thunderous bang that ripped through the air. The force slammed into Aayla like a physical wall, throwing her backward and sending her sprawling to the ground. Grass, dirt, and shards of debris rained down around her, pelting her skin and wings.

Her ears rang violently, and her vision blurred. The world around her was reduced to a disorienting haze of muted shapes and colours. She tried to shake her head clear, but the motion only made the ground beneath her seem to tilt dangerously.

Slowly, she forced herself to focus, her surroundings coming into sharper view. Several Vhurl bodies lay lifeless nearby, their forms twisted and motionless. Around her, another twenty or so stumbled through the chaos, clutching at injured limbs or staggering in confusion. Before her, a massive crater marred the once-pristine grass.

Xiaas had dropped a small explosive during the struggle with Talyn. In a desperate and careless move, one of the

Vhurls near the portal had kicked it away from themselves, sending it careening into a cluster of their own.

Straight into her path.

Aayla clenched her jaw. The disregard this species had for one another was incomprehensible. How could a species show so little care for its own kind? Aldredth's, by contrast, would sacrifice everything to protect one another. The stark contrast left her heart heavy with frustration and sorrow.

Her thoughts were interrupted as the portal began to shift. Its once-blue surface darkened, swirling ominously into a deep red. The change sent a wave of panic through the remaining Vhurls. They shrieked in alarm, their injuries forgotten as they scrambled toward the portal with reckless urgency.

Aayla's stomach sank as she recognised the warning signs. Some Vhurl portals were programmed to seal automatically once a non-Vhurl crossed through, trapping their prey on the other side while severing all ties to their pursuers. The crimson hue of the portal confirmed it. The shutdown sequence had been triggered.

In mere seconds, the gateway would collapse entirely. Anyone who failed to cross before then would be stranded on this planet with no way to escape.

Ignoring the searing pain that radiated through every fibre of her body, Aayla forced herself to her feet. Her legs wobbled beneath her, but sheer will drove her forward. With everything she had left, she sprinted toward the portal, her heart pounding with desperation.

She launched into the air as the portal flickered, its energy collapsing in a blinding flash of light. Her outstretched hands grasped nothing but empty air as she landed hard on the ground, the impact jarring her already battered body.

Aayla rolled onto her side, gasping for breath, and turned her gaze to where the portal had been. It was gone, leaving nothing but a faint shimmer in the air. Around her, half a dozen Vhurls stood motionless, their grotesque faces twisted in expressions of disbelief. Like her, they had been too slow. The portal had sealed, cutting them off from their escape.

"No!" Aayla's voice cracked, raw and trembling. Tears streamed down her cheeks as she shook her head in denial. "No, no, no!"

Talyn was gone, trapped alone on the other side with the Vhurls, and the weight of that thought crushed the air from her lungs. Panic clawed at her chest, making it impossible to breathe. She doubled over, clutching at the ground, trying to fight the overwhelming tide of fear and despair.

Then she heard the guttural, mocking laughter of the Vhurls behind her.

The crushing pain in her chest gave way to a burning rage, igniting like wildfire in her veins. She straightened, her trembling hands balling into fists. The sound of her low, guttural growl filled her ears as she spun on her heels to face them.

The Vhurls fell silent, their laughter fading into an uneasy quiet. Their hideous, toothy grins stayed etched on their grotesque faces, their eyes glinting with mocking curiosity as they watched her intently.

"Surrender now, and I won't kill you," Aayla growled, her voice low and menacing. She raised her sword, the blade gleaming faintly in the dim light as she pointed it at the group of Vhurls.

The Vhurls hesitated, their alien eyes flicking between her and one another. They muttered amongst themselves in a harsh, guttural language, though their gazes never left her.

"What do we do now?" one rasped, his voice laced with uncertainty.

"Kill her!" barked another, his tone filled with bravado that didn't quite mask his fear.

"Yes, kill her. I'm not dying for some coin," grumbled a third, and grunts of approval echoed around her.

Aayla had heard enough. She lunged at the nearest Vhurl with lightning speed, her blade slicing cleanly through him before he even had time to react. The others roared in anger and charged, their hesitation giving way to feral aggression.

The fight erupted in a blur of chaos. Aayla moved with purpose, her strikes precise and deadly, though her body screamed with exhaustion. At first, her speed and agility allowed her to dodge most of their blows, but as the battle wore on, fatigue clawed at her.

Her breaths came in ragged gasps, each one a struggle as her limbs grew heavier with every passing moment. Her wings dragged limply behind her, catching on the grass and dirt.

She ducked and rolled beneath the Vhurl's blade, swiftly spinning around to face them. The horde of Vhurls began to amass again, their dark, hulking forms blending together. Their guttural chants filled the air, a menacing rhythm that made Aayla's heart pound with renewed urgency.

Despite her best efforts, the odds felt insurmountable. The Vhurls pressed their advantage, their relentless assault showing no mercy. Aayla struck down another foe, then another, but the effort left her trembling.

Finally, only two Vhurls remained, circling her like predators sensing their prey's vulnerability. The weight of exhaustion pressed heavily upon her shoulders, her once-fluid movements now sluggish and strained. The fight had pushed her to her limits, and her strength was ebbing away like the fading light of the setting sun.

She tightened her grip on her sword, summoning the last reserves of her energy. Her vision blurred at the edges, but she forced herself to focus.

The two remaining Vhurls split apart, coordinating their attack. They came at her from opposite directions, their movements swift and calculated. Aayla turned, her sword ready, but the exhaustion slowed her reactions. Her wings dragged against the ground as she pivoted sluggishly to meet their assault, her resolve unyielding even as her body screamed for rest.

Aayla felt the presence of a Vhurl approaching from behind her just as a cold, sharp blade pierced her skin. The blade slid across her throat with a sickening ease, and she felt a warm rush of blood trickle down her chest.

A sharp gasp tore from her lungs as her knees buckled. She collapsed to the ground, her hands instinctively pressing against the wound in a desperate attempt to stem the bleeding. Her mind screamed at her to heal, but her body was too exhausted, and the blood flowed faster than she could repair the damage.

Her vision began to darken at the edges, the world around her blurring as if viewed through a fogged lens. Panic surged within her, but she forced herself to focus, pushing every last ounce of energy into a final healing attempt.

Slowly, painfully, her skin began to knit together, the bleeding slowing but not stopping. The pool of blood surrounding her grew, a stark reminder of how close she was to the edge.

The final inch of skin was sealed with a sharp breath of relief, but Aayla could barely catch her breath before the world around her tilted dangerously. She rolled over, gasping, the earth spinning beneath her as voices distorted into incoherent murmurs.

Two Vhurl figures loomed on her right, their silhouettes shifting and merging in her blurred vision. Fear clawed at her chest, but she summoned the last of her strength. With great effort, she managed to stagger to her feet, sword raised in a feeble warning.

The Vhurls hesitated momentarily, their cold, calculating eyes assessing her weak form. They took a step back, but Aayla's victory was short-lived. Her legs gave way beneath her, and she collapsed, the ground slamming into her with brutal force.

She gasped for breath, but even that small act of survival was too much. Her body was completely drained, every muscle and fibre spent. She had nothing left. The fight was over, and she could no longer summon the strength to stand.

Aayla heard the two Vhurls laughing, their cruel, mocking chuckles echoing in her ears. They knew they had her now, and she could feel their sadistic anticipation. They would make her suffer as much as possible before finally killing her.

With every ounce of willpower, she tried to rise again, but her legs betrayed her. They buckled beneath her, sending her crashing back to the ground. Desperation surged within her as she tried to raise her sword, but one of the Vhurls kicked it from her grasp, sending it skittering out of reach.

Glancing up, she saw the razor-sharp teeth of the Vhurl smiling above her, and her stomach dropped. Its foot slammed into her head and chest repeatedly. Strong hands grasped her around her throat, lifting her into the air before launching her across the field into a tree that shattered upon impact. Landing on the ground with a hard thump, she suppressed a pained groan from her broken ribs.

As the hours stretched on and the sun dipped lower in the sky, casting long, amber shadows across the land, the Vhurls unleashed their fury upon her. Their cruel laughter echoed through the air as they kicked, struck, and flung her mercilessly across every inch of the unforgiving landscape. The soft grass did little to cushion her as her body slammed into the ground again and again. Rocks crumbled and shattered beneath her impact, jagged edges slicing into her skin, while trees splintered and shattered upon impact.

Her body was a map of pain, every bruise a vivid mark of their cruelty, spreading across her skin like dark, cursed blooms and staining her flesh in angry, mottled hues of black and purple. Every bone felt fractured, her limbs trembling under the weight of the relentless assault. Blood seeped from deep gashes, pooling around her and staining the earth in vivid streaks. Her breaths came in shallow, ragged gasps, each one a struggle against the overwhelming pain.

Yet, through the unbearable agony, she remained silent. Not a single scream or plea escaped her lips. She clamped her jaw shut, biting down hard to stifle the pain that threatened to overwhelm her. She refused to grant them the satisfaction of hearing her anguish. Even as her body faltered, her spirit remained unyielding, standing strong against the storm of their cruelty.

The crowd of humans near the buildings had grown steadily, now numbering in the hundreds. Dressed in military uniforms, they stood in tense silence, their eyes fixed on the fight. Some whispered urgently into handheld communication devices, relaying updates or receiving orders.

She could sense the Vhurls' growing impatience, their cruel amusement waning as the torture dragged on. It wasn't until they finally moved to her wings that she realised they were growing tired. The Vhurls had been careful to avoid damaging them until now, knowing that Aayla would lose consciousness too soon. Aldredth were notorious for succumbing to unconsciousness when their wings were severely injured because the pain was unbearable. The Vhurls understood this well. If they mutilated her wings too early, she wouldn't be able to endure the rest of the torture, and that would spoil their sadistic enjoyment.

The Vhurl were breathing heavily when one of them violently threw Aayal to the ground. Rough hands pushed her into the dirt while another pair grabbed the tips of her wings and stretched them out. Her body screamed out at the violation while the pair of hands continued to pull her wings so tight that the delicate bones under his hands started to break.

Without warning, a massive foot slammed down onto her wings. Aayla's scream of agony ripped through the air as the blows rained down, each one amplifying the excruciating pain.

She must have lost consciousness for a moment because when she finally opened her eyes, the hands that had been pinning her down were gone.

With great effort, she rolled over, her body heaving as she vomited a violent rush of blood onto the ground. Her shaking hand instinctively reached back to touch her wings. Some bones were broken, others shattered beyond repair. Every movement was agony.

Looking around, her vision blurred, she spotted a dead Vhurl a few feet from her with his head twisted and hanging by a slither of skin. The glimmer of something behind caught her eye. It was the tip of her sword, and anger swelled deep in her stomach. It gave her a momentary burst of adrenaline.

Slowly, she crawled across the grass, every nerve in her body screaming in agony. Yet, the pain only fuelled her rage further.

Her finger brushed against the metal of her sword when a pair of large hands gripped the hair on the back of her head and pulled her upright. She twisted in his grip, slicing her sword blindly through the air as hard as she could. As she felt her sword slicing through flesh and bone, a deafening scream filled her ears. The hand gripping her hair let go, and she fell to the ground, landing hard on her side.

She saw one blurry figure stumble back before dropping to the ground. A second blurry figure lunged towards her, and she quickly kicked her leg into his face before rolling out of his reach.

Turning, Aayla tried to jump towards him on the attack, but she was too weak and lost her balance. Landing hard on her back, her shattered wings took the brunt of the fall, and she momentarily lost consciousness until a pair of strong hands wrapped themselves around her neck, squeezing the breath from her body.

Aayla struggled beneath the weight of the Vhurl, her body thrashing in a desperate attempt to push him off. Her lungs screamed for air, but the crushing pressure made each breath nearly impossible.

She clenched her hand but couldn't feel the grip of her sword. She frantically looked around and spotted her sword a few feet away. She reached towards it and called it to her hands using her powers of telekinesis, but it lay still on the ground, her energy depleted.

The Vhurl's massive hands tightened around her throat, squeezing the life out of her with each passing second. Her vision began to fade, the world going hazy as she struggled to stay conscious.

A rapid series of sharp, staccato cracks pierced the air. Gunfire. Small metal projectiles ricocheted off the Vhurl's back. He turned his head toward the source of the sound, but his grip on her neck remained unyielding.

With her vision narrowing to a pinpoint of light, Aayla drew from the last reserves of strength that kept her heart beating. She dug deep, summoning every last ounce of power to call her sword.

The hilt slammed into her palm, and with a swift, desperate motion, she swung it toward the Vhurl's neck as he lunged backwards.

Aayla's arm fell back upon the grass, and the sword rolled out of her grasp. She sucked air into her lungs with a few ragged breaths, and her head lolled to the side. A blurry, headless figure lay next to her, and a pool of black blood slowly seeped towards her hand.

She tried to fight the pull of unconsciousness, but the world around her blurred further, and a haze settled over her mind.

As her vision faded, she thought she saw dozens of humans brandishing guns moving slowly towards her.

Then everything went black.

Chapter Seven

Aayla drifted in darkness.

Voices echoed around her, but she couldn't understand what they were saying. An alarm sounded nearby, and she clenched her eyes shut against a surge of pain. It felt like she was lying on something cold and hard. She tried to move, but her body didn't respond.

Slowly, she forced her eyes open. Blurred shapes swam before her vision, and a harsh, artificial light pierced through the haze, casting long, unfamiliar shadows on the sterile white walls. Before she could fully comprehend her surroundings, dark figures loomed over her.

Panic surged through her chest, her heart pounding wildly. Instinctively, she flicked her hand toward the figures, throwing them across the room with a violent force. Their bodies collided with the wall, the impact echoing with a sickening thud before they fell to the ground, motionless.

Screams filled the air as she rolled off the cold table, landing hard on her chest on the floor below. Every movement was met with a searing pain, and her limbs felt heavy and uncoordinated. She dragged herself toward the far corner of the room, her back pressing against the wall, arms instinctively raised in a defensive posture.

Blinking rapidly to clear her blurred vision, she saw several figures running out of the room. The figures on the floor began to stir and move toward the door, only to be dragged out by others who entered. As the door slammed shut, the room was finally left in eerie silence, punctuated only by the blaring alarm and her laboured breaths.

The room was small and stark white, filled with strange surgical equipment that rhythmically blinked and hummed. The air was laced with a strong chemical smell. Monitors were dotted around the room, and two walls were lined with waist-high cabinets stacked with papers and scans of an Aldredth's body that, based on the injuries and fractures, must have been her body.

To her right was what appeared to be a large mirror, but she could hear muffled voices coming from the other side of it, leading her to suspect it might be a concealed door. Directly in front of her were two large double doors with small windows about eye height through which she could see a yellow light flashing that cast a shadow on the wall behind it.

Aayla attempted to sit up, but a wave of intense pain washed over her as the adrenaline began to fade. Glancing down, she saw she was only wearing her underwear, with several tubes protruding from her skin. Her heart raced as she quickly yanked the tubes free, tearing away the adhesive pads that clung to her skin with a sharp pull.

Based on the rate of healing of her broken bones, Aayla guessed that she had been unconscious for around four days. Her body was black and blue all over, and almost every bone felt broken. Those injuries didn't concern her too greatly because she could heal them. What concerned her most was the state of her wings.

Aayla's wings were broken and twisted, and the healing process had begun while in their deformed shape. The pain was agonising, and the only way to heal her wings now would be to rebreak the deformities, surgically insert Pallas implant supports, and strap them into shape until they had healed. Pallas implants were a form of biological smart technology that would provide both support and flexibility, dissolving once no longer necessary. But that kind of surgery would require at least two Aldredth, which was beyond her capabilities without the proper tools.

Taking several deep breaths to steady herself, Aayla knew she needed to heal her body to regain strength and escape. However, she was still drained and exhausted, and any attempt at self-healing could potentially knock her unconscious again.

She was caught between a rock and a hard place.

Lifting her head, she reached out and grabbed one of the tubes lying on the floor. She noticed clear liquid dripping from it and carefully tasted a drop. She noted with a frown that it was just salty water, no discernible drugs or chemicals. She then studied the sticky pads attached to her body, all connected to the monitors that beeped rhythmically in sync with her heartbeat.

Laying her head back down, she closed her eyes, trying to think. From everything she had seen in the room, it appeared that the humans probably weren't trying to hurt her. Several days had passed since the battle, and if they had wanted to hurt her, they likely would have done so by now.

Either way, she had no choice but to heal herself.

Placing a hand over her chest, Aayla exhaled hard before beginning the painstaking process of mending her broken body. She focused on fusing the shattered bones, growing new ones where the damage was beyond repair, and sealing the cuts along her skin whilst fighting to stay awake.

As she healed the final injuries to her body, she felt the familiar embrace of weightlessness overcome her as she drifted into a deep sleep.

Chapter Eight

As consciousness slowly seeped into Aayla's senses, her eyelids fluttered open, the world around her shifting from darkness to light in gradual, disorienting waves. Shapes and shadows slowly began to take form, but the clarity was fleeting. A dull ache pulsed through her body, a lingering reminder of the strain she had placed on her heart through too much healing. Her heart throbbed, every beat a heavy drum in her chest.

Her senses sharpened as she became more aware of her surroundings. The familiar sterile scent filled the air, accompanied by the distant hum of machinery. The bright ceiling lights stung her eyes, adding to her disorientation. Drawing upon the energy deep inside of herself, she summoned the strength to move. Her muscles protested, every inch of her body echoing with pain, but she pressed on. With considerable effort, she shifted and pushed herself up, propping on trembling arms.

She found herself back on the cold, hard table she had awoken upon previously. This time, however, large straps were looped around her wrists and ankles, pinning her down. The sharp scent of antiseptic lingered in the air, and the faint metallic taste of blood clung to her tongue. She tugged at the restraints with a small grunt of effort, snapping them effortlessly as though they were nothing more than paper. Her muscles were sore, but she was still strong enough to free herself.

Swinging her legs over the side of the table, she stood, swaying slightly as her balance adjusted. Her wings were a heavy burden on her back, aching with every movement, but bandages had been wrapped around them whilst she was unconscious. They were bulky and restrictive, but the thick layers stabilised the broken bones, preventing further damage. Aayla considered tearing them off, but the thought of further injuring her wings made her hesitate. For now, the bandages had to remain.

She began removing the tubes and sticky pads attached to her body, a series of small beeps and whirrs coming from the monitors as they lost their connection to her vitals.

As she removed the last pads, loud footsteps echoed from the corridor beyond the double doors. The sound grew louder, accompanied by the murmur of voices.

Despite the pain and disorientation, Aayla reacted swiftly and crouched into a defensive stance, her muscles protesting with each movement. Eyes narrowed, she scanned the room for anything she could use to defend herself, spotting several sharp-looking knives. She quickly palmed two, the cold steel a comforting weight in her hands.

The shuffling of feet and muffled voices grew louder as the heavy doors finally swung open. Standing beyond them was a group of about two dozen men. Most wore military attire, their large guns pointed directly at her, their expressions unreadable. The remaining individuals were either dressed in stark white coats or dark-coloured suits adorned with shiny medallions, their presence authoritative and imposing.

A man with short black hair, dressed in a dark grey suit and a blue-and-white striped tie, stepped forward. His hands were raised in a gesture of peace, and his eyes locked on hers with an unwavering intensity. He spoke in a language Aayla didn't understand, his tone calm yet commanding, as if waiting for a response.

Aayla studied the room, taking in the tense atmosphere. She had been unconscious multiple times here, and if the humans had intended to harm her, they had plenty of opportunities. Something in her gut told her they weren't a threat. It was time for her to trust them.

Slowly, she lowered her hands, slipping the knives into her underwear. Standing up, she kept her posture neutral but assertive, ensuring her body language conveyed caution while still showing willingness to engage. She bowed her head, performing the traditional Aldredth greeting but never breaking eye contact, maintaining a defensive edge.

"Greetings. My name is Aayla, daughter of Sabee and Marlia," she said slowly in Aldredth, loud enough for everyone to hear. "I am an Aldredth from the planet Nannuval. I come with peaceful tidings and mean you no harm."

The humans stared back at her, their faces blank with surprise, but it was apparent none of them understood her language. Not that she had expected them to. They exchanged confused glances, their weapons still trained on her.

Aayla paused and clicked her tongue in thought, trying to find a way to make herself understood. She pointed to the man in the grey suit and said firmly, "Human," before pointing to the floor and adding, "Earth." Then she tapped her chest and said, "Aldredth," before pointing up and saying, "Nannuval."

The man in the grey suit seemed to catch her meaning, his face lighting up with understanding. He pointed at her with an almost childlike enthusiasm and repeated, "Aldredth."

Aayla nodded in acknowledgment, though a deep sigh escaped her. This would take a long time to communicate if she didn't think of a better method. She looked around the room for something to help but found nothing.

Gesturing to her body, she mimed the act of dressing, her movements deliberate and pointed. "Where are my clothes?" she asked, her tone laced with frustration, hoping they would understand her actions if not her words. If the humans gave her clothes back, she could get her Lumina from her pocket and use it to interpret their language, try to call home, and, most importantly, send help after Tayln.

The man in the grey suit nodded thoughtfully, then turned to chat with the other humans for a long moment before spinning to her and saying something. Once he had finished speaking, he smiled and nodded, repeating a word she had heard a few times. "Yes".

It was clear that human society operated under a hierarchical system. The man in the grey suit seemed to be the leader, at least among the group in the room, as the others looked to him for direction. He stood closest to Aayla and was the only one addressing her directly. There were other humans in varying roles—some engaged in conversation, while others stood silently at the back, observing but remaining quiet unless spoken to.

Aayla returned a small smile and then decided to push her luck. Gesturing in eating motions, she asked for food. She remembered reading that humans shared physiology similar to Aldredth's, so it would be possible to share their food as long as it wasn't poisoned.

The man mimicked her gestures, rubbing his stomach as well, and said, "Food."

"Food," she repeated, hoping they were talking about the same thing. The man turned to speak with the others again, then returned to her. "Yes," he affirmed.

Just as the exhaustion from her ordeal began to hit, Aayla glanced around the room, looking for a place to sit and rest. Her legs wobbled with fatigue, and the throbbing pain in her wings and body reminded her how much she had pushed herself. Before she could move, she heard rapid footsteps approaching down the corridor.

The door swung open, and a new man entered, holding her clothes, which were tattered and stained with blood and dirt.

They placed the clothes in front of her, and she eagerly reached into one of her hidden pockets, only for her fingers to brush against shattered fragments instead.

Her Lumina was broken beyond repair, likely damaged by one of the many Vhurl blows during the battle.

Aayla's heart felt heavy, the weight of her helplessness sinking deeper with each passing moment. She could not escape the suffocating feeling of despair. Talyn's absence, his fate unknown, gnawed at her, consuming her thoughts. The helplessness was more agonising than any physical pain she had endured, and the grief was written all over her face. Her sorrow was so palpable that the man in the grey suit faltered momentarily. His hand, reaching toward her in an unspoken offer of comfort, hesitated mid-air. For a brief instant, his uncertainty mirrored her own, and the gesture was withdrawn with a soft breath. He stood there, watching her closely, clearly unsure how to address her pain.

Her legs finally gave out, and she crumpled to the floor, still searching her pockets. She found a few remaining Pixx, which she hastily consumed, the small burst of energy offering a brief reprieve. Leaning back against the wall, her eyes fluttered closed as she tried to steady her breath and calm her mind.

She took a deep breath and looked down at the soiled clothes in her lap. Aldredth were naturally comfortable in the nude. Since all Aldredth were of almost the exact same size and proportions and had no romantic inclinations towards one another except for their mates, they felt no shame or discomfort in being naked. However, given the uncertainty of her situation with the humans, she thought it was wiser to dress, if only to provide some measure of protection to her vital organs.

Reluctantly, she slipped on her once-violet chiton top and skirt, trying not to focus on the stains of Aldredth and Vhurl blood that marred the lightweight fabric.

A few moments later, three new humans, two males and one female, appeared at the doorway, each carrying trays of food and drinks. As they approached, Aayla instinctively jumped to her feet, quickly backing away to keep a safe distance between them.

"Stop, please," she said, raising her hand to her arm in a protective gesture. She shook her head vigorously, repeating the motion to communicate her discomfort with being touched. She felt foolish for the repeated gestures, but it seemed to work as the humans paused, understanding her silent plea.

"Yes?" she asked, her voice barely above a whisper, a question lingering in the air.

The man in the grey suit nodded solemnly, confirming her request with a soft "Yes." His understanding was clear, and Aayla let out a quiet sigh of relief, thankful that, for now, the humans would respect her boundaries.

The trays were carefully placed in the centre of the room, and the humans stepped back, retreating toward the doorway. Aayla moved toward them, her steps measured. With a subtle flick of her hand, she used her powers to drag the trays closer. It was customary for a male Aldredth to taste a bite of the food first, ensuring it was safe for his mate or Charge to consume. A practice born from caution and the need for vigilance.

Feeling uneasy, she surveyed the humans before her, one by one, her eyes lingering on each face. Tuning into their minds, she reached out with her telepathy. Though their words were beyond her grasp, their emotions were clear. Fragments of feelings pulsed through her, a language of its own.

One man to her left stood out. His thoughts pulsed with a dangerous edge—violent and excited. Her gaze lingered on him for a moment longer, and she made a mental note to keep close attention to his whereabouts around her.

After scanning the minds in the room, her attention shifted to a young man in military attire at the back, his sandy-coloured hair catching the dim light. He couldn't have been more than 25. His thoughts were a calming presence in stark contrast to the others. Gentleness and compassion radiated from him. Aayla offered him a small, reassuring smile. She picked up one of the cups and mimed drinking from it, her gaze fixed on him as she softly asked, "Yes?"

The young man froze, his face a portrait of shock and confusion. His wide eyes flicked between her and the others before he finally found his voice, stumbling out a hesitant "Y—Yes," followed by some words she couldn't decipher. The others in the room seemed equally unsure, glancing between them with quick, furtive looks.

Taking a deep breath, she sipped the clear-looking liquid and discovered it was water. The cool water soothed her dry throat, and she drank it eagerly, quenching her thirst. She exhaled in quiet relief and sat on the floor in front of the trays, her body still weak but managing to hold her up.

Her eyes flicked from item to item, and her senses sharpened as she began to sample the food. She offered a warm smile to the friendly young man and spoke casually about the food before her. Though he couldn't understand her words, the simple act seemed to put everyone at ease. Everyone except the man in the grey suit, who seemed displeased at being overlooked.

As she picked up various items, she gestured for their names, prompting the young man to smile nervously and respond with what she assumed were the correct terms for each.

Some items were tolerable, with simple, easy-to-consume flavours, but others were repulsive and left an unpleasant aftertaste on her tongue. She grimaced, pushing those aside. Then, she tasted something different—a soft, sticky substance resting on a bland, unappetizing food. She paused, her senses tingling. It was sweet, the unmistakable taste of high glucose. Her body responded instinctively, and she eagerly licked it, savouring the burst of sweetness that danced on her tongue.

She knew she needed to heal her wings faster and replenish her drained energy, and high-glucose food was her best chance. Aldredth thrived on high-sugar, high-energy diets to sustain their blisteringly fast metabolisms. Eyeing the friendly young man again, she pointed at the food in her hands, her meaning clear. After a quick, murmured discussion among the men, one finally spoke. "Honey," he said, his voice quiet but confident.

"Honey," Aayla repeated, her lips curving into a faint smile as she gestured for more. Several men scrambled out of the room at once, speaking into sleek black devices as they went.

While she waited, she savoured a few more sweet fruits, and the sharp tang and sugary burst briefly cut through the exhaustion. Dipping her finger into one of the sauces, she traced a picture of her sword on the ground. The humans exchanged uneasy glances, their eyes darting between each other and the man in the grey suit. His brow furrowed, his lips pressing into a thin line before he gave his head the faintest shake. The young man spoke to her in a gentle tone, his eyes cast downward and his voice laced with genuine regret as he apologised for having to refuse her request.

After a brief pause, he murmured something to one of the men behind him. A quick exchange followed among those in the room before one of the men swiftly disappeared down the corridor.

A few minutes later, the man returned carrying stacks of paper and coloured pens. Grabbing the top sheet, her hand moved with the precision only an Aldredth could achieve. She sketched Nannuval as it appeared from space, her photographic memory recreating the celestial image with perfect accuracy. Each line and detail captured a place and a moment in time, frozen forever on the page.

Drawing relaxed the tension in her shoulders, the flow of images spilling from her like a floodgate opening. One page after another, she filled them with scenes from Nannuval, the galaxy her planet inhabited, and countless detailed renderings of Talyn. His face, his wings, his eyes—each drawing an intimate capture of the man she feared might be slipping away from her.

Her heart ached with worry. She could only imagine the torment Talyn might be enduring at the hands of the Vhurl if he was even still alive. As an Aldredth, she would sense if her true mate had passed, but since Talyn was only her Guardian, she had no way of knowing whether he still lived.

Tears welled in her eyes, but she fought them back, clearing her throat and forcing herself to look up. The young man had moved closer, or rather, had been pushed closer to her, though she pretended not to notice. He stood in awe, his eyes scanning her drawings with a look of wonder.

She touched her chest and said, "Aayla," before gesturing toward him.

He glanced around at the others, a bit unsure, before mimicking her gesture, his hand resting lightly on his chest. "Seth," he said softly.

With a bow, she greeted him in her native tongue. He didn't understand the meaning, but his expression made it clear he understood the warmth in her voice and the respect in her gesture. It was strange, but humans seemed to have a remarkable sense of perception.

Another human appeared in the doorway with a tray holding several bottles of honey. He passed it to Seth, who hesitantly took it and placed it on the floor before sliding it to her. He gave her a reassuring nod, and she swiftly drank all of the bottles, to the amazement of those around her, before returning to her drawings.

The rest of the day unfolded in a blur of sketches and fragmented conversations with Seth. As she filled pages with images of Nannuval and the galaxy, she absorbed more human words, each one slipping into her mind like a small piece of a puzzle. Despite the language barrier, they managed to touch on a vast array of topics, including her people, their way of life, the Vhurl, and even aspects of human culture. The more they spoke, the more she found herself fascinated by their world, even if she only understood fragments of it.

As the hours passed, more humans came and went. Some watched her with wide-eyed curiosity, while others attempted to engage her in conversation. Their thoughts lingered in her mind, cloaked in feelings of threat, suspicion, and, perhaps, something more unsettling. Some even harboured a strange kind of desire that made her uneasy. She quickly retreated into her bubble with Seth, finding his steady presence a small comfort. Her silence toward the others, however, didn't go unnoticed. It clearly irked them, while Seth, ever the polite one, seemed increasingly embarrassed by her rejection of their attempts to communicate.

Aayla knew she would owe Seth an apology when all of this was over.

Trays of honey were brought in throughout the day, and Aayla drank deeply from them, her hunger insatiable. She consumed until her body felt on the verge of bursting. It gave her enough energy to move around, but she was still dangerously weak.

Seth had left the room for several extended periods before returning smelling like human food. He had clearly eaten a meal, but she wasn't sure how many meals the humans ate per day. As the evening wore on, she noticed Seth and several other humans yawning and rubbing their eyes, mirroring her exhaustion.

Sensing their weariness, she mimed sleeping gestures, rubbing her eyes and stretching out as though preparing for rest. Seth glanced at her, then at the others for guidance, his face tightening in concentration before he nodded. He pointed toward the cold, hard table behind her. It wasn't a bed, but it would have to do.

Aayla scrunched up her nose at the thought of sleeping on the cold, uncomfortable surface of the table. Her aching bones protested at the idea, each movement reminding her of the brutal punishment her body had endured. But despite the discomfort, she nodded and slowly sat on the table's edge.

The room gradually emptied of humans, their chatter low and indistinct as they left. Seth lingered in the doorway momentarily, his gaze drifting toward her. Unable to read his thoughts, she held his gaze briefly before he gave a small, reluctant sigh. Without another word, he turned away, his footsteps slow as he exited, closing the door behind him with a soft click.

The quiet that followed felt almost suffocating, and she found herself holding her breath, waiting for something to break the silence. But nothing came. Moments later, the light above her flicked off with a loud click, plunging the room into darkness. Finally, she was left alone with her thoughts, the weight of the day settling in her mind.

With a soft groan, she shifted, lying on her stomach to avoid putting pressure on her damaged wings. The coolness of the table beneath her felt strangely comforting as she adjusted, curling her arms beneath her head. The exhaustion that had been building throughout the day finally washed over her. Her muscles, still sore and strained, relaxed into the surface, and before long, the world around her faded.

She started to sink into a deep, much-needed sleep, her body finally releasing the tension that had held it captive for so long. Dreams came quickly—flickers of Talyn's face, fragments of distant stares, and the weight of unspoken words. Each vision was sharp, fleeting, yet intensely vivid as if her mind couldn't quite grasp onto them before they slipped away. The pain in her body faded into the background, swallowed up by the stillness of the night.

But just as sleep began to claim her fully, a strange, unsettling sound pierced the quiet. Footsteps, too deliberate, too close. Her eyes snapped open, heart pounding, but the room remained still and untouched, cloaked in darkness.

A shadow lingered by the door, and though she couldn't see it clearly, she felt its presence, cold and heavy. The muffled voices outside the door brought a tight knot of dread to her chest. She knew they were speaking about her, but she couldn't make out their words. What she did know was that she was being held prisoner in this room, her freedom carefully restricted. They had taken her weapon, her only means of defence, and without it in her weakened state, she was utterly vulnerable.

The question gnawed at her—how long would human curiosity keep her safe? How long would they keep her alive before their instincts to control and manipulate overcame their fascination with her?

She wasn't sure how much longer she could endure, how long she could remain in this cage of uncertainty and fear. The Aldredth were coming, she knew that. They would come for her, but would they arrive in time? Could she survive long enough for them to rescue her?

And what were the humans' plans for her in the morning?

CHAPTER NINE

Aayla awoke to the soft murmur of human voices, distant but persistent, tugging her from the edge of sleep. She shifted, sitting up with a wince as her sore muscles protested. Her shoulders throbbed, and the pain radiated from her damaged wings. As she massaged her shoulder muscles, they screamed in protest, and the pain from her damaged wings intensified with each movement.

When a wing was injured beyond use, like hers, it became a dead weight, heavy and unresponsive, making every slight shift feel like an effort.

A soft knock at the door pulled her from her thoughts. Seth entered, his hands raised in a gesture of peace, followed by several other humans dressed in various attire. Aayla gave him a tired but genuine smile, and Seth returned the smile, letting out a quiet laugh as he lowered his hands.

The day unfolded in a blur. Questions poured from the humans like a relentless tide, each inquiry probing deeper, some with genuine curiosity, others with an undercurrent of unease. There were more drawings, more discussions, and, inevitably, medical tests—each one an intrusive reminder of her vulnerability. Throughout it all, Seth remained by her side, his presence steady and constant, though not enough to quiet the mounting anxiety gnawing at her.

The small room felt increasingly suffocating, its four walls closing in around her with each passing minute. Aldredth thrived in wide open spaces, where the sky stretched endlessly, and their wings could catch the wind. The confinement of this tiny room, with its narrow walls and low ceiling, was a prison she could not ignore. Her agitation grew, and she began pacing restlessly, her mind racing. Every step felt like an inch closer to madness, the weight of her wings dragging her down as if trying to anchor her to the ground.

She squeezed her eyes shut, trying to block out the incessant hum of human voices around her. She focused on her breathing, forcing herself to calm down, but the unease lingered like a weight pressing against her chest. Time crawled, each second an eternity, until a voice finally pierced the fog.

"Aayla?"

The sound was familiar, warm. She turned sharply, her heart calming at the sight of Seth standing in the doorway. His hand rested lightly on the frame as he held the door open. His eyes met hers, filled with a quiet concern that spoke louder than words. The subtle tension in his expression told her he'd called her name more than once before she finally heard him, his worry evident.

With deliberate caution, Aayla stepped toward the door, maintaining a wide distance between herself and the humans. Her movements were measured, every step revealing the careful control she held over her unease. Without a word, she fell in behind Seth, who led her into a long, dimly lit corridor. The faint hum of distant voices echoed off the narrow walls, the sound both oppressive and disorienting.

The corridor was lined with doors, each fitted with small glass windows. Aayla's gaze flickered to them as they passed. Behind the panes, she caught glimpses of rooms almost identical to the one she had just left—stark, clinical spaces that seemed to leech the life from anyone within.

As they reached the end of the corridor, they arrived at an open stairway. Aayla hesitated, peering over the railing. The structure sprawled vertically in both directions, a maze of staircases and landings connecting floor after floor. She craned her neck to look above, where dim lights illuminated level after level. Her wings twitched instinctively, yearning for the open skies. Summoning her resolve, she tightened her grip on her unease and followed Seth as he began to descend.

Seth led her down the stairs and through more winding halls before finally stopping at a set of double doors. With a push, he opened them, and Aayla froze.

The ceiling was several stories tall and fitted with glass panels that let in sunlight. Aayla tilted her head back, her gaze fixed on the expanse of sky visible through the glass panels above. She stood still for a long moment, letting the sunlight wash over her, its warmth seeping into her skin like a long-lost comfort. The brilliance of the light filled her senses, grounding her in a way she hadn't felt since arriving. Finally, with a reluctant breath, she lowered her eyes to take in the rest of the hall.

There was a large seating section off to one side next to an opening in the wall that looked into what appeared to be a large kitchen. On the other side of the hall, the floor was lined with mats and exercise equipment. The middle of the room was a wide-open space.

She smiled for the first time that afternoon, the expression faint but genuine. She stepped into the centre of the room, her steps instinctively drawn to the centre of the sunlight streaming through the ceiling. Seth's voice rose behind her, explaining the space, but she hardly heard him. Instead, her hands moved to the bandages binding her wings.

Panicked voices erupted from the humans behind her as she carefully unwound the bandages. Their alarmed tones rose sharply, but Aayla ignored them and continued to unwrap her wings.

Beside her, Seth stood firm, whispering quiet, reassuring words to the humans. His presence radiated a calm authority that kept their interference at bay.

A Unix couldn't heal Aldredth wings, but thankfully, they healed relatively fast. Twice as fast as any other bone in their bodies. Removing the last of the bandages, she tried to unfurl her wings, but the broken bones had healed at incorrect angles, and her wings were now twisted in unnatural directions.

Reassessing, she instead tried to lift her wings and found, to her astonishment, that she still had limited movement, but not enough to fly. She stretched them out as far as they would go and slowly flexed them. The pain was agonising, but the exhilaration she felt at stretching her wings after having them bound for so long was worth it. The only thing more thrilling would be taking flight, but that was impossible given her current condition.

Seth spoke quietly behind her, his voice so low it was almost a murmur. When Aayla glanced back, she realised he wasn't talking to her but to himself. His eyes were fixed on her wings, wide with something akin to awe. Turning her gaze to the humans nearby, she noticed the same expression mirrored on their faces—fascination mingled with reverence, as though they were witnessing something extraordinary.

Her wings sagged under their own weight, brushing the ground. With a sharp breath, she used the muscles in her back to lift them again, holding them tightly against her body to keep the delicate feathers from scraping the floor. The effort was exhausting, but she managed.

Seth continued to watch silently before gesturing toward the large seating area. "Come," he said, his voice warm but firm. On one of the tables, a spread of honey and berries awaited her. It was clear the humans had been observing her closely, tailoring the food to her preferences.

Long, backless chairs flanked the table, and Aayla chose a spot at the end of one. She patted the space beside her, inviting Seth to sit. He accepted the gesture with a small smile and settled next to her just as the other humans filled the remaining seats.

The hall quickly came alive with the sounds of clinking dishes and the mouthwatering aroma of freshly prepared food. Trays piled high with human meals were brought to the table, and the humans eagerly dug in. Seth, however, paused, carefully offering Aayla a taste of each dish before helping himself.

Now that she had regained a minimal amount of strength, Aayla could afford to sample more delectable low-energy food. Hours passed as she ate, relaxed, and listened. While the humans' jokes often went over her head, their laughter was infectious, and she couldn't help but smile along with them.

As the sun dipped below the horizon, the light in the hall softened, casting long shadows across the walls. The humans trickled out one by one, leaving Aayla and Seth almost alone in the fading glow. He rose and gestured for her to follow.

Seth led her back down the staircase, but this time to a new room. The space was stark and utilitarian, furnished with nothing but a small bed perched on metal legs in the centre.

Seth hesitated at the door, his expression apologetic. "I'm sorry, Aayla, it's the best I could do," he said softly before stepping out with the others. As the door shut with a soft click, she circled the bed and looked around the room.

Her initial assessment had been incorrect because there was a camera in every corner of the small room. The humans clearly intended to keep her under close surveillance.

Her wings twitched in frustration as she turned her attention back to the bed. Though it was kind of them to provide one, the narrow frame was laughably inadequate for her size, let alone her wingspan. With a sigh, she stripped the mattress and sheet from the bed, dropping them onto the floor. She moved the bed frame to the corner of the room, then spread the makeshift bedding in the centre.

Lying down, Aayla stretched out as best as she could. The human mattress barely accommodated her body, and her wings hung off the sides, resting awkwardly on the cold floor. It was far from ideal, but exhaustion overruled discomfort.

Aldredth beds were like gigantic, padded mattresses that sat directly on the floor and were big enough to accommodate two Aldredth with their wings fully extended.

Sighing deeply, she could go for a nice, long bath right about now. Aldredth cherished water, bathing and swimming, not out of necessity but for the sheer joy of it. They didn't perspire or produce body odours like humans, which needed to be cleaned off frequently. On Nannuval, Aldredth would gather around the bathing pools, spending hours immersed in the warm water. It was a deeply cherished tradition. A time for connection and shared moments. The water became a sanctuary where bonds were strengthened, laughter echoed, and quiet conversations flowed as freely as the streams around them.

Washing one another's wings was also considered an extremely sensual activity shared between mates.

With a heavy sigh, she closed her eyes, her thoughts drifting as weariness took hold. The ache in her wings and the exhaustion of the past days faded into the background as sleep swept her away.

Her dreams were a whirlwind of vivid, shifting images, all centred around Talyn. In her sleep, the boundary between reality and fantasy blurred, pulling her into a world of memories and unspoken desires.

In the dreamscape, Talyn stood before her, his presence exuding the same male strength and masculinity that had always defined him. His wings unfurled, shimmering in the moonlight. Together, they soared through the skies of Nannuval, the planet beneath them a vibrant mosaic of colours and textures. The wind whispered through their feathers, a welcome contrast to the oppressive silence of the sterile human facility.

The dream shifted, and she was no longer in the sky but standing in the heart of Nannuval's lush forests, where sunlight filtered through the canopy, creating a mosaic of light and shadow on the forest floor. Talyn was there, laughing with a carefree joy that was as contagious as it was comforting. His presence was a beacon in the serenity, grounding her, filling her with a peace she hadn't felt in ages. They moved together through the trees, wings brushing the branches, their laughter mingling with the rustle of leaves, unburdened by the weight of their present reality.

Yet, the dream also carried shadows of unease. As she reached out to touch Talyn, the scene would flicker and distort, the lush greenery giving way to a desolate landscape. The familiar sight of Talyn would become a distant, wavering image, his face marred by pain and agony. The closer she reached, the further he slipped away, a fading image, as if something unseen were pulling him from her grasp. Her heart pounded with panic as the dream spiralled deeper into darkness.

In the dream's darkest corners, the nightmare took form. She saw glimpses of Talyn broken and bound in chains, struggling against the cruel forces of the Vhurl. The sight of him being tortured was agonising. She tried to reach him, but the distance between them seemed insurmountable, an invisible barrier that kept her from bridging the gap.

Just when it felt like she might drown in the suffocating weight of it all, a blinding light would appear, pulling her back to the more comforting memories of their shared moments. Talyn's reassuring presence, his soft, kind eyes, and the warmth of his touch. His lips moved as though he were speaking, and she stepped forward, hand outstretched, her fingers hovering near his chest.

But then, just as she was about to reach him, the loud sound of footsteps shattered the dream's fragile calm, dragging her back into the cold, harsh reality she had been trying to escape.

Chapter Ten

The echo of footsteps and murmured voices seeped into Aayla's consciousness, rousing her from sleep. She winced as she shifted, every muscle in her body protesting. The events of the previous day had taken their toll, and despite her need for rest, she knew better than to let her guard down. Her instincts, honed by years of surviving in hostile environments, kept her on edge. Just because the humans had been friendly so far didn't mean they would continue to be.

Reluctantly, she sat up with a low groan, her body stiff and sore. Every movement was accompanied by discomfort, and she carefully flexed her wings, wincing at the familiar ache. The delicate feathers were very sensitive, a sharp contrast to the strength they provided when she took to the skies. But for now, flight was out of the question.

A sudden, forceful knock shattered the quiet, followed by the metallic creak of the door swinging open. Aayla's eyes snapped to the entrance as Seth appeared, flanked by an older man whose stern, weathered features spoke volumes. He was a figure of undeniable authority. His presence seemed to alter the very atmosphere of the room. Behind him stood a dozen heavily armed men in black suits, their faces unreadable, their stance rigid. They were statues, muscles tensed, their eyes locked on her with unwavering focus.

Aayla quickly scanned their thoughts, detecting fear and anxiety but no trace of hostility. The tension in her shoulders eased slightly. Fear was something she could manage, though it could often prove unpredictable.

Seth stepped forward, offering her a warm, reassuring smile. He bowed deeply, his movements slow and deliberate, clearly showing respect. Aayla felt a flicker of amusement because the smart boy had been paying attention and learning her mannerisms. She smiled widely and returned the bow. There was something safe and comforting about his presence.

"Good morning," Seth greeted, his voice calm and steady as he introduced President Nick Bailey. Aayla's eyes flicked to the older man, studying him carefully. His expression was excited, and there was a hint of curiosity in his gaze as if he were trying to unravel the mystery she presented.

Two men entered, carrying a small table and two chairs, which they set down beside her with efficient precision. Moments later, Seth stepped out briefly, returning with a large tray overflowing with food and refreshments. He placed it before her on the table with a quiet reverence, and she couldn't help but notice the subtle deference in his actions. After briefly exchanging words with President Bailey, Seth bowed regretfully once more and left the room, the door closing softly behind him.

As the silence settled in, Aayla felt a surprising pang of sadness at his departure. This sudden sense of loss caught her off guard. She hadn't realised how quickly she had come to rely on his presence, the way he seemed to anchor her in this unfamiliar place.

"Aayla," a gentle, weathered voice called her name, pulling her from her thoughts. She looked up to find President Bailey observing her with a calm, measured gaze. Forcing a polite smile, she met his gaze, though the effort felt hollow.

The morning passed slowly as they sat together, attempting to converse despite the language barrier. Their exchanges were halting and awkward, but she appreciated the effort he made to communicate with her. Mainly, they engaged in lengthy discussions about Nannuval. When she casually lifted a piece of fruit from the tray with her power, she couldn't help but chuckle at the look of astonishment that flashed across his face. The way his eyes widened in surprise, the subtle shift in his posture, it was clear he had never seen anything like it before.

President Bailey seemed genuinely fascinated by her, and as the conversation progressed, Aayla demonstrated more of her abilities. She moved objects with a flick of her wrist, levitated others, and conjured small orbs of light that danced playfully through the air while carefully watching his reactions. She was cautious, revealing just enough to satisfy his curiosity without giving away too much. Trust was a delicate thing, easily broken, and she wasn't ready to lay all her cards on the table in this unfamiliar place.

But as the hours stretched on, the ache in her wings became impossible to ignore.

Wincing, Aayla rubbed at her shoulders, pressing her fingers into the tense muscles. Closing her eyes, she drew in a deep, steady breath, letting it fill her lungs before releasing it in a slow, deliberate exhale. President Bailey noticed instantly, his sharp eyes catching the discomfort in her movements. He frowned slightly, concern creasing his brow, before standing and whispering with the other humans in the room. Eventually, he turned back towards her, gesturing for her to follow.

She hesitated for a moment before slowly standing. They left the room, stepping into the labyrinth of corridors that seemed to stretch on endlessly. The building was a maze of concrete and steel, cold and unwelcoming, a stark contrast to the open skies she was accustomed to. President Bailey spoke continuously as they walked, his voice a steady stream of excited words that mostly fell on deaf ears. She caught fragments, bits and pieces of what he was saying, but mostly, the meaning eluded her.

Despite the language barrier, she could sense his attempt to put her at ease, to show her that she was not a prisoner here.

They passed through various rooms, some bustling with activity, others quiet and deserted. Aayla felt the weight of every gaze that followed her. The humans stared openly, their expressions a blend of curiosity and apprehension, their eyes lingering on her wings. She felt like a specimen under a microscope, every movement scrutinised, every expression analysed.

Finally, they stopped in front of the double doors that led into the large hall where she had spent the previous day. The two security guards flanking them held the doors open as President Bailey stepped into the room, gesturing towards the large seating area, still speaking nonstop. As she crossed the threshold, her eyes were immediately drawn to the sprawling table that was again covered in food. She hadn't realised how hungry she was until she saw the spread before her. But it wasn't the food that caught her attention; it was Seth's name, spoken casually by President Bailey as he pointed across the room.

Aayla's eyes darted across the room, drawn to a small, square ring where a group of humans had gathered around. Inside, Seth stood with his fists raised, his stance defensive as he faced off against another man. Their gazes locked, and Seth flashed her a quick, reassuring smile just before his opponent's fist slammed into his face, sending him crashing to the ground.

Aayla's reaction was immediate, driven by instinct. In a heartbeat, she was across the room, crouched protectively over Seth's crumpled form. Her heart pounded in her chest, a fierce growl rumbling from deep within as anger surged through her veins.

She flicked her hand, sending Seth's opponent hurtling into the far corner of the ring. The impact sent a jarring thud through the room.

The humans around her recoiled, fear flashing in their eyes as they stumbled backwards. Several reached for guns on her hips, but with a sweep of her power, she pulled the weapons out of their hands, the weapons skidding across the floor to rest at her feet.

The tension in the room was palpable. A thick silence, only broken by her deep growl, settled over everyone as most stood frozen in place.

Aayla barely registered the soft touch on her back before Seth's urgent voice broke through the haze.

"Aayla, no," he pleaded, his tone a mix of desperation and fear. He spoke rapidly, a string of words she couldn't quite grasp, but his movements made the message clear. He raised his hands in a calming gesture, slowly positioning himself between her and the fallen man.

Confusion flooded her as her mind raced to process the situation. Her heart hammered in her chest, and she scanned the room, trying to make sense of the chaos. Then, from the corner of her eye, she caught sight of Seth mimicking a series of slow, precise motions, and realisation dawned. They weren't fighting. They were playing. Training.

A wave of mortification swept over her as she realised her mistake. Slowly, she stood, raising her hands in a gesture of surrender. She attempted to apologise, but the words came out awkwardly, and the language barrier made her efforts seem futile. Yet, the regret in her eyes was unmistakable. Bending down to help the fallen man, she paused when he flinched from her touch, fear evident in his eyes. A heavy sigh escaped her as she straightened, feeling the weight of the misunderstanding settle heavily on her shoulders.

Her gaze drifted to the corner of the room where President Bailey stood surrounded by his security team. Their guns were trained on her, tension radiating from their rigid stance. She had indeed made a mess of the situation.

Stepping back, she watched as the humans swarmed into action, voices rising in a flurry of urgent conversation. Seth was at the centre of it all, speaking rapidly with several others, who quickly moved to confer with President Bailey. Aayla lingered on the sidelines, her heart heavy with the knowledge that her actions had only complicated an already delicate situation.

After a few tense moments, the head of security finally gave a firm nod, signalling to the rest of the team. Gradually, the team lowered their weapons, the air in the room losing its sharp edge. Aayla watched as they cautiously holstered their guns, the atmosphere slowly shifting from hostility to uneasy calm.

As the tension dissipated, the group began to disperse, a few gathering around the table set up in the corner of the room. It was clear that training had come to an end. President Bailey, now seated, gestured for the others to join him. Plates of food were laid out, including an abundance of honey and fruit, clearly prepared for her. The mood around the table slowly softened, the earlier wariness replaced by a more relaxed, communal atmosphere.

Hesitating for a moment, Aayla was unsure if she was welcome to join them. Seth crossed the room with a reassuring smile and gestured for her to follow. Despite the recent misunderstanding, there was no hostility in his eyes, only a quiet encouragement and maybe a hint of embarrassment.

As she slowly sat down, she noticed that some of the humans cast curious glances her way, though none were openly hostile. Clearly, they were still processing the earlier incident, but for now, they seemed content to let it go. She was seated directly opposite President Bailey, and Seth handed her a plate filled with delicious-smelling food. She found herself trying to focus on the meal before her. The flavours were strange but comforting, offering a brief respite from her swirling thoughts.

Around her, the humans chatted, their voices a steady hum that flowed easily between them. As she ate, Aayla studied the others, observing the subtle dynamics at play. They were a close-knit group, their interactions smooth and practised, filled with a sense of camaraderie. Despite the warmth of the meal and the casual atmosphere, she still couldn't shake the feeling of being adrift in a sea of words she couldn't understand. She glanced at Seth, who was engaged in a conversation with a few of the others, his expressions shifting quickly from serious to amused. He caught her gaze and gave her a small, reassuring smile.

Thoughts of Talyn surged, and Aayla's throat tightened as a wave of emotion threatened to overwhelm her. Her eyes stung with unshed tears, but she quickly rubbed a hand across her face in frustration, pushing the feelings away. As she leaned against the table, distracted by thoughts of Talyn, her elbow nudged the cup in front of her. It wobbled dangerously before tipping over the edge, crashing to the floor, and shattering upon impact.

Groaning, she stared at the mess she had just made.

Startled by the sudden noise, several humans instinctively rushed forward to clean up, but before they could reach it, Aayla flicked her hand with a casual, effortless motion. The broken pieces rose into the air, floating in a graceful dance. They hovered there momentarily as they reassembled, glinting in the light, before gently settling back on the table, whole and untouched as if nothing had happened.

The room fell silent, humans frozen in awe at the sight. Their shock soon gave way to amazement as they passed the reformed cup around, and their conversation shifted, picking up a new energy. Each person examined the cup with fascination, their discussions growing animated as she guessed that they speculated about the nature of her abilities.

Hours slipped by as the humans talked late into the night around her, their voices a blend of excitement and curiosity. Aayla, though still on the edge of the conversation, allowed herself to relax a little in their presence. Despite the language barrier, she could sense the change in the room, a quiet reverence replacing the earlier tension.

Eventually, the conversation wound down as the room began to clear out. Seth gave a subtle nod toward the door, and she responded with a warm smile. As they prepared to leave, several armed humans formed a protective circle around her, guiding her down the dimly lit hallway. Their footsteps echoed softly in the quiet corridor.

They led her to the room with the bed far too small for her wings. She exchanged a quiet farewell with Seth, and the door clicked shut behind her.

Exhausted, Aayla sank onto the bed. Within moments, she slipped into a deep sleep. The small room fell silent around her, the only sounds being the soft hum of the dim light and the distant murmur of the conversations she had left behind.

Aayla had only just drifted off to sleep when a low growl echoed down the hall. One that was definitely not human.

CHAPTER ELEVEN

Aayla's heart hammered against her chest as a heavy, primal sense of dread coiled tight in her stomach.

She froze, holding her breath, listening intently for any further sound. For a brief moment, she tried to convince herself it was just a lingering fragment of a dream. But then, the noise came again. Clearer and louder this time. A low, menacing growl echoed down the hall.

One that was distinctly Vhurl.

Panic surged through her as she shot upright. She darted to the door, her hand grasping the handle, testing it. Locked.

Her thoughts raced. There was no time to play their game, to wait for permission. With a surge of raw strength, she wrenched the door open, the lock splintering under her grip. The two humans stationed outside the door stumbled back in shock, their hands scrambling for their weapons.

Before they could even aim, the deafening roar of gunfire erupted from deep within the building, drowning out their movements. Aayla's pulse thrummed as the shots echoed down the hallway. She didn't stop to process it. She ran. A human stood no chance against a Vhurl, so she knew every second was costing another life.

The sound of the alarm blared in her ears, frantic voices crackling over the loudspeakers. Humans filled the corridor in front of her, and more were racing towards the fight. Her legs burned as she sprinted down the corridor, the chaos swelling around her. Gunfire rang out, punctuated by the terrified shouts of the humans.

She raced up three flights of stairs, the cacophony of gunfire and shrieks growing more intense, more desperate.

Pausing in the doorway of a smoke-filled room, she peered inside. The flickering light of a broken bulb illuminated a horrifying scene. Dozens of dead humans lay scattered across the floor, lifeless and broken. The room was eerily familiar, reminiscent of the one she had awoken in. The gunfire and screams farther down the corridor pushed her onward. There was no time for hesitation.

She pushed on, her feet moving faster now, nearing the end of the corridor, where a group of humans stood in her path. She scanned them quickly, assessing the situation. Every one of them was armed, but they were panicked and disorganised. Her eyes caught the faint glint of a small knife strapped to the belt of a man in the middle of the group.

It wasn't much, but it was her best choice.

Utilising her speed, she weaved through the humans in a blur of movement, seizing the knife without them noticing.

With the knife now in her grip, she continued forward, slipping into the room.

The room was filled with long tables, each displaying shattered artifacts in glass enclosures. At the centre of the room, a Vhurl stood with its back to her. Tubes hung loosely from its body, its hulking frame casting a shadow that seemed to swallow the room. Around him lay more fallen humans, their bodies strewn across the floor as the Vhurl loomed over them.

Aayla's pulse quickened. Though she had the appearance of strength, having awoken from a deep, restful sleep, she was still severely drained of power and burdened by her malformed wings that crippled her in battle. Engaging the Vhurl in this state would be suicide. But she had no choice.

The humans lacked the weapons to bring down a Vhurl, and without her, they wouldn't survive to tell the tale.

Gunfire erupted again, hitting the Vhurl's thick hide without so much as a dent. The creature barely flinched, but it was enough to draw his attention. His head snapped around, locking eyes with her.

The tension between them crackled in the air.

The Vhurl snarled, his lips curling back from sharp teeth. Then, he retreated a few steps, recognition flickering in his dark eyes. Aayla's breath hitched as she recognised him. This was the same Vhurl she had fought and struck down in the earlier battle. One she had thought was dead.

For some inexplicable reason, the humans had brought him here, patched him up, and made the fatal mistake of underestimating him. Now, they were paying the price.

Despite the fatigue weighing her down, Aayla forced herself to stand tall. Confidence surged through her—not because of her strength, but because she knew how to play this game. The Vhurl didn't realise how weak she indeed was.

She met his cruel gaze head-on, her voice steady and firm. "If you surrender now, I promise to let you live."

The Vhurl's eyes flickered between the humans in the room and the potential exits. His lips pulled back in a vicious snarl, baring his razor-sharp teeth.

"Where's your mate, little Aldredth?"

A chill ran down Aayla's spine, but she fought to keep her composure. The last thing she wanted was for him to sense her vulnerability, and she was hoping the Vhurl wouldn't notice that she was all alone amongst the commotion.

"You know I don't have a mate," she replied evenly, locking her eyes on his and keeping her voice steady despite the whirlwind of emotions churning inside her.

The Vhurl's snarl deepened as he took another step back. "Then where's your Guardian?"

"He'll be here soon," she said, the lie sliding out effortlessly. Anxiety gnawed at her insides. Where was Talyn? Was he safe? Was he on his way to her? She clung to that hope like a lifeline.

The room fell silent, the tension thick enough to cut through. The Vhurl tilted his head in thought before a low, rumbling laugh escaped his throat, growing louder until it echoed through the chamber. The sound sent a shiver of dread down her spine.

"You're all alone? Little Aldredth all by herself?" the Vhurl taunted, stepping forward with a slow, menacing movement.

Backing up instinctively, she lowered herself into a crouch, her growl barely audible but laced with warning. "I can take you on myself," she hissed, baring her teeth. She could definitely take him on; she just didn't think she could win.

The Vhurl's eyes roamed over her, scrutinising every inch, his twisted smile growing wider with sickening menace. "Where's your sword, little Aldredth?" he asked mockingly, taking two more steps forward.

Quickly stepping back two steps, Aayla wavered as her grip tightened around the small knife in her hand. "This is more than enough to deal with you."

The Vhurl's gaze lingered on her, eyes narrowing as he studied her with unsettling focus. He continued to examine every inch of her before letting out a low chuckle. "Your wings look a little injured, little Aldredth. Did we do that?"

He moved closer, his eyes glinting with cruel satisfaction.

Aayla felt the blood drain from her face. Instinctively, she glanced over her shoulder, her heart sinking at the sight of her deformed wings. The right one was twisted at an unnatural angle, the injury glaringly obvious even to those unfamiliar with her kind.

Even so, she was shocked that this Vhurl had been so observant. Vhurls were known for their brute strength, not their sharp senses.

Fear clawed at the edges of her resolve, but Aayla refused to let it show. She straightened, forcing herself to meet his gaze.

"Alone, unarmed, and crippled," the Vhurl sneered, lowering into a fighting stance. "This will almost be too easy."

Excitement flickered in his eyes before he launched at her.

Aayla reacted instinctively, lunging toward the towering Vhurl, her knife flashing in the dim light as she slashed at his thick, hide. The blade left shallow, glistening cuts across his chest and arms, but he barely flinched—his strength and size making her strikes feel like insect bites. Still, she pressed on, ducking low to avoid a crushing swing of his fist that cracked the ground where she'd stood a heartbeat before.

They moved in a deadly rhythm, circling, striking, dodging. Aayla twisted and turned with agile precision, her body weaving through the brutal force of his attacks like water slipping through fingers. Her knife danced across his flesh, landing quick, calculated strikes, but he remained relentless, swinging with bone-breaking force.

The Vhurls snarls grew louder, more frustrated, as she slipped just out of reach again and again, always a step ahead. But every move drained her further, and her strikes were little more than irritations to him. The confined space left her with very limited room to manoeuvre, and no chance to regain the upper hand.

Her foot slipped, and before she could recover, a massive fist connected with her jaw, sending her flying back. She slammed into the wall with a sickening thud, the impact knocking the air from her lungs.

Dazed, her ears ringing, Aayla crumpled to the ground. But survival instincts overrode the pain, and she rolled away just as his foot came crashing down where she'd been moments before.

She scrambled to her feet, backing toward the doorway. Her movements were slower now, each deflected blow taking more out of her. Desperation clawed at her chest. The knife in her hand felt insignificant, every slash barely breaking the Vhurl's thick skin.

Another punch connected, rattling her bones, and she stumbled back. This wasn't sustainable. The cramped space gave the Vhurl every advantage. She needed room, somewhere bigger, that allowed her more freedom to move and dodge.

Her pulse thundered in her ears as the Vhurl advanced, his grin widening in triumph.

Desperation sharpened her mind, and in a split second, she made her choice.

Turning sharply, Aayla bolted from the room and into the corridor. Using her powers, she gently but swiftly pushed the nearby humans safely down the hall, past the staircase, and to the far end, clearing the space before her.

She skidded to a stop at the staircase, breathless, and glanced back. The Vhurl emerged from the room like a shadow of death, his eyes gleaming with predatory intent.

Before she could act, fresh gunfire erupted from behind him. Bullets pinged off his thick hide, ineffective but enough to momentarily draw his attention. The Vhurl froze, his muscles tensing, then turned slowly toward the humans flooding the hallway. His gaze darkened with murderous intent.

One of the humans hurled a metallic sphere at the Vhurl's feet. It struck the ground with a resounding clang before detonating. The explosion rocked the corridor, filling it with acrid smoke and darkness as the lights flickered ominously. But when the dust settled, the Vhurl's mocking laughter echoed through the chaos. It was untouched and undeterred by the blast, and he continued his slow, menacing advance toward the humans.

"Stop!" Aayla shouted, her voice sharp, but the Vhurl didn't pause his stride.

Desperate to redirect his attention, Aayla raised her voice, mocking him with false bravado.

"What's wrong? Frightened? Are you too scared to take me on? Come on, show me what you've got! I'm clearly badly hurt and all on my own, but am I still too much of a challenge for you that you need to run away in the opposite direction?"

The Vhurl halted mid-step, his expression twisting into a mask of pure rage.

She really hoped this was a good plan.

Without wasting a second, Aayla spun and leapt over the staircase railing, her broken wings flaring out to slow her fall before she hit the lower platform with a jarring thud. Pain shot through her legs, but she shoved it aside, glancing up to meet the Vhurl's furious glare.

"I can taste your fear," he bellowed, his voice echoing ominously.

It was a lie, but it wasn't far from the truth in her current condition. Aayla's heart hammered in her chest, the weight of exhaustion pulling at her limbs.

With a thunderous crack, the Vhurl jumped from one level to the next, the concrete steps cracking beneath his feet.

Aayla sprinted toward the large hall, grateful to find it empty, and spun around, dropping into a defensive stance. Her breathing was uneven, so she took several slow breaths and focused on the rhythmic thrum of the Vhurl's approaching heartbeat.

Chapter Twelve

The double doors exploded off their hinges, fragments of wood and glass scattering across the floor. The Vhurl filled the doorway, his massive frame tense and coiled like a predator about to strike. The air between them buzzed with tension as they locked eyes.

The Vhurl smiled and launched towards her.

Aayla parried his relentless blows with desperate precision, her small knife slashing shallow cuts that barely slowed him and had yet to do any real damage. Meanwhile, every strike from the Vhurl landed with crushing force, sending shockwaves of pain through her battered body.

"I'm going to enjoy killing you," the Vhurl purred darkly, his voice thick with sadistic delight. "And after you're dead, I'll slaughter every last human in this building."

"I might let you live if you surrender now," Aayla retorted breathlessly.

The Vhurl threw his head back in laughter, a deep, mocking sound that reverberated through the hall. "I think I hit you too hard, little Aldredth. You're delusional."

In her peripheral vision, she saw more humans flooding the room, spreading out along the walls. They were poised to engage but stood hesitantly, having realised their weapons were useless against this monster.

The Vhurl's body was riddled with hundreds of cuts, each oozing only a tiny trickle of blood. Despite her relentless attacks, her blade was simply too small to penetrate the creature's thick, multilayered skin. She had landed stroke after stroke, but the Vhurl shook them off as if they were nothing. His fists, like battering rams, hammered at her defences with relentless power, each blow leaving her more weakened than the last. She could feel her bones breaking under the impact, her ribs aching with every breath.

What little energy remained in her was rapidly fading with each passing second.

Aayla parrying his blows with all her strength, but the fight felt increasingly hopeless. The Vhurl's attacks came in like waves, crashing into her repeatedly. He struck her with enough force to fling her across the room, slamming into walls and tables. With every strike, her vision blurred, her strength waned, and her breaths became ragged gasps for air.

Intermittent bursts of gunfire filled the air, but the Vhrul was so lost in his bloodlust that he didn't even pause.

Time seemed to blur, and the world was reduced to a whirlwind of frenetic movement and the relentless thud of blows. Her knife felt heavy and sluggish in her weakening grasp. The realisation settled in, a bitter truth that victory was slipping further from her reach.

The Vhurl, by contrast, moved with terrifying ease. His hulking form loomed before her. His gleaming eyes showed no concern, only a twisted sense of amusement as if she were no more than a bothersome insect to be swatted away.

Even as her broken body screamed in protest, her bones shattered, and her muscles on the verge of collapse, Aayla refused to surrender. The darkness closing in on the edges of her vision threatened to consume her, but she pushed it back with sheer force of will. Every breath was a struggle, each movement a defiance of the pain wracking her body, yet she drew upon her last reserves of strength. Desperately, she searched for a weakness in the Vhurl's attack, seeking some way to shift the tide of battle, but nothing came to her.

Still, she fought on, refusing to yield, knowing that giving in would mean far more than her own death.

A fist slammed into Aayla's face, sending her hurtling backward into a table that shattered beneath the impact. She hit the floor with a sickening thud, the knife slipping from her grasp and skidding just out of reach. Stifling a groan, Aayla twisted, stretching for the blade, but the Vhurl was faster. He landed in front of her, looming over her, and delivered a brutal kick to her head. The sickening crack of bone echoed through the room as her head recoiled from the impact. Pain exploded in her skull as her vision darkened, her body teetering on the edge of collapse.

Even as the abyss beckoned, Aayla gritted her teeth and clung to consciousness.

Dizziness washed over her, disorienting her as she struggled to regain her balance. Before she could react, massive hands clamped around her throat, hoisting her effortlessly into the air. She dangled at eye level with the Vhurl, his snarling face inches from hers. The rancid stench of his breath filled her lungs as he sneered.

"So much for the special little Aldredth. I thought you were supposed to be the strongest of them all."

Gunfire erupted again, but the sound felt distant, muffled by the pounding in her ears. Aayla gasped for air, choking in a ragged whisper, "No... I'm still just a child."

The Vhurl's lips curled into a cruel grin, and his grip tightened. Her lungs burned as the last traces of oxygen slipped away, her vision blurring. With a snarl, he hurled her across the room like a ragdoll. She slammed into the wall, the impact stealing what little breath she had left. Gasping, she crumpled to the floor, fighting to pull air into her battered lungs.

Before she could recover, the Vhurl loomed over her, his shadow casting her into darkness. His foot came down hard on her wing. Agony erupted through her body, a scream ripping from her throat as the already shattered bones were ground further under his weight. The Vhurl laughed, the sound dripping with sadistic delight as her vision flickered white with pain.

"Aayla!" a familiar voice broke through the haze.

She turned her head, teeth gritted against the searing pain, to see Seth standing in the doorway holding up her sword.

Extended her trembling hand, she dug deeper into her energy than was safe to go, and called the sword to her. The weapon responded instantly, ripping through the air and slamming into her palm with a metallic hum.

The Vhurl's momentum faltered, his expression contorting in surprise before quickly giving way to alarm as Aayla's sword arced through the air in a deadly sweep. The blade bit deep into his thick hide, eliciting a guttural roar of pain. He staggered backward, his balance faltering.

Aayla advanced, her movements fuelled by raw determination and the last reserves of her energy. Her blade flashed again and again, carving through his multilayered skin with brutal precision.

With one final, decisive blow, she severed his head clean from his shoulders. The Vhurl crumpled, his massive body hitting the ground with a thunderous thud. Black blood pooled around him, the severed head rolling lifelessly across the floor.

A grim smile tugged at Aayla's lips, but her triumph was fleeting. A sudden, sharp pain lanced through her chest, dropping her to her knees. Clutching at her heart, she gasped for breath as it beat erratically.

The realisation hit her like a physical blow. She had pulled too deeply from her life force to sustain herself in battle, and now her body was beginning to fail.

Darkness crept at the edges of her vision, growing thicker and heavier with each passing moment. Aayla swayed, unable to resist its pull. As the world blurred into nothingness, she toppled forward, her body giving out entirely.

Just before her body hit the cold floor, everything went black.

Chapter Thirteen

Aayla dreamed of the day she first met Talyn.

She had walked silently through the grand hall of Sabor and Frela's family estate, her small hand clasped tightly in her father's as her mother strode beside them. Sabor and Frela led the way, their steps eager, guiding them toward the Training Centre at the back of the estate. Aayla felt the weight of the new sword on her back, a gift from the day before on her second birthday. Its weight somehow felt foreign and familiar at the same time.

Aldredth children were socialised as much as possible from their birth in the hopes of finding their mate. They embarked on journeys across Nannuval, meeting other children, for it was only in person that a true mate could be recognised. Even newborns were capable of identifying their mates. If an Aldredth hadn't found their mate by the time they were ready to leave their home world, another suitable unmated Aldredth would be assigned to them. Females were called Charges, and males were called Guardians. They remain paired until they find their true mate.

That morning, Aayla had been told she would meet her new Guardian, Talyn. He hailed from the lineage of the original founding fathers, a line that had nearly been declared the royal bloodline when the monarchy was first established. Talyn's family was renowned for producing exceptionally skilled warriors. His family's name was synonymous with strength and loyalty, their legacy etched into Aldredth's history as protectors of Unix and Lazuil rulers.

Sabor and Frela, like all previous generations, were intensely proud of their heritage. They carried the weight of their responsibility with strict discipline, knowing the demands of their lineage left no room for failure. Aayla expected no less from Talyn, knowing his upbringing would reflect the same pride and, most notably, the strict devotion to duty.

Yet, the thought of meeting him filled her with unease. She feared his rigid adherence to rules might constrain her spirit, especially since she was someone who always forged her own path.

With a nervous knot in her stomach, Aayla turned the corner and saw him for the first time. Talyn sat cross-legged in the centre of the Training Centre, his wings spread wide behind him, their soft gold shimmer catching the morning light. His focus was fixed on the sword that he was meticulously polishing in his hands.

For a moment, her world shifted. She stood frozen, captivated by him, oblivious to everyone else and the sounds around her, lost in the rhythm of his heartbeat. When he glanced up, their eyes met, and it felt as if time itself had stopped. Her heartbeat quickened, but it wasn't fear; it was recognition, deep and unshakable. She felt like she was looking into her own soul and wanted to cry with joy.

Before the thought had fully registered, she ran to him, throwing herself into his arms. His hold was strong yet gentle, and she felt like she'd found a lost part of herself she hadn't even known was missing.

"He's my mate!" she declared, her voice trembling with certainty.

Turning to her parents, she saw their expressions shift from surprise to horror. Frela's voice broke the silence, sharp and panicked. "Impossible! Don't ever say such things!"

"But it's true," Aayla insisted, shaking her head. "We're—"

"No, Aayla," her father interrupted, his tone quiet but desperate. "It can't be. He's not of royal blood. Even suggesting it could lead to his death. You know it's impossible, so you must not say such things." His expression was begging her to stop.

Tears welled in her eyes as Talyn's arms tightened protectively around her. "I don't understand," she wept. Turning to him, she searched his face. "Do you feel it too? Do you think I'm your mate?" Her voice trembled.

Tayln's deep green eyes searched hers, and he opened his mouth to respond, but before he could answer, his father stepped forward. "Maybe we should pair Aayla with our eldest instead—"

"No," Talyn snapped, his wings flaring slightly as he glared at his father.

Frela paled, her voice trembling. "I'm sorry, Talyn. We can't pair you together if you keep talking about being mates. If anyone hears that, you'll be immediately executed."

Talyn growled softly but said nothing, his jaw tight. His father shook his head, his hands on his hips, as his voice carried a note of finality. "If you can't distinguish your feelings of love for your Unix from those of a mate, you're unfit to be her Guardian. That's final."

Talyn stared hard at the floor, tension rippling through him, before he looked back at Aayla. His expression was unreadable. "No, I can do it. Nothing is stopping me from acting as Aayla's... Guardian," he said quietly.

The word felt like a dagger to her heart. Guardian. That's all he felt for her. Pushing away from him, tears streaming down her face, she ran as fast as her legs could carry her from the room. She flew off the balcony, circling the estate, blinded by tears until she collapsed in a meadow of long grass. Folding her wings behind her back, she sat down, hidden in the grass, and buried her face in her knees as sobs rocked her body.

The grass swayed in the gentle breeze above her head as if it were dancing in the sky.

Aayla sensed Talyn approaching before she heard the soft rustling of his wings as he landed behind her. Walking forward silently, he sat beside her and wrapped his arms around her in a gentle embrace.

"Are they taking you from me?" she whispered, her voice trembling.

Talyn cupped her face, lifting it so their eyes met. "If you agree you were mistaken, they don't see any reason why I can't be your Guardian. But... if you don't admit it, then..." His voice trailed off, leaving an unspoken weight in the air.

They sat silently for what felt like an eternity, watching the grass dance in the breeze. Finally, Talyn broke the quiet.

"I'm sorry I can't be what you want me to be. I wish I could tell them you're my mate, but—"

"No, you're right," Aayla interrupted, her heart sinking. If Talyn didn't see her as his mate, there was no way he could truly be hers. Their parents must be right, she must be mistaken, and maybe, with time, she would understand why she felt this way. "I think I made a mistake."

Talyn's expression shifted to one of shock and confusion. "You did?"

Nodding, Aayla looked away, finding it easier to think when she wasn't getting lost in his deep green eyes. "I'm sorry for what I said. I don't know why I thought... but I promise I won't say it again."

"O... okay..." Talyn's face paled, a ghostly look settling over him. "If it was a mistake, then we'll pretend it never happened and not speak of it again. If that's what you wish?"

"I do," she replied softly, feeling the heaviness of her words settle between them.

CHAPTER FOURTEEN

In all of Aldredth's history, no Aldredth had ever aged beyond 25 without finding their mate. Aayla was currently 21, and Talyn was 22. The reason she hadn't found her mate yet was simple—she had been actively avoiding it since the day she met Talyn.

From the moment she met Talyn, she was certain he was her mate. She also knew it wasn't possible. Still, the pull she felt toward him was undeniable, a tether that tightened every time they were near.

Whenever someone arranged a meeting with other unmated Aldredth's, Aayla always found a reason to be unavailable, dodging the inevitable. But now, with only a handful of eligible males left, the pressure was mounting, and their persistence to meet her was becoming overwhelming. She dreaded the moment everyone else found their mate, leaving her still unbonded. What would her people think when they realised she was broken? Surely, only a broken Aldredth would look upon an Aldredth male who was not their mate with such desire in their heart.

Worse, she felt guilty for keeping Talyn from his true mate. He refused to meet other unmatched females until she found her mate. Ever self-sacrificing for her.

Her thoughts fractured as familiar voices whispered in the back of her mind, pushing away her longing and guilt. She strained to hear, but the voices were distant as if echoing from across a great void.

She concentrated on the voices until they grew louder and felt close enough to touch. Her eyelids fluttered open, the bright light burning her eyes.

"Ayala, thank the stars! Can you hear me?" a familiar voice called out, relief dripping off their words.

"Yes," she mumbled, her voice raspy as her vision swam with blinding white.

"It's okay, you're safe now. We've got you".

As Aayla blinked, the blurred figures before her sharpened into focus. Martok, a Lazuil of royal blood with shimmering turquoise wings, knelt beside her, his hands cradling hers with gentle care. His mate, Skyla, stood close by, her scarlet wings tucked protectively at her side. Around them, a small group of Aldredth filled the human room where she had first awoken.

She tried to sit up, but a searing pain shot through her body.

"Stay still," Martok urged softly. "You're badly hurt, and you have to heal before we can move you. I thought I almost lost you..." His breath hitched at the end, and she knew they all would have been suffering greatly at the sight of her injuries.

"No," Aayla rasped, fighting through the pain. "I need to find Talyn. They took him. They have him—"

"He's safe." Martok quickly reassured her, pushing her gently back onto the bed. "The Vhurls were gloating about capturing an Aldredth to auction off to the highest bidder. We thought it was you. We didn't realise it was Talyn until after we rescued him. As soon as we figured out our mistake, we came for you. I'm so sorry we weren't here for you."

Relief swept over her like a tidal wave, and tears stung her eyes. "Thank you," she whispered, her voice trembling.

Martok looked into her eyes, and his words felt like a warm embrace in her mind. *Have they treated you well?*

She looked towards the doorway but didn't see any humans in the room. Returning his gaze, she gave him a reassuring smile. "Yes, they've cared for me as best they could."

A collective sigh of relief rippled through the Aldredth around her. Mated Aldredth stood side by side, their wings overlapping in an intimate embrace. Even in the cramped space, they maintained a respectful distance between pairs to avoid wings brushing and allowing room to manoeuvre if they needed to defend themselves.

Skyla gently patted Aayla's arm. "Are you able to heal yourself?"

Aayla nodded. "Enough to move, yes. I'll finish the process later."

Several Aldredth exchanged disapproving glances with their mates. They hated the idea of her enduring pain for even a moment, but she was resolute. She needed to remain conscious until they were safe aboard their ship, just in case something happened and one of her people required her healing abilities.

Skyla and Martok exchanged a long glance, communicating silently before Martok's wings rustled faintly, and he finally nodded.

Shutting her eyes, Aayla placed her right hand on her chest and focused on the rhythm of her heartbeat. She willed her body to heal, directing her energy toward the fractured bones that hindered her movement. Exhaustion weighed heavily on her, and the process took longer than usual. Pain rippled through her with every pull of energy, sharper and more demanding than she had anticipated.

Opening her eyes, she offered a reassuring smile, though the Aldredth around her didn't seem convinced. Nevertheless, they all responded with cautious smiles of their own, and Martok stood, extending his arm to help her up.

"Careful. Just take it easy," he said, his gaze scanning her with concern, lingering on the bruises and unhealed cuts. "I'll carry you."

"No," Aayla replied gently, her voice steady but strained. "I'm well enough to walk."

She swung her legs off the bed, but the moment her feet touched the cold floor, her knees buckled.

Martok's warm arms caught her before she could fall, cradling her against his chest. "Do you want to try again?" he joked, laughing.

She gently patted his cheek, her smile widening at the sound of his laughter. "You know, I think I might just take you up on that offer after all."

Martok cradled her in his arms as they moved into the hallway, flanked by the other Aldredth, who had formed a protective circle around them. The corridor was filled with humans wearing a mixture of different uniforms, their expressions a mix of curiosity and awe.

Martok inclined his head at President Bailey, who stood in the centre of the corridor. "Thank you for taking care of her."

The President's face brightened at the acknowledgement. "It was an honour. And I'd like to reiterate that we would be deeply grateful to begin a dialogue between our civilisations. We have so many questions to ask you. There is so much we wish to learn."

Martok nodded. "And we would be honoured to answer those questions in due course. We'll be in contact soon."

The humans parted to allow the Aldredth to pass and followed them as they exited the building. The metallic doors swung open with a click, and Aayla blinked rapidly, momentarily blinded by the bright sunlight after the dim interior.

Before her lay a vast expanse of lawn, with a small army of Aldredth forming a protective ring around the perimeter while a few stood in the centre, engaged in quiet conversation. Beyond them was an ocean of humans of all different ages and sizes. Some were cheering, some were screaming, and others stood seemingly frozen in awe. Sirens wailed in the distance, carried on the soft breeze. The roar of the countless sounds and voices merged into a cacophony of noise.

Martok carried Aayla with deliberate care toward the centre, while the Aldredth they passed lowered themselves in deep bows in a traditional gesture of respect. Aayla responded to each with a soft smile and a nod of acknowledgment.

The grass was alive with colour as the wings of each Aldredth shimmered in the light, their vibrant hues painting the air like a living tapestry. Each set of wings was as unique as a human fingerprint. Their hair and eye colours, too, varied, often revealing family connections passed down from parent to child.

"What's the situation?" Martok asked Rune, an Aldredth of Vajjer blood, and his mate Ceeda, of Aurra blood. Rune's vibrant orange wings edged in deep plum, brushed against Ceeda's magenta wings streaked with threads of golden yellow as they stepped forward.

Both Rune and Ceeda bowed deeply toward Aayla. "It is an honour, Unix," Rune said solemnly.

Aayla nodded in acknowledgment. "Thank you for your help," she said, her voice softening as she lowered it. "Are there any injuries?"

"No, my Unix," Rune assured her. "Everyone is safe."

Ceeda nodded, "Yes, there haven't been any incidents, but there are many negative thoughts wishing us harm. It would be wise to move quickly."

"Agreed," Martok said firmly. "Give the order. We return to the ships."

Martok nodded to his mate, and they flared their wings before they took to the sky, soaring straight up toward the shimmering ships hovering just beneath the clouds.

As their feet touched down inside the ship's entryway, Aayla glanced below and saw the Aldredth executing a perfectly coordinated retreat. The weakest took to the sky first, while the strongest remained behind to cover their exit. In Aldredth society, strength comes with responsibility. The strongest amongst them, which was the Unixs, followed by the Lazuils, always protected those weaker than themselves. They led from the front, standing as the first line of defence and the last to leave any battlefield. The ruling class did not hide behind their army—they led it into battle. First in, last out.

Except, of course, when they had to rush a gravely injured Unix to the nearest MedBay.

The Aldredth ships were sleek and curved, their design prioritising functionality and beauty. Spacious interiors allowed wings to spread freely, with large, open corridors and chambers. Martok carried Aayla swiftly through the ship's halls, his movements efficient and purposeful.

"Soval, Aeryn, is that you?" Aayla exclaimed, her tone brightening as Martok gently lowered her onto the soft, raised bed in the MedBay.

Soval, an older Aldredth of Emba blood with olive-hued wings, stepped forward, his smile warm but tinged with worry. His mate, Aeryn, also of Emba blood, stood beside him, her deep purple wings shimmering like velvet under the soft light. They were the ones who birthed Aayla, cared for her during the first few years of her life, and she had been stationed with them on several different planets over the years.

Soval smiled widely. "It's so good to see you, Aayla. We've been so worried." He ran a scanner over her body, and his expression darkened as he studied the readings. "You look surprisingly well considering everything. But your wings..."

She knew exactly what he was thinking. "Do you need to excise them?"

Aeryn zoomed in on the scanner's display, her brows furrowing as she examined the damage. Soval rubbed his chin thoughtfully. "We might be able to save them. That's a big might."

"Do whatever you need to." Aayla nodded without hesitation. She reached out, taking Soval's hand in hers. The calming influence of a Unix's touch flowed through him like a gentle tide. The tension in his features softened, his shoulders relaxing under the soothing energy. It was one of the many abilities unique to a Unix.

Soval squeezed her hand, smiling softly. "Get some rest. We'll be right here when you wake up."

Aeryn handed Soval a vial of sedative, and he first tested its contents for safety. It was an instinctive gesture of protection hardwired into the DNA of male Aldredth. After confirming it was safe, he slowly injected it into Aayla's arm while Aeryn gathered the tools to reset her wings.

They would first need to break and realign the malformed bones, using small struts to hold them in place. The struts would dissolve in a week, giving the bones enough time to start knitting together. They would then inject a bone growth stimulant into the other sections of her wings where the bones had shattered to accelerate the healing. She needed to sleep through this process, as it was excruciatingly painful.

The sedative took effect quickly, and Aayla's eyelids grew heavy. She gave them a faint, drowsy smile. "Feel free to make some improvements while you're back there," she joked, her voice fading.

Soval chuckled softly. "We'll see what we can do. Now sleep, Aayla."

With a final smile, Aayla closed her eyes. The darkness embraced her gently, and the hum of the ship faded into silence as she drifted into unconsciousness.

CHAPTER FIFTEEN

Aayla's mouth felt parched, her wings ached, and the weight of exhaustion kept her eyes shut. The quiet, muffled sounds around her faded as she became acutely aware of a familiar presence beside her—Talyn's energy.

Her heart leapt as she bolted upright, her pulse racing. She found Talyn slumped in a chair at her bedside, his head and arms draped across her legs, fast asleep. He had big, dark bags under his eyes, and his complexion was ashen, drained of life, as though he hadn't slept in days.

"He hasn't moved from your side since he arrived," Aeryn's soft voice broke the silence.

Aayla turned toward Aeryn, seated by a display screen at the far side of the room, reviewing her bloodwork. She managed a faint smile. "How long have I been out?" she rasped.

Aeryn stood and walked over, running a scanner over her. "Eight days. You gave us all quite a scare. Talyn arrived seven days ago."

Aayla's gaze shifted back to Talyn, and she reached over and gently threaded her fingers through his hair. His eyes snapped open at the touch, and in an instant, he sat upright, cupping her face with trembling hands.

"Aayla," he breathed, his voice trembling with raw relief. "Thank the stars! Are you okay? How do you feel? Does anything hurt? Do you need water, food, anything?" His questions came in a frantic rush, his eyes scanning her face like he didn't believe she was real.

She pressed her hands over his, her touch grounding him. "I'm fine," she whispered. "I was so worried about you. Did they hurt you?"

"Forget about me," Talyn said, his voice a mix of anger and guilt. "I've barely eaten or slept. I'm so sorry for leaving you unprotected. This is all my fault." His anguish was palpable, and it took all of her strength not to reach out and embrace him.

Talyn shook his head and dropped his gaze to the floor.

"I... I think maybe you need a better Guardian than me..." His voice trailed off, and he looked pained by the very words.

"What? Never!" Aayla's voice was firm, filled with disbelief. "This isn't your fault, Talyn. There is no one better than you. You have nothing to be sorry for—"

"I've seen the scans," Talyn interrupted, his eyes locking onto hers. "I know how badly you were injured."

Aayla froze, her heart sinking. She had hoped their separation had shielded him from the truth of her injuries. But Soval's scans would have revealed everything, including all of the fresh heals.

"They probably make it look worse than it—"

"They recorded it!" Talyn shouted as if he had been trying to keep the words hidden.

A sense of dread washed over Aayla. "Recorded what?"

"The whole thing," yelled Talyn as he started pacing the room. "Every second, from the moment I left you until Martok found you. The humans recorded everything that happened. Apparently, that species records every part of their lives, so we have multiple angles of everything they did to you."

Her breath caught. "Did... did you watch it?" she whispered.

Talyn stopped pacing the room and braced his hands on the end of the bed. When he looked up at her, his eyes were filled with raw anguish. "Yes," he said, the word hanging heavy in the air between them.

Aayla felt her stomach churn. Talyn would never forgive himself for this. She could see the weight of it crushing him, his guilt a burden that would haunt him forever.

Tears welled in her eyes as she turned to Aeryn. "Why did you let him watch it?"

Aeryn's gaze dropped to the floor, guilt etched into her expression. "I'm so sorry," she murmured, meeting Aayla's eyes again. "We didn't realise how bad it was. But as your Guardian, we didn't have the right to stop him even if we had known."

Aayla's stomach churned. In Aldredth society, every moment of life was meticulously recorded. However, one unbreakable rule stood firm that no Aldredth was ever shown footage of their mate enduring torture or significant pain. The emotional bond between mates was too profound, and the guilt of failing to protect their partner would be an unbearable weight, a shadow that would haunt them for eternity. Guardians, by contrast, were permitted to view such recordings. Though deeply committed, their role lacked the intimate, unshakable attachment shared by bonded mates.

However, Aayla knew Talyn would carry the guilt in the same way. It would eat away at him. Knowing that hurt her more than any torture the Vhurl had inflicted.

Talyn straightened, pacing the room in tense, measured strides before turning to face her. His eyes were filled with a mix of desperation and fear. "It's a miracle you're even alive. I couldn't live with myself if something happened to you. I can't risk you," he said, his voice thick with emotion.

Aayla shook her head firmly. "And I won't live without you by my side. That's non-negotiable. I trust you with my life."

Talyn's expression darkened. "I almost cost you your life—"

"And I'd rather die than live without you!" Aayla yelled, her voice raw with emotion. She stood her ground, her gaze locked on his, unwavering. Her chest heaved with each breath as if her very heart depended on his next words. Slowly, she extended her arms toward him, a silent plea.

For a moment, Talyn hesitated, torn between running into them or away from them. His jaw clenched, but then, with two giant strides, he closed the distance between them, pulling her into his arms and hugging her tight against his body.

Aayla put her arms around him and crushed him against her with equal intensity. They closed their eyes and pressed their faces together as Talyn's wings surrounded her. Their bodies were pressed together, and she could feel every contour of his muscular body against hers, igniting a deep yearning inside her. She wanted more, needed more. The heat of his breath ghosted over her lips, and she imagined the warmth of his kiss, the feel of his lips against hers. She wanted to rip his clothes off and feel their naked bodies pressed together.

But too soon, Talyn leaned back, his gaze meeting hers. His deep green eyes held her captive, like staring into a piece of her own soul. She could have lost herself in them for hours.

Something flickered across his face—a fleeting emotion she couldn't grasp. Talyn gently rested his forehead against hers, his lips parting as if to say something, when the door swung open. Martok and Skyla entered the room, shattering the quiet intimacy of the moment as Talyn quickly folded his wings tightly against his back.

"Thank the stars, you're finally awake!" Martok said as he came over to stand by her bedside, his face lighting up with relief. Nearby, Skyla was communicating telepathically with Aeryn, likely discussing Aayla's latest test results.

Talyn silently stepped back into a protective stance, his eyes scanning the room for any potential threat, even in a place as safe as the MedBay. Only mated Aldredth had the right to stand at their mate's side. Guardians, on the other hand, were expected to be close enough to protect their Charges but distant enough to be an unobtrusive presence and not interfere or be in anyone's way. Always in the shadows.

When two Aldredth's mated, they both carried the status of the highest-ranking partner. The Unix bloodline was the highest-ranked, followed by the royal Lazuil bloodline, Vajjer, Aurra, Vorax, and Emba. Guardians, however, ranked below even an Emba, regardless of their bloodline. This was because their sole purpose was the protection of their Charge. Charges, by contrast, were ranked according to their bloodline.

As her Guardian, Talyn didn't carry Aayla's status as a Unix, nor his as a Vajjer. In the eyes of the others, he might as well have been invisible.

A deep anger stirred within Aayla at the sight of Talyn standing off to the side, overlooked and unacknowledged by everyone in the room. But she quickly pushed the anger back down, turning her attention to Martok.

"Thank you for everything you've done," she rasped, her voice hoarse from the long sleep. "What's the current status?"

Skyla walked over to join them and briefly communicated telepathically with Martok before he turned back towards her. "The Vhurl involved in the incident have all been eliminated. No Aldredth casualties."

Aayla opened her mouth to speak, but Martok raised a hand, cutting her off, "And no injuries requiring your attention," he added firmly.

Letting out a sigh of relief, she smiled at Martok. "Well done, both of you. What about the humans?"

"We're still in orbit around Earth," Skyla replied. "We've been in communication with them and are preparing for an in-person meeting once you've fully recovered."

"I'm well enough to—"

"To do nothing," Martok interrupted, his tone brooking no argument. "No one is going near that planet until you completely recover."

Aayla opened her mouth to protest, but Martok knew what she would say and shook his head. "I will make you undergo a fitness test if I have to."

Knowing she wasn't in any shape to pass, Aayla sighed in defeat and patted his arm. "Okay, we will wait. But I will wait from the comfort of the garden if you don't mind."

Carefully, she twisted and swung her legs over the edge of the bed, groaning as stiff muscles protested the movement. Talyn was instantly at her side, his hands steadying her as she stood, their wings gently brushing together as she swayed. Her body felt weak from her extended time in bed, but she masked the discomfort, walking slowly from the room.

Aldredth bowed their heads to her in a sign of respect as she passed, and Aayla inclined her head in acknowledgement.

Aayla's wings trailed heavily along the floor, her back muscles straining with each attempt to lift them. She fought to keep them raised, but the aching tension in her shoulders made it impossible, every movement sending a dull throb of exhaustion through her body.

Talyn walked silently beside her, his presence a warm caress on her soul.

As they reached the entrance to the garden, Talyn hesitated, his steps slowing as if weighed down by an unspoken thought. "Do you intend to go back to Earth? Or are we returning to Neptuinea?"

Neptuinea was an allied planet on which they were meant to be stationed. The planet was chosen based on several factors, such as the distance to the nearest Unix, the likelihood of needing a Unix, and safety.

Aayla paused, turning to face Talyn. "I haven't decided yet. But I already have a connection with some of the humans, which could be advantageous."

Talyn's brow furrowed in thought. "Earth is a dangerous planet," he mused. "And the closest Unix is quite far away."

"It is," Aayla agreed. "It would be a prime location for a Unix to be stationed. Would you be upset if we didn't go back to Neptuinea?"

Talyn's expression softened, and he let out a low chuckle. "I'll be happy as long as I am with you. Besides, Earth looks like it might be fun," he teased, a mischievous grin playing on his lips.

Aayla smiled back, her heart-warming at the sight of his grin. "All right then. Let's do it."

Talyn's smile widened, and for a moment, Aayla was mesmerised. He was easily the most handsome male she had ever seen. How others didn't seem to notice was a mystery to her.

The door to the garden slid open, and the sound of laughter spilled into the air, light and full of life.

"Aayla! My Unix!" boomed a familiar voice. Reluctantly, Aayla broke her gaze with Talyn and turned, smiling in greeting at Rune, who stood before her, bowing deeply, his eyes alight with excitement.

When Rune rose, he nearly bounced on his feet. "My goodness, you're finally awake! How are you? Do you need anything?"

She smiled softly, his energy infectious. "Thank you, Rune, but I've only just woken up. I intend to be back asleep shortly," she teased, her voice light but still a bit hoarse.

Ceeda danced over to Rune's side, her movements graceful and full of joy. She bowed deeply before Aayla, her magenta and golden yellow streaked wings shimmering in the light, but Aayla waved her hand dismissively, grinning. "Please, continue your dance. I'll catch up with you at dinner."

Rune and Ceeda shared a playful glance before twirling away in perfect harmony, their laughter echoing through the garden. Aayla's heart squeezed at the joy on their faces as they nestled into each other with wings overlapping in an intimate caress. It stirred something deep within her—a longing to feel her mate wrapped around her.

Or, more precisely, a longing to feel Talyn wrapped around her.

Out of the corner of her eye, she caught Talyn watching Rune and Ceeda intently, his expression thoughtful and unreadable.

The garden was alive with vibrant colour and tranquillity. Aldredth moved about, bowing respectfully to Aayla as they passed. The garden was a sanctuary for their people—a place of peace and relaxation. It wasn't uncommon for Aldredth to drift off to sleep beneath the warm, artificial sun. The projection was flawless. Above her, the bright sun shone high in a sky so blue it could have been real. The warmth on her skin, the soft breeze—it was just like being on Nannuval. The space teemed with life. Big brittlebush and pleech trees were ringed with rainbow snowwood, fairymoss, and dragon feverfew. The plants formed private nooks scattered throughout the garden, and a soft, flowing creek wound its way through, connecting the tranquil spaces.

Gardens were cherished treasures among the Aldredth, so much so that they replicated them aboard their ships and on any planet where indigenous plant life was scarce. These green sanctuaries were essential to their well-being, a symbol of life and tranquillity that nourished their soul wherever they travelled.

"That spot looks nice," Aayla said, pointing to a small patch of long grass encircled by brittlebrush trees.

Talyn smiled, leading her to the clearing. His wings brushed gently through the soft grass as they walked, and Aayla's eyes were drawn to them, captivated by their beauty and quiet strength. Tearing her gaze from his wings, she lay down, the soft earth beneath her grounding her in a way that brought immediate comfort. The scent of fresh soil filled her senses, and her tension began to melt away.

Aayla stretched out on her back, her wings spread out beside her. Tilting her head to the side, she watched the breeze gently jostle Talyn's hair. He lay beside her on his side, gazing into her eyes with an intensity that made her pulse quicken.

Her gaze dropped to his lips, and a shiver of longing rippled through her. She imagined the feel of his mouth trailing down her neck, sending a flush of warmth across her cheeks. The yearning inside her grew stronger, nearly overwhelming, and she shifted, pressing her legs together as her heart raced.

Quickly, Aayla shut her eyes and turned her face back toward the sun, forcing herself to stay grounded before she did something she would regret.

The warmth of the sun soaked into her feathers, its soothing heat lulling her into a state of peaceful exhaustion.

As sleep began to pull her under, she felt Talyn's touch—a gentle caress as he brushed a strand of hair from her forehead.

His fingers trailed softly down the side of her face, lingering on her cheek. His touch was like a promise she could feel deep in her soul.

Chapter Sixteen

The next few days blurred into a whirlwind of meetings.

Aayla debriefed the senior Aldredth on her experiences during her time on Earth, and they updated her on events that unfolded while she was unconscious. Seven transporters were urgently dispatched from the nearest colonies to Earth after her location was discovered, with another fourteen from surrounding areas placed on standby. In her absence, several enemies seized the opportunity to create unrest on three of the planets, but those disturbances were quickly quelled, resulting in no loss of Aldredth or native lives. However, due to rising tensions, three transports returned to the nearby planets to help maintain peace.

Meanwhile, virtual meetings with human representatives culminated in an agreement on a meeting location and time for first contact, set to occur in less than an hour. Though given the circumstances, Aayla figured it was more like a second contact.

The ships had remained in Earth's orbit throughout the discussions, with additional Aldredth vessels joining to rotate crews. The initial Aldredth to respond to the distress call were the closest to Earth, but once Aayla was safe, they ensured that only the most experienced and strategically adept Aldredth were left behind to handle delicate discussions with a class-2 hostile planet.

The humans had expressed concerns about public panic and requested a small landing party to dispel fears of invasion. Aayla was chosen to lead the team, accompanied by three carefully selected Aldredth pairs. The composition was deliberate, blending skills and personalities to create a versatile, effective unit.

The first pair selected was Daxion and Cythara, a Vajjer and Vorax mated pair. At 675 and 674 years old, respectively, they were considered middle-aged by Aldredth standards and parents to two young adult children. Daxion had striking dark teal eyes and wings that transitioned from black at his spine to a deep blue along the length of each feather. He had led some significant battles and was an intimidating presence. In contrast, Cythara was a shorter Aldredth who radiated excitement, perfectly balancing Daxion's more serious demeanour. She had light brown eyes and vibrant, yellow-orange wings.

The second pair, Rythar and Ophelian, were Vorax mates aged 591. Unlike Daxion and Cythara, they had yet to have children. Rythar, a jokester and big brother figure, had dark auburn eyes and mottled sage-coloured wings, while Ophelian, a quiet observer, possessed dark brown eyes and olive-green wings tipped with orange streaks.

Finally, the last pair selected to join the landing team was Rune and Ceeda, the young Vajjer and Aurra pair who had rescued Aayla from Earth. Aged 254 and 253, respectively, this experience would be invaluable for them. Rune's deep blue eyes and orange wings edged in deep plum complemented Ceeda's silver eyes and magenta wings streaked with golden yellow. Their unyielding, youthful determination would be a powerful asset.

The Aldredth selected for the landing team were chosen to represent a broad range of strengths, including strong fighters, elemental masters, a clairvoyant, and a healer. To minimise risk, no Lazuil accompanied the unit. There was no need for two high-level targets in the same place, especially when a Unix could speak on behalf of all Aldredth.

Aayla and Talyn were by far the youngest in the group, at 21 and 22 years old, respectively. In the eyes of the Aldredth, they were mere children. Almost babies. No one under 100 years of age was usually permitted to undertake significant appointments.

Normally, sending such a young Aldredth pair into a dangerous mission was unheard of, but it was one of the many responsibilities associated with being a Unix. Unlike others, Unix began their training in infancy, thrust into high-stakes responsibilities long before their peers. Unix didn't have the luxury of a carefree childhood, so Aayla's training had been accelerated from birth, preparing her for field action at an age far younger than most. She had been paired with Talyn at two, and by ten, they were already handling life-or-death missions.

Of course, Aayla had a say in her path. She could reject any training or position, but the drive to protect her people was woven into her DNA. There was no sacrifice she wasn't willing to make to ensure their safety.

Aayla watched as Talyn reviewed the security details for their landing for the third time. She could sense his unease, the tension radiating from him. She knew much of it stemmed from the haunting memory of her torture. He had lost her once on this planet, and he wouldn't let it happen again.

Her thoughts wandered as her gaze lingered on him, captivated by his breathtaking beauty. She wondered what it would feel like to have his intense eyes locked onto hers as he thrust himself deep inside of her. She envisioned his hands gently caressing her wings, trailing down to the sensitive spot at their base. A shiver of imagined sensation sparked through her.

A flush crept across her cheeks just as Talyn glanced up, their eyes meeting. In that moment, the room dissolved around them, leaving only the two of them. Talyn's gaze held a magnetic intensity that seemed to spark the air around them, his eyes ablaze with emotions that were both fierce and intoxicating, igniting a whirlwind of feelings that made her pulse quicken.

"Aayla, what do you make of this?" a voice called, breaking through the moment and pulling her reluctantly back to reality.

She blinked, turning toward Daxion, who was studying the monitors with a furrowed brow. Cythara stood tucked beneath his wing, her hand resting lightly on his chest, but her gaze was only half-focused on the screens. As an Vorax, her mind didn't assess situations in the same tactical way that a Vajjer did, so she didn't contribute significantly to the planning.

As Aayla approached the monitors, she saw several news reports displaying a large anti-Aldredth group gathered outside the building where they planned to meet the humans.

"That group is significantly larger than we had anticipated," Daxion stated. "We'll need to stay in the air when we move. The ground is too dangerous to navigate."

"Agreed," Aayla replied, her tone measured. "Rune and Ceeda can set up surveillance from the roof of the building. Rythar and Ophelian will join us inside." She studied the screen again, her mind already piecing together contingency plans. They had requested a meeting space with high ceilings and open rooms, but she suspected the chosen government building in the city centre would feel more cramped than they were accustomed to.

Small, cramped environments made the Aldredth uncomfortable. While a confined space wouldn't prevent them from using their wings for offence or defence, it would severely hinder their movements. Akin to entering a dangerous situation with their arms tied behind their backs.

"Ask everyone to gather here in five minutes so we can finalise our preparations," Aayla instructed. Daxion nodded and strode off without hesitation.

She sensed Talyn walking up behind her, the familiar warmth of his presence enveloping her and sending a thrill through her chest as she turned to face him.

"Are you ready for this?" she asked.

Talyn gave her a crooked smile, the faintest trace of humour lighting his eyes. "I wouldn't miss this fun for the world."

She allowed herself a small smile in return, but the gravity of the situation loomed. First contact was always precarious, but this one was exceptionally high risk as they were uncertain what data the humans had collected from Aayla during her unconsciousness. Or what advancements they might have made since. The humans may have lacked weapons capable of easily harming the Aldredth before Aayla's arrival, but that didn't guarantee they hadn't developed something deadly in the time since.

Aayla and Talyn continued scanning the media updates until the landing team assembled, their focused gazes waiting for her instructions.

"Thank you all for coming," she began. "Rune and Ceeda, you'll handle surveillance from the roof. Daxion and Cythara, stay close to me as primary support. Rythar and Ophelian, you'll hang back in the room for secondary support."

"What's our level of intervention?" Ceeda asked.

"The humans have agreed to our terms of lethal engagement for any direct threats against an Aldredth," Aayla explained. The agreement was a non-negotiable condition for any first contact, ensuring they could defend themselves with deadly force against any threat or act of violence.

"However," she added, her tone firm, "we have no authority over human laws. We won't intervene in human-on-human violence unless explicitly requested. Our role here is strictly observational."

She saw unease ripple through the team. It wasn't in the Aldredth's nature to stand idly by while harm unfolded, especially when they had the power to prevent it. However, respecting the humans' sovereignty was crucial to building trust. Therefore, until the humans requested their assistance, they would remain observers. A decision that weighed heavily on them.

Talyn leant forward over the map in front of them, "I think it's best if we hover the ship instead of landing it on the grass near the meeting location."

Aayla considered his suggestion and nodded. "Agreed. The ground is too risky right now. We'll hover the ship and fly down instead."

Ophelian tilted her head. "Are we still using the front entrance?"

No, it's too dangerous. It would be an unnecessary risk. We should enter through the balcony instead. Talyn communicated telepathically.

Glancing at him, she nodded. *Okay. Balcony, it is.*

"No," Aayla said aloud, shaking her head, "We will enter through the balcony entrance."

The humans had chosen a building with a large front entrance and a balcony, which they welcomed the Aldredth to use. It was a generous gesture, and while the humans didn't know their preferences, their effort to accommodate was appreciated.

"Remember, they aren't familiar with our customs, so wherever possible, use only non-lethal engagement," she reminded everyone. "If there are no further questions, let's head to the transport ship and begin our descent."

As the team began dispersing, Martok and Skyla approached, bowing deeply. Martok's turquoise wings shimmered like sunlight on water, while Skyla's scarlet wings absorbed the light, giving them a matte-like finish.

"We'll monitor your camera feeds and remain on standby," Martok assured, referencing the microscopic, nearly invisible cameras embedded in the Aldredth insignias on their clothing. All Aldredth wore the same microscopic cameras embedded in their clothing. Security is something they took seriously. While the feeds weren't continuously monitored, they could quickly access specific recordings or review recent footage when necessary.

"Thank you, Martok," Aayla replied warmly. "But let's hope your assistance won't be needed today."

She gently patted Martok's cheek before pressing her forehead against Skyla's.

A Unix's touch was both calming and euphoric, but it was mostly a sign of great respect and trust.

Martok and Skyla smiled deeply at the touch as Talyn and Aayla made their way toward the sleek silver transport ship that they would navigate through Earth's atmosphere and hover above their meeting location. Once in position, they would fly down into the building below. The ship would be too high for the humans to reach, but regardless, its security system was coded to Aldredth DNA, ensuring that only their kind could enter.

The rest of the landing team fell into step behind them, their movements purposeful and precise. As they approached the ship, they paused to exchange final farewells with the many Aldredth gathered along the corridor, offering nods of respect and quiet encouragement. Once aboard, the team settled into their positions, and the transport ship began its slow, steady descent toward Earth.

CHAPTER SEVENTEEN

The journey was slower than usual, a deliberate choice to avoid alarming the humans. Any sudden movements would attract unwanted attention, so they moved with measured grace, keeping their pace steady and controlled.

For the same reason, their swords remained sheathed across their backs, though still within easy reach. Arriving with empty hands was a deliberate gesture of peaceful intent. Initially, the humans had insisted on no weapons for first contact, but the Aldredth had made it clear that going anywhere unarmed was non-negotiable. Since the age of two, each Aldredth had carried their sword, an extension of themselves, a piece of their very being. It wasn't just for protection but a symbol of their duty to keep those around them safe. Without it, they felt exposed, vulnerable, naked. Even when they slept, their sword was always nearby.

Finally, they arrived at their hovering location, prompting Aayla and Talyn to step away from the control panel and join the others near the doorway.

Talyn took his place at the front alongside Aayla, with Rune and Ceeda flanking their left, Daxion and Cythara to their right, and Rythar and Ophelian watching their backs. It was tradition—the strongest stood at the front, leading the way. Their strength came with the responsibility to protect those weaker than themselves. It was an honour they carried with pride.

As the door slid open, a soft breeze lifted Aayla's hair, and she gazed down at the crowd of humans below. Every inch of space was packed with people, some even hanging from the sides of buildings just to catch a glimpse of their arrival.

The roar of the crowd hit them like a wave—cheers mixed with heckles, banners waving in celebration and protest. The energy was electric, and the atmosphere was tense with anticipation.

Aayla's eyes swept over the crowd, scanning for any signs of danger. Nothing posed an immediate threat from their current height, but her instincts remained on high alert.

It's time, she sent telepathically to Talyn, turning to him. She expected his usual reassuring smile, but instead, she found him looking back at her, his face etched with concern.

"Promise me you won't do anything reckless down there," he said quietly, his deep green eyes locking onto hers with intensity. "I wouldn't be able to live with myself if anything happened to you."

His words struck her, his gaze so full of emotion that it made her heart skip. For a moment, she felt completely disarmed, caught in the depths of his eyes. Her throat tightened, and she could only manage a nod. "I promise," she whispered.

Talyn studied her for a second longer, his gaze searching, before he turned back to the scene below.

The silver shimmer of the protective barrier at the ship's entrance flickered in her peripheral vision. It was designed to block anyone without Aldredth DNA, a solid barrier to outsiders while allowing them to pass through like it wasn't even there. It could even be adjusted to permit or block specific elements, depending on their security needs.

Aayla glanced at the others. "If everyone's ready, let's move. Stay sharp and stay safe."

She gave Talyn a playful nudge, locking eyes with him, her gaze sparkling with mischief. *Do I need to warn you not to be too overprotective?*

He shot her a dry look. *I'm not overprotective. I'm just... aware of your tendency to dive headfirst into chaos.*

Someone's got to keep things interesting, she teased with a wink, her wings unfurling in one fluid motion. As she stepped through the shimmering barrier, she gave a single powerful beat and launched into the air. The others followed in perfect synchrony, their wings beating together in a harmonious rhythm.

As they descended toward the humans, Aayla could see the awe and wonder in the faces of those below. Talyn flew beside her, his wing tips so close they nearly brushed against hers before he swooped ahead, positioning himself protectively in front of her, his body a shield between her and any potential danger ahead.

The vibrant forest green colouring of his wings caught the sunlight, their beauty taking her breath away.

They circled the area, eyes scanning balconies and rooftops for any sign of trouble. Once satisfied that everything was clear, Talyn and Aayla descended softly onto the cold, black tiles of the balcony.

Talyn stood just ahead of her, slightly to the left, always alert, always protective. Aayla's eyes moved over the five armed men in black suits standing before them. To the far right, two men in black pants and white shirts stood with bulky camera equipment, capturing every moment of their arrival for the world to see.

Listening to their thoughts, Aayla quickly assessed that while the humans were undeniably anxious, their excitement was far more prominent, and none posed any immediate threat.

Her eyes shifted to the balcony's perimeter, scanning for anything unusual, when Talyn stiffened beside her. A low, primal growl reverberated from his chest, drawing her attention to a man standing on the far left. Talyn's eyes were locked on him, glaring with intensity. Aayla followed his gaze and dipped into the man's thoughts, catching flashes of desire directed toward her.

It caught her off guard—she hadn't anticipated humans finding them attractive. She mentally kicked herself for overlooking such a basic element of human behaviour. Unchecked desires had a way of spiralling into dangerous territory, leading to unpredictable behaviours, and they couldn't afford that kind of risk in such a delicate situation.

Talyn, stand down. He's no threat to me, she warned him telepathically, sensing his rising protectiveness flaring to new heights.

No threat? Talyn shot back, his voice dripping with dry sarcasm. *So that's not a gun on his hip? And judging by the way he's looking at you, I'd say his intentions are anything but 'harmless.'*

His thoughts are purely... sexual. There's no hint of violence. Let's chalk this up to a cultural misunderstanding, she countered, keeping her tone calm. *He's harmless.*

If he's harmless, why am I imagining hurling him off this balcony? Talyn retorted, his gaze still locked onto the man with a level of intensity that could melt steel.

Aayla stifled a laugh as Talyn finally stopped growling, though his glare lingered, causing the human to shift nervously under the scrutiny. The human's earlier bravado faltered, and his gaze quickly dropped to the floor.

With a warm smile, Aayla spoke aloud to diffuse the tension. "Apologies for that. My Guardian can be... a bit protective."

As the humans processed her words, she felt the silent arrival of Daxion and Cythara landing behind her on the right, with Rythar and Ophelian positioning themselves to her left.

Overhead, she spotted Rune's striking orange wings streaked with deep plum, and Ceeda's vivid magenta wings edged with golden yellow, as they continued to circle the building. They would complete another loop before taking positions on the rooftop.

The human standing at the centre stepped forward and bowed deeply. "Thank you for coming. If you would please follow me, I'll lead you to the President."

"Thank you for the welcome," Aayla replied, inclining her head in a graceful gesture of respect.

They passed through the wide, ornate doors into a grand hall adorned with glittering crystal chandeliers and polished wood panelling, the air thick with opulence. But their human escorts didn't linger, leading them swiftly toward a smaller, unassuming doorway at the far end of the hall. They entered a smaller, dimly lit room with low ceilings, dark carpets, and plain black walls, contrasting with the hall's opulence. Three wooden chairs stood in the centre, two empty and the third occupied by the man she recognised as the President of the United States, Nick Bailey.

Security personnel lined the room's perimeter alongside several reporters and media advisors, their eyes sharp. The Aldredth had requested a complete guest list to avoid any unwelcome surprises, and thankfully, it seemed that the humans had complied.

An ugly debate had raged among the human nations while Aayla was asleep, recovering from her injuries. Without a single global leader, the humans were divided on who should represent them. The Aldredth had offered several solutions, including inviting all regional leaders, but logistical and safety concerns led to the compromise of meeting with the United States, where the first contact had been made. Several conditions were attached to the meeting, including a requirement for it to be broadcast live to every nation, free of charge. Furthermore, President Bailey was prohibited from making any agreements on behalf of Earth's population. The global leaders will collectively review any Aldredth proposals at a special summit to follow.

These terms were ones the Aldredth were more than willing to accept.

Talyn took his place in front of Aayla as they entered the room, his instincts sharp and alert. He moved purposefully, circling the chairs while scrutinising every corner for potential threats, before settling behind one of the empty seats, his presence both imposing and protective.

Daxion and Cythara followed closely, slipping into the room with the quiet confidence of seasoned warriors, positioning themselves against the wall to the right. Meanwhile, Rythar and Ophelian took their post near the doorway on the left, eyes scanning the perimeter, ready for any sign of trouble.

The only sound breaking the heavy silence was the faint rustling of feathers, a quiet reminder of their presence.

Aayla stepped forward, offering a warm smile. President Bailey shot up from his chair, bowing with an awkward eagerness.

"Greetings, Aayla. On behalf of the people of Earth, I welcome you with open arms and peaceful intentions," he said, his voice warm with sincerity. After briefly pausing, he added, "It's wonderful to see you again, and you look radiant."

Aayla inclined her head in return, her expression composed yet friendly. "Thank you, President Bailey. It's an honour to be here, and I'm pleased to renew our acquaintance—though I must say, I prefer these circumstances much more than our last meeting."

"Please, call me Nick," he said quickly, gesturing to the chairs. "Please, take a seat."

Aayla carefully sat down, lifting her wings and draping them elegantly over the back of the chair.

"Is that seat comfortable for you?" the President inquired, his gaze lingering on her wings with a hint of concern. "I must apologise. It seems my team didn't think about the accommodations for your wings. I take full responsibility for that oversight."

Aayla waved a hand lightly, offering a reassuring smile. "It's quite comfortable, thank you. Our seating usually has concave backs for our wings, but we are quite adaptable."

President Bailey nodded, visibly relieved, though his gaze shifted uneasily to Talyn. "Would your... companion like to sit as well?"

A quiet laugh escaped Aayla. She glanced back at Talyn, catching the faint hint of a smile tugging at his lips. "Thank you, but that won't be necessary." She replied, her warm smile lighting up the room. "Allow me to introduce myself properly. I am Aayla, the daughter of Sabee and Marlia. Beside me is Talyn, son of Sabor and Frela. To my right, we have Daxion and Cythara, and to my left are Rythar and Ophelian."

As she spoke, each member of her group inclined their heads in a respectful greeting, their vigilant stances unwavering.

Aayla paused, choosing her words carefully. "Talyn does not occupy the seat next to me because he is my Guardian, not my mate."

She could see the small frown forming on President Bailey's head, and she knew she was already starting to lose him.

"Let me begin at the start," she said, her tone more formal. "We are Aldredth, from the planet Nannuval in the Tuxrai galaxy. Renowned as the peacemakers of the universe, we are spread across the universe, dedicated to protecting the vulnerable from more violent species. Aldredth are found on countless planets, but only at the invitation of the resident species. We strive to preserve peace and justice, and we offer our protection to those in need, especially against more violent species. Take the Vhurl, for example. You've already seen what a species like that can do. They thrive on death and destruction, revelling in torture and slaughter or plundering resources from other planets simply because they can."

President Bailey's eyes widened, his mouth slightly open as he nodded. He was utterly captivated by her words.

For the next few hours, the room buzzed with vibrant conversation, all centred around Nannuval. They dove into the intricacies of its landscapes, its unique characteristics, and the striking contrasts it presented compared to Earth's familiar terrain.

As their dialogue unfolded, they ventured beyond Nannuval's boundaries, exploring the mysteries of neighbouring planets, each rich with its own distinctive attributes and environments. Aayla observed with keen delight as President Bailey's eyes sparkled with imagination, his curiosity ignited by tales of the diverse species and civilisations scattered across the cosmos. They exchanged ideas and insights with infectious enthusiasm, the conversation flowing seamlessly between them.

With each passing moment, the connection between their two civilisations deepened, fuelled by a shared passion for discovery and a mutual appreciation for the boundless wonders that lay beyond their respective worlds.

"As you might have noticed, while Aldredth are similar in physiology to humans, we possess wings for flight, special abilities, and a different digestive system. Everything we consume is absorbed into our bodies, leaving no waste, unlike human bodies that produce urine and faeces," Aayla explained.

President Bailey appeared unfazed, likely due to the numerous scans he'd been briefed on during her time under human care. Leaning forward with genuine interest, he asked, "What happens if you eat something you can't digest?"

"If we consume something indigestible, like metal or stone, we must expel it—how shall I put it? Vomit it up. It's less than ideal, so we are quite cautious about what we eat," she replied with a slight smile.

"What kind of food do you enjoy?" he inquired, a hint of eagerness in his voice.

Aayla's eyes sparkled as she smiled. "Actually, we eat the same types of food as you. Our physiology is quite similar to yours. For instance, we have a heart, lungs, stomach, and sexual organs. We just lack the same intestinal system."

She lightly touched her lower abdomen. "In female Aldredth, our uterus and wing muscles fill the space beneath our stomachs, while in male Aldredth, that space is filled solely by wing muscles."

He glanced at her abdomen before his gaze drifted higher, inadvertently lingering on her breasts for a beat longer than appropriate. Flushing slightly, he quickly averted his eyes and stammered, "S—so, you have the same... um, sexual organs as we do?"

Aayla stifled a laugh, surprised at how quickly the conversation veered into such territory. "Yes, we possess the same sexual organs, and our pregnancy and gestational periods are similar as well."

"Why are we so alike?" he pondered, intrigue written across his face.

"That's... a complex story. Millennia ago, the early Aldredth acquired the ability to traverse the universe, spreading out to settle on uncolonised planets. The early Aldredth who settled here flourished under your yellow sun, evolving into the humans you are today. Meanwhile, we developed under the intensity of our powerful red sun, which shaped our evolution and gifted us with unique abilities."

President Bailey leaned back, exhaling sharply. "So, you're telling me we're related? We didn't evolve from apes?"

"You did evolve, but not from apes. I believe you refer to them as early Homo sapiens. They were, in fact, Aldredth," Aayla clarified, choosing her words carefully, aware of the weight they carried.

Aayla paused, contemplating how to phrase the next part of the conversation to avoid causing unrest among humanity. She understood that revealing too much information too quickly could have far-reaching consequences, potentially destabilising their society.

"The universe is vast, home to countless civilisations. A small number of them were settled by the Aldredth, while the rest evolved from their own ancestors or those of neighbouring species. The makeup of planets and suns in each galaxy has influenced how each species has evolved. It's quite fascinating."

President Bailey nodded, his brow furrowed as he processed her words, unsure of what to believe. Sensing the tension in the air, Aayla decided it was time to shift the topic.

Chapter Eighteen

"On Aldredth," Aayla began, "we have six distinct bloodlines."

"What are these bloodlines? Are they familial?" he asked, curiosity rekindled.

"Not exactly. They're more akin to the different blood types in humans—like A, B, or O. Our bloodlines reflect the molecular composition of our blood, inherited genetically from our parents. I belong to the Unix bloodline, which grants me the ability to heal other Aldredth. Only those of the Unix bloodline can heal themselves and others. Then there's the Vajjer bloodline, known for their extraordinary combat skills and being the strongest fighters among us. The Vorax bloodline excels in elemental manipulation, while the Aurra bloodline possesses remarkable powers of second sight and premonition. The Emba are the gentlest of our kind, gifted scientists and medics, and the Lazuil bloodline is of royal descent."

"Are these the 'special abilities' you mentioned earlier?"

"Yes, that's correct. Being of royal blood, the Lazuil lead the Aldredth, except in the presence of a Unix, as we have the authority over all other bloodlines. However, since so few Unix exist, the Lazuil assume leadership in our absence."

Aayla noticed President Bailey's gaze shift thoughtfully toward the Aldredth around her, no doubt trying to discern which bloodlines were present among them.

Twisting to gesture to Talyn, she maintained eye contact with President Bailey. "In this room, we have Talyn, who is a Vajjer. Over to my right is Daxion, who is a Vajjer, and Cythara, who is a Vorax. To my left are Rythar and Ophelian, who are both Vorax's. Stationed outside are Rune and Ceeda, a Vajjer and Aurra, respectively."

President Bailey shifted slightly, his brow furrowing. "So, there's no Lazuil present?"

Aayla shook her head. Was he disappointed? Did he prefer to be speaking with a Lazuil instead? She knew the royal bloodline held great significance in human society, so perhaps he viewed it as superior to a Unix. Or maybe he had ulterior motives regarding the Lazuil and was disheartened by their absence today.

"A Lazuil isn't necessary when a Unix is present," she replied politely. "I am considered the highest-ranking individual in the room. I take pride in being a Unix and in my ability to heal other Aldredth. Yet," she added with a wry smile, "as you have seen, that makes me a high-value target."

"A target for what?" he asked, curiosity piqued.

It was an excellent question and a challenging one to answer. Aayla frowned in thought. "Some species seek to imprison me for profit. Others want to kidnap me to use as leverage. And then there are those who simply wish to... kill me, just to inflict pain upon the Aldredth."

Talyn shuffled behind her, and she caught the pained look on his face as he absorbed the implications of her words. He carried the weight of all the threats she faced and the scars of those already inflicted.

His gaze locked onto hers, fierce determination lighting his eyes. *And I will protect you with my life.*

Her heart raced, a thrill surging through her as she lost herself in his gaze.

Realising she'd been staring at Talyn too long, Aayla quickly cleared her throat and returned her attention to the humans.

President Bailey was enthralled in the conversation, but his focus had shifted to her wings, which she had draped over the chair and spread slightly on either side of her. Her subtle movements were no doubt making them shimmer in the light, and this had caught his attention.

"I can't help but admire the stunning array of colours in your wings. Yours, in particular, are... luminous. Do the colours of your wings or hair signify anything about your bloodline?"

Slowly, Aayla unfurled her wings, the pure white feathers catching the light, each golden edge sparking in the light. They were not merely appendages for flying. They were the embodiment of freedom and empowerment.

To an Aldredth, wings were a prized possession, defining their very identity. With every beat, they felt the rush of wind against their feathers and the exhilarating weightlessness of flight. Without wings, they would be grounded, stripped of their freedom, and extremely vulnerable to attack.

"No, the colouring holds no intrinsic meaning. It's entirely random, unique to each of us, much like your fingerprints. Our wings are extremely sensitive. They have the most nerve endings, which allows us to feel and navigate the subtle air currents around us."

She flapped her wings slowly, a graceful display. "Because of their sensitivity, we don't allow others to touch our wings. Only mates may do so, as that touch can feel very sexual in nature. It's an intimate caress sharing amongst lovers."

She extended her wings to their full expanse, then folded them gracefully away, catching Talyn's soft gaze lingering on her with an intensity that warmed her inside. She watched him for a moment before he noticed her looking at him, and he abruptly snapped his attention forward.

Flushing slightly, she cleared her throat, "In contrast, the colour of our eyes and hair is genetic, making familial relationships easily recognisable. The resemblance can be striking at times."

President Bailey didn't respond immediately. Instead, he narrowed his eyes, glancing between her and Talyn, a flicker of curiosity in his expression.

"Let me tell you more about the Aldredth," Aayla continued. "We are honest people, valuing truth and kindness. We would willingly give our lives to protect others. As you may have noticed, Aldredth can move much faster than humans—almost too fast for the naked eye."

He pointed to her chest. "Is that your logo?"

"Yes," she said, a smile tugging at her lips as she placed her hand over the gold-embroidered Aldredth crest over her heart, the heart of all Aldredth. "We call it a crest."

The elaborate gold crest featured intricate geometric patterns reminiscent of constellations, interwoven with Aldredth symbols denoting virtues such as unity, compassion, and honour. It was a crest of beauty, and they were proud to wear it.

She tapped the centre of the crest. "Each Aldredth crest features one of six animals native to Nannuval, representing our bloodlines. An Aldredth carries their bloodline's emblem on their clothing and sword. Our names are sewn underneath the crest, and once bonded, our mate's name is sewn beside it."

Aayla's heart sank as she felt the empty space beside her name. Dropping her hand, she forced a smile, pushing down the ache in her chest. "If I had to choose six animals you'd be familiar with that best represent our bloodlines, I'd say the Unix resembles a Pegasus, the Vajjer a dragon, the Vorax a

Siberian tiger, the Aurra a stag, the Emba an Arctic fox, and the Lazuil a blue glaucus."

Aayla looked over at Talyn, their eyes meeting for a brief moment. *So, how am I doing? Do you think I've made an impression on the humans, or should I start performing tricks?*

Talyn smirked. *If you start doing tricks, just promise me you won't juggle anything sharp. We can't have you stealing the show with a trip to the MedBay.*

With a warm smile, Aayla turned back to the humans. "When two Aldredth of different bloodlines have a child, the child usually inherits the stronger bloodline. The only exception is the Unix bloodline, which occurs randomly and can't be inherited. We still don't understand what triggers the Unix lineage, which is unfortunate because we could use a few more of us," she added with a dry laugh.

Rubbing his chin thoughtfully, President Bailey surveyed the various Aldredth in the room before returning his attention to Aayla. "If the Unix bloodline can't be inherited, what bloodline would your children have?"

Aayla turned her head to look at Talyn, who stood tall and confident, his commanding presence radiating strength. In that moment, she felt a pang in her chest because the thought of having children with anyone else was simply unimaginable. Yet, the harsh reality weighed heavily on her mind. Not only was it impossible for Talyn to be her mate, but the grim truth was that Unix often fell in battle long before they had the opportunity to start families, a tragic fate that came with being a high-value target.

Taking a deep breath, she faced President Bailey again. "If I were fortunate enough to have children, they would inherit my mate's bloodline."

President Bailey narrowed his eyes and leaned forward, curiosity piqued. "What do you mean, if you're lucky enough?"

"Unlike humans, Aldredth can only bear a maximum of three children. We must reach middle age before we can conceive, but unlike humans, we're born with one to four eggs. Most of us only have two eggs, resulting in two extremely cherished children. In contrast, humans are born with millions of eggs and experience cycles and periods throughout their fertile lives."

"Do you experience periods or something similar?"

Aayla shook her head lightly. "No, we don't. Every egg we possess is fertilised as it matures, and they mature at different times, so we're never pregnant with more than one child at a time. However, many Aldredth are killed in battle before they can have children."

The heaviness of the topic made her restless, the pain of loss echoing in her heart.

"Children are our greatest blessing and most valued commodity. If I could have a thousand children, I think I would," she declared audaciously, catching Talyn's quiet laugh behind her.

"In times of great war and unrest, our numbers can dwindle significantly. However, normally, our population remains relatively steady, experiencing only slight increases over time."

With furrowed brows, President Bailey sat in contemplative silence for several long moments. "Is war common?"

Exhaling hard, Aayla hesitated before answering. "More common than I would like. Our primary weapon is a sword," she said, pulling the blade from her back and holding it across her palms for better visibility. "This sword is more than just a weapon. It channels and amplifies our abilities, reducing the drain on our energy when we use them.”

Aldredth always kept their swords sheathed on their backs, except when bathing or sleeping. Occasionally, they concealed their swords with a layer of glamour to help the Aldredth blend into their surroundings or soften their aggressive appearance. Crafted from a rare metal found only on Nannuval, the swords were not only deadly sharp but also served as powerful amplifiers of Aldredth magic. The hilt was a matte golden colour adorned with precious gemstones collected from across the universe, which caught the light in a dazzling display of colours. The polished silver blade bore intricate engravings that seemed to dance in the light, while the top of the pommel depicted the Aldredth crest.

“Your sword is beautiful,” President Bailey remarked, studying it intently. “What do the stones and engravings represent?”

Turning the sword over in her palms, Aayla looked at the various stones on the hilt. “The stones are gifts or souvenirs from our travels, like memories. The engravings along the blade represent an Aldredth scrawl that assists with the amplification of our powers.”

“Amazing.”

Sheathing the sword on her back, Aayla smiled softly at him. “Another difference between our cultures is the role gender plays. Aldredth cherish and adore their females. Male Aldredth are inherently stronger than their female counterparts, and no amount of exercise or training can change that. Don’t get me wrong, a person’s worth isn’t measured by strength, but our physical differences are clear. Therefore, males see it as their duty and honour to protect females.”

President Bailey frowned. “We protect our females, too.”

Aayla raised an eyebrow, challenging him. "Sometimes."

Aayla gestured at the Aldredth behind her. "You may have noticed that all males are similar in height and build, as are the females. This is because we are nearly identical in appearance. The only distinctions are the strength of our abilities and bloodline. Unlike humans, our similarities foster a culture without competitiveness or shame over our bodies. We also don't feel attraction to any Aldredth except our mates, allowing us to be quite comfortable in our nudity." Aayla suppressed a snicker. "But don't worry, we'll keep our clothes on to avoid shocking you."

Talyn growled menacingly, and Aayla's hand snapped to her sword as she twisted toward him. He glared with murderous intent at a human standing against the far wall.

The other Aldredth in the room had crouched lower into fighting stances, hands poised on their swords.

Aayla turned her gaze to the human in question, locking eyes with him. As she listened to his thoughts, a wave of revulsion washed over her. He was picturing her naked, his hands roaming over her body, envisioning her beneath him, moaning in pleasure, then wrapping his fingers around her throat, relishing the sight of her gasping for air.

The human security personnel in the room finally registered the shift in the atmosphere, their reaction times slower. They began to reach for their weapons just as Aayla raised her hands.

"Stop!"

CHAPTER NINETEEN

"He's no threat," Aayla said firmly, her voice cutting through the tension in the room.

The Aldredth immediately sheathed their swords in unison and relaxed their stances, deliberately softening their expressions, trying to ease the nerves of the human delegation. All except Talyn, whose face still burned with fury.

At least he had stopped growling.

Talyn, Aayla thought softly. *It's all right. Breathe.*

Talyn shot her a heated look before closing his eyes and taking a deep, controlled breath. *I knew I should have tossed him off the balcony when I had the chance,* he thought dryly. When he opened his eyes, his expression was neutral, though Aayla could still feel the simmering anger beneath the surface.

The humans, picking up on the atmosphere, slowly released their grip on their weapons, casting uneasy glances at one another.

Aayla turned back to President Bailey, offering a tight smile. "There's another ability I should have mentioned earlier. Aldredth can communicate telepathically with each other, though it usually demands focus and eye contact. The exception is with our mates, whose thoughts we can hear as long as they're nearby, and Unix, who can project their thoughts across great distances. We can also... hear the thoughts of other species."

The President paled slightly, so Aayla quickly added, "We don't invade people's minds without permission. It's a matter of courtesy unless necessary for safety. But sometimes, if someone's thoughts are loud enough, it's like they're shouting, and we can't help but hear." She nodded toward a human in the back of the room. "For example, that one was thinking some rather unpleasant things about me... quite loudly."

All heads turned toward the man, who flushed a deep red as the room fell into awkward silence. His colleagues stood frozen, unsure of what to do next.

Aayla's voice hardened. "He should either control his thoughts or leave."

President Bailey nodded to a tall man beside him, who immediately escorted the red-faced offender out of the room.

"We apologise profoundly for the insult," President Bailey said, his hand over his heart.

"It's okay," Aayla replied, glancing at Talyn. "I have an extremely protective Guardian, and this is a highly tense situation."

President Bailey exhaled in relief, rubbing his chin thoughtfully. "If I may ask a rather odd question... You've been incredibly open with us. Why?"

"We value truth," Aayla replied without hesitation. "We're here to help you, and we're trusting you with the truth in the hope that the trust is returned. Do you intend to use the information we have given you against us?"

"No," President Bailey chuckled nervously, glancing briefly at Talyn before turning back to her. "So, tell me, what's the difference between a mate and a... Guardian?"

"Aldredth only have one mate, and we mate for life," Aayla began.

She explained how finding a mate was the most significant event in an Aldredth's life. Mates shared a bond deeper than anything imaginable. It was the joining of two souls to become one, their life forces intertwined. Once bonded, mates shared an identical energy signature, proof of an unbreakable bond.

From birth, Aldredth searched for their mate, recognising them instantly when they met.

"Mating is a permanent, irreversible bond. When one mate dies, the other can't live on," Aayla said softly, a shiver running through her. "And... they wouldn't want to."

She glanced at Talyn. "I can't imagine a worse pain than being separated from your mate, knowing they've gone somewhere you can't follow."

"Is it the pain of losing them that kills you?"

"Partly," Aayla admitted, "but mostly, we lose the will to live. We want to leave this existence and reunite with them."

President Bailey tilted his head, intrigued. "When you say 'this existence,' do you know what happens after death?"

Aayla hesitated, exchanging glances with the other Aldredth in the room before rubbing the back of her neck. "Yes, but... we don't think you're ready for that conversation yet. There is something after death, but it's important to understand that this life is the purpose of your existence. What happens next depends on how you live this life."

"So," he began excitedly, "there's something after? How do you know?"

"It's complicated," Aayla explained. "We can communicate with the recently deceased. They've shared a great deal with us, though they've also warned that some knowledge cannot be passed to the living. Perhaps you'd like to see for yourself once you're ready?"

"That... sounds amazing," President Bailey said, though there was caution in his voice. "But what would that cost us?"

"Nothing at all. We are happy to help others in any way we can. We are happiest helping others. That's why we are the peacemakers of the universe. Sitting back and not assisting when we are able eats away at us, weighing on us like a suffocating blanket. Many species consider us self-sacrificing, but we are just trying to be the positive energy we wish to see in the world around us."

President Bailey nodded thoughtfully, and Aayla hoped she hadn't overwhelmed him. After a pause, he glanced at her. "So, Talyn is your Guardian?"

"Yes, that's right," she replied.

"Which means... he isn't your mate."

A flicker of unease stirred in Aayla. "He's my Guardian."

"But could he ever become your mate?"

She hesitated, then answered carefully, "I can't be mated to a Vajjer for two distinct reasons," she began. She could feel Talyn's presence behind her, strong and silent, a pillar of unwavering support. Her heart ached as she spoke the words she had long accepted but still struggled to say aloud. "First, for reasons we still don't fully understand, Unix only mate with Lazuil. Other bloodlines mate with each other freely, but a Unix has never bonded with anyone outside the Lazuil line."

She paused, letting the weight of that truth settle in the room before continuing. "Secondly, long ago, a Unix and a Vorax were bewitched and falsely believed they were mates. They walked into enemy hands, were tortured, and eventually killed, but not before their betrayal led to the deaths of countless Aldredth. That betrayal and the devastating loss it caused left a scar so deep on the Aldredth that they created a second law—any non-royal claiming to be the mate of a Unix will be executed immediately."

Her words hung in the air, heavy with the gravity of their history.

President Bailey slowly nodded, absorbing the information. "I see. So, because Talyn is a Vajjer, it's forbidden. He can't be your mate."

"Exactly," she said.

He studied her, his gaze sharp. "Yet you haven't directly said that Talyn isn't your mate."

Annoyance flickered through Aayla at his persistence. "I've already answered that."

"Actually, you haven't. You've been careful with your words. I asked if Talyn is your mate, not who you're allowed to mate with."

Frowning, she replied sharply, "I am unmated."

"But do you believe Talyn could be your mate?" he pressed.

The question struck a nerve. Aayla shifted uncomfortably, her pulse quickening. "It's forbidden," she repeated, her voice lower, almost defensive.

President Bailey leaned forward slightly, his gaze narrowing. "Is there a reason you're avoiding a simple answer?" he asked, his tone edged with suspicion.

Around her, the Aldredth turned to face her, their expressions curious, and her heart raced. Clenching her hands on her lap, she took a deep breath.

"I've already told you. I am not mated."

"Do you wish you were? Do you love him?" President Bailey pressed again, his voice even more pointed now.

Grinding her teeth in anger, she glanced behind her at Talyn. His chiselled features, accentuated by the warm light, exuded a rugged allure. With each subtle movement, muscles rippled beneath his clothing, hinting at his power and agility. His piercing eyes shifted to look directly at her, drawing her in with an irresistible magnetism. As she gazed into them, time seemed to stand still, and the world faded away, leaving only the intimate connection between them.

The quiet sound of someone clearing their throat snapped her back to reality, and she turned to face President Bailey again.

”Yes, I love him,” she admitted, her voice steady but guarded. “I love him more than you could ever know. Just as I love all my people, they are mine to love and protect. Aldredth are open about our love—it’s part of who we are. But that love is not the same as being mated. It’s not the same as being bound by the deepest connection.”

President Bailey’s eyes gleamed with challenge. “Then why have you not simply said that Talyn isn’t your mate?”

Rubbing the back of her neck, Aayla glanced around the room again. The Aldredth were fixated on her with their heads subtly tilted in curiosity. She tuned into their thoughts, navigating the confusion swirling among them. They were perplexed by President Bailey’s questions and unsure if they had overlooked something critical. Suddenly, their collective gaze shifted to Talyn, and Aayla’s heart plummeted, her blood turning to ice.

Her hands clenched in her lap, her fingers tightening around the fabric of her skirt as she forced herself to speak. “Talyn... Talyn’s not my m—mate,” she stammered, the words tasting like ash in her mouth. As soon as the sentence left her lips, the Aldredth seemed to relax, convinced by her answer. They returned to their watchful positions as if nothing had transpired.

President Bailey, however, leaned back in his chair, his frown deepening. “That doesn’t sound very convincing.”

A rush of anger surged through Aayla, and she stood up abruptly, towering over him. Her voice was now filled with fire. “I have answered your question,” she growled, eyes blazing. “And I will not allow you to twist my words to endanger my Guardian.”

President Bailey flinched slightly, visibly startled by her outburst. His security detail tensed, their hands instinctively hovering near their weapons, prepared to defend him if needed. But Aayla no longer cared about appearances, not when Talyn's life was on the line.

"You continue to ask about my bond with Talyn as if you're trying to uncover some secret," she continued, her tone fierce. "If I were mated to him, his life would be forfeit. He would be executed without hesitation. Your questions are a direct threat to his life, and I will not sit here and let you play these dangerous games." A low, guttural growl rumbled in her chest, her protective instincts roaring to the surface. "How dare you threaten my Guardian. We defend our own with our lives, and I will not hesitate to defend him from any perceived threat."

President Bailey shrank back in his chair, his face pale with alarm. "I—I didn't mean to threaten your Guardian," he stammered, his voice faltering. "Truly. We're ... a naturally inquisitive species."

Aayla's fiery gaze bore into him for a moment longer before she slowly exhaled, trying to regain control of her emotions. Shame and guilt began to creep in as she realised the extent of her reaction. She closed her eyes briefly, taking a steadying breath, before opening them again and offering a tight, strained smile.

"Perhaps we should take a short break," she suggested, her voice calmer now, though still edged with tension.

President Bailey nodded quickly. "Yes, of course. I apologise if I offended you. That was not my intention."

With a polite nod, Aayla turned and walked towards Talyn, who stood waiting nearby. His expression was one of quiet concern. *Are you okay?* He asked telepathically before reaching his hand out to caress her face.

Don't, she warned, glancing towards the humans. *We can't give them any reason to misinterpret things. Their accusations are playing with your life.*

Talyn's expression softened before his lips twitched into a faint smile. *Or we could do the opposite*, he suggested with a playful glint. *Show them exactly what an Aldredth's love looks like. Make it so public that they can't question it.*

Your way does sound like much more fun, she admitted with a smirk.

She stepped closer to him without hesitation, her arms wrapping around his torso. Talyn held her tightly, and she savoured the warmth and strength of his embrace, relishing the feel of his body pressed against hers. She felt the soft press of his lips against the top of her head and looked up at him, their eyes meeting. His hand gently cupped her face as they leaned in closer, nuzzling into each other, a quiet but intimate display of affection.

Behind them, Rythar, Ophelian, Cythara, and Daxion approached, watching the humans who were engaged in hushed conversations. Aayla reluctantly pulled away from Talyn to face them, though the warmth of their moment lingered.

Daxion stretched his dark blue wings, and Aayla looked at how the black faded across his wings from his spine to the tips. She couldn't help but think that they looked like the night sky. "Do we need to extract?" he asked, his intense gaze scanning the room.

Aayla shook her head. "No, it was a misunderstanding that got out of hand."

She glanced at the humans, still whispering among themselves. "I believe the president when he said it wasn't meant as a threat."

Cythara bounced lightly on her feet, her yellow-orange wings like a bright sun to Daxion's night. They fluttered with barely contained excitement. "I think you're doing great. It's fascinating how curious humans are about everything. I wish we could ask them questions, too. There's so much I want to know."

"The plan is to have them like us. That won't work if you bore them to death with questions," Rythar joked with a laugh as one sage-coloured wing draped over Ophelian, who was tucked tight against him.

Aayla turned to Ophelian, her sharp gaze always observant. "What do you make of the situation?"

Ophelian's dark brown eyes scanned the room before resting on Aayla. "They like us. A lot," she said quietly. "But we need to be careful. If we're not, they might end up fighting each other for access to us."

She knew that was a very real possibility and one they would need to carefully manage in future meetings.

If the humans requested another meeting after today, that is.

Aayla glanced over her shoulder at Talyn, who stood nearby. As a Guardian, he was meant to stand behind her, not beside her, and she hated it. She usually ignored formality and had him by her side, but he was a stickler for the rules. From birth, He had been raised to be her Guardian, her subordinate, and his training had been very strict in the name of family honour. Honour that their family was chosen to guard a Unix. She hated the notion that he was anything except her equal.

"How are Rune and Ceeda?" she asked, shifting the conversation.

"They're enjoying the view. Several human-on-human disturbances were reported, but nothing was of threat to us."

Talyn replied. *And they miss your antics,* he added with a crooked smile.

She could picture them on the roof, relishing this opportunity. Rune would have his orange-coloured wings, edged in a deep plum, spread out slightly to enjoy the wind over his feathers. Ceeda would be tucked in by his side, close enough for their wings to overlap but far enough apart that she, too, could have her magenta and golden-yellow streaked wings spread out to catch the wind. They mirrored each other perfectly and were a formidable pair.

Talyn stepped forward, offering her his hand. "That's almost five minutes."

With one final nod at the others, Aayla took his hand, letting him guide her back to her seat as the other Aldredth resumed their positions. As she sat down, Talyn leaned over her, his hands resting on the back of her chair.

Let's really give them something to talk about, he smirked as he leaned down and passionately kissed the side of her neck just below her jawline. Her body heated at the contact, and electricity sparked through her veins, igniting a primal fire deep within as her heartbeat quickened.

His lips lingered on her neck for a moment longer, and she felt them curve into a smile.

You are wicked, she grinned.

Shrugging nonchalantly, he stood up. *Any excuse to kiss you.* With a cheeky wink, Talyn stepped back into his protective stance behind her.

Chapter Twenty

Her neck still tingled from where Talyn had kissed her. She offered President Bailey a wide smile, though her mind struggled to recall what she had been about to say moments earlier.

"Sorry, where were we?"

President Bailey's eyes flicked between Aayla and Talyn, the weight of unasked questions clear in his gaze. Aayla raised an eyebrow, daring him to voice his thoughts. After a moment, he thought better of it and instead signalled to his aide before looking back at her with a wide smile.

"Thank you for continuing our conversation today. I know we've been talking for hours, and I truly appreciate your time."

Placing a hand over her heart, Aayla responded sincerely, "We're always happy to help."

President Bailey lifted a small slip of paper. "I have a few questions prepared by the various leaders of our planet. But before I dive in, I'd like to ask one more personal question, if I may. Please don't answer if it's inappropriate. I mean no offence."

Aayla tensed, readying herself for yet another inquiry about Talyn.

"I'm curious about Aldredth mates. How does it... work?" he asked cautiously.

Relief washed over her that the focus had finally shifted from Talyn.

Of course," Aayla began. "You already know that a mate is like the other half of our soul. The bond between our life forces usually happens during our first moment of intimacy, but it can also be triggered by powerful emotions. For Aldredth, sexual desire doesn't awaken until adulthood, and it's not a gradual process—it's more like a switch that flips when two key conditions are met. First, the Aldredth has to be at least 16 years old, and second, they must have found their mate. Until then, if children meet their mate, they bond through simple gestures like hugs, rather than anything... physical."

President Bailey nodded, absorbing her explanation. "And how do you complete this, uh, mating bond?"

"It's not a conscious choice, but it requires a moment of physical contact," she explained. "When Aldredth are intimate, it can last for hours, and it's not just about physical pleasure. The real connection comes from sharing our auras. We push our energy into each other, and that's where the real pleasure lies. Unlike humans, who reach a single climax, we experience continuous waves of pleasure throughout the entire time. It's said to be overwhelming, almost intoxicating." She shrugged lightly, "Not that I'd know firsthand."

President Bailey's brows lifted. "That sounds intense."

Aayla shrugged. "It's hard to explain to someone who can't feel their own aura, but yes. It's... powerful."

"It sounds incredible," President Bailey admitted, his curiosity piqued. "So, you've never experienced it yourself?"

She had dreamt about it, but being unmated, she shouldn't feel such desires. "No," Aayla answered. "We're only intimate with our mates, and since I'm unmated, I've never experienced it."

"Would you consider yourself a virgin, then?"

She tilted her head thoughtfully. "In human terms, yes. But in Aldredth society, we don't have a word for that. You're either mated or unmated."

Her gaze drifted involuntarily to Talyn, who stirred emotions she knew she shouldn't be feeling. His eyes met hers, burning with something unspoken. Realising she'd lingered too long, she shifted her gaze to Daxion and Cythara. "Did I explain that well enough?" she asked, trying to sound casual.

Daxion chuckled, exchanging a knowing look with Cythara. Desire flickered between them before he turned back to Aayla with a playful smile. "Very basic, but you covered the essentials. You'll understand better soon."

Not wanting to let the humans dwell on that, Aayla quickly added, "Sex is celebrated in our society. It strengthens the bond between mates, leads to children, and is... quite enjoyable. I'm at the age where I'll probably meet my mate soon."

Bailey blinked, studying her as if seeing her anew. "Can I ask how old you are?"

"Of course. I'm 21. Aldredth live for around a thousand years, so I'm still considered a mere child. Daxion and Cythara are 675 and 674 years old, and Rythar and Ophelian are both 591."

President Bailey's jaw practically hit the floor. "A thousand years... I had no idea. How old is Talyn?"

Aayla smiled softly. "He's 22. Normally, Aldredth aren't assigned to dangerous duties until they're at least 100, but as a Unix, I don't have that luxury." Sighing heavily, she paused before continuing. "There are so few of us, and my people need me now. I—"

A wave of horror hit her, though it wasn't her own. She spun around, seeing the same expression mirrored on every Aldredth's face in the room. All except Talyn, who stared at the floor, looking utterly stricken. She longed to comfort him, but Daxion's horrified whisper cut through her thoughts.

We don't ask that of you, do we?

Before realising it, she moved toward him, her Unix instincts taking over. Cupping his face, his eyes fluttered closed as her energy soothed him, the tension in his features softening.

Her voice was quiet and gentle. *Don't ever think that. No one ever has or ever could compel me to do anything I do not want to do. Everything I do is driven by love, just as your actions are driven by love for your mate.*

She brushed Cythara's cheek, then moved to Rythar, placing her hand over his heart before pressing her forehead to Ophelian's. With each touch, she felt their tension ease.

Finally, she turned to Talyn. Walking toward him slowly, she wrapped him in a tight embrace. He clung to her, burying his face in her hair. After a long moment, she pulled away, kissing his chin softly before returning to her seat.

"Is... everything all right?" President Bailey asked nervously.

Aayla smiled, trying to ease his worry. "Yes, everything is fine. They care deeply for me, and as a Unix, I feel their heightened emotions. It's part of who I am—to bring peace to those around me. What I should have said earlier is that the compulsion I feel to help my people is... suffocating. Doing nothing goes against my very nature. I know they wish they could protect me, keep me hidden until I'm at least 100, but they can't change who I am or what I need to do."

President Bailey nodded solemnly, clearly moved by her words. After a moment of heavy silence, he raised the paper again, attempting to break the tension.

"Well then, before we run out of daylight, I'd better get to these questions."

"Yes, please," Aayla replied, grateful for the change of topic.

Clutching the paper tightly, President Bailey read the first question slowly. "First question. Have you ever visited Earth before, and if not, why have you never made contact until now?"

Aayla had expected this. Her response was measured and calm. "No, we've never landed on Earth, and neither have any other species. We follow a strict no-contact policy to avoid interfering with the natural evolution of your world. We were watching to see how your species evolved, as you are capable of both great kindness and great cruelty. We do not assist violent civilisations, at least not those beyond saving."

Her gaze sharpened. "We've watched your planet for centuries, concealing its existence from other species. You're a young planet with minimal technology and limited weapons. To most civilisations, Earth would be an easy target. Some species would exploit you—steal your resources, your planet, your people, or worse, destroy you for their amusement. My crash, however, has exposed Earth to dangerous attention. I don't want to alarm you, but Earth is now in grave danger. This is one of the reasons we've stayed in your orbit."

A murmur rippled through the room. The humans at the back whispered frantically, but President Bailey sat unmoved, his eyes searching hers for any hint of deception.

"That leads me to the second question. What are your short- and long-term plans?" His tone remained steady, though tension strained his voice.

"That depends on you," Aayla replied warmly. We'll offer you four options to consider. The first is that you want no further contact with us, in which case we'll leave immediately. The second is that you request our protection, but we remain off-planet. The third option allows for our protection with us stationed on Earth to defend you from external threats, but we don't interfere with your society. Lastly, the fourth option offers both protection and assistance. We would not only defend you but also help maintain peace and order—again, under your governance."

Her tone darkened. "However, no matter what you choose, one condition is non-negotiable. Any attack on an Aldredth will be met with immediate execution. This rule applies to every planet and every species. If I can't guarantee the safety of my people, we cannot help you. I'm sure, as a former military commander, you understand."

President Bailey's face remained stoic, but something flickered in his eyes—understanding, perhaps, or acceptance.

"Understood. Moving to my third question. Are there other races we can communicate with?"

Aayla hesitated, pressing her lips together. "That's... complicated. For the most part, yes. However, most species will only communicate or trade through us. We act as peacemakers, and our presence guarantees their safety. A few species might be willing to deal with you directly, but I must warn you that while their intentions may seem friendly, they are not. The degree of their betrayal will depend on how they perceive your strength, and I fear most would view your planet as... weak."

President Bailey frowned, clearly offended by the implication, but moved on quickly, his tone clipped. "Final question. Can we exchange technology?"

"We would be willing to share our resources should you decide to collaborate with us," Aayla replied. "However, we've learned from past mistakes. We once gave advanced technology to a young planet at their request, but the leap was too much, too fast. They advanced too quickly, destabilised their world, and destroyed themselves. Since then, we've implemented a more controlled rollout of technology to prevent that from happening again."

As Aayla spoke, her mind drifted back to the records of the failed planet, an image of devastation that haunted her even now.

President Bailey folded the paper in his hands and leaned forward, his voice low but sincere. "Thank you for your time today. You've given us much to consider. How long do we have to make a decision?"

Aayla smiled softly, folding her hands in her lap. "Take as long as you need. We'll leave a communicator with you. When you're ready to speak again, you can contact us. In the meantime, we'll remain close by for as long as possible."

President Bailey stood and unconsciously extended his hand before catching himself. With an awkward smile, he quickly dropped it and offered a respectful bow instead.

"It has been an honour, Aayla."

Aayla rose gracefully, her wings folding tightly against her back. She smiled, inclining her head in a sign of respect. "The honour has been ours. Whatever your decision, we wish you and your people the best."

Turning to face the room, Aayla watched as the humans bowed in unison. With one last nod, she turned, and Talyn silently moved into position in front of her, leading the way toward the balcony.

On the balcony, Talyn reached into his pocket and produced a sleek communicator, handing it to President Bailey. "This is how you can contact us when you're ready," he said.

Above, the sky darkened with the approach of dusk. Rythar and Ophelian were the first to take flight, their wings slicing through the air with precision, the sound of feathers catching the wind sharp and swift. Daxion and Cythara followed, their movements fluid as they rose into the twilight, silhouettes against the fading light.

Aayla turned to Talyn. *Are you ready?*

Always, he replied as he flashed her a brief smile.

Without a word, their wings unfurled, each feather catching the last golden rays of the sun. A single, powerful stroke of their wings sent them soaring above the building, the force of their ascent stirring the air in their wake.

Gliding effortlessly, they circled the building as Rune and Ceeda rose toward the ship. Below, the humans craned their necks, eyes wide with awe, watching the Aldredth move like silent, ethereal guardians before angling gracefully toward their waiting transport.

When all but Aayla and Talyn had boarded, Talyn swept beneath her. In perfect synchrony, they ascended together, their movements fluid and precise, vanishing into the deepening hues of the evening sky.

CHAPTER TWENTY-ONE

With a final, powerful beat of her wings, Aayla glided through the shimmering protective barrier of the landing dock, her feet touching down lightly on the cold floor.

"Well, that could've gone better," Rythar quipped, his voice laced with amusement.

Aayla turned just in time to catch Ophelian nudging him playfully. Rythar feigned a wince, laughing heartily before pulling Ophelian close and quickly kissing her cheek.

"What? I'm joking!" Rythar insisted, his grin widening. "Sort of."

Daxion approached, his expression calm but his tone slightly amused. "Could've been worse. All things considered, I'd call it a success."

Aayla sighed, acknowledging that Rythar had a point. There were tense moments she wished she'd handled better, but in the end, the humans had listened. Peace had been maintained. Everyone left the meeting safe. That, to her, was victory enough.

"Good job, Aayla," Martok's voice called from across the dock. He approached with Skyla at his side. "It got tense for a minute there, but you kept things under control."

Despite the praise, she still felt embarrassed about losing her temper. They didn't understand the intricacies of Aldredth customs, and she should have been more patient. But when she thought Talyn was in danger, control had slipped through her fingers.

"Actually, I'm the reason there was a situation in the first place," she admitted, her voice tinged with guilt.

Skyla frowned slightly but spoke gently, "Even so, we mustn't diminish our victories."

Martok gave Skyla a wide smile before kissing her gently. He then turned his attention back to Aayla. "Senior Lazuil are waiting for you via video conference in the Command Centre."

"Thanks, Martok," she said softly, brushing a hand over his and Skyla's cheeks in appreciation as she made her way to the Command Centre.

Inside, Aayla stood before a wall of screens, each displaying the faces of senior Lazuil members. Despite the few awkward moments earlier, she couldn't help but feel a rush of excitement from the encounter with the humans.

As the other landing party members joined her in the room, her eyes instinctively found Talyn at the back, arms crossed, his gaze fixed on her with a quiet intensity. She gave him a quick smile before focusing on the task at hand.

"All right, everyone," she said, leaning forward slightly. "Let's debrief."

The words were met with nods and murmurs of agreement. Each person took turns sharing their insights, their voices carrying a mix of curiosity and cautious optimism.

The hours slipped by as they dissected every detail of the meeting, from cultural nuances to potential missteps, discussing how best to navigate this potential alliance. They discussed humanity's reception to their presence, and the talk turned to human culture, their fragile political state, and the implications of establishing a colony on Earth if approved.

As the conversation drew to a close, Aayla began to feel the exhaustion creeping in. "Goodnight," she bid the others as they disconnected one by one.

The day had dragged on far longer than she anticipated. On Nannuval, Aldredth days lasted 32 hours, but in Earth's orbit, they'd adapted to a 24-hour cycle, sleeping in sync with the humans.

As she and Talyn walked silently down the corridor to their private quarters, she could feel the strain of the day tugging at her. The door slid open with a soft swoosh, revealing a spacious interior designed for beings with large wings like theirs. It was open and airy, with high ceilings and no doors separating the various living spaces.

The sitting area at the front held oversized chairs perfect for lounging and smaller chairs centred around a table. The right side of the room featured an expansive bed with an oversized, plush mattress adorned with soft, fluffy blankets and pillows. It was large enough for two Aldredth to sleep side by side with their wings fully extended—a necessity for them.

Aldredth often slept nude. Clothing was an unnecessary formality, discarded quickly for intimacy. However, unmated Aldredth, like Aayla and Talyn, usually kept their underwear on.

They didn't require frequent bathing like humans since Aldredth didn't produce body odour, but bathing was a luxury they indulged in for the relaxation it brought. Rather than personal bathing areas, they shared one immense communal swimming and bathing pool area, where floating weightlessly and the social aspect of the experience were considered divine.

As Talyn sealed the door behind them with a soft press of the keypad, Aayla turned to him, her mind swirling with thoughts, yet none found their way to her lips. The sight of him in the dim light left her momentarily spellbound. Her thoughts scattered like leaves in the wind, swept away by the quiet power of his beauty, leaving her momentarily speechless.

Sensing her shift, Talyn's brow furrowed in concern. "Is everything all right?"

She hesitated. "It's just... do you realise the others were starting to believe what the humans said today? They thought we might be secretly mated. They were watching you, trying to figure out if you were some kind of threat they'd overlooked."

Talyn sighed, running a hand through his hair. "I know," he said quietly. "I heard it in their thoughts."

"I was terrified," she whispered, her voice trembling slightly.

Without a word, Talyn wrapped her in a tight embrace, holding her as if to shield her from the weight of the world. They stood like that for a long time, neither of them needing to speak, until finally, he pulled back and pressed a soft kiss to her forehead.

"It's late. Let's get you into bed," he said gently. "And for the record, I'm not going anywhere."

"I'll hold you to that," she said, a smile tugging at her lips.

"Please do," he teased, guiding her toward the bed.

As she undressed, she couldn't resist stealing a glance at Talyn from the corner of her eye. In the dim light, Talyn's silhouette was striking, every muscle defined beneath the moonlight streaming in from the window. He moved with a quiet grace, his body a sculpted work of art that seemed almost surreal in its beauty. As he undressed next to the bed, the fabric of his clothing slid off his sculpted physique, accentuating the strength beneath. Each flex of his muscles seemed to dance in harmony with the moon's gentle caress, creating a mesmerising spectacle of masculine beauty against the backdrop of the night sky.

He turned towards her, and she quickly averted her gaze, her heart racing. She was hoping he hadn't noticed her staring.

Sliding into bed, exhaustion overtook her. She lay on her side, facing Talyn, who mirrored her position, his eyes locked on hers. He always stayed awake until she drifted off, a silent sentinel by her side.

The simple act of being near him soothed her, no matter how chaotic the day had been. With closed eyes, she felt his fingers brushing her cheek with a tenderness that made her heart swell.

"Goodnight," he whispered. His voice was the last thing she heard as she drifted into a peaceful sleep.

Chapter Twenty-Two

The next few days flew by in a blur, with Aayla dedicating herself to training. Not because she believed war was imminent, but because she was a child of immense potential, a precious asset, and one that others would eagerly seek to harm.

Standing at the entrance of the loading dock, Aayla's gaze drifted to Talyn. The wind playfully tousled his hair as he scanned the sky, ever vigilant for signs of danger.

"Do you see anything?" she asked, her voice breaking the stillness.

"No," Talyn replied, lost in thought. "Everything looks clear."

She turned her attention to the landing team, each member poised and ready for flight. The humans had deliberated over the proposals and were set to announce their decision at the upcoming meeting at Buckingham Palace with the Queen of England. This time, a different ruler would have the honour of hosting them.

Flaring her wings, Aayla looked over her team one last time. "Please don't take any unnecessary risks down there. Stay safe."

Talyn turned to her, his eyes glinting with playful mischief and a teasing smile tugging at his lips. *Let's try not to threaten the humans, shall we?*

A wide grin spread across her face as she shrugged playfully. *I can't promise anything.*

With a leap, she fell for a moment, feeling the exhilarating rush of wind against her skin before snapping her wings open and circling down gracefully. She caught a glimpse of the other Aldredth taking off behind her, their movements fluid and synchronised, a beautiful dance against the backdrop of the clear sky.

The flight was brief, and soon they were gliding over Buckingham Palace. A vast crowd filled the area outside its gates, stretching as far as the eye could see. People of all ages clamoured for a glimpse of them, many holding signs and shouting excitedly. The noise was deafening, but the energy was electric, igniting a spark of hope within Aayla.

As she descended slowly into the courtyard, she made a point of executing a dramatic and graceful flap of her wings, showcasing their elegance before folding them against her back.

Waiting in the courtyard was a contingent of the Queen's Guard, clad in black trousers, vibrant red uniforms, and towering furry hats.

The Lord Steward stepped forward to greet Aayla with a respectful bow. "Welcome, Aldredth, to Buckingham Palace. Her Majesty is very excited to meet you. Please, follow me."

Aayla nodded, her gaze drifting to the throng of people on the other side of the gate. She took in the diversity of faces, the excitement palpable in the air. Unable to resist, she waved, earning a chorus of delighted screams.

As they followed the Lord Steward through the grand halls of Buckingham Palace, Aayla marvelled at the opulence surrounding her. They finally entered a grand room adorned with rich tapestries and ornate furnishings. Tall windows were dressed in velvet curtains that allowed streams of natural light to cascade into the room, illuminating the intricate details of the antique furniture and gilded decorations. Portraits of past monarchs lined the walls, their watchful gazes seemingly overseeing the proceedings. In the centre stood a long, polished table surrounded by plush chairs upholstered in sumptuous fabrics.

At the head of the table sat the Queen, her demeanour warm as she smiled happily. The table was lavishly set with silver trays brimming with bite-sized delicacies and ornate silver teapots surrounded by delicate china cups.

The Lord Steward announced their arrival as they entered the room, and the Queen rose from her seat, her smile warm and inviting. "Greetings on behalf of the United Kingdom, and welcome to my home, Buckingham Palace."

"Thank you for the invitation. Your home is truly beautiful."

Gesturing to the plush chairs around the table, the Queen took her seat once more. "Please, have a seat."

Aayla sat at the far end of the table while Daxion and Cythara stood against the wall to her right, and Rythar and Ophelian stood against the opposite wall to her left. Talyn positioned himself protectively behind her.

A small number of royal staff lined the wall behind the queen, while four Royal Guards stood sentinel in the corners of the room.

The Queen gestured toward the spread of food. "My chef has prepared some refreshments for our meeting. Please, help yourselves."

A royal staff member discreetly approached, quietly placing a plate of delicacies and a cup of tea before the Queen before retreating to the wall.

As Aayla surveyed the array of delectable treats before her, her eyes widened in awe. "You spoil us with your generosity. We would be honoured to taste your offerings."

With a flick of her hand, she used her telekinetic powers to levitate three plates, elegantly arranging small bites of food on each. The Queen's eyes widened in surprise before she regained her composure.

"Is your ability to move things with your mind unique to the Unix?"

"No," Aayla explained, her voice steady. "All Aldredth can manipulate the molecules of objects around us."

As she twisted her hand, sending a plate toward Daxion and Rythar, Talyn stepped closer. He inspected the food on her plate first, his hands gently brushing over the items, instinctively sensing for danger, before discretely tasting some. Satisfied, he nodded to Aayla, then with a slight flick of his wrist, he levitated one of the teapots, pouring tea into three cups. He lifted one to his lips, inhaling the delicate aroma before taking a small sip. He set the cup down in front of Aayla before sending the other two to Daxion and Rythar, who had passed the plate of food to their mates.

The Queen watched them with a slight frown, "The food is quite safe, I assure you."

"Thank you for this feast. It's an Aldredth tradition for our males to check our food before consumption, even on our home planet. We mean no offence," Aayla explained, her tone respectful yet firm.

Sampling a small, sweet pastry, she looked to Talyn, holding it up in invitation. With a smile, he leaned in and took a bite, their eyes locking in a moment that stretched on before he stepped back.

"Your Guardian is welcome to have a plate of his own," the Queen offered, her voice gentle.

"There's no need. We share our food, so only one serving is required per pair," Aayla responded, her voice filled with assurance.

The Queen seemed satisfied with this answer and pleased to see the food offerings accepted. She took a delicate sip of her tea and set the cup down silently.

"I'm sure you're eager to hear our decision, so let's not waste any time," the Queen began, her voice steady and direct. "After thorough discussions among the world leaders, we've reached a conclusion. I'm pleased to announce that we've chosen the fourth option. We're inviting you to establish a base on Earth, and we'll work out the details together. In exchange, we request both your protection and assistance."

Aayla couldn't suppress her wide smile at the fantastic news. "We are beyond happy to hear that."

"What are the next steps?" the Queen asked eagerly.

"We've considered Earth's unique circumstances and tailored an approach that we think will work best for you. No two planets are the same, so our approach is unique to Earth's needs. For a planet of this size and population, we estimate that three Aldredth bases will be necessary. However, we'll start with just one to allow everyone to adjust to the idea."

The Queen, listening with a calm expression, gave a slow, thoughtful nod.

"We've selected tower locations based on the distance to areas where our help will be needed the most, population clusters, and political reasons," Aayla explained. "With these considerations in mind, we propose the first base be built in the United States due to our existing relationship, followed by Nigeria and China."

Though the Queen's face remained composed, Aayla noticed the slight downturn of her lips, a sign she may have hoped for a base in her own country.

"We'll coordinate with the leaders of those nations to finalise the exact locations," Ayala asserted, her tone steady and commanding. "Construction can begin as soon as the approvals are in place. In the meantime, we're ready to provide immediate assistance where required. We will reach out to each respective leader to confirm our assistance."

The Queen gave a thoughtful nod. "How many Aldredth do you plan to station on Earth?"

"We'll need around 30 to start construction, and we propose at least 20 to stay on Earth permanently. Ideally, more would follow, but we're happy to begin with a smaller contingent."

The Queen took a sip of her tea and nodded. "That sounds reasonable."

"We're also interested in employing human staff," Aayla added. "We know your economy is money-based, so we'll offer appropriate compensation."

Aayla, you need to see this, Talyn interrupted, stepping forward as the Queen spoke. He showed her a message on his Lumina from Ceeda, a warning about a troubling sense of unease. Aurra's could see the future in their premonitions, but they could also feel a shift in the energy around them, a harbinger of impending danger. Whilst it wasn't enough to halt the meeting, it made clear that they would need to remain vigilant.

Thank you, Talyn. Please tell Rune and Ceeda to let me know if they sense anything else.

The Queen's eyes tracked Talyn's movements before her gaze returned to Aayla. "You don't use money in your society?"

"No, we—"

Aayla was hit with a blinding vision of an explosion outside. She clutched her head in pain, her breath coming in sharp gasps. The scene unfolded in agonising slow motion, every detail etched into her mind with crystal clarity. Thankfully, it felt like the future, not a reflection of the past, but the pressing urgency hinted at an imminent threat.

"Bomb... outside," she managed to gasp, eyes wide with the effort of pushing the words out.

In a heartbeat, the Aldredth responded. They surged out of the room in a blur of motion, blades already drawn, their formation fluid and lethal. They burst through the gates just as Rune and Ceeda took up defensive positions, standing shoulder to shoulder, eyes sweeping the crowd for the source of the threat.

Ceeda turned sharply. "The man in the black shirt and blue pants, with the black case."

Aayla moved swiftly, stepping in front of Ceeda as Talyn flew forward at full speed, landing in a crouch mere feet ahead. His wings folded instantly against his back as he rose, and with a flick of his hands, he parted the panicked crowd like a tide, revealing the suspect.

The man froze, wide-eyed, caught in the open. Then, as if breaking free from a trance, he lunged for his black bag. But he was too slow.

With a sharp motion of her hand, Aayla's telekinesis slammed into him, lifting him violently into the air as if gravity had forgotten him. The bag tore from his grasp and sailed across the space toward her. Suspended in the air, the bomber thrashed, fury and fear twisting his features.

"The penalty for an attack on an Aldredth is death," she declared coldly.

With a single twist of her wrist, there was a sickening crack. The man's body went limp, his neck snapped cleanly, and he crumpled to the ground in a heap.

Aayla held the bag suspended for a moment before placing it gently at the feet of the nearest Royal Guard.

Talyn stepped forward and used his powers to lift the bomber's corpse, carrying it effortlessly and setting it beside the bag.

"There's a bomb in the bag," Aayla said. "Can you please dispose of it—"

Before she could finish, Ceeda's voice sliced through the air like a blade. "It has a backup timer!"

Time seemed to stall for a split second—then Talyn moved.

He surged forward, his palm slamming down as he conjured a protective shield around the bag, his wings flaring slightly with the force of the magic. A heartbeat later, the bomb detonated. The explosion erupted in a thunderous roar, a blinding fireball engulfing the space within the shield. The shockwave slammed into the barrier with a deafening boom, sending cracks like lightning across its surface.

Talyn gritted his teeth, his jaw clenched tight as he absorbed the brunt of the impact through the shield. Sparks danced across his fingertips and veins of golden light pulsed along his arms as the magic strained under the pressure. The force of the blast pushed him back half a step, boots skidding against the ground, but he held.

The firestorm raged for a breathless moment—then began to die down. Smoke curled around the edges of the barrier. Ash drifted through the air.

With a final, shuddering exhale, Talyn dropped the shield. The remains of the bomb lay inside—charred and melted metal, nothing more. His chest rose and fell with the effort, but his eyes were steady.

"It's contained," he said, voice low but firm.

The crowd beyond the gate screamed and ran in panic. Aayla stepped to Talyn's side, her gaze flicking to the scorched earth where the bag had been. The threat was gone, but the message was clear.

They had been targeted. And whoever was behind it had just declared war.

Are you okay? He asked, glancing at Aayla.

I'm fine, Aayla said, turning to the Royal Guards. "Apologies for missing the backup. We didn't intend to offer you a live bomb."

The guards stared at her, speechless. That could have gone better.

After quickly checking on the others and confirming there were no further injuries, Aayla turned to Talyn. Their eyes met—no words were needed. She gave him a silent nod, the kind that carried both gratitude and resolve, and took the lead, guiding the group back toward the gates.

They paused at the perimeter where the Royal Guards had assembled in force, their weapons drawn and eyes alert. Aayla and Talyn stepped forward to speak with them, voices calm but firm as they explained the situation. Reassurances were given. The threat had been neutralised. There was no ongoing danger. Slowly, the tension in the ranks began to ease, though wariness still lingered behind guarded expressions.

Once the immediate crisis had passed, the group made its way back into the building. The corridor was quieter now, the hush of aftermath settling like dust after a storm. When they reached the meeting room, Aayla stepped inside first and paused.

The Queen stood near the far wall, flanked by a contingent of elite guards dressed in deep black armor, their presence silent but formidable. Her expression was tight, jaw set, and her eyes were fixed on the door as if she had been waiting. The tension in the room was palpable, a coiled wire ready to snap.

"My deepest apologies, Your Majesty," Aayla said calmly. She searched her mind for the most diplomatic explanation. "Rune and Ceeda detected a dangerous individual outside intending to do harm to them, whom we have now neutralised. Shall we continue our conversation, or would you rather adjourn?"

After a brief whispered discussion with her advisors, the Queen allowed herself a small, uneasy smile. The weight of recent events lingered in her eyes, but she masked it with practised grace. "Let's continue," she said softly, her voice steady despite the undercurrent of tension.

They resumed their seats as the others returned to their places, the atmosphere tense but focused. The Queen straightened her posture and addressed Aayla.

"You were explaining how your society operates without money."

"That's right," Aayla said, steadying herself. "In Nannuval, we don't use money. Everything is shared, and while we do trade resources with other civilisations, it's purely an exchange of goods—no currency changes hands."

She paused, letting the idea sink in before continuing.

"We also don't have assigned jobs or tasks that we're obligated to perform. Anything I do, or anywhere I go, is completely my choice. Everything we do is of our own free will. I don't command the other Aldredth like a superior would. I can make requests, but ultimately, they have complete freedom."

Aayla glanced across at Daxion. "For instance, if Daxion and Cythara decided to leave Earth and pursue something else, they wouldn't need permission. They'd inform me out of respect, and I would accommodate their decision accordingly."

She paused, her gaze briefly lingering on Talyn before shifting back to the Queen.

"Or, if Talyn decided he no longer wanted to be my Guardian, he could request to be assigned to a new Charge."

Turning with a mischievous smile, she saw Talyn's look of disgust and laughed out loud. "Or he is welcome to stay with me for as long as he likes."

Talyn raised an eyebrow at her. *You think you're funny, don't you?*

I'm hilarious, she replied with a wink.

Talyn's expression softened. *I'll never leave you. You're stuck with me.*

Good, she replied, her smile widening.

"Before we finish, may I ask about your customs around bowing?" the Queen asked, curiosity evident. "I've noticed that your people bow to you, but you don't bow in return."

Aayla nodded. "Yes, that's true. In our society, Aldredth bow as a sign of respect. In our society, the strongest Aldredth protects those weaker than themselves. As the strongest Aldredth in this room, it's my duty to lead my people into battle and be the last to leave the battlefield. It's not required of me, but it's something I must do. Just like how cheating, lying, or stealing might give you a bad feeling, if I were to stand aside when I could help, it would gnaw at me. That sense of duty is likely why we've expanded our protection to other civilisations. We find joy in helping those around us," she finished with a shrug.

The Queen smiled softly. "That's quite noble."

Aayla returned the smile. "It's a mindset we hope to inspire in your people as well. Humans are capable of great kindness but also great cruelty. I've seen footage of strangers banding together to lift a car off someone injured, but I've also seen people walk past someone hungry and homeless without a second glance. Your society has the potential to evolve in either direction. Now that we've made contact, we'd like to help guide humanity toward the kindness already within you."

The Queen seemed moved by her words. "I'm very grateful I was able to meet you today. I look forward to future conversations."

"As do I."

With that, the Queen gave a final respectful bow, bidding the Aldredth farewell. The Lord Steward led them outside, and as they took flight back to their ship, Aayla's thoughts turned to the next step—contacting the world leaders to finalise the details.

The first call would go to the President of the United States.

CHAPTER TWENTY-THREE

Only six days later, Aayla stood in New York, gazing up at the building that would soon be demolished to make way for what had been dubbed 'Aldredth Tower', a beacon of their presence on Earth.

It had been a whirlwind few days. After another meeting with President Bailey, she proposed that the tower be constructed in New York due to its dense population and strategic importance. His team responded swiftly, offering several potential sites. After flying past each location, she had chosen one in the Bronx, a decision rooted in her desire to uplift underprivileged neighbourhoods. Research had predicted that proximity to Aldredth Tower would cause property values to skyrocket. By placing the tower in an area that needed financial revitalisation, they could inject much-needed resources into the community.

While Earth revolved around money, Aayla understood the importance of setting up a financial system before the tower was finalised. Several major banks had sent proposals to them via the leaders of their prospective countries. After some deliberation, JPMorgan Chase had been selected to handle all Aldredth currency on Earth.

Aayla's research revealed that humans placed great value on rare and beautiful stones, often trading them for significant sums of money. Recognising an opportunity, she proposed an exchange of precious stones and gems sourced from distant planets in return for Earth currency. It was agreed that these trades would occur every six months to prevent flooding the market and diminishing their value. The first round of trade, conducted with multiple nations worldwide, generated over two billion U.S. dollars. A small portion of this was allocated to purchase the land for the Aldredth Tower, while the remainder was entrusted to JPMorgan Chase for management.

JPMorgan Chase was in the process of creating an exclusive credit card for the Aldredth that would be accepted globally. The ultra-thin cards, crafted from solid gold, would be elegantly embossed with the Aldredth emblem. Each Aldredth would receive a card upon arrival on Earth, making transactions seamless during their stay on the planet.

That morning, Aayla had finalised the card's design in a conversation with the bank before leading an Aldredth team to Earth with Talyn by her side.

The sun was beginning to rise behind the tall buildings, and there was a cold, crisp chill in the air.

The sky above was alive with colour, transformed into a mesmerising canvas adorned with a myriad of colourful wings. Each fluttering movement painted sweeping streaks of vibrant hues, creating a breathtaking spectacle that danced with vitality and energy.

A sizable contingent of Aldredth had recently arrived on Earth to establish their new station, and among them were Aayla's cherished friends, Jaxion and his mate, Kythera.

Jaxion was a younger male Aldredth of Vorax blood, just 189 years old. His pale blue eyes glinted with resolve, and his navy-blue wings, rippling with light grey waves, shimmered in the morning light. Beside him, his mate Kythera, a year younger at 188, stood ready with her moss-green eyes fixed on the sky above. Her chocolate-coloured wings, edged in soft pastel pink, unfurled gracefully behind her.

Aayla had been stationed with the pair during their assignment on Orvax-3 and several adjoining planets, where they had forged a close bond through shared adventures and no small amount of mischief. Their camaraderie had been a source of joy and support during those times, and the memories of their escapades still brought a warm smile to her face.

Seeing them again felt like a gift. Aayla couldn't help but feel a surge of excitement at the thought of working alongside them once more. They were not only trusted allies but also the kind of friends who could make even the most daunting missions enjoyable.

Aayla stood side-by-side with Talyn and couldn't hide the exhilaration she felt at this new beginning, whilst Talyn remained vigilant, cautiously scanning the surrounding crowd.

Humans had turned out in thousands, eager to witness the arrival of the Aldredth and the groundbreaking construction that was about to unfold. The atmosphere buzzed with anticipation, filled with a cacophony of voices and the rhythmic clicks of camera shutters. Above them, a small army of Aldredth soared gracefully. Their radiant plumage shimmered like jewels, casting a kaleidoscope of colours against the backdrop of the endless sky.

From fiery oranges to serene blues, and verdant greens to sunset pinks, the sky became a tapestry of nature's most enchanting palette.

The building in front of them, a once-abandoned factory, spanned an entire city block. The Aldredth would begin demolishing it with their powers, neatly stacking the materials for recycling or disposal by human crews. In just three days, the new tower would rise from the rubble, constructed from Aldredth materials.

Aayla wouldn't personally contribute to the construction. Instead, she focused on ensuring the site's security.

A cheer rose from the crowd, signalling the start of the demolition. Aayla activated her Lumina—a sleek device that responded to touch, voice, and even thought, interpreting the body's electric signals. With a quick flick, she expanded a small hologram of Martok and Skyla stationed on the opposite side of the building.

"How's everything looking on your side?"

"All clear so far," came Martok's response. "The human police are doing a good job keeping the crowds back."

Aayla nodded, satisfied. The police had fenced off the area immediately after the site was confirmed, preventing the eager public from getting too close. "Good. Just remember, the humans are still learning about us and our customs. Some might get too curious and try to touch you, but it's nothing malicious."

"We're handling it," Skyla reassured her. "Nothing to worry about."

Just as Aayla ended the call, a wave of unease swept over her, tightening her chest. Her instincts flared. Something was wrong. She scanned the sea of civilians in front of her.

Talyn noticed her sudden tension; his voice was gentle but worried. *What do you sense?*

I'm not sure... but something feels wrong.

As the sun's golden rays stretched across the sprawling landscape, her eyes followed Talyn's sharp gaze, catching a glimpse of irregular movement in the distance. A group of figures moved stealthily through the crowd, their trench coats and heavy clothing out of place for the day's warmth. Their movements were nearly concealed by the throngs of unsuspecting civilians. Positioned strategically, they were preparing for an attack.

"Ambush!" Aayla shouted into her Lumina, drawing her sword.

The assailants were buried too deep within the crowd for her to reach without endangering the innocent civilians around them. In a swift, synchronised motion, they reached beneath the folds of their trench coats. Her heart raced as their hands emerged, revealing the glint of something hidden. As they drew the objects out with a deliberate flourish, she recognised the unmistakable form of the assault rifles. The weapons gleamed ominously in the light, drawing startled glances from those nearby.

In an instant, chaos erupted. The crowd scattered, screams filling the air as the attackers raised their weapons, aiming not at Aayla but at the Aldredth in the sky.

Aayla reacted instinctively, launching herself into the air with a powerful burst. Talyn was right beside her, matching her every stroke. The wind roared past, whipping through her hair as they soared higher, a blur of speed and motion.

Gunfire echoed through the streets as Talyn cast a protective shield around them, expanding it to cover the Aldredth flying behind. Aayla focused her energy, telekinetically stopping the bullets mid-air, holding them just inches from Talyn's shield.

Amidst the chaos, humans scattered in all directions, desperately seeking refuge from the violence erupting around them. Yet even in the confusion, a few brave humans stepped forward, managing to tackle a couple of the armed assailants to the ground.

Despite her best efforts, a few bullets slipped past Aayla's defences on her far left, striking Talyn's shield, freezing in place. As the attackers paused to reload, she twisted her hard and telekinetically ripped the guns from their hands whilst the bullets fell to the ground with sharp, metallic clinking sounds.

The guns hovered in the air, and Talyn wasted no time, lifting the assailants into the air with his power, their limbs pinned rigidly to their sides. Suspended helplessly, they dangled high above, unable to move as their weapons floated just out of reach.

Aayla folded her wings and dropped like a bullet before snapping them out to their full width. Her wingspan created a massive shadow as she swept gracefully down in a deliberate show of strength before hovering in front of the assailants.

"The penalty for attacking an Aldredth is death," she stated, her voice unwavering. "Do you have anything to say for yourselves?"

One of the men, his face twisted with anger, yelled, "We won't let you destroy us with your tricks!"

Aayla sighed, her heart heavy with sorrow at their distrust. "We're not here to trick you. We only want to help, and it's unfortunate you couldn't see that."

With a snap, Talyn broke their necks, lowering their lifeless bodies to the ground. Aayla landed beside one of the men, reaching for his hood.

Be careful, Aayla. We don't know if they were under someone else's control.

Slowly, Aayla lifted the hood from his face but saw no signs of mind control—no telltale thin black veins spreading outward from the site of infection. It was one of the reasons the Aldredth were so cautious about physical contact. Mind control magic could easily pass through touch with some species.

With a deep sense of loss weighing on her, she stood up and glanced over at Martok, her voice calm but firm. "Make sure the human authorities take custody of their bodies."

Martok nodded in silent agreement, and Aayla flared out her wings in preparation for flight.

With one final glance over the crowd, she pushed off with a powerful beat of her wings, Talyn by her side. Together, they circled the construction site several times, their sharp eyes scanning the swelling crowds for any other signs of danger.

In the days that followed, the old building was reduced to rubble, and the ground beneath was excavated, making way for the new Aldredth Tower. Talyn scrutinised every media headline and broadcast in the aftermath of the attack. One evening, after hours of monitoring, he turned to Aayla, his gaze thoughtful but resolute.

"We need to prioritise early engagement with the humans. Let them see the full extent of our abilities and prove our intentions by standing with them, not from the shadows."

His reasoning was flawless, and damn if she wasn't a little proud of that sharp mind.

Though they had planned to focus their resources on the new tower's security, Aayla agreed. Together, they embarked on a mission across the planet, aiding wherever they could.

In Canada, they rescued civilians from a burning apartment block and saved passengers from an overturned ferry. In Russia, they freed hostages from terrorists, and in India, they thwarted muggings, rapes, and robberies. They extinguished a raging bushfire in Australia, helped victims of a derailed train in Libya, caught an out-of-control aeroplane in France, and rescued tornado victims in Texas.

Throughout their journey, they ate at human cafés and stayed in modest hotels, making a point of being among the people and intentionally immersing themselves in the community. This was a deliberate effort to build trust and demonstrate solidarity.

Aayla glanced around the small hotel room in Boston, her wings shifting uncomfortably as her eyes rested on the bed that was far too small to accommodate their large wings.

"You can take the bed," Talyn said, coming up behind her and running his hand gently through his hair. He'd insisted on sleeping on the hard floor next to her throughout the trip while ensuring she was comfortable on the mattress.

"Not tonight. You're taking the bed," she said, folding her arms.

Talyn gave her a firm look. "Never."

She stared him down, but he only raised an eyebrow in challenge. With a sigh of defeat, she glanced around the room. "Are you sure we can't sleep on the ship for one night?"

"The media's praising how sociable and approachable we've been. Leaving the hotel after checking in might raise some questions."

His logic was sound, though she still hated seeing him so uncomfortable.

Talyn cupped her cheek, brushing his thumb over her skin. "Besides, Aldredth Tower will be ready by tomorrow, so it's just one more night before we can sleep there."

She nodded, a small smile touching her lips. "All right. Let's go grab something to eat before calling it a night."

His eyes gleamed with mischief as he opened the balcony door, holding out his hand. "It's a date."

Aayla laughed and took his hand, "I like the sound of that."

Unfurling their wings, they soared into the sky, gliding effortlessly on the currents before making a dramatic descent to the street below. Their landing was wildly showy and showcased their striking presence.

Strolling past rows of brightly lit shops. A crowd quickly gathered, people snapping pictures and eagerly approaching them to ask questions or trying to shake their hands.

Despite Talyn's concern, Aayla felt energised by their excitement and graciously shook hands with anyone who asked, even though the risk, however small, remained.

She felt a loose feather and, with a gentle tug, pulled it from her wing, tucking it into her pocket with the intention of gifting it to a human later. Aldredth occasionally shed feathers as part of their natural renewal process. During their time on Earth, Aayla had witnessed two feathers fall, both igniting fierce competition among humans eager to claim them. This time, she was determined to ensure the feathers didn't fall carelessly.

Talyn paused in front of a quaint shop bustling with locals. The faded facade boasted vibrant colours and bold shapes, while flowerpots of various sizes adorned the windows. A balcony on the second level featured decorative metal tables and chairs, surrounded by more pots overflowing with colourful blooms.

What do you think of this place?

Looking across the eclectic decorations, she heard the quiet melody of music overlaid with the hum of lively conversations from inside. *It feels like a happy place.*

They had lingered so long that the restaurant owner emerged, bursting out of the doors in excitement. He was an older gentleman with grey, curly hair, a rounded figure, and flushed rosy cheeks.

"Welcome! I'm Juan, and this is my humble restaurant. Please come inside and try our finest dishes on the house. It would be my honour!" His face lit up with a broad smile, brimming with excitement, before he quickly composed himself and bowed deeply in greeting.

Aayla smiled and subtly glanced at Talyn. His eyes surveyed the building. *I don't sense any danger.*

"We would be honoured," Aayla said, turning to Juan, "but we insist on paying."

"I couldn't possibly—"

"Your offer is generous, but we insist," she said gently. "May we sit on the balcony?"

"Absolutely! Anywhere you like!" Juan said, beaming. "I'll bring menus right away."

Aayla extended her wings, preparing for flight, and gave him a warm smile. "Thank you."

They flew to the balcony, choosing an open spot where the people below could still see them. Talyn made a leisurely circuit around the balcony, offering friendly smiles to the two other couples seated there while checking for potential threats. Once he felt assured of their safety, he stopped beside a table on the balcony's edge, making them visible to the bustling street below.

"After you, my Unix," he said, bowing playfully with a charming flourish. *It looks safe.*

"Thank you, Talyn," Aayla replied, her lips curving into a smile as she settled into her seat, her wings gracefully draping over the back of the chair.

Juan hurried over to their table with an armful of menus as Talyn sat opposite her. "Here's our dinner menu, dessert menu, and wine list for you," he said, beaming with enthusiasm.

Talyn smiled warmly and replied, "We would be honoured if you could select a few specialties for us."

Juan, a bit flustered, gathered the menus with a bow. "Of course, I'll bring out our most popular dishes."

Aayla smiled at Talyn as Juan rushed away. Gazing into his eyes, she felt herself drawn into the depths of his presence, and the connection between them pulsed stronger. Swallowing hard, her gaze shifted to his lips, and she wondered what it would be like to lean in, feel his lips against hers, and taste him. The thought sent a shiver down her spine, her heart fluttering.

With his every breath, every subtle movement, she felt an irresistible pull, as if drawn by an invisible thread weaving between them.

A soft cough broke the spell, and Aayla jumped slightly, embarrassed to see that Juan had returned with a procession of servers carrying trays of food. She had become so transfixed by Talyn that she hadn't sensed their approach.

Talyn chuckled under his breath, flashing her a crooked smile.

"Apologies for the interruption," Juan said with a smile, "but your food is ready." He motioned to a line of servers behind him, each carrying an array of plates.

Delicious, aromatic dishes soon covered the entire table. Talyn scrutinised each one before generously serving Aayla a portion of every dish.

They spent hours eating and talking as the crowd below swelled. For someone as serious as Talyn could appear, Aayla watched as he waved and engaged with the humans even more than she did, taking time to acknowledge their presence. His warmth and easy manner captivated them. The humans seemed to really resonate with him. He had an uncanny ability to engage people, effortlessly bridging the gap between their worlds.

As Aayla finished the last sip of her drink, she watched Talyn light up while chatting with the crowd. He answered questions from the crowd, laughing with them. She wasn't sure who was having more fun—him or the humans.

When he turned back to her, his wide smile brightened the space between them, and he reached across the table to take her hand. "Are you ready to go?"

Her skin tingled at his touch, and she blushed slightly. "Yes. I couldn't possibly eat another bite."

As they rose to leave, Juan hurried over from the balcony's edge, where he'd been pretending not to watch them.

"Can I get you anything else?" he asked.

"No, thank you. The food was wonderful," Aayla said. "Please give our compliments to the chef."

Talyn handed Juan the gold credit card. "Please add 100 per cent gratuity to the bill."

Juan started to protest, but Talyn raised his hand to stop him. "We insist, as a token of appreciation for your excellent service."

Bowing deeply, Juan replied, "I'm truly honoured. I'll be right back."

As Juan hurried back inside, Aayla turned to Talyn, looping her arms through his as they strolled along the edge of the balcony. "We should do this more often. Just the two of us."

A smile tugged at the corner of his lips, "I would like that very much."

They stood at the balcony's edge, watching the bustling crowd below, their laughter and chatter mingling with the evening air. Aayla felt a sense of contentment wash over her, the vibrant energy of the humans resonating within her.

When Juan finally returned, they exchanged warm farewells, gratitude evident in their smiles. With a final wave, they launched into the night sky, gliding effortlessly back to their hotel balcony, their movements graceful and fluid against the backdrop of the twinkling stars.

As they settled in for the night, Aayla faced Talyn, their faces mere inches apart. She hadn't convinced him to take the bed for himself, but she had successfully persuaded him to share it by threatening to join him on the floor. The bed was so small that they were practically sleeping on top of each other, their wings draping over the edges onto the floor.

As sleep enveloped her, the warmth of his breath brushed against her lips, igniting a thrilling heat that coursed through her, stirring feelings deep within.

Chapter Twenty-Four

As the sun rose the following day, Aayla and Talyn stood in front of Aldredth Tower, the new landmark shimmering in the dawn light. A media crew buzzed around them, setting up for interviews before the official opening later that day. Cameras flashed, and reporters jostled for a word, eager to capture every detail.

Aldredth Tower loomed majestically against the skyline, a dazzling beacon of modernity that captivated the eye with its sleek lines and shimmering facade. Rising high into the heavens, it seemed to defy gravity, its form stretching towards the clouds with an air of confidence and grace.

Every facet of the building gleamed like a polished gemstone, catching and scattering the sunlight in a dazzling display of brilliance. The glasslike exterior refracted light into a kaleidoscope of colours, casting a mesmerising glow that shimmered across the structure like a constellation of twinkling stars come to life.

Light-coloured pavers gleamed softly under the sun, their surfaces imbued with a subtle radiance that illuminated the pathway around the entire exterior of the building. Each paver bore a delicate hue reminiscent of the pale glow of dawn. As sunlight kissed their smooth surface, they reflected a gentle luminosity, casting a warm and inviting aura over the surrounding space. In the evening, when bathed in the soft glow of outdoor lighting, these pavers would continue to enchant, their pale hues glowing softly in the twilight.

The light-coloured materials created a sense of openness and airiness, brightening the landscape with their soft, neutral tones.

The sleek lines of the building were softened by lush greenery that adorned the building and cascaded down its sides like a lush waterfall. From afar, it appeared as if nature itself had embraced the building, weaving a tapestry of foliage and flowers that enveloped it in a cloak of natural beauty. The plants on the outer edge were native to Earth, but the plants around the middle of the building were new varieties sourced from other planets. Careful consideration had been made to ensure the species selected would be viable in Earth's atmosphere but wouldn't be at risk of spreading or cross-pollinating with Earth's native plant species.

At every level, gardens and green spaces flourished, their vibrant hues contrasting against the sleek lines of the building's modern facade. From manicured lawns to cascading vines, each garden was a testament to the harmonious coexistence of architecture and nature, a living testament to sustainable design.

As the sunlight filtered through the foliage, dappling the ground below with patterns of light and shadow, the building took on an ethereal quality as if it were a living, breathing organism. The air was already alive with the hum of bees and the chirping of birds, adding to the sense of tranquillity and serenity that permeated the space.

At its summit, a rooftop oasis was designed with a lush garden retreat offering panoramic views of the city below. Here, amidst the swaying trees and fragrant blooms, Aldredth could escape the hustle and bustle, finding solace and rejuvenation in the embrace of nature that they so valued.

It was more than just a building. It was a symbol of their power and a sanctuary in the heart of the city where nature and modernity converged in perfect harmony. Its form seamlessly melded with function to create a masterpiece of modern design, shining as an example of what could be achieved when you embrace the beauty of the natural world.

Aayla knew that the building would take on a new life as the sun set, its luminous exterior coming alive with the glow of sparkling lights. It would become a beacon of progress in the heart of the city, an icon of collaboration between their people.

The tower was constructed from a material similar to glass but far more resilient, its surface sparkling like crushed diamonds while providing perfect insulation. The entrances, including the many balconies dotting its exterior, were protected by the same force fields used on Aldredth ships. These fields were coded to permit entry based on DNA, currently allowing only Aldredth and other friendly species. Soon, as humans joined their workforce, their DNA would be added to the registry, granting them seamless access through the invisible shields.

That was, of course, if the humans were interested in working with them. Yet, judging by the ever-expanding crowd that had gathered since the construction of the building just five days ago, Aayla felt increasingly confident in their willingness to collaborate.

Navigating through the throng of dignitaries surrounding her, she exchanged warm greetings and pleasantries before stepping onto the smooth pavers to commence the opening ceremony officially. Her heart raced with excitement, fuelled by the bright lights and the enthusiastic cheers of the crowd, all contributing to the whirlwind of activity around her.

Aayla couldn't help but marvel at the sea of faces before her, each one brimming with anticipation and enthusiasm. The energy in the air was electric, a palpable pulse of collective excitement shared among everyone gathered for this momentous occasion.

The cheers of the crowd washed over her like a warm embrace. It was a humbling experience to be the focal point of such adoration and attention.

A silver microphone had been set up by the humans in front, and although Aldredth didn't normally "open" buildings, she was more than happy to celebrate this momentous occasion. Taking a deep breath, she glanced behind her at Talyn, who winked with his trademark cheeky disposition, making her heart flutter.

With a radiant smile, Aayla turned to face the crowd, and the deafening roar gradually fell to a hush. "Ladies and gentlemen, esteemed guests, and honoured representatives of Earth. Today marks a historic moment for both our civilisations. For millennia, the stars have watched over us as we journeyed through the cosmos, separated by the vast expanse of space. But today, we stand united, bound together by the shared dream of friendship and cooperation. It is with great joy and excitement that we, the representatives of the interstellar community, gather here to inaugurate our first building on Earth. This structure, conceived as a symbol of our burgeoning friendship, is a testament to the power of unity and collaboration."

Silence enveloped the crowd, the gravity of her words resonating in the air. "But let us not forget that this is just the beginning. As we embark on this new chapter of our shared history, let us do so with open hearts and minds. Let us embrace the challenges that lie ahead with courage and determination, knowing that together, there is no obstacle that we cannot overcome. So, let's raise our voices in celebration as we inaugurate this building and herald the dawn of a new era of friendship and cooperation between our two great civilisations. May it serve as a symbol of hope and inspiration for generations to come."

The crowd roared in agreement.

"Thank you and may peace and prosperity reign on Earth and throughout the cosmos." Finishing, Aayla stepped back and watched President Bailey cut a symbolic ribbon that adorned the front door of Aldredth Tower.

"You did great," Talyn commented, walking up to stand beside her. *I mean, I could have done better, but it's still not too bad.*

Aayla couldn't suppress her wide smile. *You're so cheeky. It's lucky I love you enough to keep you around.*

She playfully bumped him with her hip, and he chuckled in response. *So, it doesn't have anything to do with my attractive looks? I'm gutted.*

Laughing at his exaggerated mock sorrow, she felt the humans walking up behind her, but she found it hard to tear her gaze away from him as if he had cast a spell that made everything else fade into the background. As Martok and Skyla strolled over to join them, Aayla finally tore her gaze from Talyn.

Together, they led a small media team on a tour of the impressive new building.

As they entered the expansive foyer, the grandeur of the entrance elicited audible gasps from the group. Sunlight flooded through the towering glass walls, casting a warm golden glow on the polished white stone floors below. The air buzzed with the sound of footsteps echoing in the vast space, harmonising with the hum of conversation that floated through the atmosphere, creating a lively backdrop to their exploration.

At the centre of the foyer rose a magnificent atrium that soared nearly to the ceiling. Balconies encircled the atrium at each level, designed to accommodate winged species. Small glass panels lined the balconies for safety, ensuring the well-being of all visitors. At the back of the foyer, two sleek glass elevators gleamed, offering a modern touch alongside a grand decorative staircase that elegantly ascended to the first three levels. Access to the higher floors was provided by a smaller staircase tucked away at the rear of the building, seamlessly blending functionality with aesthetic appeal.

The foyer served as the grand entrance to the building, leading into the first three levels, which housed the Dining Hall, Command Centre, and Training Centre.

As they moved through each level, the extra-high ceilings and expansive open spaces finished with plush furniture impressed the human dignitaries. The humans couldn't help but notice the absence of interior poles or columns, lending an air of openness to the environment, while minimal interior walls ensured unobstructed sightlines throughout the building.

They toured the Aldredth sleeping quarters, MedBay, Bathing Pools, and several meeting spaces, each thoughtfully designed for comfort and functionality. Finally, they arrived at level 12, which showcased rooms specifically tailored for various species, such as restrooms for humans and sleeping pods for the Xaraphor, a species hailing from the Azulon galaxy.

The tour concluded on the rooftop, where the humans marvelled at the thoughtfully designed, serene garden sanctuary.

Everyone was captivated by the array of unique spaces, and lively discussions sparked excitement, making it clear that the conversations could have easily stretched for hours. However, time was not on their side, as they were already late for an exclusive lunch reserved for dignitaries in the Dining Hall.

The grand Dining Hall exuded a sense of sleek modernity and refined elegance, blending cutting-edge design with timeless sophistication.

Floor-to-ceiling glass windows adorned the walls, offering panoramic views of the lush surrounding landscape while bathing the hall in natural light. A unique particle mixed into the glass rendered it almost invisible from the inside. From the outside, the windows shimmered like solid, impervious silver walls. This innovative material enhanced privacy for the Aldredth and served as a protective measure against potential attacks. The reflective surface also captured the beauty of the outdoor balcony gardens, creating a seamless connection between the interior and exterior worlds.

Gleaming polished wood floors complemented the space, and in the centre of the hall, a long, sleek table stretched out, its surface glistening under the ambient light. The table was laden with a wide selection of human, Aldredth, and exotic delicacies.

Sleek, low-backed chairs, elegantly upholstered in a silk-like fabric woven from fine threads, surrounded the table. The air buzzed with the subtle hum of conversation crystal as guests indulged in the unique dining experience, all set against the breathtaking backdrop of the outside views.

As Aayla stepped into the room, all eyes turned to her, and one by one, the Aldredth and humans rose to bow. It was a mark of respect she received daily, but thankfully, tradition only required the bow once per day. Otherwise, she'd be trapped in an endless cycle of nodding and pleasantries. Still, it never failed to strike her how, in these moments, she felt so honoured.

She caught sight of a few Aldredth she hadn't greeted yet and gave them a warm wave. With purposeful steps, she moved around the room, stopping by each person to offer them a smile, gentle touch, and kind words.

The room seemed to glow in her presence. As a Unix, she carried an unspoken power that radiated through the space, a presence that commanded respect and devotion. The

Aldredth looked up at her with eyes full of reverence, like children silently seeking the approval of a beloved guardian. With just a glance or a touch, she could make them feel seen, valued, and connected, and in those brief interactions, she could sense how deeply they depended on her for reassurance and strength.

Aayla slipped gracefully into a vacant seat at the centre of the long, polished table. Across the room, Talyn stood by the doorway, his eyes finding hers even from a distance. His posture was relaxed, shoulders loose, yet there was an unmistakable vigilance about him. He stood at ease, exuding quiet confidence, his presence a calming yet formidable force in the room.

While his demeanour seemed casual, Aayla knew better. Beneath his calm exterior, Talyn was always on alert, subtly scanning the room, especially with so many unfamiliar faces gathered. His watchfulness wasn't overt, but she could sense the unspoken protection he offered. Always ready, always aware.

The coldness of the cutlery beneath her fingertips mirrored the knot tightening in her stomach as Aayla glanced at the empty seat beside her. Usually, she brushed aside the outdated formalities that insisted only mates could sit next to her. It was a relic of old traditions that had no place in their evolving society. In her mind, Guardians like Talyn deserved the respect and place of honour they'd earned right by her side.

Of course, Talyn adhered to the rules. His strict training made him uncomfortable with breaking protocol. But Aayla had always been willing to challenge those boundaries, especially for him. With so many dignitaries present today, though, she reluctantly swallowed her frustration. She forced a polite smile at the guests seated across from her, masking the simmering anger that burned just beneath the surface.

As the conversation flowed, Talyn moved around the table with a purposeful grace, expertly selecting dishes for Aayla while discreetly inspecting them first. As he leaned in close to place the food before her, she felt the warmth of his breath against her skin, sending a delightful shiver through her. His familiar scent wrapped around her, enveloping her.

If you keep feeding me like this, you might need to roll out of here.

Talyn's lip curved. *I'd gladly be your personal roller.*

Aayla's smile widened as she watched Talyn make his way back to his spot by the doorway. Her slender fingers toyed with the silverware, absentmindedly prodding her food, while her gaze discreetly strayed towards Talyn as she participated in the conversations around her.

He stood in the doorway with an air of quiet authority, his tall frame commanding attention. His clothes hugged his body, accentuating his muscular physique. Despite her efforts to engage in the conversations around her, Aayla found herself irresistibly drawn to him, captivated by the subtle allure of his presence.

No matter how hard she tried to concentrate on the decadent dishes before her, her attention kept drifting back to him. Each stolen glance only deepened the enchantment.

Aayla heard her name called. Turning to her right, she realised everyone was watching her, their expectant gazes waiting for a response.

Chapter Twenty-Five

"Sorry, I missed that. What was the question?" Aayla asked, a blush creeping across her cheeks as she looked towards Daxion.

"Have you seen what the human media is publishing about your recent activities? It seems they're quite enamoured with you," he said, a teasing glint in his eye.

"Both of you," Cythara interjected, a smirk playing on her lips.

Aayla stole another quick glance at Talyn. "I know Talyn has been keeping up with the developments, but I haven't had a chance to read what's been published myself. Maybe I'll take a walk later to catch up. It would be nice to explore the neighbourhood a bit more."

Mainly, it would be nice to know what the humans were saying about Talyn based on Daxion's comment.

The conversation flowed effortlessly for hours. As lunch drew to a close and the room began to empty, Aayla made her way over to Talyn, her steps lightening as he welcomed her with a warm, familiar smile.

Wrapping her arms around him, she buried her head against his chest, inhaling his comforting scent. She knew she shouldn't be so intimate, but the distance created by the lunch had left a hollow ache inside her that only his touch could mend. After a moment, she leaned back to meet his gaze. He quickly masked his look of surprise, adopting a casual, relaxed stance that radiated a comforting, masculine warmth.

"Let's visit the Command Centre quickly, and then maybe we can take a walk to see what the humans have been saying about us," Aayla suggested.

Talyn gently brushed a strand of hair from her face and chuckled softly. "That sounds perilous."

"But first, you need to eat something. Come, sit."

She took his hand and led him to the table, but he grabbed an apple instead, taking a quick bite.

"This is all I need," he said with a grin. "I'll eat while we walk to the Command Centre."

"No," Aayla responded sharply, her tone leaving no room for debate. "You deserve to enjoy all of the food. Now sit."

She sat down, tugging him with her. Talyn hesitated, clearly uncomfortable with breaking formality, but she acted as if she didn't notice. Silently, she served him a plate of food, then fixed him with a raised eyebrow, daring him to argue. Reluctantly, he picked up his fork and ate under her watchful gaze.

Once Talyn had finished eating, they made their way to the Command Centre, where they checked the status of Earth and all the planets under their protection. At least one Aldredth pair was always stationed in the room, continuously monitoring communications.

Aayla spent the next couple of hours refining strategies, navigating logistical challenges, and engaging in the intricate dance of diplomacy. Every decision was weighed with care, the weight of countless lives and the fate of entire planets resting on their actions. As a Unix, her opinion was especially valued, as strategic thinking came naturally to her. Unix were known for their unparalleled foresight and tactical genius.

Throughout the discussions, Aayla found herself stealing subtle glances at Talyn. Sometimes, she caught him watching her as well, though he quickly shifted his gaze to something else in the room whenever their eyes met.

Skyla entered the room, nestled under Martok's wing. "How's everything looking in here?" she asked with a warm smile.

"Going well so far," Aayla replied, briefly explaining recent developments. "How's the security around Aldredth Tower holding up?"

Martok studied the plans on the screens momentarily, his eyes flickering over the details. Then, with a grin, he turned back to Aayla. "The human police force is still assisting. They'll stay on until we get our own system in place, but it's been smooth so far."

"That's great news. Can you initiate a recruitment process for the humans in two days? Give them enough time to travel here if they're not close by. And, can you also arrange an audience with Seth?" She wanted to personally thank Seth for his support and gauge his interest in a potential position at Aldredth Tower.

Martok nodded, his expression serious. "Will do, my Unix."

After addressing all the pending questions and assigning tasks, Aayla bid farewell to the remaining Aldredth in the room.

Exhaling deeply, she rubbed a sore spot at the base of her neck, only to feel Talyn's hand overlap her own. His fingers kneaded gently into her tense muscles, and a wave of relaxation swept over her. She hadn't even heard him approach, but his touch brought an instant sense of relief. As warmth radiated from his touch, Aayla closed her eyes, sinking deeper into tranquillity with each soothing stroke.

Her lips parted slightly, and she leaned back against his firm body. His presence enveloped her completely as if the rest of the world had melted away, leaving just the two of them in that moment.

Aayla lost track of time, lost in the rhythm of his movements, as a symphony of sensations cascaded through her body. His voice was barely more than a breath against her neck. "You've been working too hard."

She wanted to think of a funny retort, but the words dissolved, carried away by the warmth of his touch.

His fingers stilled, and then his lips pressed softly against her neck, sending a shiver down her spine. *Let's go rest in the garden.*

His lips lingered for a moment before they were replaced by the cold embrace of the air, leaving her skin tingling and pulling her out of the blissful trance.

Clearing her throat, she turned to face him. "I can't," she murmured, "there's too much to do."

He started to protest, but before he could speak, she leaned in and pressed a gentle kiss to his jaw. "As soon as everything's settled, I promise to take a small Mir'ka."

Mir'ka was a period of rest during which Aldredth were not allowed to undertake any duties or be contacted to assist with any duties unless they were of the utmost importance. It could be a self-chosen or enforced break, and it lasted as long as required.

Talyn raised an eyebrow, unimpressed by her response. "A big Mir'ka," he insisted.

"A medium Mir'ka," she conceded with a coy smile.

Realising he wasn't going to win this battle, he decided to shift the conversation. "Where to now?"

"I believe there's a small news agency down the street. Shall we go for a walk?" she suggested.

He flashed her a quick smile before leading her onto the bustling street. As they strolled, a crowd began to swell around them. They paused occasionally for photos, but mostly, they waved and exchanged friendly hellos with those nearby, enjoying the warmth of the moment as they continued their walk.

Nestled on the street corner a few blocks from Aldredth Tower, a small shop was tucked amongst the tall buildings. Its weathered facade was covered in faded signage adorned with bold lettering. As they stepped inside, a bell tinkled cheerfully, announcing their arrival to shelves lined with stacks of newspapers, magazines, and a collection of essential pantry items.

The aroma of ink and paper fills the air, mingling with the faint scent of freshly brewed coffee from a nearby corner cafe. The space would be quite cozy for a human, but the narrow aisles looked uncomfortably tight for their enormous wings.

Behind the small wooden counter stood the shopkeeper, an older gentleman with grey hair and a friendly face weathered by years of welcoming customers with a warm smile. His fingers deftly handled the newspapers, folding them with practised precision before neatly stacking them for display.

The shopkeeper's face lit up with genuine warmth as they entered. With a friendly wave, he beckoned them further inside, his enthusiasm palpable in every gesture.

"Welcome, welcome! Is there anything specific you're looking for, or would you like to browse around?"

His enthusiasm was infectious, and Aayla couldn't help but smile widely. "Thank you for the warm welcome. We'd like to review some of your news articles if that's all right."

"By all means!" he replied, hurrying around the counter to gesture toward the aisles lining the front windows. "Please help yourselves, and don't hesitate to call out if there's anything I can assist you with."

Despite its small size, the shop was a treasure trove of information, catering to a diverse clientele with a wide range of interests. There was something for everyone, from local news and politics to sports, entertainment, and more.

Aayla thanked the shopkeeper and walked over to the shelves by the window. She perused the electric array of periodicals, magazines, and tabloids before her, each vying for attention with vibrant headlines and eye-catching images.

Her eyes widened at the images before her. "I can't believe it! There are photos of us on almost every single one."

Talyn didn't look surprised as he picked up a folded newspaper and scanned its contents. "They're beyond fascinated by you," he remarked matter-of-factly.

Glancing over the covers, Aayla noticed his face featured nearly as prominently as hers. "And you."

Pictures depicting Aayla and Talyn filled every cover. The stories detailed everything they had done on Earth and talked positively about their influence and hope for the future. However, the tone shifted dramatically as she moved from reputable media to tabloid magazines. The stories transitioned from their accomplishments to sensationalised tales that fixated on the idea of her secret love affair with Talyn, overshadowing their actual achievements.

Snickering, Aayla couldn't resist reading further. The tabloids documented the number of times they exchanged glances or touched each other, even going so far as to compare their interactions to those of other mated Aldredth couples, presenting it as proof of their hidden romance.

"Look here," Talyn exclaimed excitedly, holding up a magazine. "They caught us kissing, apparently!"

Aayla leaned in to see the images he was referring to. The photos showed them hugging and kissing each other's cheeks, but the angles were misleading, making their gestures appear more scandalous than they really were.

Frowning in disbelief, she turned to him. "That's a blatant lie. Why would they do that?"

Shrugging nonchalantly, he set the magazine down and picked up another. "Because lies sell more papers, and they're only interested in profit, not the truth."

"But why would lies sell more magazines?"

"Ah, now that's the real question. Is it because they discovered something no one else did? Is it because humans love an underdog story? Is it because they're hopeless romantics? Or is it something else entirely?"

Turning back to the magazines with a frustrated sigh, Aayla flipped through a few more until she landed on one that claimed Talyn was secretly in love with her. The article based its conclusions on stolen glances, joyful touches, and the longing they claimed was evident in his eyes.

With a wide smile, she turned the magazine toward him. "Apparently, you're in love with me."

A fleeting look of shock crossed his face before giving way to a bold smile. "That's no secret. I love you completely, and I think I'm pretty open about it."

Running her hand down his arm, she couldn't resist teasing him. "Apparently, you look at me all the time."

"I would hope so. I'm pretty sure that's one of the requirements of being a Guardian." He crossed his arms, smirking at her.

"And touch me whenever you can," she added playfully.

He shrugged casually. "I can't help how much I love you."

Snickering, Aayla flicked through a few more pages before suddenly tensing, slamming the magazine shut, and dropping it back onto the pile.

Talyn reached over and flipped the magazine open, landing on a page that made his eyes widen. "Talyn's Perfect Match," he read aloud.

"Utter rubbish," she snapped, recalling the article that ranked the most popular human females, ultimately declaring a charity worker turned supermodel as Talyn's ideal partner. "Humans and Aldredth can't mate."

Chuckling, he gently nudged her. "You're not jealous, are you? Of a human threatening to take me from you?"

She huffed in response, which only made him laugh harder as he closed the magazine and returned it to the stack.

With a smug smile, he leaned against the shelves, facing her. "Don't worry, I'm not leaving you."

"You're free to mate with whomever you choose," she replied curtly, turning to leave the shop.

"Except I'm not," he whispered so quietly that she almost missed it.

Abruptly, she turned back to face him, her gaze piercing. "What did you say?"

A sheepish look crossed his face, and he found himself unable to meet her eyes.

"Apologies, it was a... poorly worded comment."

Talyn walked quickly out of the shop, pausing to pay the shopkeeper for the various articles they had browsed, adding a little extra as a gesture of gratitude for his hospitality. As a Vajjer, he was free to mate with anyone, except a Unix. Aayla watched him closely, and for a fleeting moment, she wondered if his comment had been directed at her. She quickly pushed the thought away. In their youth, he had made it clear that he didn't consider her his mate, making the idea seem ridiculous.

Perhaps he was referring to the threats he had faced whenever someone suggested he had a relationship with her. She couldn't blame him for being angry about it.

Yet, the curiosity lingered, and his words echoed in her mind long after they left the shop.

Chapter Twenty-Six

The sun warmed her wings as they walked in silence, but the unease in the pit of her stomach lingered.

Aayla dared a glance at Talyn, noticing the solemn expression on his face. She hesitated, stopping in her tracks. Sensing her pause, Talyn turned back, his head tilting slightly in quiet curiosity.

She stared down at the cracked grey concrete beneath her feet, gathering the courage to meet his gaze again. "When you mentioned the humans taking you from me... You don't think you'll have to leave me after you're mated, do you?"

Talyn's brows knitted in confusion, and Aayla rushed to explain, only just realising how bad that had sounded out loud.

"I mean, you and your mate are more than welcome to stay here on Earth with me to keep assisting me if you'd like."

He stared at her for a long time, the wind gently rustling his hair. She couldn't quite read the emotion behind his gaze, but his solemn expression stirred something deep inside her. Eventually, he reached out to caress her cheek and smiled softly.

"I'd love that," he said quietly. "But I have to tell you... Even after you're mated, I'm not going anywhere. I'll still be close, whether you want me to be or not."

"Good," she murmured, placing her hand over his, holding it against her cheek as a smile spread across her face.

"Good," he echoed softly.

Aayla's Lumina beeped, drawing her attention. Glancing at it, she saw a message that Seth would visit Aldredth Tower later that evening, leaving them with a few hours to spare. It was the perfect opportunity to take to the skies and help the humans.

The joy they felt from helping was like a rush of adrenaline to her system. Over the next few hours, they stopped robberies, helped car crash victims, extinguished a fire, and identified several child abusers—all handed over to human authorities for justice. The last one had such vile thoughts swirling in his mind that it had taken every ounce of Aayla's restraint not to snap his neck on the spot.

As the sun dipped lower on the horizon, they touched down in front of Aldredth Tower. A cool breeze stirred the leaves of nearby trees, and Aayla gave a respectful nod to the human police officers stationed at the entrance, who bowed slightly as she landed.

As they entered, the lobby buzzed with energy as the Aldredth busied themselves with preparations for the upcoming interviews. Aayla had just started ascending the stairs when she heard Martok call her name. He stood on the upper balcony with Skyla, chatting with a small group of Aldredth. After offering a quick farewell nod to the group, Martok and Skyla flew down, landing silently beside her on the steps.

"Good news," Martok beamed. "I have two potential Lauzil mates arriving on Earth in the next couple of days."

Talyn stiffened beside her, and Aayla's jaw clenched. "Absolutely not," she replied sharply before immediately resuming her ascent without another glance.

Martok and Skyla exchanged confused looks before hurrying up the stairs to catch up with her. "I don't understand," Martok pressed. "Why don't you want to meet them?"

Twisting sharply, her eyes narrowing as her words came out clipped. "Because I'm far too busy to deal with such things right now."

Skyla's mouth dropped open, her shock evident. She exchanged a worried glance with Martok. "We're talking about finding your mate, Aayla. There's nothing more important than that. Is something wrong?"

Aayla closed her eyes, drawing a steadying breath. It wasn't their fault she dreaded the idea of finding a mate because, deep down, she wanted Talyn by her side forever. She reminded herself that it was a natural desire to find one's mate, something she should want. Or, at the very least, something she needed to pretend to want so as not to worry her people.

"I'm sorry," she sighed, opening her eyes and forcing a smile for Skyla and Martok. "You're right, of course. Everything's fine. I've just been extremely busy with everything lately. Could they come in a few months instead?"

If she could delay their arrival, it would buy her time. Time to cancel the visit later or conveniently be off-planet when they were scheduled to arrive—an old trick she had used more than once.

Martok hesitated, exchanging a quick glance with Skyla, the two clearly communicating telepathically. When he turned back to Aayla, his expression softened, almost apologetic. "I'm sorry, but I think we should arrange the meetings as soon as possible, given your... age."

Aayla stiffened, biting back a retort. She was nearing the point of becoming the oldest Aldredth to have never found a mate, a milestone she dreaded. Eventually, questions would arise. Why hadn't she found a mate? And worse, what was wrong with her?

"Right," she muttered, her voice strained. "Okay, arrange them if you must."

As she walked away, anxiety coiled tightly in her stomach. She felt powerless to change her fate, trapped between two impossible decisions. No matter what she did, it seemed her future was slipping out of her control.

She was so lost in thought that she stepped into the lift without realising it. Standing there with her hands on her hips, her head hung low in frustration, she did not realise where she was. Only after a moment did it dawn on her where she was.

Huffing in frustration, she ran a hand over her face. "What floor are we going to?"

Talyn stood beside her, arms crossed, watching her silently for a long moment before finally leaning over to touch the sensor. "Level 7."

Aayla could feel his gaze on her, sharp and unyielding. "Do you have something to say?" she muttered.

His eyes narrowed, sweeping over her slowly. "Why agree to it if you don't want to?"

"I didn't say I didn't want to," she grumbled, almost too softly to be heard.

Talyn raised an eyebrow, and Aayla exhaled sharply, rolling her eyes. "Fine. It's just... they always seem to pick the worst possible times." As if there's ever a good time.

She paused, biting her lip. "And is it wrong to want to keep you around for a little longer?"

Talyn smirked as the lift doors slid open, following her out. He stopped in the hallway, arms still folded, watching her intently.

"Why didn't you just say no?"

Aayla's stomach twisted. Saying no would only draw attention to her, raising suspicions about whether she was the only Aldredth with no desire to find a mate. That spotlight was something she couldn't afford.

"Aldredth don't say no to a chance to meet their mate," she said, her voice quieter now.

Talyn pressed his lips into a thin line. "You've said no before," he reminded her, the challenge in his eyes unmistakable.

Blushing, she thought over the many times she had pretended to be too busy to meet. In truth, she couldn't bear the idea of anyone replacing Talyn by her side.

"Those were different situations. We were providing confidential protection services, so parading potential mates around would have jeopardised the safety of those around us." Shrugging, she tried to portray a calm persona despite the raging turmoil inside.

Talyn's eyes narrowed, clearly unconvinced. After a long pause, he gestured down the corridor. "We're late."

Keeping her gaze low, Aayla hurried ahead, her steps quickening as she approached the meeting room midway down the hall. The room was sleek and modern, flooded with natural light from the floor-to-ceiling glass walls. Smart sensors adjusted the lighting and temperature as they entered, responding to their presence, while soundproof walls ensured privacy. The furniture was modular to allow for easy rearrangement. This room was for the meeting of friends, so it featured several plush lounges and chairs.

Standing in the middle of the room, staring wide-eyed at the surroundings, was Seth.

Genuine happiness flooded through her at the sight. "Seth! It's so good to see you again!"

He bowed deeply, but she couldn't help herself—she pulled him into a tight embrace instead. His cheeks flushed a bright crimson, almost as if they were on fire. "Thank you for inviting me here! This place is amazing, and I'm so glad to see you looking better."

"No, thank you. I haven't had a proper chance to thank you for your help, and I'm sorry about that."

"There's nothing to apologise for, really," Seth insisted, his voice warm and sincere.

"Seriously, thank you for everything."

As she stepped back, Talyn extended his hand to Seth, warmly clasping it in a human gesture of respect.

"And I am indebted to you as well," Talyn added, gesturing to the plush lounges behind them. "Please, have a seat."

Shaking his head as he settled down, Seth looked embarrassed by the praise. "I did what any decent person would have done."

Aayla nodded, her smile fading slightly as she sat on the lounge opposite him. "And there were definitely some less-than-decent people there. I didn't know what they were saying or thinking then, but now that I've learned your language... I was right to trust my instincts about a few of them."

Talyn went deadly still beside her, the tension in his body palpable. Aayla could feel his thoughts spiralling into darker territory as memories of her torture consumed him.

She turned to him, silently extending her hand in invitation. He hesitated for a moment, then warmly grasped her hand, allowing her to pull him onto the lounge beside her. After giving his hand a final reassuring squeeze, she turned back to face Seth.

"I also have an ulterior motive for inviting you here today," Aayla began, her tone shifting slightly. "You are probably aware that we will be undertaking interviews in one day's time for several positions in Aldredth Tower. We also need to recruit a human security force to assist us. I was hoping you'd consider the role of Team Leader and help me recruit other trained personnel."

"You want me? But I'm only a private," Seth said, clearly taken aback.

Talyn leaned forward, his wings nearly brushing hers. "You're stronger than you give yourself credit for," he said, shaking his head slightly. "You have immense potential, but more importantly, you have the qualities we need in someone standing by our side."

"And I already trust you with my life," Aayla added with a soft, reassuring smile.

"I'd love to work with you," Seth began, excitement clear in his voice. "Would this be a part-time position or—"

"Full-time," Talyn cut in. "We'll offer you a fair salary, but you'd need to resign from your current role. Is that something you'll need time to think over? You do not need to give us an answer today."

"Being in the army is something I've trained for most of my life, and I love it..."

Seth paused, nodding thoughtfully as he glanced around the room. "But the chance to work with you is something I can't pass up. So, no, I don't need time to think it over. My answer is... yes."

Chapter Twenty-Seven

Bouncing excitedly on the chair, Aayla clapped her hands. "Really? You'll do it?"

"Yes," Seth replied, his voice wavering slightly. "The idea terrifies me, but I'm more excited about the possibilities than I can even express right now."

"Excellent news," Talyn smiled. "From my initial assessment, we will need a team of about 25 men. If you have any recommendations, that would be incredibly helpful. Otherwise, we'd appreciate your assistance in the interview process to ensure we form a cohesive team."

"I've got a few names in mind, but I'd be more than happy to help with the interviews," Seth said, his smile widening.

His enthusiastic smile was infectious and made them all feel lighter, the stress and anxiety of the previous conversation long gone.

Over the next hour, they discussed the finer details of the appointment. The human security force would be responsible for securing the building and protecting the humans working within Aldredth Tower. They'd also handle missions outside the tower when deemed safe by the Aldredth, providing critical support. Additionally, the team would offer an extra layer of support and protection for Aldredth and visiting guests from other planets.

A uniform had already been meticulously designed by Talyn's parents, Sabor and Frela, who were renowned for their expertise in crafting Aldredth attire. The uniform would serve as a visual reminder that the security force was working with the Aldredth. Therefore, they were granted the same protection as an Aldredth, meaning that any threat to their lives could be punished by immediate execution.

The uniform consisted of a sleek, form-fitting black and gold shirt and tactical pants made from advanced, lightweight material unique to the Aldredth. It offered both flexibility and an extra layer of protection. This fabric, the same used for Aldredth clothing, was durable yet comfortable, enhancing both movement and safety. Subtle, intricate patterns embroidered in dark thread across the fabric depicted ancient Aldredth symbols and sigils.

Over the shirt, the security personnel would wear a tailored black utility vest made from the same resilient Aldredth material. The vest, designed for both functionality and durability, was equipped with an array of concealed pockets for tactical gear. On the chest, the Aldredth crest was elegantly embroidered in gold thread, a prominent symbol of their affiliation with the Aldredth and a clear indication of their protected status.

Sturdy black boots designed for stealth and agility completed the uniform. These boots allowed the wearer to move swiftly and silently during patrols. Like the rest of the uniform, arcane runes were subtly etched into the surface, only visible upon close inspection.

Next, they discussed the logistics of the team and the type of people and skills they thought would be best suited. It was agreed that the humans would undertake all of their training in Aldredth Tower's Training Centre. Talyn would lead the training to improve their skills and enhance their abilities beyond standard human training.

Employment hours were discussed, and each recruit was offered flexibility to choose their preferred schedule. Seth recommended starting with a four-day-per-week, rotating shift, which seemed ideal for balancing their workload.

The humans were welcome to live in the tower if they desired, or if they didn't have a home nearby. Otherwise, the purchase of accommodation nearby would be funded by the Aldredth if they preferred their own space.

Seth owned a house some distance from Aldredth Tower, sharing it with five other roommates. He spoke fondly of the freedom that came with having his own space, even amidst the bustling environment. Nodding, Talyn discreetly contacted Rune and Ceeda, requesting they bring up a few of the accommodation options they had already shortlisted.

They had just finished discussing Seth's recommendations for the security force's primary weapons—handguns, daggers, and tasers—with a full armoury available at Aldredth Tower when a soft knock interrupted.

"Come in," Aayla called.

Ceeda strolled into the room, closely followed by Rune, and casually perched on the couch's armrest. "I have the accommodation options you requested," she said, handing over her Lumina.

The device, a sleek sheet of near-indestructible glass, lit up with a few taps, revealing a wide array of housing options—from standalone homes to high-rise penthouses.

Aayla expanded the selection before passing the Lumina to Seth. "Look at these options and see if anything takes your fancy. Just pinch and flick to scroll through the options," she said with a smile.

As Seth scanned the options, his eyes widened in disbelief. "You can't be serious. These places look like they cost a fortune! This one must be at least three to four million dollars. You can't spend that much money."

Aayla frowned in confusion. "Why wouldn't we want you to live somewhere nice?"

He shook his head, placing the Lumina on his lap. "It's just too expensive."

Exchanging a glance with Talyn, she shrugged. "What's the point of having money if we don't share it? If you don't like any of these places, we can look for alternatives, but I won't be searching for cheaper options."

Seth paused, his finger tapping his leg, before he nodded thoughtfully. "Okay, I guess it's at least a good investment for you."

"Actually, no. We won't be the owners of the property. You will."

Looking concerned, Seth rubbed his neck. "So, I would own the house for as long as I work for you."

Talyn was frowning hard. "No, you own the house no matter how long you work for us. It's yours to keep permanently."

"Well... that's a terrible investment then." Seth smiled, clearly taken aback.

Aayla couldn't help but laugh. She understood the risk involved in offering a property with no strings attached, but the Aldredth didn't impose restrictions on their gifts, and the kind of people they hoped to hire wouldn't be motivated solely by the promise of a house.

Before the meeting finished, Seth's eyes lit up when he selected a beautiful penthouse in a prestigious nearby high-rise. With a nod, Rune and Ceeda departed to finalise the purchase.

Aayla then took out her Lumina. With a soft hum, it emitted a faint glow as she touched it against Seth's arm. A quick prick was all it took, drawing a single drop of blood that disappeared as the Lumina began its scan. The device processed the sample instantly, integrating Seth's DNA profile into their secure database.

This tiny drop of blood would do more than just open doors. Now, Seth's genetic signature would also allow him to bypass the Aldredth's security shields, granting him unrestricted access to the facilities he needed for his work. Additionally, his DNA imprint enabled other privileges such as encrypted communication lines, medical assistance, and, when required, remote access to the Aldredth's resources.

Afterwards, they walked him outside and said their goodbyes, agreeing to meet again in two days. Seth needed time to wrap up a few details with the army before returning to assist with the interviews.

Aayla watched him walk off, her gaze drifting to the sky, which had transformed into a vast canvas of pastel hues, soft pinks and purples stretching across the horizon like strokes of watercolour. She took in a deep breath, feeling a sense of calm in the quiet beauty.

"It can be quite beautiful here," she murmured.

Warm hands slipped around her waist, and she felt his familiar breath whisper against her ear, sending a delightful thrill through her. "Not as beautiful as you."

She laughed, nudging him playfully. "You're such a tease—"

Their Lumina erupted with a sharp alert. Kythera's voice crackled through the static, urgent and strained, reporting a Kramxion attack in progress. A nearby town was under siege, and she and Jaxion were trapped, desperately needing backup.

Aayla and Talyn didn't pause before taking flight.

The Kramxion were much larger than the Aldredth, their bodies covered in rough, bumpy, pale grey-white skin that exuded an intimidating presence. They wore black strips of leathery material wrapped tightly around their muscular forms, with additional strips securing their elbows and knees.

A terrifying aspect of their physiology was their ability to generate bolts of electricity from within, powerful enough to scorch Aldredth and deliver a crippling shock. For humans, that same surge would stop a heart instantly.

Each Kramxion also carried small blades strapped to their chests, reserved for close combat or finishing blows.

Talyn and Aayla flew as fast as they could, the urgency of the situation propelling them through the air. They arrived minutes later, descending onto a residential street to find devastation. Several houses stood significantly damaged, windows shattered, and debris strewn across the front yards. The air was thick with the acrid scent of smoke and fear.

Human police officers, desperately outmatched, fired their weapons at a small army of Kramxion advancing down the street. The sound of gunfire echoed, punctuating the chaotic atmosphere, but the bullets merely bounced off the Kramxion's tough skin, leaving no mark as if they were made of stone.

The officers' faces reflected disbelief and desperation as they realised their weapons were ineffective against the towering figures.

In a terrifying display of strength, the Kramxion moved with ruthless efficiency. They easily flipped police cars over, tossing them aside like toys, the metal groaning as it crumpled under their power. The overturned vehicles collided with nearby houses, sending splintered wood and shattered glass flying everywhere.

Police officers scattered in panic as the Kramxion tore through their barricades, sending them flying like leaves in a storm. Jaxion and Kythera leapt in front of the humans, expertly deflecting the relentless barrage of energy bolts.

Aayla and Talyn landed hard in front of them, swords drawn, and threw up a protective shield that flickered to life.

"Stop now and leave Earth immediately!" Aayla commanded, her voice steady and authoritative, cutting through the chaos. The weight of her presence and the power radiating from her shield created a momentary pause in the violence, drawing the attention of the advancing Kramxion.

One of the Kramxion uttered a guttural yell, and all of their attacks ceased. The creature shuffled to the side, its eyes narrowing as it focused on Aayla. "The Unix! I heard a rumour you were on this planet," it taunted, a twisted grin spreading across its face.

"This is your last chance," she warned. "Leave now."

"I think not," the Kramxion spat, its voice dripping with contempt. "You've hidden this planet for far too long. I rather like it here. These defenceless bags of flesh will make excellent target practice for my men. I might even keep a few as pets."

Talyn's growl rumbled low in his throat, a warning barely contained as the Kramxion tried to provoke her.

"This planet is under our protection, so that won't be happening. Leave now."

Out of the corner of her eye, Aayla spotted four more Aldredth drop in behind her, their presence shifting the balance of strength slightly. Although the Kramxion vastly outnumbered them, the Aldredth's speed and agility gave them a crucial advantage.

Aayla gripped her sword tightly, feeling the weight of the blade in her hand as she surveyed the Kramxion before her. She knew they were facing a formidable challenge, regardless of the numbers.

The Kramxion smiled menacingly before stepping back to hide behind the others in front of it. "Bring her to me alive. Kill the others," it commanded, a sinister glint in its eyes.

Aayla exchanged a silent nod with Talyn, their unspoken bond a testament to the trust forged through countless battles.

In an instant, they launched toward the Kramxion, using their speed to strike while deftly evading the incoming blows.

With a graceful flourish, Aayla leapt amidst the action, her sword slicing through the air with deadly precision. She moved with speed and agility as she sliced through their thick skin, severed limbs, and deflected searing energy blasts that would have torn her wings apart.

Beside her, Talyn fought with raw, unyielding strength. His sword swung in wide, brutal arcs that cleaved through the Kramxion's thick hides like a scythe through wheat. When a Kramxion lunged for him, he met it head-on, steel crashing against bone with a thunderous crack. He pivoted with ease, cutting down two foes in a single, powerful sweep. His wings unfurled briefly, granting bursts of speed and leverage that allowed him to strike from unexpected angles, then folded tightly to keep his movements streamlined.

The battle stretched on, each moment a test of endurance as they steadily dwindled the Kramxion's numbers. Aayla's breath grew ragged, and adrenaline surged through her veins as bolts of energy zipped past her, kicking up dirt and debris that momentarily obscured her view.

Despite the chaos surrounding her, Aayla remained focused, carefully strategising her next move. She relied on her training, the instincts honed through experience, and the unyielding trust she had in the Aldredth fighting alongside her. The tide of battle was shifting.

Then, without warning, a sudden crack shattered the rhythm of battle. Jaxion, who had been shielding Kythera moments before, was struck squarely in the chest by a blast of energy. The force slammed into him with brutal impact, sending him hurtling backward like a ragdoll. Time seemed to freeze as he crashed against an overturned car, his body sliding to a halt amidst a cloud of dust and scattered debris.

"Talyn!" Aayla shouted, urgently drawing his attention to Jaxion's crumpled form.

In an instant, they flew over to Jaxion, and Talyn threw up a protective shield, creating a barrier against the surrounding chaos. Aayla knelt beside Jaxion, gently cupping his face to turn it toward her, desperate to connect.

Jaxion was groaning in pain as his skin was being eaten away from the point of the blast. Kythera knelt by his head, her expression a mix of horror and desperation.

"Keep looking at me," Aayla commanded, locking eyes with him as she slowly began to heal his injuries. She felt the familiar warmth of energy flow through her hands, the magic intertwining. As she focused, Jaxion's skin gradually continued to knit back together, the agony in his eyes softening as he felt her presence.

Once the last of the damage had healed, Aayla released him, breathing deeply as her heart raced.

"Thank you, my Unix," Jaxion murmured, placing a hand over his heart in gratitude. Without hesitation, he propelled himself into the air, Kythera by his side. They rejoined the battle with renewed determination.

Talyn cupped her face gently in his hand, concern etched across his features. *Are you okay?* His worry was palpable despite his attempts to mask it.

Healing was a painful process for a Unix, but they always concealed their discomfort to avoid concerning their people.

"Yes, I'm fine. Let's get back in there." Aayla assured him, her voice steady.

They launched back into the heart of the battle, and despite the hail of blasts raining down upon them, Aayla and Talyn pressed on, their determination unyielding. They moved as one, their movements synchronised as they danced amidst the chaos of battle.

As the battle raged on, they covered each other's backs with precision, anticipating each other's moves with flawless accuracy. Aayla was a formidable force on her own, but together, they were a force to be reckoned with, their skills complementing each other perfectly.

Only two Kramxion remained, one of whom was the leader who had stayed at the back to avoid the heat of the battle. As they pressed forward, victory tantalisingly close, a sudden ambush erupted around them, catching them completely off guard. Bullets whizzed through the air, and Aayla found herself directly in the line of fire.

Without hesitation, Talyn leapt in front of her, his movements swift and selfless. Time seemed to slow as bullets struck him in the shoulder and chest, each impact echoing in her mind like a thunderclap.

"No!" Aayla cried out, her heart racing.

Talyn staggered back, wounded but still standing, his determination unbroken. With a fierce resolve, he deflected an energy blast aimed at them, the sheer force of his will shining through the pain.

With adrenaline surging through her veins, Aayla turned to see that the bullets had come from a small group of humans hiding behind overturned cars. In a burst of energy, she pushed one of the vehicles over, crushing them beneath its weight.

Spinning back to Talyn, her heart dropped as she saw him collapse beside her. Jaxion and Kythera landed in front of them, shielding them from attacks whilst the other Aldredth finished off the remaining Kramxion.

As the chaos of battle began to fade, all Aayla could hear were her ragged breaths, heavy with dread. Blood poured from Talyn's chest, soaking the ground beneath him. Her heart raced as she watched the light in his eyes flicker, the familiar spark dimming with each laboured breath. Panic surged within her, an icy grip that threatened to consume her.

"Talyn!" she cried, the name tearing from her lips like a desperate prayer. "Stay with me!"

He lay there, chest rising and falling unevenly, and for a moment, it felt as if the world had slowed to a standstill. She pressed her hands against his chest, the warmth of his blood soaking into her skin, and time stretched painfully as the reality of his wounds settled over her like a suffocating blanket. Every second felt like an eternity as she struggled to will him to respond, to fight against the shadows creeping into his gaze.

"Look at me," she urged, forcing her voice to remain steady despite the rising tide of fear threatening to drown her. "It's going to be all right. Just look at me!"

Talyn's eyes fluttered open, but they lacked focus, drifting to something beyond her reach, something she couldn't see. A wave of desperation washed over her as she realised he was slipping away. "No, no, no! Talyn, don't you dare leave me!" The words tumbled out, frantic and raw.

But as she called to him, she felt the life force within him fading like a candle flickering against the wind. Blood bubbled from his lips, and he struggled to speak, his voice barely a whisper, "Aayla..."

Chapter Twenty-Eight

"Shut up and look at me!" she ordered fiercely, her heart racing with the knowledge that every moment counted. He was fading, and she could feel it. "Shit!"

Closing her eyes, she reached out with her mind, feeling his unique energy signature and following it around his body. The bullets had struck a major blood vessel leading to his heart. He had bled out so much that his body now barely had enough blood to keep his heart beating. "No, not like this," she pleaded, a primal fear rising in her chest. "Please don't leave me."

Normally, to heal someone, she hijacked their energy to will their body to slowly knit itself back together one cell at a time. Direct eye contact facilitated her ability to control their energy. However, when her patient couldn't meet her gaze, she had to infuse her own energy into them, aligning it within their body. This method was agonisingly slow, painful, and draining.

Excruciating pain radiated around her body like sharp electric shocks as the wounds slowly healed. She forced herself to dig deeper into her energy as she felt Talyn's energy fading.

"Stay with me, Talyn," she begged. Tears blurred her vision as she poured her energy into him, feeling his life force slip further away with every heartbeat. "You have to fight! Fight for me!"

Soval swiftly scanned Talyn with his Lumina, and a detailed hologram of Talyn's body flickered to life before them. They zoomed in on the injuries, their expressions tightening as vital readings flashed overhead. He'd stopped breathing, and his heart struggled with weak, erratic beats that grew slower with each second.

Aayla's entire body felt ablaze, but she pressed on, knitting his tissue together layer by layer, starting from the deepest wounds and working outward.

Around them, the chaos of the battle faded into a muffled background, the world narrowing to just her and Talyn.

Everyone kept a wary distance from Aayla and Talyn, aware that even the lightest touch could derail the delicate process. Sometimes, the touch of another could wash their energy over the injured person, and a Unix-like Aayla would struggle to differentiate between the clashing energies. Any interference risked slowing the healing, and with it, the life hanging by a thread.

As the final layers of skin fused, Aayla leaned back, gasping for breath, her body trembling from the effort. The moment her hands left Talyn, Aeryn took a blood sample, her Lumina flashing a red alert for critically low energy and blood levels.

Talyn's eyes remained closed, and a chilling silence enveloped them. A sickening dread pooled in her stomach, and she felt the weight of despair settle over her like a heavy fog.

Aeryn glanced at her mate, Soval, who rolled up his sleeve without hesitation. He inserted one end of a tube with needle-like tips into his arm, connecting the other end to Talyn's. Blood flowed swiftly into Talyn while Aeryn injected Pixx into his other arm to boost his energy.

Cupping Talyn's face, she felt the faintest flicker of energy—a whisper of life. He was still there. She closed her eyes and reached for his energy again, desperate to pull him back from the brink, pushing every ounce of her will into him.

"Come on, Talyn," she whispered, her voice barely audible. "Please..."

Her heart pounded as she willed him to open his eyes, desperate for any sign of life. He lay motionless, his breaths shallow, his skin unnervingly pale. The moments stretched painfully, and fear clawed at her chest.

Then, at last, his eyelids fluttered. Relief surged through her, nearly overwhelming her, but she held herself steady. His gaze was unfocused, his eyes searching, caught between worlds. Aayla saw the confusion flickering across his face, the shadows of pain.

His hand instinctively reached out to grasp Aayla's, and she pressed it firmly against her chest, letting him feel the strong, grounding rhythm of her heartbeat.

I'm here, she whispered. *We're safe.*

She felt his fingers curl weakly around hers, his grip faint but real. A tiny flicker of awareness lit his eyes, and she could see him fighting through the haze, anchoring himself to her touch. Her chest ached with a mixture of relief and lingering fear as she watched him, unwilling to let go.

In that quiet, fragile moment, with his hand resting against her heart, she knew they'd come terrifyingly close to losing each other.

Gradually, the haze seemed to lift, and Talyn's focus sharpened. He took a deep breath and slowly sat up, noticing the tube connecting him to Soval for the first time.

After a few more moments, the tube was removed. The Pixx had taken effect, and though still unsteady, Talyn rose to his feet shakily and ran his hands over Aayla.

"Are you hurt?" he asked, his voice low and full of concern.

"No, I'm fine." Shaking her head, a shadow of worry crossed her face. "But the humans tried to kill us. I don't understand why."

Talyn gently stretched his shoulder, his expression darkening. "There are still many who don't trust us, and they took advantage of our distraction. That was too close."

"I know." She exhaled shakily. "You almost died."

"No," he corrected sternly, "you almost died."

His gaze locked onto hers with such intensity that it became overwhelming, and she had to look away, feeling something indescribable stir deep within her.

Martok and Skyla landed abruptly beside Aayla.

"I'm sorry we were delayed," Martok said, his gaze sweeping across the scene. His eyes froze on the dark pool of blood surrounding Talyn, and a spark of worry flashed over his face. But as he took in Talyn's steady breaths and the hint of colour returning to his skin, Martok's shoulders eased, tension melting away.

"Seems like you have everything under control," he nodded, a note of respect in his voice.

"They attacked while we were distracted by the Kramxion."

"Opportunistic," Skyla murmured thoughtfully.

Martok's eyes narrowed with a cold edge. "What about human casualties?"

Aeryn let out a heavy sigh, a hint of sadness in her eyes. "Numerous injuries, several serious... but thankfully, no friendly fatalities."

Aayla glanced around at the others. "Are any Aldredth injured?"

Martok shook his head. "Nothing that needs your attention. I'll take it from here. You should head back and get some rest."

Aayla hesitated at the thought of leaving before she was sure the scene was secure. Talyn had suffered a significant injury, and she wanted him checked in the MedBay. She also felt a responsibility to assess the other injured Aldredth.

Aldredth knew that healing was painful, but they didn't grasp the full extent of that pain, and as a result, they only sought her help for serious injuries. However, she believed every wound, no matter how small, deserved her care.

"Okay, let me know if anything changes."

Martok nodded in acknowledgment, and Aayla and Talyn slowly lifted off into the sky, rising leisurely as if savouring the moment. They glided back to Aldredth Tower, riding the gentle currents of the wind to conserve their energy, careful not to reveal how exhausted they were.

As they entered the MedBay, Aayla let out a sigh of relief at the sight of only two Aldredth seated on beds, being attended to by Graca.

Graca, an Emba healer, moved toward the far bed with her usual graceful, calm demeanour. At 351 years old, her pale lavender eyes had seen centuries of battles and wounds. Her hot pink wings, flecked with vibrant yellow bursts, were striking against her mate Loxian's bright red wings. Loxian was a 352-year-old Aurra with dark grey eyes.

Aayla's smile faded as her gaze drifted past Graca to the far bed, where Rune lay. The upper edge of his right wing was damaged. An injury outside her healing abilities. Her heart sank as she noted his pain, though he tried to keep his expression steady, likely for Ceeda's sake.

Graca injected him with a blend of pain relief and a sedative, letting him slip into a deep sleep so he'd be spared the worst of the pain. The silver lining was that he would still be able to fly once the pain had passed, though he'd need extensive retraining to regain full strength.

Graca noticed the shift in Aayla's expression. "He'll be all right, Aayla," she said softly. "It's a painful injury, but he's strong."

Aayla nodded at Graca's words, though worry lingered in her eyes. When Graca finally finished tending to Rune, she turned her attention back to Aayla and Talyn, her eyes sharp but kind. "So, who's my patient?"

"Talyn—" Aayla started.

"Aayla—" Talyn said at the same time.

Graca laughed, a warm sound that lightened the tense air. "Both of you, up on the bed."

After a thorough check, Graca administered additional Pixx to boost their energy and gave a firm order for them to rest for the remainder of the day.

Following Graca's advice, Aayla led Talyn up to the rooftop garden. She thought about retreating to the bed in their private quarters, but she craved the sun's warmth after such a draining event.

They found a sunny patch of grass, and she sank down beside him, feeling the gentle warmth of the sun on her skin and feathers.

Talyn lay stretched out on his back beside her as he relaxed into the grass. Aayla rolled onto her side, pressing herself close and resting her head against Talyn's chest, letting the steady rhythm of his heartbeat lull her. Talyn wrapped an arm around her, his embrace warm and grounding.

The warmth of his body and the gentle rise and fall of his breath filled her with a rare sense of peace. She let herself sink into the moment, each beat of his heart grounding her until her own breathing slowed, lulling her toward sleep.

The next day, Aldredth Tower buzzed with activity as interviews for various positions began. Humans had been told to come as they were, without needing to bring resumes or wear formal attire. Still, many arrived clutching neatly prepared resumes or dressed in their best, eager to make a strong impression.

The relaxed approach had been intentional. Requiring resumes might exclude those who hadn't prepared or lacked access to a printer, and a casual dress code helped ensure no one felt disadvantaged by an inability to afford formal attire. Here, their skills and character mattered most, not the polish of a resume or the price of a suit.

Humans lined up in long queues that stretched down the block, eager for a chance to work at Aldredth Tower. The interview process began with groups of people entering the large meeting rooms, where each seat was set with a sheet of paper and a pen. On the paper were a series of simple yes/no questions like, "Are you kind to others?" and "Do you help others when you can?"

The Aldredth didn't focus on specific answers but instead used these questions as a way to glimpse each person's basic personality. As the humans filled out their sheets, several Aurra quietly listened to their thoughts, tuning into each person's thinking and sensing their truest qualities. It was more about the spirit behind their responses than the words themselves.

After a couple of minutes, those selected to continue were asked to step into the next room, while others were thanked and informed that there were no suitable positions at the present time.

In the next room, selected candidates sat for one-on-one meetings with an Aurra, who asked only two questions—"Tell me about yourself," and "What type of job interests you at Aldredth Tower?" This step was meant to deepen the understanding of each individual, ensuring their intentions were genuine and their values aligned with Aldredth's mission.

Those who passed these conversations moved to a final stage—meeting with Aayla and Talyn.

Aayla couldn't help but smile at the look of surprise on each human's face when they entered the third room and found her waiting at a welcoming table filled with food. She greeted each candidate warmly, discussing the specific role she thought suited them best and finalising their accommodation arrangements.

Throughout the day, she assembled a diverse team, hiring people for roles ranging from administrative and executive assistants to chefs, media advisors, political advisors, and security force members. For security positions, Seth joined her, lending his expertise to assess each candidate's minimum skills and experience. His presence added weight to the interviews, ensuring only the most qualified and trustworthy candidates were selected for Aldredth Tower's protection.

The personal approach left each new hire feeling valued, and Aayla found herself both energised and encouraged by the day's progress.

Most new hires would start working the following day, while some needed a few more weeks to give notice to their current employers. With careful planning, they had filled enough positions to keep Aldredth Tower fully staffed every day of the week, from early morning to late at night. However, no one worked more than four days or 25 hours a week. The Aldredth valued quality of life outside of work, so they offered exceptionally generous salaries—sometimes six times what the humans previously earned—to ensure financial stability without requiring long hours.

For those interested, the Aldredth had designed a range of optional uniforms to clearly signify affiliation with the Tower while adding a layer of protection for employees.

The uniforms featured a sleek, modern design that seamlessly blended functionality with style. A striking combination of bright white and gold contrasted with deep black created a timeless, professional appearance. Ultra-fine gold-like threads were woven throughout the fabric, subtly catching and reflecting light to create an understated, elegant shimmer. Made with advanced Aldredth reflective materials, the uniforms glowed faintly, even in dim light, enhancing both visibility and sophistication.

The uniform options included a tailored jacket with a high collar and discreet gold accents along the seams and cuffs, adding a touch of sophistication. The slim-fit pants complemented the jacket while maintaining comfort and ease of movement. Gold-threaded piping ran down the outer sides of the pants, enhancing the overall sleek look. A selection of skirts, dresses, blouses, and coats had also been created. To complete the collection, a lightweight, breathable business shirt made from moisture-wicking fabric would ensure comfort during extended wear. This blouse and the shirt featured gold-threaded buttons that added a refined touch without overpowering the design.

Every person who accepted a position requested at least one piece from the collection, with almost all requesting an entire wardrobe. Wearing the uniform became a source of pride for them, and the Aldredth, in turn, took pride in seeing their new team embodying the Tower's vision and values.

Each human had also signed a non-disclosure agreement, binding them to keep their salary, private details, and any information obtained during their employment strictly confidential.

By the day's end, millions had passed through Aldredth Tower. As the sun dipped, casting an orange glow, Aayla looked down the street where the once-long queues had dispersed. Only the media, curious "Aldredth watchers," and a few rejected applicants who refused to leave remained.

"You have quite the celebrity status," Talyn joked, nudging her with his hip.

She laughed, slightly baffled. "I thought all Aldredth held the same significance, but somehow, the two of us seem to have a special standing. I wonder why that is?"

Talyn tilted his head thoughtfully. "Maybe it's because we're closer to their age. Or maybe it's because we're the only unmated ones, making us... intriguing."

Shrugging, Talyn ran his hand through his hair before flashing a smile at Aayla. "It's getting late, so how about we get you naked?"

She raised an eyebrow, and he laughed, shaking his head. "I don't know about you, but I'm dying for a bath. Shall we?"

Laughing, she looped her arm through his. "I would love that."

They spent the rest of the evening immersed in the expansive Bathing Pools, a serene retreat that stretched the length of the entire floor. The open space lacked internal walls, lending it an airy, boundless feel. To the left of the lift, a rainfall shower area provided a place to rinse off any grime from the day. Nearby, an open shelving unit offered space for clothes and weapons.

The pool was divided into sections, each designed for unique purposes. The front section was shallow, with a scattering of smooth, irregularly shaped stones forming seating and lounging areas in the water. In the middle section, the water was only ankle-deep, with large, smooth stone beds beneath overhead rainfall showers, perfect for the intimate act of washing a mate's body and wings. That type of washing was a deeply sensual act that anchored bonds.

To the right, a smaller pool filled with a cleansing solution provided a quick option for unmated or time-pressed Aldredth. By simply immersing themselves, the solution would efficiently lift away any impurities. Meanwhile, the back section offered a deeper area, perfect for diving and swimming unimpeded.

Even though Aldredth were terrible swimmers due to their heavy wings, there was something about floating in the water that they found incredibly cathartic. They swam and bathed mostly for enjoyment because Aldredth didn't perspire or produce body odours like humans that needed to be cleaned off frequently.

The water shimmered, its surface aglow with soft lighting built into the pool's lining, which shifted in mesmerising patterns. The pool's smooth white surface accentuated the light blue hue of the crystal-clear water.

The ceiling above the pool had been treated to mirror the bright starry night sky as seen on Nannuval. As the Aldredth floated in the pool, they could gaze up at a real-time sky, watching clouds drift, connecting them back to their home world.

The glass walls surrounding the room were darkly shaded to add to the atmosphere. Every detail in the room worked together to evoke a sense of tranquillity and escape. It was a space where time seemed to stand still, a sanctuary of modernity and elegance where they could immerse themselves in a world of pure relaxation and indulgence.

Aayla and Talyn spent most of the time in the front section of the pool, relaxing and taking naps before they finally retired to their private quarters for the night.

She'd barely drifted off to sleep when a medical emergency call jarred her awake. A male Aldredth, critically injured in a fierce battle on a distant planet, had been swiftly transported through space portals, with Aayla being the nearest Unix to provide the urgent care he needed.

Aayla hurried to meet the ship as it landed beside Aldredth Tower and dashed into the ship's MedBay to tend to his injuries, healing him and several other minor wounds among the crew. It was anticipated she'd be called to help with off-world medical emergencies about once a week while stationed on Earth.

Moments after she disembarked, the ship took off again, leaving her with the small aftershocks of a draining session.

"I really should start charging for these late-night house calls," she joked softly, already feeling the weight of exhaustion settling in.

"Or at least start a loyalty program," Talyn said, flashing a crooked smile.

Aayla chuckled weakly, leaning against him as a wave of fatigue swept over her. "I can picture it now, sign up today and get a free cupcake with every third medical emergency."

Talyn's laughter filled the air, light and infectious, but the healing had been so draining that when she swayed again slightly on her feet, he quickly scooped her up and carried her back to their bed. She rested her head against his solid chest, inhaling his familiar, calming scent as sleep claimed her once more.

CHAPTER TWENTY-NINE

Aayla awoke to the soft light of dawn filtering through the curtains, casting a gentle glow across the room. Aldredth did not have curtains over their windows on Nannuval, but she had liked the way they delicately fluttered in the breeze, so she had asked for sheer lace curtains to be added to the balcony doors of her private quarters.

She felt the warmth of the morning sun on her skin, a comforting presence that beckoned her into wakefulness. Talyn lay beside her in a deep sleep, his form outlined in the soft hues of early morning. Aayla gazed at him, a smile playing on her lips as she took in the sight of his peaceful slumber.

The room was filled with a serene calmness, broken only by the steady rhythm of their breathing. Aayla could have remained in that tranquil moment forever.

With a tender slowness, Aayla reached out to caress Talyn's cheek, her fingers igniting with a warm tingle at the contact. Stirring at her gentle touch, he grasped her hand and brought it to his lips, placing a soft kiss on her fingertips.

"Good morning, beautiful," he murmured, his voice husky with sleep.

Aayla felt a blush creep across her cheeks, warmth spreading through her. "That's why I love waking up next to you. You always flatter me with the sweetest compliments."

Talyn flashed her a wide smile and pressed a kiss to her palm. "It's not flattery if it's true. It's just a fact."

Aayla snuggled closer to Talyn, closing her eyes as she inhaled his intoxicating scent. "I could stay here in your arms all day."

"You're describing my idea of heaven," he chuckled, pressing a kiss to the top of her head. "But I need to get some food into you, so unfortunately, we have to get up."

"Right now?" she asked, a hint of reluctance in her voice.

With a mischievous smile, he hugged her tighter. "Well… maybe in a few minutes."

Eventually, they rose and strolled down the corridor toward the Dining Hall. When the lift doors opened, Martok stepped out alongside Skyla. His face lit up at the sight of Aayla, and he bowed graciously.

"Aayla! Good morning. How are you on this fine day?" he greeted enthusiastically.

Aayla paused before him and Skyla. "Wonderful, thank you. We were just on our way to the Dining Hall. Would you like to join us?"

"Sorry," he replied, patting his stomach, "we've already eaten and are heading to meet some of the new staff. It's fantastic to see so many new faces joining us."

"Absolutely. We'll drop by later to greet everyone. Well, we'd better be off," Aayla said, nodding goodbye as she turned to walk away.

"Aayla, wait! I have good news," Martok called after her, his tone brightening. "A potential mate will be arriving within the hour."

Aayla stiffened at the mention, her heart racing, while Talyn stood frozen beside her.

"Thank you for letting me know. We'll be in the Dining Hall when he arrives," she replied, forcing a grim smile as she tried to ignore the confusion in Martok's eyes. Clearly, he expected her to be excited, but all she felt was a tightening anxiety in her stomach.

They made their way to the Dining Hall and took their seats at one of the two long tables that stretched the length of the room. Groups of Aldredth were clustered together in lively conversation. As a social species, they craved each other's company, and eating was more about social connections than nourishment.

Leaning into Talyn's side, Aayla tried to immerse herself in the boisterous chatter of her people, but her gaze kept drifting toward the doorway. Each passing second felt like an eternity. She fidgeted nervously, tapping her fingers rhythmically on the tabletop in a subconscious attempt to distract herself from the impending encounter.

When her Lumina finally buzzed, she jumped in surprise. Glancing at the message, her breath caught. Bazura had arrived at Aldredth Tower and was on his way up.

When two unmated Aldredth met for the first time, tradition dictated that it take place in a secure location at an agreed-upon time. This precaution arose from the intense, consuming nature of a mate bond, which left both individuals monetarily vulnerable to attack due to their distraction. Additionally, the bonding process could cause male Aldredth to become dangerously volatile to any nearby males they considered a threat, necessitating close supervision.

Footsteps echoed down the corridor, growing louder with each step. Aayla rose slowly and moved to stand in front of the doorway, her hands folded, her heart pounding faster with each approach.

Beside her, Talyn stood rigidly, his expression tense.

The air felt thick with tension, and a knot of anxiety tightened in her stomach. When Bazura entered, she noticed Talyn watching her closely.

Bazura and his Charge, Elizia, bowed deeply. "Greetings, my Unix. Thank you for inviting us here."

Bazura was twenty years old, had dark blue eyes, and pale silvery-grey wings. But most importantly, Aayla felt no pull toward him.

Exhaling heavily, she offered him a small smile. "Greetings, Bazura. It's good to meet you. And you, too, Elizia. Thank you for coming."

Aayla stepped closer, resting a light touch on their cheeks. She felt the tension ease from their shoulders as her presence calmed them, their breathing steadying under her hand. Curious, she cast a quick glance back at Talyn, catching a relaxed softness in his expression. Almost like a look of quiet relief.

Bazura beamed with excitement. "Would you like to join us for some food?"

"Sorry, we just finished eating." Seeing his face fall, she inwardly scolded herself. They had travelled far to see her, and Aldredth treasured meeting a Unix, so he'd likely been excited for this moment.

She softened her expression. "How about lunch together instead?"

His face lit up again. "I would love to. Thank you."

With a parting nod, Aayla turned and began down the corridor, aware of Bazura's silent gaze following her every step.

Talyn paused in front of the lift. "Where to?"

"I'm in the mood for some training. I might go to the Training Centre. What about you?"

Pressing the touchpad on the lift, Talyn gave her a crooked smile, "I'll go to the Training Centre as well. If you're in the mood to lose, we can spar?"

With a wide grin, she nudged him as she walked past. "Pretty sure you meant win."

They spent the rest of the morning training. All Aldredth undertook regular, usually daily, rigorous training to maintain and sharpen their skills. They enjoyed the physical exercise and found it cathartic. As a Unix, Aayla's training demanded even greater intensity, but she relished the challenge.

Together, Aayla and Talyn were a formidable duo, pushing each other to new heights. With weapons in hand, they moved in perfect synchrony, their movements fluid and precise. Each step was calculated, and each strike was aimed with unwavering accuracy. As they navigated the obstacle course around the Training Centre, they relied on each other's strengths, seamlessly alternating between offence and defence.

Aayla was breathing hard, her legs starting to feel like jelly, but she crouched into a fighting stance in front of Talyn. He launched at her, their strikes evenly matched, their blades clashing with resounding echoes.

Sensing an opening in Talyn's defence, she swiftly maneuvered her sword with practised finesse, aiming to disarm him.

With lightning-fast reflexes, Talyn executed a well-timed feint, drawing Aayla's attention toward a false opening. As she moved instinctively to counter the perceived threat, Talyn seized the opportunity to strike.

In a swift, fluid motion, his sword arched toward hers, targeting the vulnerable point where her grip was weakest. With expert precision, his blade applied just enough pressure to leverage Aayla's sword from her grasp.

As her sword was dislodged, it clattered to the ground, leaving her momentarily vulnerable and disarmed. Talyn maintained his focus and composure, ready to capitalise on the advantage gained. With one final strategic strike, he utilised his superior strength and executed a swift hip toss, leveraging his weight and momentum to flip her onto the training mat.

Caught off guard, Aayla found herself airborne for a split second before landing with a thud on the padded surface below, wings spread out wide. The breath was knocked from her, but before she could breathe, Talyn was lying across her with one hand holding her hands above her head and his other hand clutching his sword, pressed against her neck. His face was barely an inch above hers, and he panted hard with a radiant smile.

"Looks like I win this round."

The weight of his body pressed against hers, their breaths coming in rapid and uneven rhythms. With each inhale and exhale, she felt the rise and fall of his chest against hers, a steady rhythm that seemed to synchronise with the beating of her heart. His breath was warm against her skin, igniting something deep inside her.

As they lay there, his weight a comforting presence, Aayla couldn't help but notice how he fit perfectly against her, as if they had been designed for one another. She savoured the closeness, their gazes locked in an unbroken connection that felt like it lasted an eternity.

A thunderous voice boomed from a distance, shattering the silence. "Are you ever going to let her up, or do I have to make you?"

CHAPTER THIRTY

For a fleeting moment, Aayla swore she saw Talyn flush a deep shade of crimson before he stood in one quick, fluid motion and extended his hand toward her. She grabbed his hand, and he pulled her to her feet with his trademark cheeky smile.

She grinned back at him, but her stomach twisted as she turned to see Bazura striding confidently into the room. She had completely forgotten about him in the heat of their training.

Bazura beamed with excitement as he stopped in front of her. "I was wondering if you were ready for that lunch now?"

Looking down, she bit the inside of her cheek, reminding herself that she needed to play her part and pretend to be interested in finding her mate.

"I would love to. We were just finishing up, so I'm all yours now."

Glancing at Talyn, she noticed a pained look on his face. As their eyes met, he quickly looked away, resuming a look of casual disinterest. It happened so fast that she couldn't tell if it was real.

Clearing her throat, she turned her attention back to Bazura. "What have you been up to this morning?"

"We took a lovely flight over California and provided assistance wherever possible. It's quite a lovely planet in places."

"Absolutely. In that case, I suggest we go to Maine. I think you'll quite like it there."

They all flew to Maine and found a cozy rooftop cafe nestled between old buildings. Bazura and Elizia sat across from Aayla while Talyn stood behind Bazura, leaning casually against the wall, seemingly at ease but actually on high alert.

The conversation flowed from past adventures to recent events, and Aayla enjoyed the company. Yet, an unmistakable emptiness settled in her chest at the sight of the empty seat beside her. Despite her best efforts, her gaze kept drifting back to Talyn, though he seemed entirely focused on Bazura with a look of suppressed anger.

Frowning, Aayla offered Talyn a tentative smile when his eyes finally met hers. *Is everything okay?*

Yes.

His curt response only made her more uneasy, and she noticed his attention shift back to Bazura, a guarded intensity lingering in his expression as they finished their lunch.

Aayla's gaze then moved to Bazura and Elizia. Unlike her and Talyn, Bazura and Elizia sat with a noticeable space between them, even when walking side by side. They rarely glanced at one another, sharing a calm companionship more like old friends than bonded pairs.

Looking around, she wondered if the humans had noticed it too. She and Talyn were unusually close for a Guardian and Charge, always near, always touching in subtle ways. It had never bothered Aayla. She cherished Talyn's presence and touch too deeply to question it.

After lunch, they flew around the city, admiring the sights and pausing regularly to help with various incidents, including a robbery, a car accident, a police chase, a domestic disturbance, and a few street scuffles spiralling out of control. Together, they worked seamlessly, a swift force that left the streets safer in their wake.

It was late, and as the day wound down, the office buildings around them emptied, workers spilling into the streets. Aayla was walking along the main avenue when her gaze caught movement across the road. A small, thin young woman with curly, bright red hair rushed along the footpath with several worn bags hanging off her arms. Yet it wasn't just her movements that drew Aayla's attention. It was the warm, kind aura that seemed to radiate from her like a gentle light.

Looking at Bazura, she touched his arm. "There's something I need to take care of this way. I'll meet you back at Aldredth Tower."

She brushed a gentle hand over Elizia's cheek in farewell, then turned and set off quickly in the direction of the red-haired girl.

Talyn matched her stride, the agitation he'd shown all afternoon melting into a look of intrigue. *What did you see?*

Someone I want to talk to. The girl with the bright red hair up ahead.

They trailed her at a careful distance, watching as she hurried several blocks, darted across intersections, and finally ducked into a narrow storefront with a vibrant sign that read The Smith Family in bold red, white, and blue.

Aayla and Talyn exchanged a look and slipped inside, the shop doorbell chiming softly.

The shop was cramped, shelves lined with trinkets and knick-knacks, leaving no room for their wings. Their sudden appearance cast a hush over the small crowd of humans browsing inside. Gasps rippled through the room, and in seconds, all eyes were on them, wide with awe and curiosity.

Just then, an older woman, her face alight with surprise and excitement, burst from behind the counter. She nearly tripped over her own feet as she came forward, eyes darting between Aayla and Talyn with a grin that was both welcoming and reverent.

"Well," she said, her voice quivering with delight, "we don't usually get visitors like you in our little shop."

"Good afternoon," Aayla greeted warmly. "I'm looking for a young woman with curly red hair who just walked in."

The older lady's gaze sharpened. "And why are you looking for her?"

Aayla's smile softened as she took in the older woman's cautious gaze, admiring her protectiveness. "I promise, there's nothing to worry about," she said gently. "I'd simply like to have a word with her—if she's willing, of course."

The woman seemed to weigh Aayla's words, then finally gave a slow nod. "All right, wait here."

Talyn flashed her a gentle smile, easing her concern, and within moments, the young woman with vivid red curls emerged from the back, her eyes widening as she took them in.

"Hi, I'm Becca. You... wanted to speak to me?"

"Yes," Aayla replied, her voice reassuring. "If now is a good time, we'd love to introduce ourselves and wanted to ask you a few questions."

Becca glanced at the growing crowd of curious onlookers, then nodded, gesturing behind her.

"Absolutely. Let's step into one of our private rooms where it's quieter."

Aayla and Talyn held their wings tight against their back and carefully followed her through a narrow hallway into a private room at the back of the shop. As the door closed, the murmurs and stares faded, replaced by a quiet, almost charged atmosphere.

"How can I help you?" Becca asked softly, her voice tinged with curiosity.

Up close, Aayla couldn't help but notice how fragile the young woman appeared. Her small frame was even tinier upon close inspection. Aayla was sure humans weren't meant to be that thin, but she would save that question for another time.

"Thank you for agreeing to speak with us," Aayla began with a smile. "I saw you on the street, and you radiated such kindness that I felt drawn to meet you."

Becca's cheeks flushed a deep red. "That's... really kind of you to say."

Sitting there, she suddenly realised she didn't know what to say, so she scanned her brain for an easy conversation starter. "We recently held interviews for positions at Aldredth Tower. Did we see you at the interviews by any chance?"

Becca's gaze dropped, her hands fidgeting slightly as she replied, "No, I didn't apply. It sounds like an amazing opportunity, but... I didn't go for an interview."

Aayla tilted her head, sensing there was more to her story. "May I ask why not? Did you have reservations about working with us?"

"Oh, no!" Becca blurted out, her cheeks reddening further. "It's just... I don't have any degrees or special skills. I didn't think you'd be interested in someone like me."

"On the contrary, you seem exactly like the kind of person we're looking for," Aayla replied warmly. "Tell me more about yourself. What do you do here?"

Becca glanced around, a soft smile tugging at her lips. "I'm an administrative officer here. This is a wonderful charity that is focused on helping young people overcome educational inequality due to poverty. I also work part-time at the RSPCA and volunteer at a soup kitchen."

Aayla knew she was right about Becca. "They are all worthwhile organisations to work for. Tell me more about yourself. Do you have any hobbies?"

As Becca talked animatedly about her love of hiking, her eyes lit up with an infectious enthusiasm. Aayla whispered telepathically to Talyn, *What do you sense?*

She has a profoundly kind and gentle soul, but she's been through a lot. What are you thinking?

There's something about her. I can't put my finger on it. But I want to offer her a position with us. She's precisely the type of person I want by my side.

A smile tugged at Talyn's lips. *I think that's a great idea.*

As Becca wrapped up her story, Aayla leaned forward, meeting her gaze. "Becca, I'd like to offer you a position at Aldredth Tower. Is that something you would be interested in?"

Becca's eyes widened in astonishment. "Really? Me? What kind of position?"

Aayla shrugged and glanced at Talyn, who simply mirrored her gesture. "Honestly, I'm not sure yet. What are your skills?"

"Well..." Becca pondered, "Not many. I had to drop out of university at the end of my third year, and I undertake coordinator-type duties in my current position."

Talyn tilted his head, curiosity in his gaze. "Why did you leave university?"

Becca hesitated, her fingers nervously tracing the edges of her nails. "I, ah, had to take a few jobs to pay my bills, and I missed too many mandatory classes, so I didn't have enough credits to graduate," she said softly, disappointment lacing her words.

"What course were you enrolled in?" Aayla asked gently.

"Law. I wanted to go into family law, to provide legal aid for people who couldn't afford it," Becca replied, her voice brightening slightly at the thought.

"That's a noble goal." Aayla's gaze softened, and she nodded thoughtfully, considering the potential opportunities. "I think you'd make an excellent advisor. Would you consider becoming mine?"

Becca blinked, caught off guard. "Really? What would I even do as your advisor?"

"Well, you'd help me understand human nuances I might miss, give me advice, and take on tasks when I'm unavailable."

Aayla noticed Becca frown, doubt clouding her expression. Sensing her uncertainty, Aayla added gently, "Mostly, I need someone I can trust, and I just feel you're the right person."

Becca was still frowning as she struggled with the idea.

Aayla smiled softly before standing up. "Please take a week to think about it and let me know your answer. I hope it's a yes. How about you come to Aldredth Tower next Monday?"

Becca quickly rose, giving a respectful bow. "I have work Monday, but could I meet you first thing Tuesday morning before my shift starts?"

Aayla walked around the table and extended her hand. As they shook, she almost smiled at Becca's shocked expression. "I look forward to seeing you then."

When they landed back at Aldredth Tower, Aayla felt a surge of excitement at the sight of so many human faces throughout the building. Though about half of them were still transitioning from their previous jobs, the building already felt alive with vibrant energy and activity.

She nodded greetings at the two security personnel stationed at the front entrance and walked inside to greet the staff operating the front desk before flying up to the upper balcony on her way to the Command Centre.

The air in the Command Centre hummed with the low murmur of voices. With deft precision, the Aldredth navigated through layers of information, deciphering patterns and anomalies with the practised ease of seasoned professionals.

From the doorway, Aayla surveyed the scene with a watchful eye, her gaze sweeping across the room with the natural authority of a leader.

Seth glanced up from the screens in front of him, a grin breaking across his face as he waved. He jogged over, handing her a Lumina. "There's a strong anti-Aldredth uprising brewing in Iran. We need to exercise extreme caution before any Aldredth attempts to enter that region."

The data displayed on the screen disturbed her. She passed the Lumina to Talyn, watching his expression shift as he scanned the information, a small frown formed between his brows.

They delved into a lengthy discussion about the origins and implications of the data when a sudden growl from Seth's stomach interrupted their focus.

"Sorry, Seth, I didn't mean to keep you for so long. Come on, let's all get some dinner," Aayla suggested.

"I'll be down shortly. I just have a few more things to check," Seth replied, still engrossed in his work.

"Oh no," Talyn chuckled, "I've told myself that a thousand times. Come, we have enough hands to carry the load, and everything else can wait."

With a mischievous grin, Talyn playfully shoved Seth down the corridor, prompting a burst of laughter and light-hearted protests.

"You know," Seth said between bouts of laughter, "you remind me of a rambunctious kid I once had stationed under me. The kid had more energy than a hyperactive puppy."

Talyn raised an eyebrow, intrigued. "Oh really? What happened?"

Seth smiled warmly. "I remember one night when he sneaked into the mess hall, determined to whip up what he proudly called a culinary delicacy. An old recipe from his grandmother, or so he claimed."

Laughing, Seth shook his head. "The only thing he managed to cook up was a flash fire that completely singed his eyebrows off and burnt down half the kitchen. He had a knack for turning the simplest plans into unforgettable chaos."

The laughter echoed in Aayla's ears as Talyn and Seth's playful banter continued into the Dining Hall and throughout their dinner. Aayla watched them happily, her heart swelling with warmth as she observed the camaraderie between them. They were already closer than brothers, their friendship marked by a delightful mix of teasing and genuine affection. It was a bond that had formed so quickly and powerfully that it was almost tangible.

Talyn and Seth exchanged playful jabs, recounting tales of their training mishaps, when a few other human security recruits wandered over, drawn by the laughter.

They all jumped in, sharing their most embarrassing moments as laughter erupted, creating an atmosphere filled with warmth and light-heartedness.

Seth animatedly gestured as he described how he'd once nearly tripped over his own gun during a mock combat drill, much to everyone's amusement.

David, a former soldier under Seth, leaned forward with a wide grin. "Seth, remember that time back in training when you almost knocked over that stack of weapons?" He laughed, leaning back in his chair. "What was it you said? You were just demonstrating the art of distraction?'"

Talyn playfully slapped Seth on the back. "You two should consider a career in comedy," he quipped.

"Hey, we have plenty of time for both!" Talyn shot back, a glint of mischief in his eyes.

Aayla couldn't help but smile at their light-heartedness. As the dinner progressed, the conversation flowed effortlessly from one topic to another, punctuated by hearty laughter. Aayla savoured the delicious food before her, but it was the company that genuinely nourished her spirit.

Looking around, she saw that the entire Dining Hall was filled with laughter and conversation from the dozens of people in the room. Humans and Aldredth intermingled, sharing both food and company. Food was available at all times of the day and night, so anyone could drop in whenever they desired, but it was the companionship that the Aldredth truly valued.

Happiness swelled in Aayla at the sight of the humans enjoying food side-by-side with the Aldredth. She thought it might have taken a while to see such acceptance of their presence.

As the conversation wrapped up and Aayla prepared to leave, she asked Talyn about humans' rapid acceptance of them. He believed that it was a bond formed through mutual trust and faith. The Aldredth didn't treat the humans as lesser than them. Instead, they treated the humans as valued friends—equals.

She was feeling lighter than she had in a long time as she lay down to dream that night.

As exhaustion washed over her like a gentle tide, her eyelids grew heavy, each blink lingering a little longer than the last. Her breathing slowed, deepening into a steady rhythm as she surrendered to sleep's inevitable pull. Thoughts scattered like autumn leaves in the wind, drifting aimlessly through her mind before dissolving into the darkness of unconsciousness, followed by a blinding white light.

When her vision cleared, Aayla found herself standing in the middle of a desolate road, watching in helpless, slow motion as a blade pierced Talyn's chest, straight through his heart. She lunged forward, arms outstretched, but he was already collapsing, his gaze frozen, lifeless, staring into a distance he could no longer see.

Awakening with an ear-splitting scream, she jolted awake, bolting upright in bed, heart pounding wildly against her ribs. Talyn was there, holding her with one arm, sword raised with the other to defend her from the invisible threat.

Her breath came in ragged gasps, and tears flowed down her cheeks as the remnants of the nightmarish vision lingered like tendrils of smoke in her mind. She clutched Talyn tightly to her chest and couldn't stop the sobs that escaped her lips.

"What is it? What did you see?" Talyn asked, his voice edged with fear as his eyes frantically searched her face.

Tears continued to stream down her cheeks, her body convulsing with the force of her sobs. Each breath came in ragged gasps, her shoulders heaved with the weight of her grief, her hands clutching at Talyn's chest.

"You... you... You're going to die."

Chapter Thirty-One

Several Aldredth had burst into the room soon after Aayla's scream, but all except Martok and Skyla had since departed.

Martok knelt patiently on the floor before her as she remained curled in a tight ball on Talyn's lap. His strong arms held her securely, grounding her as silent tears continued to fall.

"Can you tell me what you saw?" Martok asked gently.

Aayla opened her eyes, staring distantly as she tried to piece together the haunting images. "I... I was standing in the middle of a street. Shadowy figures surrounded me. It was only a few seconds, but everything felt like it was in slow motion. I think I was in the middle of a battle because I could feel the weight of my sword in my hand."

Talyn stroked his hand down her back reassuringly, and Skya nodded silently.

"I saw Talyn," she whispered, her voice thick with emotion. "He was completely overwhelmed by shadowy figures. I could barely catch a glimpse of him through them."

Martok rubbed his chin thoughtfully. "Did you see anything to identify them?"

Aayla shook her head, clearing her throat. "No, I couldn't make out their faces or clothing, but I believe they were Yvoran. I saw a Yvoran blade pierce Talyn's heart. I tried to reach him, but... he was dead before he even hit the ground."

She took a shaky breath, steadying herself as the vision's vividness weighed on her.

Martok waited patiently until her gaze lifted to meet his before he asked softly, "Do you know when it will happen?"

She pondered the question, searching for a sense of timing in the vision. Unix and Aurra's visions could vary, unfolding immediately or lingering far into the future.

"It felt... close," she said, voice low. "Maybe in a few days or within a month."

Visions showed a glimpse of the future as it would unfold if left unchanged, but they also offered a chance to alter fate. The future wasn't set in stone. Events could shift with the right actions.

Exhaling deeply as he stood, Martok nodded, satisfied. "Good. Now, get some rest. We have this under control."

After they left, Aayla lay awake for hours, her head resting on Talyn's chest, listening to his strong, steady heartbeat. Only then, lulled by its reassuring rhythm, did she finally surrender to sleep.

The following morning, there was a flurry of activity in the Command Centre. The Aldredth worked with other civilisations across the galaxy to track down any new information on the Yvoran or whispers of an upcoming attack.

As an added precaution, they agreed that if a Yvoran strike on Earth occurred within the coming months, Aayla and Talyn would not engage. The thought of standing by while her people fought left her feeling ill, but she agreed that if they couldn't prevent the attack, she would prevent Talyn from joining in the fight to save his life.

To keep her mind occupied, Aayla threw herself into organising an intergalactic summit on Earth, inviting dignitaries from friendly civilisations across the galaxy. Set to take place in a few months, the gathering required intensive coordination with human leaders, who granted permission to increase the number of Aldredth on Earth for enhanced security. Such events were often prime targets for attacks, and they planned to have the planet well-guarded with Aldredth to deter any threats.

The next few days flew by as they settled into a busy routine. Alongside her duties supporting the humans, Aayla began conducting daily media interviews and hosting nightly balls and gatherings, each dedicated to honouring different causes, individuals, or initiatives. During the evening dances, her gaze often drifted toward Talyn, who stood on guard along the edge of the room, always vigilant and poised.

Usually, the Aldredth took turns patrolling, ensuring some were on duty while others joined the festivities. This rotation allowed everyone a chance to relax. However, as an unmated Guardian, Talyn was permanently stationed on guard, blending into the shadows to oversee events unseen.

Talyn spent a large portion of his time during the evening events coordinating with the human security force. Meanwhile, during the day, he led a rigorous training program for them, overseeing them. Now that Aldredth Tower was complete and fully staffed, Aayla and Talyn often found themselves involved in separate activities.

As a Guardian, Talyn wasn't required to accompany her when she was around a large number of Aldredth or in the secure environment of Aldredth Tower, especially during lengthy briefings, confidential meetings, or while she trained. During those times, he would typically head to the Training Centre himself or oversee other security details.

While Talyn led his training sessions, Aayla also usually took the chance to visit patients in the MedBay, check on others around the Tower, or unwind in the rooftop garden.

Balancing these responsibilities alongside their daily training, media interviews, and support work kept them both busy. By the time the dancing ended at the end of each night,

Aayla was generally exhausted but never too tired to relax with Talyn in the Bathing Pools before finally retiring for the night.

Yet tonight felt different. The energy in the grand hall was electric, with laughter and music swirling around them. The charity ball was a chance for joy, and she longed to share that joy with Talyn, even if just for a moment.

As the song drew to a close, Aayla glanced at Talyn for what felt like the thousandth time that night. He remained stationed at the back of the room, ever watchful, his eyes scanning the crowd.

As he watched her, a small smile formed on his lips, but he quickly averted his eyes under her gaze.

Nervous, she walked over and paused beside him, facing the lively crowd. "It's a lovely party, isn't it?"

His smile widened as he met her gaze. "Indeed, it is. And you look beautiful tonight, as always."

"I'm only missing one thing. Dance with me."

He frowned, looking away. "That wouldn't be proper. I am your Guardian, and my place is here."

She moved in front of him, forcing him to meet her gaze. "Your place is by my side, and my side is on the dance floor."

Talyn was silent for a long moment. "You don't take no for an answer, do you?" He smiled softly.

"No. Now, don't make me order you," she teased, extending her hand toward him.

Her heart raced as she watched him hesitate, longing and confusion flickering across his face before he finally reached out to take her hand.

"I'm... sure one dance won't hurt."

One dance turned into two, then three, and eventually ten. The feel of his body pressed against hers, moving with hers, rubbing sensually, was intoxicating, making the rest of the world fade away.

The way he looked at her, the way he touched her, ignited a fire within her. A deep yearning for more.

Laughing, content in each other's arms, she could have continued to dance all night. But as the last guests began to retire, the spell started to fade.

Leaning closer, Talyn's warm breath brushed against her ear. "What does a man have to do to get a beautiful lady like you into his bed?"

Laughing uproariously, she kissed his neck. "You are ridiculous. Come now, take me to your bed."

That night, as she fell asleep beside Talyn, she had the most wondrous dreams of dancing in his arms high in the sky.

CHAPTER THIRTY-TWO

Talyn had cherished the feeling of Aayla in his arms as they danced yesterday, but today, watching her dance with effortless grace only deepened his longing. Her wide smile and the way her wings flared with joy made his chest tighten, a bittersweet reminder of how much he wanted to be closer to her.

Talyn glanced at his Lumina as it buzzed with an incoming message and grimaced at the display.

With a sigh, he looked over to Jaxion. *Watch her for me. I need to step out for a minute.*

Jaxion nodded as Talyn walked briskly to an empty meeting room and mentally braced himself before answering the waiting call.

"Talyn," his mother's voice came through, crisp and authoritative. "Tell me, are you fulfilling your duty at the ball?"

"Yes, Mother," he replied, his tone respectful despite the irritation brewing beneath the surface. "I'm ensuring all security protocols are followed."

"Is that all?" she pressed, her tone icy. "You know how critical your position as Guardian is. Our family's honour is on the line. You must demonstrate strength and vigilance, not only for yourself but for the honour of our family's name. There are eyes on you."

Talyn's jaw tightened. "I am aware of my responsibilities. I have been diligent."

"Diligent is not enough," his father's voice interjected, cold and disapproving. "You are a Guardian, Talyn. You should be setting an example. The family has a reputation to uphold. Do not forget that your actions reflect upon us all.”

“Father, I’m—”

“Do not interrupt,” his mother snapped. “You need to focus on your duties. We have heard the rumours coming out of Earth of your casual, flirtatious relationship with Aayla. That is not how we trained you. This is not a time for distractions or emotions. Remember, your position comes with great responsibility.”

Talyn clenched his fists, fighting the urge to retort. It was always the same from them. The suffocating expectations, the unyielding pressure to be perfect. “I understand. I will not let you down,” he replied, keeping his voice steady.

“See that you do. We expect a full report after the event,” his father added, and the call abruptly ended.

As he lowered the Lumina, Talyn felt the weight of his parents’ expectations pressing down on him. Their concern was never about his well-being. It was solely about the family’s honour and how he represented them. He stood alone for several moments before walking back towards the ball. Pausing at the door, he looked across the room at Aayla, who was laughing with a group of dignitaries, her joy a stark contrast to the constraints he felt from his family.

He sighed heavily, staring hard at the floor. He was so lost in the storm of his thoughts that he didn’t notice Aayla walking over to him.

“Talyn?” Aayla’s voice broke through his thoughts, drawing him back to the present. She noticed the tension in his expression. “Are you okay?”

She despised how his parents viewed him as her expendable bodyguard first and their son second. Every chance she got, she sought to draw him away from the rigid training and discipline that had shaped his upbringing, inviting him instead into the warmth of her light. Wanting him to savour the joy of every moment with her.

"Just family matters," he said, forcing a smile. "Nothing to worry about."

But as he took her hand, the weight of his parents' expectations seemed to dissipate. At that moment, she instinctively understood that what he truly needed was the grounding reassurance of her touch. The weight of his parents' expectations seemed to melt away with her shy smile. Captivated by her presence, he lost track of everything outside their bubble. The pressures of the world grew distant, fading into the background, leaving only the warmth of her company.

"It's getting late. We should call it a night," Aayla said with a soft smile. *Or... we could go for a fly instead. Just the two of us, lost in the freedom of the open night sky.*

Talyn smirked, heat curling through his veins at the thought of dancing with her in the moonlight. *As tempting as that is, you've been overworking yourself. You need to rest.*

Okay, she conceded, *after I check in at the Command Centre.*

Deal. Talyn nodded.

They quickly left the ballroom, pausing briefly at the Command Centre before retreating to their private quarters. Once Aayla had drifted off to sleep, Talyn remained awake, his gaze fixed on her peaceful form bathed in the soft glow of moonlight. The urge to reach out, to trace his fingers over her skin, was nearly blinding, but he clenched his fists and rolled onto his back. The ache inside him grew unbearable at night, with her warmth so close yet untouchable—his own private torment.

His eyes flickered back to her, lips slightly parted as she breathed softly. It took every ounce of his strength not to lean in and claim her mouth with his own.

Unable to bear it any longer, he slipped out of bed, dressed quickly, and hesitated at the door, stealing one last glance at her sleeping form before stepping into the hallway. She was safe in her room and didn't need a Guardian by her side.

He had no destination in mind, only the need to escape the war raging inside him.

The crisp night air bit against his skin as he ascended to the rooftop garden. He wandered through the garden, hoping the solitude would clear his head. Instead, voices—low and familiar—drifted through the quiet.

Rounding a large brittlebush tree, he found a group of security team members gathered around a crackling fire, laughter mixing with the night breeze. As soon as they spotted him, the conversation died.

"Talyn, is everything okay?" Seth asked, brows furrowing.

"Sorry, I just came up for some fresh air. I didn't mean to disturb you." His eyes scanned the garden, but his mind was too entangled in the storm raging inside him.

Seth offered a warm smile. "You could never disturb us."

Talyn stared at the ground, shame twisting like a blade in his chest. He didn't deserve their respect, not when his thoughts strayed where they never should. Aayla deserved a Guardian who was steadfast, honourable, and untouched by forbidden longing. Someone who protected her without questioning their place at her side. But no matter how hard he tried to convince himself to walk away, he couldn't. The thought of leaving her, of not being the one to keep her safe, was unbearable. He was a coward, a selfish fool. And yet, he stayed.

Clearing his throat, he turned. "I'll let you get back to it."

"Talyn—" Seth's voice stopped him.

He glanced back, meeting Seth's concerned gaze.

"Something's wrong," Seth said, quiet but certain.

Talyn dropped his gaze, his throat tight with the weight of unspoken words. If only he could let it out and admit the feelings clawing at his insides that were tearing him apart piece by piece. But he knew the truth. The moment he spoke, duty would demand they report him. There would be no leniency, no second chances. His fate would be sealed, and his execution would be swift and unquestioned.

And the worst part? He wouldn't even fight it. Because deep down, he knew he deserved it.

"Stay," Seth said quietly, then grinned. "We have alcohol."

Talyn's gaze flicked to the bottles in their hands. Maybe that was precisely what he needed. A distraction. A numbing. "If I'm not imposing?"

"Never." Ethan handed him a dark brown bottle. Talyn took a sip, the unexpectedly earthy flavour coating his tongue, grounding him for just a moment.

"Thank you." Smiling softly, he sank into one of the padded seats beside the others, his wings unfurling quietly behind him. At first, their conversation was just background noise, drowned out by the storm in his mind. But soon, the warmth of their easy banter pulled him in, and before he knew it, a small smirk tugged at his lips.

"So, tell me," Ethan grinned, "can Aldredth get drunk? Do we need to worry about you falling off the roof?"

Talyn smirked. "Our bodies metabolise alcohol faster than yours. I'd have to drink a lot, and even then, the effects wouldn't last long. So no, you don't have to worry about me falling off the roof... unless, of course, gravity decides to be extra needy tonight."

Laughter erupted around the fire.

Seth shifted slightly, his expression thoughtful. "Can I ask... why aren't you with Aayla right now?"

Talyn stared at the bottle in his hands. "She's safe, asleep in her bed. I just couldn't... sleep."

A long silence stretched between them.

"It can't be easy, being her Guardian," Seth said quietly.

Talyn smirked. "That's the easiest part. I get to spend every day with her. I couldn't be luckier."

"I heard more Lazuli's are coming to Earth to see if they're her mate. That's good news, isn't it?" David asked cautiously.

Talyn's jaw clenched. "Fantastic."

Seth's eyebrows shot up. "You don't want her to find her mate?"

"Of course I do," Talyn exhaled sharply, turning the bottle in his hands, watching the firelight reflect off the glass. "Finding our mate is the most significant moment in our lives. I want her to experience that happiness, that fulfilment. I want everything for her."

"Do you wish you could be her mate?" David asked.

Talyn's fingers went white against the bottle. He looked away, jaw tight. Of course, he wished that. But Aayla deserved someone much better than him.

"What do you think her mate will be like?" Ethan asked into the silence.

Talyn's throat burned. "She's brilliant. Beautiful. Powerful. Perfect in every way." He inhaled sharply. "So, her mate? He'll be the strongest, the fastest, the best fucking male among us." The words were laced with bitterness, with a fury he barely contained. "I bet he's perfect."

His fingers clenched at the thought of another male touching Aayla in ways he had only ever dreamed of, and the bottle shattered in his hand.

"Shit," Talyn muttered, waving his hand over the fragments and fusing them back together before setting the empty bottle down.

When he looked up, he found everyone staring at him with varying degrees of confusion and concern.

"Sorry. I should go." He stood abruptly.

Seth was on his feet in an instant. "Wait."

Talyn hesitated.

"Here." Seth held out a fresh bottle. "You know, I could break a bottle with my bare hands, too."

"Is that so?"

"Yep," Seth grinned. "But I'd need one hand for the bottle and the other to let gravity do the heavy lifting when I drop it."

Despite himself, Talyn let out a quiet laugh and took the bottle, sinking back into his seat.

They talked for hours, their conversation flowing like a steady current, weaving through stories of wild missions and hilarious mishaps. The laughter was infectious, echoing in the night air as they shared memories that ranged from embarrassing to downright absurd. With each passing minute, the atmosphere lightened, and the group grew more relaxed, slipping into a rhythm of camaraderie. The quiet rooftop was filled with warmth, and for a brief time, the weight of their responsibilities faded into the background, replaced by the comfort of good company.

"Anyone who's free meets here every night just to hang out and relax," Seth said as Talyn finally stood to leave. "If you're around, you should join us again."

Talyn paused, touched by the offer. "I'd love to." He knew he'd have to make it a new nightly routine, heading to the roof after ensuring Aayla slept safely and peacefully. It would be his time to unwind, to breathe, and to connect with something other than the weight of his duties.

Sliding back into bed beside Aayla, he felt lighter than he had in weeks. The weight on his shoulders was still there, but just a fraction less crushing. He breathed in her intoxicating scent and, for the first time in a long time, drifted into a peaceful sleep.

CHAPTER THIRTY-THREE

Aayla and Talyn lingered over breakfast in the Dining Hall, surrounded by the vibrant buzz of morning chatter. The hall was filled with laughter, the clink of cups, and the warmth of easy camaraderie as Aldredth and humans mingled freely.

She watched Talyn across the table, throwing his head back in laughter as Seth and the others from the security team recounted some wild tale. The light in his eyes made her heart ache, a fleeting reminder of simpler times.

Her Lumina buzzed, cutting through the lively atmosphere. Glancing down, she frowned slightly at the message. Becca had shown up unexpectedly at the entrance, leaving word that she couldn't meet today. But the guard had reported that she appeared injured, and he was concerned.

She flashed the screen to Talyn, their easy-going moment slipping away as they both stood without a word. Together, they left the hall, moving quickly down the corridor, wings catching the light as they flew from the closest balcony and circled the building.

Aayla spotted Becca moving quickly along the path away from the building. Gliding over, they landed behind her, calling her name.

Becca froze mid-step, shoulders tense, before turning around with a hesitant slowness. Her hair fell over her face as if she were trying to shrink beneath it, her arms wrapped tightly around herself. Aayla's gaze moved over her, settling on the dark bruise that had formed around her right eye, barely concealed beneath thick layers of makeup, and the split lip, swollen and raw.

"Who did that?" Talyn's voice came out in a low, menacing growl.

Becca shifted uncomfortably, her gaze darting away. "It's... It's not as bad as it looks." She forced a smile, though it didn't reach her eyes. "I just wanted to let you know I'm not feeling well enough to meet today. I called in sick to work, too."

Aayla felt anger rising within her, but she forced herself to remain calm, her voice gentle but firm. "Becca... tell me what happened. Please."

Becca hesitated, drawing a shaky breath. "My father... he saw photos of us talking in the tabloids, and, well, he's got a bit of a drinking problem."

Clenching her fists, she tried to keep her voice carefully measured. "Do you live with him?"

"Oh, no." Becca shook her head quickly. "I left home years ago. My mom passed away when I was born, and I think... he's always blamed me for that, even if he never said it outright. He drinks to... cope, I guess."

Talyn's jaw tightened, his voice laced with barely controlled fury. "Why did he hurt you?"

Becca flinched slightly at his tone, and Aayla placed a calming hand on Talyn's arm. Becca swallowed, eyes dropping to the ground. "He wanted me to use my connection with you to help his business... and I refused."

Tilting her head thoughtfully, Aayla asked, "What does he do?"

Huffing in exasperation, Becca ran a hand through her hair. "He rips people off. That's what he does. Look, I didn't want you to see this because I didn't want you to see me as some helpless victim. I escaped him once, and I am more than capable of doing it again."

Aayla offered her a crooked smile. "I can feel that spark in you, so I know you can. But before we go any further, I need to ask whether you were coming here today to say yes or no?"

Becca looked at the ground for a long moment before raising her gaze with fierce determination in her eyes. "Yes."

"Good," Aayla grinned. "That means you're under our protection now. He'll never touch you again."

"Unfortunately," Talyn interjected, crossing his arms, "you weren't wearing an Aldredth crest before, so we can't kill him. But now? If he so much as looks at you wrong, it's a different story."

Becca's cheeks reddened slightly, her mood visibly lightening. "Thanks, but honestly, I can handle myself."

Aayla's voice softened. "I know you can. But now that you're with us, you don't have to handle it alone. We protect our own. It's just what we do."

Becca smiled, a spark of humour in her eyes. "So, an all-for-one, one-for-all kind of thing?" When they stared blankly, she added, "It's a Three Musketeers reference."

Aayla chuckled. "Sorry, I'm not aware of that reference, but that's why I need you as my advisor."

Talyn sent a quick message on his Lumina, then turned to Becca, his tone firm but reassuring. "Let's get you inside to finalise the employment contract and—most importantly—get an Aldredth crest on you. I don't want you left alone, so a security team member will stay with you today. As for tonight, you'll stay at Aldredth Tower until we've changed the locks at your place. We'll arrange for someone to help you gather any essentials you need from home."

Becca's gaze drifted to the security team stationed nearby, and a flicker of unease crossed her face. Aayla could see how the sight of the towering, uniformed guards might seem intimidating, especially after everything Becca had just been through.

A thought struck her, and Aayla turned towards Talyn. *Can you check if Seth is free?*

Talyn's eyes brightened with understanding as he sent off a message. *He's on his way.*

"I have an idea that might make you feel more comfortable if you'll give us a moment," Aayla said gently to Becca.

A few minutes later, Seth strode over, his easy smile vanishing as his gaze landed on the bruise shadowing Becca's face. His eyes flashed with anger. "Who did that?" he asked, voice low and simmering.

"Someone," Talyn replied darkly, "we intend to hold accountable. I'll need your team on it, Seth, so that he can face justice through the human courts."

Seth's jaw tightened in silent agreement before he turned toward Becca, his expression softening. He introduced himself, his voice warm and steady, and Aayla didn't miss the faint blush creeping across Becca's cheeks.

As Aayla laid out the plan, Seth listened intently, his gaze steady on Becca. He'd protect her until she wore the Aldredth crest, escorting her to collect belongings from her apartment, and would personally show her around Aldredth Tower.

Seth offered a reassuring smile as Becca nodded, her shoulders visibly relaxing.

"Welcome to the family, Becca," he said, his voice filled with quiet strength.

Seth couldn't keep his eyes off Becca, and the two of them exchanged shy smiles. As they walked off together, Seth burst into laughter—louder than necessary—at something Becca said, his face lit with genuine amusement.

What's going on there? Aayla pondered.

I think, Talyn chuckled, a mischievous glint in his eye, *they like each other.*

Really? Aayla's gaze drifted back to the pair as they disappeared into Aldredth Tower. *They'd make such a wonderful couple. She's so grounded and genuine, and he's got a heart of gold.*

Talyn shrugged, though his smile lingered. *Human love is complicated, but it will be fun watching that unfold.*

Laughing, Aayla nudged him playfully. *Just don't give him a hard time.*

With a quiet chuckle, Talyn leaned in, gently kissing her cheek. *I wouldn't dream of it.*

Their Luminas suddenly buzzed to life with an alert, startling Aayla. Her pulse quickened as adrenaline surged through her. She barely looked at the message before exchanging a quick look with Talyn. They both registered the urgency at once. President Bailey was under attack. An ambush had been reported on his campaign trail, and the team was under heavy fire, urgently requesting backup.

"We're closer than anyone," Talyn said, his voice tight but steady. "We have to go now."

Aayla nodded, her wings already unfurling, instinct kicking in as the message settled in her mind. "Let's go."

Without another word, they both leapt into the sky, their powerful wings beating against the cool morning air. The city stretched beneath them as they climbed higher, gaining altitude and speed, their wings synchronised in a practised rhythm. The urgency of the alert pulsed in Aayla's veins, sharpening her focus, and every beat of her wings seemed to bring them closer to the flickering chaos of the ambush site.

The wind roared around them as they pushed their speed to the limit. From above, Aayla spotted a faint glint of movement at the rally site below. The crowd had erupted in chaos, scattering in all directions as flashes of gunfire lit up the scene. The President's security had formed a defensive line, their focus sharp as they tried to contain the sudden attack.

They landed on the edge of the rally site in perfect unison, wings folding back swiftly as their feet touched the ground. Aayla's gaze locked onto the President's position, sheltered but under heavy fire, with his security detail holding off multiple attackers from behind makeshift barricades.

Talyn's hand went to his sword, his stance immediately alert. "Flank left," he murmured, his voice low and controlled. "We cut them off from either side."

Aayla nodded, slipping into position, her eyes scanning for threats as she moved. Together, they plunged into the fray, instincts honed and muscles primed for the fight. As Aayla threw herself into defending the President, she knew that no matter the chaos around them, Talyn would be right there with her, fighting at her side until the last threat was neutralised.

They moved through the chaos with blistering speed, their abilities instantly turning the tide of the ambush. With a sweep of her hand, Aayla sent several attackers flying through the air, their weapons torn from their grip as they crashed into nearby structures. Talyn's strength was a force of nature, and his blows incapacitated the attackers before they had time to react. His telekinetic powers twisted and crushed the attackers' weapons in midair, rendering them useless before they could fire another round.

The President's security team, initially pinned behind cover, quickly adapted to the shift in momentum. As the ambushers were overwhelmed in a matter of moments, the detail regained its footing. They formed a tight defensive circle around the President, now able to focus on securing the area. Aayla and Talyn moved in perfect sync with them, covering blind spots and providing suppression fire with their own unique abilities, pushing the remaining attackers into retreat.

Captain Marek, a stern-faced man, locked eyes with Talyn and gave him a sharp nod of acknowledgment. "We appreciate the assist!" he shouted over the sounds of the remaining gunfire, directing his team to fall into formation around the President.

Talyn nodded back, his gaze sharp and calculating. "Form a perimeter," he instructed, recognising that they'd need a coordinated effort to hold off any remaining hidden attackers. The security detail reacted immediately, falling into place with disciplined precision, reinforcing the defence as they tightened the protective circle around the President.

A bullet grazed one of the agents, but his partner instantly shielded him with his own body, dragging him back behind a barricade without losing their rhythm.

Ayla stepped in front of the agents, shielding them with her body. Talyn launched himself at the remaining attackers, his movements fluid and lethal. With a series of swift, precise strikes of his sword, he cut down the last of the assailants, each slash executed with devastating efficiency.

"Clear!" Aayla called out, her voice steady and commanding. She motioned for the detail to sweep the area, ensuring no threats were left.

Captain Marek, now more composed, gestured for two of his agents to sweep the perimeter while he stayed by the President's side, who, despite the chaos, now wore a look of quiet resolve. "Sir, we're almost through," Marek said, keeping the President low and protected.

The security team quickly fanned out, cautiously checking for lingering threats while maintaining their protective formation around the President. After several tense moments, they appeared satisfied that no further threats lingered, and the area was now quiet and secure.

"Are you injured, Mr. President?" Aayla asked, her voice steady as she scanned him for any signs of harm.

President Bailey shook his head, his face showing gratitude mixed with exhaustion. "Not a scratch, thanks to you," he said, his voice shaking slightly. He glanced at Captain Marek and nodded. "Good work holding them off."

Marek met Aayla's gaze with a look of respect. "We wouldn't have managed it without you two," he said, his tone gruff but grateful.

As the security detail continued their sweep, Talyn's gaze stayed trained on the perimeter, his stance still alert. Even with the immediate danger gone, Aayla could sense his tension, the way his focus lingered on every shadow as if ready for another ambush. She placed a steadying hand on his arm, a silent reminder that, for now, they were safe.

With the President and his security team finally secure, Aayla and Talyn fell back, watching as the detail regrouped. Marek gave them both a nod of thanks before several black vehicles quickly pulled up, rushing President Bailey to safety in a blur of motion.

They flew back to Aldreth Tower in silence, and after an intensive training session, Aayla exhaled as she slipped into the warm waters of the Bathing Pools, the gentle heat working its way through her sore muscles. Every part of her body ached, a steady reminder of the she had been pushing herself too hard lately. She could still feel the echo of Talyn's hand on her shoulder from when he'd pulled her out of harm's way earlier, his touch firm but protective.

The steam drifted around the pools, softening the edges of everyone lounging there. Seth and a few other security team members reclined near her, their laughter and easy banter breaking the usual formality of their roles. Seth had a way of drawing people in, and even now, his warm chuckles rippled over the water, lightening the atmosphere, while the others leaned back, eyes half-closed in well-earned peace.

Aayla glanced across the pool to where Talyn sat, his shoulders just breaking the surface, and his wings flared out behind him. Despite the relaxation that seemed to reach everyone else, she noticed a subtle tension in his frame, the way his muscles still seemed tense. Talyn was, as always, vigilant, his eyes shifting from face to face, catching every movement in the room. She knew that the day's events weighed on him. The responsibility, the risks, and the consequences always played out in his mind long after the mission was done.

But there were fleeting moments when his gaze softened, and Aayla thought she caught him watching her, his expression unguarded as if he was seeing only her. She turned her head towards him and, just for a second, felt the warmth of his gaze, even though he quickly looked away when she turned to meet it.

Aayla's lips quirked in a slight smile. She wasn't sure if he realised how often she did the same, letting her eyes linger on him when he wasn't looking. The steam gave her cover, and she studied how his light brown hair curled slightly with the heat, how the water's reflection played over his skin, softening the lines that were usually so sharp with purpose.

"You did well today," Seth said, his voice breaking into her thoughts. He was looking at her, a knowing look in his eyes. "Both of you."

"Thanks, Seth," she replied, offering him a genuine smile.

Talyn's usually serious expression softened into an easy grin. He nudged one of the human guards, grinning as he said, "You know, you lot practically live here now. The Bathing

Pools, the Dining Hall, the rooftop gardens—you spend more time in Aldredth Tower than in your own homes.”

Ethan laughed, shaking her head. “Best spot on the planet, and the company’s not too bad, either.” He shot a playful glance at the others, who nodded in agreement.

David leaned in, smirking. “It’s true, though. Out there, we’re instantly recognisable. That Aldredth crest practically turns us into celebrities. Here, at least, we can have some privacy.”

Seth chuckled, stretching out and propping his arms up on the pool’s edge. “Nothing quite like being off-duty and not having every civilian staring at you.”

Aayla watched them, feeling both a quiet amusement and an unexpected fondness for the human security team’s candid camaraderie. She’d never had anything quite like this before. This casual, comfortable connection.

Mark raised an eyebrow at Talyn, gesturing around the pool. “Admit it, Talyn, you like this place just as much as we do. There’s nowhere else you’d rather be.”

Talyn chuckled, glancing around as if considering. “It’s true,” he replied, his voice dropping to a more sincere tone. “We’re family here, all of us. There’s no place I’d rather be.”

Aayla couldn’t help but smile as she met Talyn’s gaze. The gentle look in his eyes told her he meant it—not just about the team, but about her, too. A soft chuckle rippled through the group, and Aayla found herself laughing along with them, the tension from earlier slowly easing from her body. Yet a part of her remained aware of Talyn, feeling his presence even when she wasn’t looking directly at him.

As the night wore on, the pool slowly emptied, friends and allies bidding goodnight one by one. Finally, just the two of them were left, lingering in a comfortable silence. When they eventually rose to head to their private quarters, a quiet anticipation hung in the air, almost tangible, like a breath held between them.

They slipped into bed, the soft sheets cool against their skin. Talyn settled beside her, but there was a tension in the way he lay, his muscles tight despite the exhaustion of the day. Aayla's heart fluttered slightly in her chest, an unfamiliar feeling stirring deep within her as she turned onto her side, facing him. They were close, closer than they'd been in a long time, and the space between them felt both impossibly small and full of possibility.

Aayla could feel the quiet pulse of his presence, the way his breath slowed as he settled into the stillness of the room. They didn't speak, but the weight of the moment hung between them, pulling them closer even without words. Talyn's eyes met hers once more, and for a heartbeat, everything else seemed to fade away.

Chapter Thirty-Four

Talyn stood at the head of the Training Centre, issuing commands to the squad, his voice steady and commanding. His job was to protect and serve. Not to feel. And certainly not to feel anything for Aayla. Yet every time she entered the room, every time she was near him, his self-control wavered.

Today was no different.

The feel of her beside him in bed yesterday had almost broken him, and waking up beside her, sleeping soundly, was agonising. He longed to reach out and touch her.

He was almost glad when it was time for him to lead the training session with Seth's team so he could escape her intoxicating presence before he lost control and touched her in ways that were forbidden.

As he demonstrated a new defensive manoeuvre, he felt her presence the moment she walked through the door, his pulse quickening despite himself. His body was going through the motions, guiding the squadron through the drills, but his mind was a mess. Every now and then, he thought he sensed her eyes flicking toward him. Not for long, just enough to catch a glimpse before she quickly turned away.

He could feel the squad watching him, too. Seth had sharp eyes and shot him a questioning look as they sparred, catching Talyn's sudden lack of focus. "You seem... off," Seth said quietly, lowering his voice as they clashed, their movements swift and precise.

"I'm fine," Talyn muttered under his breath, swinging wide and nearly overextending in his haste to look casual. He quickly corrected himself, inwardly cursing his lack of composure.

Aayla moved with an effortless grace unlike anyone he had ever seen. She was strong, independent, beautiful, and utterly out of reach. He could look at her all he wanted and scan the room to ensure her safety like any good Guardian, but he wasn't supposed to see her. Not the way he did.

His eyes flicked to her as she stretched, her wings unfurling slightly as she commenced a new training routine. He clenched his jaw. He shouldn't be watching her like this. His job was to protect her, not to desire her. And yet, there he was, heart beating a little too fast, trying to remind himself of the boundaries he had sworn to uphold.

Aayla glanced over, catching his gaze for just a second. Talyn immediately looked away, heat creeping up his neck. She had caught him staring again, and he couldn't help but wonder if she knew. Did she know how hard he was trying to hide it? How, despite everything, he couldn't stop himself from feeling what he wasn't supposed to?

"Talyn?" Seth's voice interrupted his thoughts, pulling him back to the present. Seth had noticed his distracted state and watched him with a raised eyebrow.

Talyn nodded curtly, his wings rustling restlessly as he turned back to the squad. His muscles tensed with the effort of pretending everything was fine. It wasn't. Not with Aayla here, so close and yet so far from what he could ever allow himself to have.

He continued pushing the squad through the drills, his voice steady even as his thoughts were anything but. But the second Aayla let out a soft grunt of effort during her routine, his head snapped toward her, his body reacting instinctively. He quickly turned away, hoping no one saw how obvious it was that she had a hold on him.

He twisted his body, wings spreading out behind him as he went through a difficult manoeuvre, feeling the stretch of his muscles. But still, his gaze wandered, and his eyes lingered on Aayla.

As the squad went through the rest of their drills, Talyn kept his eyes forward, trying to ignore the magnetic pull he felt whenever she moved. His heart was betraying him, and he knew it. He wasn't supposed to care for her like this, and he wasn't supposed to let his feelings slip into the job. But his chest ached every time he caught sight of her. He had no right to those feelings, and he knew it.

Talyn stole another glance, trying to convince himself it was only out of duty. He was her Guardian, and he had to make sure she was safe. But deep down, he knew it was more than that. And he hated it. He hated that he couldn't stop himself from caring and wanted more when he wasn't allowed to.

Aayla caught him staring again, and this time, instead of looking away, she held his gaze for a fraction too long. There was something in her eyes, something she wasn't saying, but Talyn forced himself to remain stoic. Sure, he could look at her, but only because it was his job, because protecting her was all he could ever do.

He couldn't let himself cross that line.

But when her lips parted slightly, as if she were about to say something, Talyn's heart skipped a beat. He quickly turned away, his jaw clenching, reminding himself of the boundaries. He could never love her, not like that.

She was definitely off-limits.

Talyn began a solo routine, pushing himself harder to forget how his skin tingled whenever their eyes met. He focused on each movement of his arms and wings and the way his muscles stretched and contracted. He was finding it harder to pretend. He caught himself staring again and again, unable to stop. His breath hitched every time she shifted, stretched, or bent into a new form. He forced his eyes back to his squad, but it was useless. She was too much a part of him, ingrained in his thoughts.

"Talyn!" Seth's voice broke through his reverie, catching him off guard. He barely dodged a wayward blade, his reaction slower than usual. Seth smirked. "You sure you're with us today?"

Talyn shot him a glare, but it was almost impossible to hide the truth from Seth's watchful eyes. "I'm fine," he said through gritted teeth, turning sharply to refocus on the drill. But he wasn't. Not with Aayla here, not with her every move drawing him in, whether he wanted it to or not.

The squad finished their final round of exercises, each member sweating and breathless but grinning. Talyn gave a nod of approval as they straightened up and began to pack away their gear. He kept his commands short, his mind buzzing with the unresolved tension of Aayla's presence in the room.

"Good work today," he said, his voice even. "Get some rest. Same time tomorrow."

The group exchanged weary, good-natured farewells, a few offering Talyn a brief slap on the shoulder as they left. Seth lingered a moment longer than the others, giving Talyn a knowing look but saying nothing before finally stepping out.

When the last of the squad had gone, the Training Centre felt too quiet. Too still.

Talyn rubbed the back of his neck, watching Aayla still working through her routine at the far end of the room. He hesitated, then walked toward her, his footsteps echoing in the large room. As he approached, he kept his expression neutral, arms crossed casually in front of him, though his heart raced in his chest.

"So, what's your plan after this? Trying to find someone who can actually keep up with you, or just settling for my mediocre company?" he said, a crooked smile playing on his lips.

Finishing her last stretch, she turned to face him and paused, her eyes steady but unreadable. He couldn't let his gaze linger on her too long or let the feelings he had buried bubble up to the surface. Not now.

"Just finishing up here," she said, clearing her throat, her tone light and calm. "I'm thinking of going for a swim afterwards."

Talyn nodded, swallowing down the ache in his throat at the thought of her naked body. "I'll meet you there once you're done."

"I won't be long," she replied softly, a warm smile lighting up her face.

Talyn's gaze flicked away, a mix of emotions swirling inside him. "Take your time," he said, his voice barely above a whisper. "I'll be outside when you're ready."

He turned to leave, needing to put space between them before his composure faltered. As he neared the door, his steps slowed involuntarily. His hand hovered over the doorframe, and for a second, he lingered, heart pounding. He wanted to look back, to see her one last time before he left, but he didn't dare. If he turned around, he wasn't sure what his face would give away.

Instead, Talyn took a deep breath and strode through the door. The cool air of the corridor washed over him, starkly contrasting the heat building inside him.

He needed to get control of himself and his emotions before he did something that couldn't be taken back.

Chapter Thirty-Five

Aayla slipped into the pool, the cool water providing a welcome relief after the morning training session. The day had started like so many others, routine and predictable, but today, something was different. Her thoughts were scattered and unfocused. Every strike during training had felt hollow, every move sluggish. The rhythm that usually came so naturally to her was lost, slipping through her fingers.

She couldn't stop thinking about him.

Talyn. His presence. His quiet, watchful gaze. The way he seemed to always be aware of her, even in the smallest of moments. She had been so distracted that she had executed her moves with less precision than usual, the thought of him lingering at the edges of her mind. And it was enough to make her lose focus.

The sensation of the water surrounding her was soothing, the gentle flow washing away the lingering discomfort in her muscles. But even here, in the calm of the pool, she couldn't escape the restlessness inside her.

Talyn noticed, of course. He always did. He didn't say anything, just shot her a look. One that made her heart beat a little faster, one that made her feel as though he could see straight through her. And for a moment, she almost wished he would.

"Something on your mind?" he asked, his voice low, concerned yet steady, as he moved to sit beside her in the Bathing Pool.

Aayla offered him a faint smile, though it didn't quite reach her eyes. "Just tired," she replied, not meeting his gaze. She didn't trust herself to look at him too long. Not today.

He didn't press further, though she could feel the weight of his silence. It was enough for him to know something was off, and that was enough for her, for now.

Aayla swam a few laps, trying to shake the feeling of his gaze, the pull of his presence. The coolness of the water helped, but it didn't do enough to calm the storm that was quietly building inside her.

After a quick stop at the Command Centre, they took to the skies, flying wingtip to wingtip against the brilliant cityscape.

Moving in sync, they rode the same drafts, gliding effortlessly through the air. When Aayla looked over to Talyn, he glanced back with a smile that was for her alone. They didn't speak as there was no need for it. They were in perfect harmony as they dipped, weaved, and rode along the winds.

They made their way downtown to offer their help to the local police force and enjoy a morning mingling among the humans.

They had just finished lunch and were heading to a media interview when Aayla received a message that made her stomach drop.

Another potential mate was arriving on Earth.

The ship would land on an oval near Aldredth Tower, and Aayla decided to fly over to greet him as soon as he arrived, wanting to get it over with. The landing locations for ships varied each time to thwart potential attacks. Sometimes, they would only hover in the sky without ever touching down.

Beside her, Talyn turned into a rigid, unmoving statue, his breath seemingly caught in his throat as they watched the ship slowly descend.

Aayla's palms felt clammy, and anxiety churned within her, making her fidget restlessly. As the doors began to open, she took a couple of steadying breaths to calm herself.

A couple of Lazuli's she recognised stepped out of the ship, bowing in her direction before parting to make way. Behind them emerged a young Lazuil Aldredth male, his black hair contrasting with dark teal eyes and cream-coloured wings streaked with black.

When their eyes met, he paused, and Aayla felt... nothing. Releasing the breath she hadn't realised she was holding, she smiled softly and began walking toward him.

"Greetings, and welcome to Earth."

He smiled warmly and bowed as she approached. "Greetings, my Unix. My name is Bilor. It's an honour to meet you finally... even if you aren't my mate."

Laughing, Aayla glanced at Talyn, who looked thoroughly unimpressed by the joke.

"Unfortunately, not," she replied playfully. "But I hope you enjoy your visit to this planet regardless."

"The chance to be in the presence of one of our Unix is truly a great privilege." Bilor held his hand out and gestured towards a young female Aldredth standing behind him. "This is Kilea, my Charge."

The Vorax female had silvery-grey hair and pale orange eyes, with lilac-coloured wings that faded from dark to light across their length.

"It's an honour to meet you, my Unix," she said, bowing gracefully.

"I'm currently on my way to a media interview, but I'd be happy to give you a tour of the city afterwards if you'd like," Aayla said.

Talyn's teeth ground together at her words, but Bilor's grin widened at the invitation.

"That would be wonderful! Would you mind if we also observed your interview? I have not undertaken one before, and it sounds like a great learning experience."

"Of course!" Aayla mentally kicked herself for focusing so much on wanting to escape their meeting that she hadn't considered the opportunity for her people. "We should get moving if we don't want to be late."

Talyn flared out his wings in preparation but held back until Aayla lifted off. With a powerful thrust, he launched into the sky. Bilor and Kilea flew alongside Aayla while Talyn swept up and over them, his shadow a kiss against her senses.

When they arrived at Aldredth Tower, they were greeted by a female reporter who was eager to interview Bilor and Kilea as well. The interview went exceptionally well, and everyone seemed to enjoy it, even as the topic kept circling back to the distinctions between Guardians and mates.

As they were preparing to leave Aldredth Tower, Aayla's Lumina received an alert about a possible attack underway. Heart racing, she raced back to the Command Centre, where chaos reigned. The room was packed with Aldredth, their voices overlapping in urgent discussions.

Catching Martok's eye through the throng, she called out, "What's happening?"

"Three unidentified ships are inbound to Earth. They'll be here in minutes."

Her gaze snapped to the screen, displaying a frozen image of one of the ships. The markings were too blurred to discern their origin. A wave of dread washed over her as she whispered, "Is it the Yvoran?"

Martok held her gaze for a tense moment before responding, "I don't know."

Composing herself, she turned to Talyn, her voice firm despite the adrenaline coursing through her. "Get everyone on alert. We need all our resources mobilised. Equip the human security forces with ammunition that is effective against a Yvoran but keep them at a safe distance. I don't want anyone getting hurt."

With a resolute nod, Talyn vanished into the crowd as Aayla concentrated on the screens ahead of her. The tension in the room was palpable.

"It's confirmed," Daxion's voice rang out, cutting through the noise. "They are Yvoran."

As the confirmation of the Yvoran threat washed over her, Aayla felt the colour drain from her face, and a heavy weight settled in her chest. Her breath caught in her throat, and her hands trembled slightly as her fingers curled into fists, an unconscious effort to steady herself. The room around her blurred and sounds faded into a distant haze as she concentrated on the message, which brought back vivid memories from her vision.

"That's settled," Aayla replied as the floor seemed to sway beneath her. "Martok, you'll lead the attack while Talyn and I stay back to run the Command Centre."

A wave of nausea churned in her stomach at the thought of being left behind, but she steeled herself, knowing it was a sacrifice she had to make to keep Talyn safe.

The Aldredth filed out of the room as the Yvoran ship touched down in Toronto.

The Yvoran were a formidable fighting alien race with an average height of eight feet. They had robust, muscular frames covered in thick, chitinous exoskeletons that served as natural armour over their vital organs.

Their skin ranged in hues from deep crimson to dark charcoal. It was often adorned with tribal-like markings that denoted their rank and achievements in battle and glowed faintly in low light.

The Yvoran's faces were a fearsome sight, dominated by a pair of glowing, slit-pupil eyes that could see in complete darkness and across various spectrums. Their mouths were filled with sharp, serrated teeth capable of tearing through the toughest materials. Prominent mandibles extend from their jaws, used both as weapons and for intricate communication through a series of clicks and hisses.

Each Yvoran had four arms, two primary and two secondary, all ending in clawed hands capable of both delicate manipulation and brutal combat. Their limbs were extraordinarily strong, allowing them to wield their heavy weapons with ease or engage in devastating hand-to-hand combat. Their secondary arms often hold smaller blades, providing them with versatility in battle.

The Yvoran's combat tactics were as varied as they were ruthless. They were masters of guerrilla warfare, using their environment to their advantage with a cunning intelligence that belies their fearsome appearance. Their society is built around a strict martial hierarchy, with honour and prowess in combat being the highest virtues. Young Yvoran are trained from birth in the arts of war, honing their skills in individual combat and coordinated group strategies.

Luckily, the Yvorans weren't particularly technologically advanced in relation to their weaponry, as they relied too heavily on their physical strength, which Aldredth utilised to their advantage.

In battle, the Yvorans were relentless, their war cries echoing across the battlefield as they charged with unyielding ferocity. They showed no mercy to their enemies, driven by a deep-seated cultural belief that only the strongest deserve to survive.

Their primary weapon of choice was a large blade that looked like serrated chunks of black stone. The stone was a mineral mined from the Yvoran home world that acted like a poison when it pierced Aldredth flesh, making each strike far more dangerous than the physical damage inflicted by the blade.

"There's something wrong here," Talyn murmured, a deepening frown forming between his brows. "Why Toronto? There's no strategic site or population centre of significance there. We're missing something. I can feel it."

Aayla knew he was right. The answer felt like it was just beyond her reach, hidden in plain sight.

In the dimly lit Command Centre, her gaze was fixed on the array of screens displaying a different angle of the unfolding battle. Each monitor now displayed a different angle of the battlefield, a symphony of chaos slowly tipping in favour of the Aldredth.

Her posture was rigid, every muscle coiled with focus as she scrutinised the unfolding scenes. On the central screen, the Aldredth were making steady progress, their movements coordinated and precise, a testament to their rigorous training. As they pushed forward, outmanoeuvring the Yvoran, a flicker of pride stirred within her at the skill and bravery of her people.

Talyn leaned closer, his hands gripping the edge of the control panel, knuckles white with intensity. She knew that he hated the fact that they were left behind because of him. His sharp eyes darted from one screen to the next, assessing strategies, anticipating counterattacks, and issuing commands into his Lumina with a calm authority that inspired confidence in the Aldredth on the ground.

As the battle raged on, she felt confidence swell within her. The tension in her shoulders eased a fraction, though her vigilance remained sharp, knowing any slip could shift the tide. In her mind, she cycled through contingencies, ready to adjust to the slightest change in the battle's dynamics, her instincts attuned to any hint of danger that might still lurk, unaccounted for.

"Wait," Talyn murmured, narrowing his eyes. "Where's the third ship?"

Aayla's gaze darted to the screens, and she felt a chill run through her. He was right. All three ships had initially landed close together, yet now only two remained.

"I didn't see anything take off," she said, her mind racing. "How could we miss that?"

A horrified expression crossed Talyn's face, "Because it never landed, it was an illusion. See," pointing to the monitor, the third ship appeared to flicker for a fraction of a second after it had landed. "It was a projection this whole time."

"Fuck. Where's the real—"

A deafening boom rattled the entire building, cutting her off.

"It was a trick!" Talyn shouted, sword already drawn, as he punched an emergency evacuation alert into the system.

Panic surged through Aayla, and she could feel her breath quickening. "We can't engage, Talyn. If this was their plan all along, we're not prepared."

He turned to her, eyes fierce, and cupped her face with a steadying hand. "We're the only Aldredth here, Aayla. We have no choice."

She held back tears as she whispered, "Then promise me. Promise you'll protect your right side."

"Only if you promise you won't do anything stupid," he demanded, his gaze desperately scanning her face.

She opened her mouth to speak when another explosion shook the building.

Talyn grabbed her hand, pulling her from the room as they sprinted through the debris-strewn passages. Smoke thickened the air as they reached the foyer, turning it into a haze of shadows and flickering light.

Aayla gripped her sword tightly, its blade gleaming with deadly promise as they burst through the building's entrance and into the open air.

The Yvoran ship towered ominously in front of Aldredth Tower, its massive frame casting a long shadow across the street as Yvoran warriors poured out.

Aayla scanned the surroundings, quickly assessing the best route to draw the enemy away from the vulnerable civilians hidden within and around the building.

Taking a deep breath, she called out, "Yvoran!"

Her voice rang through the streets, echoing off the tall buildings. Instantly, every Yvoran's gaze snapped toward her, their fierce eyes locking on her with a deadly intensity.

Talyn nudged her shoulder. With a swift nod, they took off, pounding down the street at full speed before extending their wings and soaring into the sky with one powerful stroke. The Yvoran snarled and followed, their shouts growing louder as they gave chase, leaving the civilians out of immediate danger.

They zigzagged through the narrow streets, weaving between buildings and leading them far from the highly populated area. Every fibre of her being was attuned to the pursuit, her mind a blur of strategies and escape routes. Adrenaline pulsed through her veins, sharpening her instincts and fuelling her resolve.

They finally landed in an open park, soft grass under their feet. Turning, Aayla and Talyn faced the approaching wave of Yvoran warriors.

"Leave Earth now, or you forfeit your life," Aayla called, her voice steady, cutting through the noise.

An enormous Yvoran stepped forward, his gait slow and deliberate as he paused just a few feet from Aayla and Talyn.

"You know what?" he replied, glancing around as if unimpressed. "I don't think I will."

Talyn let out a low, menacing growl as Aayla tightened her grip on her sword. "This is your last warning," she said coldly.

The Yvoran let out a mocking laugh, raising his voice. "And walk away from the chance to capture a child Unix? Insanity! I thought your presence here was nothing more than a rumour, but here you are. The Aldredth's most valuable target, their best bargaining chip, standing here right in front of me so... vulnerable."

The Yvoran glanced at his warriors, his voice dropping into a sinister command. "Remember, bring her to me alive."

Amid the chaotic battlefield, Aayla and Talyn stood back-to-back, their swords gleaming in the harsh sunlight. The clang of metal against stone and the shouts of battle filled the air, a symphony of conflict that underscored their desperate struggle. But unlike the Yvoran around them, Aayla and Talyn still had the significant advantage of their wings.

Talyn moved with calculated precision, his wings beating powerfully as he leapt into the air after Aayla to gain a strategic height advantage.

Aayla soared gracefully above the fray. Her wings shimmered as she used her aerial agility to dart in and out of combat, striking with pinpoint precision before retreating to safety. Her blade sang as it cut through the air, a blur of steel and motion. She parried an Yvoran's attack with a deft twist of her wrist, her movements a blend of agility and strength. With a fierce cry, she spun and delivered a precise strike that felled another Yvoran.

Beside her, Talyn surveyed the battlefield, diving down with lethal speed to strike unsuspecting foes. His sword slashed through the air with deadly accuracy. Each swing was purposeful, every parry and thrust executed with a mastery that spoke of countless battles fought and won. He deflected an incoming strike with a swift, practised motion, then countered with a powerful blow that sent his opponent sprawling.

The Yvoran army surged around them, a relentless tide of aggression and violence. But they stood their ground, their swords flashing in the sunlight. Each enemy that came at them was met with a flurry of strikes and parries, their blades moving in perfect harmony. When the battle became too dense, they would take to the skies, regrouping and diving back down like bolts of lightning.

Their movements synchronised in a deadly dance both on the ground and in the air, and despite being outnumbered, they were slowly dwindling the Yvoran numbers. When Aayla was pressed, Talyn was there to fend off the attackers. They communicated through quick glances and subtle nods, their understanding born of years of fighting side by side.

Blood and dirt mingled on their skin, their breaths coming in ragged gasps, when a Yvoran blade sliced through the tip of Aayla's wing as she fought off a different counterattack.

Crying out in pain, she felt the poison spreading across the entire wing, numbing it so that it dragged like a dead weight behind her.

"Aayla, are you all right?" Talyn shouted, throwing up a protective shield before quickly assessing her wing.

I can't fly, she gasped, clutching her shoulder, terror raking through her body.

Hang on, backup is close.

Dropping his shield, they continued fighting on the ground. Even though Talyn could still fly, he would never leave her side, so her injury had grounded them both.

As the remaining Yvoran swarmed them, Aayla realised she'd been separated from Talyn in the chaos.

Time seemed to freeze as she saw Talyn surrounded, just as in her vision.

Glancing down, she noticed that they had moved off the oval and were now standing on the side of the road.

Her heart pounded in her chest as she saw several blades swinging in slow motion towards Talyn. He had twisted to defend his right just like she had warned him, but his left was completely open.

She had tried to protect him, but she had failed. Without thought, she leapt in front of the blade, using her body as a shield to protect Talyn.

The blade drove deep into her chest, puncturing her lung. It felt like her skin was on fire where the blade pierced her, as the poison seeped into her body.

Swinging her sword with every ounce of strength she had left, the Yvoran was too close to evade her strike, and his head rolled to the ground with a sickening thud.

Pain blurred her vision, and the metallic taste of blood filled her mouth. Her body gave way, and she felt herself falling backward into darkness.

Chapter Thirty-Six

Aayla's consciousness drifted between the realms of the living and the dead, the passage of time slipping away like sand through her fingers.

The rhythmic beep of a heartbeat was the first sound that penetrated the fog in her mind. It was steady, almost soothing, and a stark contrast to the confusion swirling in her thoughts. Her eyelids felt impossibly heavy, but with a concerted effort, she willed them open.

A blinding white light flooded her vision, forcing her to squint. As the ceiling above her slowly came into focus, a dull ache radiated through her body.

Definitely not dead, Aayla thought, her mind clear but groggy.

She tried to move, but her limbs felt sluggish and weak as if she had been asleep for a long time. Slowly, she turned her head towards the steady beeping of the heart monitor that had pulled her from the haze. Talyn sat in a chair beside her bed, hunched over, his gaze fixed on his hands. He looked utterly lost and broken.

Then, as if sensing her awareness, Talyn's eyes snapped to meet hers. Instantly, he was on his feet, cupping her face with trembling hands.

"Thank the stars, you're awake!" His voice, thick with relief, washed over her, grounding her in the present.

Her lips felt dry as she attempted to speak, her voice barely more than a rasp. "What happened?" she croaked.

"Despite your stupidity, we defeated the Yvoran with only minor injuries. Thankfully, no casualties," Talyn's voice was strained, his relief tempered by anger. "You've been unconscious for days. We almost lost you, but you'll be okay now. Just... take it easy."

Aayla nodded weakly, her eyes fluttering shut as she processed the information. The relief in the room was palpable, like a weight lifted from her chest. No casualties.

Soval appeared and quickly checked her vitals while Talyn stood off to the side, his posture rigid, his anger simmering beneath the surface. Sensing the tension, Soval and Aeryn excused themselves, leaving the two of them alone.

"Talyn, what's wrong?" Aayla croaked.

He stood against the wall, unmoving, arms folded tightly across his chest. He looked at the floor for a long time before meeting her eyes, the fury in his eyes unmistakable.

"You almost died. For me. What were you thinking?" he snapped.

Offended, Aayla struggled to sit up. "What was I supposed to do? Stand there and watch you die?"

"Yes!" He yelled, his anger boiling over. "I'm meant to die to protect you, not the other way around."

Aayla's eyes narrowed, her voice rising. "I won't watch you die."

"But I get to watch you die!" Talyn exhaled sharply, pacing the room in frustration before stopping in front of her. "If I die, you'd be sad. But if you die, hundreds of thousands of people—people you could have saved—will die."

Her gaze dropped to the bed, the sting of his words cutting through her. He was right. She hadn't considered the consequences of her death, how it would deprive the Aldredth of a Unix they desperately needed. There were already too few of them.

"The whole point of my life is to protect you. If that means I have to die, then so be it," Talyn said, his voice thick with resolve.

Aayla's heart clenched. "You are worth more than just being a shield for me."

"No," he growled, "That is precisely all I'm good for."

Aayla recoiled, horrified by the thought. "How can you think that?" But Talyn continued to pace the room, consumed by his turmoil.

Was it possible that, while she had been unconscious, the others had blamed him for failing her? No. She quickly dismissed the thought. Aldredth didn't place blame on each other, not like that. He would undoubtedly blame himself, and his parents would probably be displeased to hear he had failed in his duties. They followed an ancient sense of duty that she didn't agree with. Talyn had more value than anyone could determine, and to her, he was irreplaceable.

"I think you need a better Guardian," Talyn whispered, his voice barely audible.

Aayla's chest tightened, the weight of his words hitting her harder than any battle wound.

"I don't want to live in a world without you," she whispered, her voice trembling.

The words hung in the air, and Talyn stopped in his tracks. The anger in his eyes faded, replaced by a deep sadness. "And I can't live in a world without you," he replied softly, sitting on the edge of her bed and taking her hand.

Leaning forward, he kissed her forehead gently, and Aayla pulled him onto the bed, wrapping her arms around him tightly. They stayed entwined, lost in the quiet comfort of each other's presence until the soft sound of footsteps in the corridor interrupted the stillness.

"I come bearing food!" Ophelian announced cheerfully as she entered, her gaze hardening as it lingered on Talyn. "For both of you."

Aayla glanced at Talyn as he stood, noticing the gauntness in his face and the dark shadows etched beneath his eyes.

She folded her arms, frowning at him. "By the look of you, I'd say you haven't been eating or sleeping."

"I wasn't exactly in the mood," he replied with a pointed raise of his eyebrow, challenging her gaze.

Huffing in exasperation, Aayla turned to Ophelian and Rythar. "Anything important I missed?"

"Well," Rythar said, a gentle smile playing on his lips, "you had countless messages pouring in, all hoping you'd pull through. Every friendly civilisation sent its wishes for a quick recovery. Truthfully, you had every Aldredth worried sick, fearing the worst." He let out a heavy sigh. "I was terrified you might not make it."

Aayla dropped her gaze, a hint of shame in her expression. "I am truly sorry."

Rythar's smile widened. "Apology accepted, of course. Plenty has happened, but nothing that can't wait until you're fully back on your feet."

He gave a quick wink before heading out after a final check of her vitals with Soval.

Aayla savoured the meal with Talyn before they left the MedBay, stepping straight into a massive celebration. Across every planet, Aldredth rejoiced for their child Unix's recovery, and Earth was no exception. Aldredth and humans alike had gathered to celebrate.

The festivities, hosted by Aldredth Tower, stretched over three unforgettable days filled with unrestrained joy and revelry. The first day opened with a grand feast, tables laden with vibrant, sumptuous dishes beneath decorations that sparkled in every corner. Music filled the air, drawing dancers to the floor with energy that refused to fade.

As dawn broke on the second day, the celebration moved outdoors with games and activities, building excitement until music and dancing swept through the evening again. That night, a spectacular fireworks display lit up the sky. Each burst met with gasps and cheers from the Aldredth crowd.

The third day blended seamlessly into the previous ones, a tapestry of lively brunches, music, dances, and animated conversations. By dusk, the festivities wound down, leaving a gentle sense of contentment and euphoria in the air.

Exhausted yet content, Aayla and Talyn collapsed into bed, the echoes of the celebration still buzzing in their minds as if the joy of the night lingered in their very bones.

Aayla fell asleep quickly, but her mind was filled with nightmares of the Vhurl crushing her wing when she was stranded on Earth and laughing as he ground it beneath his foot. Her heart raced erratically, and she trembled through the pain until a strong, comforting presence enveloped her like a heavy blanket. Her heart rate slowed, and her soul calmed as thoughts of Talyn filled her mind.

She envisioned his deep green eyes, captivating her soul with their intensity. His smile ignited a warmth within her, tightening something deep inside. The strength of his muscular physique, a sign of the overwhelming strength of his body, and the graceful shimmer of his wings as he moved were vivid in her memory.

A small smile tugged at her lips as she dreamt about the carefree moments they had spent together on Nannuval, free from worry and lost in each other's company.

Taking a slow breath, Aayla felt safe in a warm embrace that made her heart sing. As she slowly opened her eyes, she saw Talyn's distinctive, vibrant forest-green and gold wing draped across her, its powerful muscles forming a heavy, comforting blanket.

Aayla was lying on her side, with Talyn's body pressed against her back, curving around her protectively. One of his arms was wrapped securely around her, his face nestled against the nape of her neck, and his lips brushed against the sensitive spot just behind her ear.

They often touched and embraced, but the intimacy of this position was unmistakable.

Both wore only a thin strip of underwear, their naked skin pressed together, creating an intoxicating sensation. Aayla's wings were folded behind her, trapped against Talyn's muscular chest. The feeling of his bare skin against her sensitive feathers was almost painfully pleasurable. Her wings were overwhelmed by a surge of sensations as if his skin was searing her with waves of ecstasy.

The intimacy of their embrace made her press her thighs together as a deep need throbbed inside of her.

She contemplated waking him or shifting out of his hold, guilt gnawing at her for feeling like she was betraying his trust. But instead, she inhaled his intoxicating scent, biting back a moan of pleasure.

Hesitantly, she lifted her fingers and gently stroked the edge of Talyn's primary feathers. They felt warm and buttery soft beneath her fingertips. The touch sent a jolt of ecstasy up her arm.

Though she knew she shouldn't have done it—such intimate caresses were reserved for mates alone—her hand moved of its own accord, unable to resist the urge.

Talyn moaned softly, tightening his grip around her, his face nuzzling against her neck, kissing her skin lightly. He languidly thrust his hips against her, and a wave of desire crashed over her, thick and intoxicating, making it hard to breathe. She pressed her thighs tighter together, biting her cheek to suppress a moan as heat pooled between her legs.

Talyn froze, his body stiffening behind her. A moment later, the warmth of his presence vanished, replaced by the cold bite of the air that chilled her to the bone. Shifting, she sat up to face him and sucked in a breath.

Talyn's eyes were ablaze with an intense, unyielding hunger. His breathing was deep and erratic, and his gaze pinned her like a predator sizing up its prey.

Swallowing hard, she tugged the sheets up to cover her body. "Talyn?"

His voice emerged as a deep, guttural sound, strained as if he had to drag the words out. "I'm sorry, Aayla. Please forgive me."

He jumped off the bed, hastily pulling on his pants and snatching his shirt as he strode toward the door.

"Wait, where are you going?"

"I think it's best if I leave." He said without a backwards glance.

Aayla shifted, drawing her legs up against her chest, her wings spreading out behind her. "Come back to bed." It was a soft plea.

Pausing at the door, his shirt clutched in his hand, he slowly turned to look at her. His eyes still burned with fire as his wings snapped open behind him, glowing with such power that it made her eyes water. He turned his body toward her, and she bit her lip, captivated by his sculptured muscles as he prowled toward her with lethal focus.

Her heart raced as she met his gaze, feeling the weight of his deep hunger reflected in his eyes. Sucking in a deep breath, she shivered under his intense scrutiny.

Talyn halted, his jaw clenching and closed his eyes as he took a deep, steadying breath. Abruptly, he turned to leave. "I need to leave before I do something that we'll both regret. I'll be in the Training Centre if you need me," he said, his voice taut.

CHAPTER THIRTY-SEVEN

The following day, Aayla stirred awake to find the bed beside her empty, the cool sheets a stark contrast to the warmth of the night before. A soft sigh escaped her lips as she sat up, the quiet of the room enveloping her. Without hesitation, she made her way to the Training Centre, knowing exactly where to find Talyn.

There he was, shirtless, his body slumped with exhaustion. His movements were slow, and the lines of fatigue on his face were more pronounced than ever. He had clearly pushed himself through the night.

Without saying a word, Aayla stepped into the room and silently opened her arms, her heart aching for him. Talyn looked up, his eyes momentarily meeting hers, and without hesitation, he walked into her embrace. She held him tightly, feeling the weight of his weariness as he buried his face in her shoulder. The world outside seemed to disappear in that moment, and for a brief second, all that mattered was the comfort they found in each other's presence.

"I'm sorry for my behaviour last night." He whispered.

"There's nothing to apologise for," Aayla replied gently, her voice full of warmth. "I was just as caught up in the moment as you were. But, if we can agree to forget it ever happened, I think it's time for breakfast. We've got a busy day ahead of us."

Talyn nodded, his tension easing slightly as he followed her out of the Training Centre. They walked side by side, the silence between them comfortable, though filled with the unspoken understanding of everything that had passed between them.

As they made their way toward the Dining Hall, the soft clatter of footsteps echoed down the corridor. Rune and Ceeda spotted them from a distance, and with smiles lighting up their faces, they hurried over.

When they reached Aayla, Rune beamed and bowed with deep respect, his enthusiasm impossible to contain. "Good morning, Aayla!" he greeted, practically bouncing on his feet. "I've got some exciting news for you. Another potential mate has just arrived! I was on my way down to greet them. Would you like to come with me?"

Ceeda, standing beside him, gave a small, knowing smile, her eyes twinkling with curiosity. "It seems like today might be even more eventful than we thought," she said lightly.

A sudden wave of unease washed over Aayla, and her appetite seemed to vanish with it. She forced a smile, though it felt thin and unconvincing, and nodded. "Of course. After you."

Rune paused, noticing the shift in her demeanour, his brow furrowing in confusion at the subtle change in her. He studied her for a moment, but before he could say anything, Ceeda gave him a gentle nudge, silently urging him to keep moving.

Talyn remained by her side, his silence thick with tension. Aayla sensed his anxiety and a strange, unspoken weight that pressed between them. As they neared the foyer, she offered him a reassuring smile, but his gaze stayed fixed ahead, his expression unreadable. A knot twisted in her stomach, and she couldn't shake the feeling that he was wrestling with something he wouldn't share.

They paused in the foyer, waiting for the visitors to arrive. Aayla stood as still as she could, fighting the restless energy that urged her to fidget. It was almost unbearable, but she forced herself to remain calm.

"They're here!" Rune exclaimed, his excitement palpable.

Aayla's gaze snapped to the door just as a young Lazuil Aldredth stepped inside. He smiled broadly, and his dark red wings, edged with gold, caught the light as he moved. His hair was a striking shade of blond, and his light copper-coloured eyes gleamed with warmth.

Aayla's heart skipped a beat at the sight of him.

It was Giorgieon. Her childhood friend. The one person who had always been there for her before Talyn had entered her life. Though they had never met in person, their bond had been forged through endless hours of conversation, even long after she was paired with Talyn. Giorgieon had been her closest friend, a constant in her world. When she was younger, the reality of being a Unix felt isolating at times, but Giorgieon was always there for her.

He was powerful, a young Lazuil who travelled often, but despite his busy life, their friendship had always been a cherished constant. They had shared so much, and their connection had never been weakened by distance or time.

Giorgieon's smile grew when he saw her, and Aayla's heart ached with the sudden flood of emotions. It was a feeling she hadn't realised she'd missed so much.

Giorgieon threw his arms open wide. "Aayla!" he exclaimed, his voice filled with excitement.

She ran to him without hesitation, enveloping him in a tight hug. "Giorgieon, is that really you? I can't believe it! After all this time, we finally get to meet in person!"

Her smile widened, but when she glanced at Talyn, her heart froze. The shock and raw heartbreak in his eyes were impossible to ignore. She suddenly realised how it must have looked, her running straight into the arms of another potential mate upon first meeting.

Stepping back quickly, she created some distance between herself and Giorgieon, then turned to Talyn. "Talyn, come meet my old friend, Giorgieon."

Talyn's gaze flicked between her and Giorgieon, his expression unreadable. Aayla noticed how his eyes lingered on her face, registering the emphasis she had placed on the word "friend."

Slowly, Talyn walked over, his steps measured, his eyes never leaving her. She reached out, looping her arm through his. Turning to Giorgieon, she introduced him with a soft smile. "Giorgieon, this is my Guardian, Talyn."

Giorgieon's confusion was evident. It wasn't typical for Charges to introduce their Guardians, let alone pull them into casual conversations. He raised an eyebrow. "Guardian."

Talyn narrowed his eyes at both the short tone Giorgieon had used and the use of his position over name as a subtle reminder that he didn't belong in this conversation. He narrowed his eyes, his response clipped. "Lazuil."

The two men glared at each other, eyes narrowed, jaws clenched, and palpable tension crackled in the air between them.

"Okay..." Aayla murmured, glancing uneasily between them, uncertain of the tension simmering in the air.

Turning back to Giorgieon, she offered a soft smile. "How long are you here?"

Giorgieon's gaze warmed as he looked at her. "Not long, unfortunately. I'll have to leave tomorrow."

"Tomorrow?" Aayla's heart sank. "That's so soon."

"I'm sorry." Giorgieon sighed, regret flickering across his face. "I'm needed on Pelixaois to meet my new Charge. I only detoured quickly to see you and ensure you were all right. But if you'd like, I could return in a few weeks and stay as long as you want."

She nodded, appreciating the gesture, even as she tried to hide her disappointment.

Giorgieon's Charge had recently found her mate, and under normal circumstances, he would have been assigned to the unpaired Charge. However, the available unpaired Charge was an Emba who would spend most of her time on peaceful planets, while Giorgieon, as a Lazuil, needed to gain experience in dangerous territories. Thus, an unusual decision was made. Rather than pair him with the Emba, he would be assigned to a powerful Aurra whose Guardian had also found his mate that same day.

"At least you're here now," she said, her smile brightening as she pushed the disappointment aside. "Would you like to join us for breakfast?"

"I'd love that," he replied warmly, his gaze steady and genuine.

As they headed toward the staircase, Giorgieon walked on her right while Talyn stayed so close on her left that their wings occasionally brushed against each other.

Giorgieon and Aayla reminisced over childhood memories with boisterous laughter. But every so often, Giorgieon would cast a pointed glare at Talyn.

"Tell me," Giorgieon said, his tone dripping with challenge, "does your Guardian always forget his place?"

Talyn's eyes narrowed as he met Giorgieon's gaze. "My place is by her side," he growled. "Yours is on Pelixaois. Or did you forget where you belong?"

"Enough!" Aayla's voice rang out as Giorgieon opened his mouth to retort. "I don't know what's gotten into you two, but knock it off. I don't like it."

Giorgieon bowed smoothly, his expression softening. "Apologies, my Unix."

In the Dining Hall, Aayla and Giorgieon quickly fell back into their easy rapport, sharing stories and laughter that lasted for hours and drew the attention of others around them.

Talyn, however, took an unexpected seat beside her, breaking his usual protocol of positioning himself along the edge of the room. She shot him a questioning look, surprised by his choice, but he either didn't notice or chose to ignore it. While Aayla and Giorgieon laughed, Talyn sat stoically at her side, his expression unreadable as he watched her.

As breakfast wound down, Giorgieon leaned forward with a grin. "Where to next?"

Talyn reached over, tucking a loose strand of Aayla's hair behind her ear before leaning in to press a slow, lingering kiss to her neck. *How about we take a flight while Rune and Ceeda give Giorgieon a tour?*

Be nice, she said with a smile, catching Talyn's gaze in a shared moment that lingered until Giorgieon cleared his throat pointedly.

Blushing, Aayla straightened up. "Sorry. Let's all go for a tour of the city."

"I'd love to," he smiled softly before turning to Talyn, "You can leave your Guardian here."

Talyn's expression hardened as he leaned forward across the table. "Watch your mouth unless you want me to shut it for you."

Giorgieon shot to his feet, slamming his palms on the table. "You'd do well to learn some respect, or I'll be happy to teach it."

"Enough!" Aayla's voice rang out, cutting through the tension. "What is going on with you two?"

They continued to stare each other down until she shook her head, exasperated. "Honestly, I expected better from both of you."

Giorgieon's expression softened as he turned to her, offering his arm. "Apologies. Shall we?"

Looping her arm through his, Aayla pretended not to notice the seething glare he sent over his shoulder at Talyn.

The rest of the morning passed in laughter and banter, with only minimal taunting.

They roamed the bustling streets of New York City and eagerly explored iconic landmarks like the Statue of Liberty, Times Square, and Central Park, taking in the city's dazzling lights and energetic atmosphere. As they marvelled at towering skyscrapers and flew low through the streets, they stopped to mingle enthusiastically with the curious locals, exchanging stories of their home planets and enjoying the diverse food stalls. The presence of a new Aldredth brought an extra spark of excitement to the city as New Yorkers embraced the new visitor with a blend of fascination and hospitality.

However, their morning of exploration was cut short when a sudden alert on their Lumina called them back to Aldredth Tower. An imminent attack was threatening a planet under Aldredth's protection, and they were needed at the Command Centre for an urgent briefing session.

"Thank you for such a wonderful morning, Aayla," Giorgieon said, his tone sincere. "I couldn't have asked for better company."

"I can think of an improvement," Talyn muttered under his breath.

Giorgieon shot a sharp glare at him but then turned back to Aayla with a smile. "Why haven't we done this before?" he mused, gently brushing his fingers against her cheek.

Before she could respond, Talyn's sword flashed in a blur, its flat edge driving Giorgieon back with controlled force. In the same breath, the blade hovered at Giorgieon's throat. His warning was clear.

"Keep your hands off her," Talyn growled.

"How dare you!" Giorgieon shouted in outrage.

"Enough!" Aayla's voice rang out, her anger reaching a boiling point. "I'm done. The way you two are treating each other is completely unacceptable. If you can't speak respectfully, then don't speak at all. I won't stand for this kind of rudeness, and I am not some object for you two to fight over!"

She turned to Giorgieon, fury in her eyes. "How dare you touch me without permission?"

Spinning to Talyn, whose smug expression only fuelled her frustration, she continued, "And you know how important Giorgieon's friendship is to me. Yet you persist in arguing with him over nothing, knowing it only causes me pain. If you force me to choose between the two of you, of course I'll choose you." Swallowing hard, her voice barely above a whisper, she said, "But right now, I need you to leave."

Talyn looked shocked, and his confusion was evident on his face.

She took a steadying breath and cupped his face gently, softening her tone just enough. "Giorgieon is only here for a few more hours, and I don't want to spend them listening to you two argue. I need to attend this briefing, and Giorgieon will be there to keep me safe. Please, go and do something else. I'll catch up with you later."

Despite his crushed expression, Talyn forced a faint, strained smile. "Of course. I'll see you later."

Aayla turned on her heel, walking briskly toward the Command Centre. But just before she entered, she heard Giorgieon's voice, laced with a taunting edge.

"Don't worry," he whispered, "I'll keep her safe."

CHAPTER THIRTY-EIGHT

Talyn was seething. How Giorgieon acted like Aayla belonged to him made Talyn want to punch him in the face.

He had come to the Training Centre hoping to burn off some of the frustration, but hours of relentless training had only left him breathless and no closer to feeling any better.

Seth approached, rolling his shoulders as he started his warm-up stretches beside him.

"I heard what happened," Seth said, a mischievous glint in his eye. "Want me to tase him? I'm sure I could accidentally mistake him for an enemy." He shrugged casually with a small smile.

Talyn let out a surprised laugh, rubbing his hand over his face. "Thanks, I needed that," he admitted, the tension easing a little in his chest.

Glancing at the clock, he made a snap decision. He would go check in at the Command Centre and see how things were unfolding.

Talyn made his way slowly there, pausing to lean against the doorframe as he peeked inside. The conversation was still in full swing, with the maps and screens alight with activity, and it was clear they'd be in there for a while. With a deflated sigh, he turned to leave when he heard quiet footsteps behind him.

"Talyn, wait."

Turning, he straightened when he saw Giorgieon standing in front of him with arms crossed and a serious expression on his face.

"What can I do for you, Giorgieon?"

"I wanted to talk," Giorgieon said, glancing around to ensure they were alone before stepping closer. "I don't know what your problem with me is, but I'll tell you what my problem with you is. It's the way you treat Aayla like she's your mate, and the fact that you're a danger to her."

Talyn's chest tightened, his instinct to defend himself rising, "I don't—" But before he could finish, Giorgieon raised a hand, cutting him off.

"Stop. Let me finish. The reason I came here was because I heard about how she almost died protecting you. How messed up is that? It's your job as Guardian to protect her, and if you can't do that, if you're putting her in situations where she risks her life to save you, you need to step down. For her sake. Because the difference between you and me is that everything I do is in her best interest, while you make decisions based on your own wants."

"That's not true," Talyn said quietly.

Giorgieon's voice grew more intense. "Tell me I'm wrong. Tell me I'm wrong, and she hasn't been in danger because of you. Tell me that wasn't the only time she almost died because of your decisions."

Talyn swallowed hard, the weight of guilt crashing over him. Giorgieon was right. It was the very thought that had been gnawing at him since Aayla had been injured.

"I get it," Giorgieon continued, his tone softening slightly. "I know what it's like to be around her. It feels incredible being around a Unix. I don't blame you for wanting to keep her all to yourself. But the fact is, you're not her mate. I don't even know if I am. I might be, I might not. And I don't think Aayla knows either because her mind is so wrapped up in you that she can't see past that to figure out how she feels about someone else."

Talyn shook his head as he looked back up at Giorgieon. "You're wrong. You know the moment you find your mate. If you're unsure, then the answer's no."

Giorgieon stepped closer, his voice firm. "How would you know? Look, the point is that your presence is dangerous to her. If you truly loved her, you'd step back and let someone else protect her."

The words cut through him, raw and piercing. Talyn tried to find something to say, some defence, but the words wouldn't come. He stood frozen, the weight of Giorgieon's words pressing down on him like a heavy, immovable stone.

After a long pause, Giorgieon turned without another word and walked back into the Command Centre.

Talyn stood in the corridor for a long time, staring at the floor, the silence swallowing him whole. His mind raced, but no answers came.

"Talyn, are you okay?" Jaxion asked, his voice full of concern.

Talyn looked up, realising Jaxion and Kythera had just emerged from the Command Centre. That meant Aayla wouldn't be far behind them. He needed to get out of there before she saw him.

"I'm fine," he replied quickly, though the words felt hollow.

Without another word, he turned and headed for the roof garden, needing space, needing to breathe. He stopped at the edge, gazing out over the bustling city below, his mind a whirlwind.

As the hours passed, Giorgieon's words echoed in his ears, and he knew with painful clarity that he was right.

He should have stepped back long ago. He should have left a thousand times over. He had no place in Aayla's life like this. He'd crossed so many lines already, from longing for something that wasn't his to wishing—irrationally, shamefully—that she wouldn't find a mate so she could stay with him. It was all wrong. He felt the weight of his selfishness, the bitterness that had been growing with each passing day.

The things he thought about her ashamed him, and he felt unjustified anger every time a potential mate looked at her. Now, the fact that he was putting her in danger was a step too far. He was supposed to protect her, yet he only put her in danger. The thought was unbearable. Aayla deserved someone stronger, someone who could give her the protection and peace she needed.

Not him.

He loved her too much to keep failing her. That realisation twisted his insides.

He took a deep breath, squared his shoulders, and walked toward the Command Centre, his footsteps heavy. By the time he arrived, only Martok and Skyla were left in the room, and the buzz of the earlier meeting was gone.

"Martok... I need to talk to you," Talyn said, his voice trembling slightly despite his efforts to sound steady.

Martok looked up, concern flickering across his face. "Of course, Talyn. What's going on?"

Talyn paused, a cold weight settling in his chest. Taking a shaky breath, he struggled to get the words out. "I need to... step down as Aayla's Guardian."

Skyla gasped, her expression one of disbelief. She stepped forward quickly, her hands reaching out to cup his face. "Why? What's wrong?"

"I'm not well," Talyn admitted, his voice strained. "I think I need to return to Nannuval for a while, for a Mir'ka. Aayla needs a stronger Guardian than I can be. I recommend

Giorgieon, at least temporarily or permanently, if that's what she wants."

The words tasted like ash in his mouth. His hands trembled uncontrollably. The weight of the decision crashed over him, but he knew it was the right thing to do.

Martok and Skyla exchanged a look, both troubled by his words. "Is there anything we can do to help?" Martok asked, his voice quiet.

Talyn shook his head. "No. I need to speak to Aayla. After that, I'll leave right away."

They both nodded, but there was no mistaking the concern in their eyes. As Talyn stepped out of the room, the hallway felt suffocating. He leaned against the cold wall, his vision blurring, and for a moment, he could hardly breathe. His heart was torn in two, but he knew this was the only way forward.

He gritted his teeth, pushing the pain down, and walked away, the weight of his decision heavy on his shoulders.

He found Aayla in the Dining Hall, surrounded by the others. The moment she spotted him, her face lit up, and for a fleeting second, it almost shattered his resolve.

She always looked at him with such quiet admiration, like he was someone deserving of her affection. Her eyes, full of warmth and depth, stirred feelings in him that he had tried so hard to bury. Feelings he couldn't deny, no matter how hard he tried to pretend they didn't exist.

Watching her walk over to him, the way her body swayed gracefully made his heart beat faster.

"There you are!" she exclaimed, her voice full of genuine relief. "Where did you go? I was looking for you."

He inhaled sharply, his chest tightening. "I... needed some time to think." He turned his face away, afraid to let her see the turmoil in his eyes. "There's something I need to tell you."

Aayla glanced over her shoulder as the other Aldredth began to leave the room. "Can it wait? We're heading back to the Command Centre now. The situation has taken a turn for the worse."

"It can't wait," he said, his voice coming out sharper than he intended. She stopped in her tracks, her eyes widening in shock as she studied his face. His pulse hammered in his ears as he forced himself to speak the words he had been dreading. "I've asked to resign as your Guardian. Effective immediately."

Aayla's face drained of colour. She stood frozen, her mouth slightly parted in disbelief, unable to process what he had just said.

"Why?" Her voice cracked, desperate. "Is it because of what happened before? I'm sorry, I— You can't leave me. You can't..."

"No, Aayla," he interjected, running a hand through his hair, frustration clawing at him. "It's not because of what you think. It's me. There's something wrong with me. My presence is putting you in danger. You need a new Guardian. A stronger Guardian than me."

"I don't understand..." Her voice trembled, and she reached out to grasp his arms, her fingers tightening around him as if trying to hold him there. "If there's something wrong, I can help you. You've never put me in danger, Talyn. I don't understand any of this."

"I'm not..." His words faltered, and he swallowed hard. He could feel his control slipping. "You're not safe with me."

"That's not true!" Aayla's voice was fierce, her eyes wide with disbelief. She shook her head as if trying to will him to take back the words.

"It is," he said, his voice cracking. He looked down, unable to meet her gaze. "Giorgieon was right. You've almost died because of me. More than once."

Aayla's expression shifted to confusion, her brow furrowing. "Wait... What did Giorgieon say?"

"Nothing I haven't already been thinking for a long time," Talyn admitted, the weight of it all pressing down on him. He felt hollow, defeated.

Just then, Aayla's Lumina buzzed. She glanced down at it, frowning at the message.

Talyn's hand, trembling, reached up to gently caress her cheek, a quiet goodbye. "You need to go."

Aayla hesitated, her gaze lingering on him for a moment longer, her heart torn. "Promise me you'll be here when this is over," she said, her voice thick with emotion. "We're not done talking. Not yet."

He leaned forward and kissed her forehead, his lips lingering far longer than he should have, his heart aching with every second. "I promise. I won't leave until we've had a chance to talk. But you can't change my mind, Aayla."

As her Lumina buzzed again, her frown deepened. She glanced at him one last time, but the urgency in her expression pushed her to hurry away, leaving him standing there, hollow and alone.

CHAPTER THIRTY-NINE

Aayla was so distracted by Talyn's announcement that she barely registered anything being said around her.

"Aayla?"

Turning toward Daxion, she realised he was waiting for her response.

"I'm sorry, what was the question?"

Daxion repeated himself, a faint frown forming as he noted her distraction. She tried to refocus on the meeting, but her thoughts kept drifting back to Talyn.

They spent hours in the Command Centre discussing the aftermath of an attack on a friendly planet, which had led to mass injuries and the kidnapping of two Aldredth. They had allocated all their resources to finding the pair and eventually tracked them down to an adjoining planet. The reconnaissance team faced heavy resistance, but eventually, they rescued the captive Aldredth.

As the meeting drew to a close, Aayla hurried to the door, hoping to find Talyn, but the corridor was empty. A quick check of her Lumina showed that he had just started a regular training session with the human security force. Sighing, she knew it would be a couple of hours before he was finished, and she didn't want to disturb him.

Giorgieon walked up beside her and paused. "Is everything okay?"

Staring at the floor, she struggled to put her emotions into words. "Talyn doesn't want to be my Guardian. What did you say to him?"

"I... I think it would be better to talk somewhere more private."

He led her to an exterior balcony, and she shivered slightly as the cold air hit her skin. Giorgieon stood at the balustrade, gazing over the city as the golden glow of sunset bathed everything in its light.

"He told you about our conversation?"

"No," she rubbed her chest, trying to soothe the ache there. "He told me he was resigning as my Guardian and said you were right."

"Ah." Giorgieon watched the city for a moment before turning back to her. "I told him that his presence puts you in danger, and if he truly loves you, he should want better for you."

Aayla felt a surge of conflicting emotions. She wanted to feel anger and rage towards him for driving Talyn away, but she knew he was only concerned for her. It was a decision Talyn made of his own free will and one he wouldn't have made if he disagreed with it. That was what hurt the most.

"There is no better for me than him," she said, her voice thick with emotion, before turning back toward the sunset.

"Maybe," Giorgieon shrugged. "But something is wrong here. I just can't put my finger on it."

Wrong? That was precisely what Talyn had said that something was wrong with him. And what about her? For years, she had buried her feelings for Talyn, pretending everything was normal. But in the end, it looked like it was about to come out anyway.

"I'm also not sure if his relationship with you is hindering you from finding a mate."

The words hit her like a physical blow, and she turned to look at him, shocked. "How?"

"I don't know," Giorgieon exhaled deeply. "I was wondering if his presence might be distracting you somehow. Honestly, I think I'm just really disappointed that you're not my mate. It's not because I wanted to mate with a Unix, but because I was genuinely looking forward to finding that connection, the one everyone talks about. I'm sure you understand that," he added, managing a wry smile.

Grinning tightly, Aayla turned back to the sunset, now streaked with red. "Of course," she said, the words heavy with a lie that seemed to pile onto the growing stack of untruths in her life.

"Although, I'm still not convinced you're not my mate," Giorgieon continued with a hint of uncertainty in his voice. "I feel more connected to you than I've felt with anyone else. But you're a Unix, so it's impossible not to feel drawn to you like a moth to a flame. I guess there's one way we could check for sure. We could always kiss?"

"Yeah," it was true that in rare circumstances, some potential mates had been known to kiss one another to test if they had a mating bond. However, she always felt that if you needed to test it, then the answer was a resounding no.

Lost in thought, she barely registered Giorgieon stepping closer to her. Before she could react, he gently grabbed her chin, turned her head toward him, and pressed his lips softly against hers.

The moment his lips touched her, Aayla recoiled internally, a wave of revulsion surging through her. Her body tensed in shock, and her mind raced with disbelief. Without thinking, she used her energy to push him away with force, sending him crashing painfully to the ground.

Feeling a deep sense of violation and anger rising within her, tears welling up in her eyes as she breathed heavily and raised her sword in his direction.

Giorgieon landed heavily on his back, sliding a small distance before he clutched his chest where she had struck him. "I'm sorry," he choked.

"How dare you!" she cried, her voice shaking with raw emotion.

"I'm sorry," he said again, sitting up carefully. "I thought you agreed to it."

Aayla backed away, her arms trembling. She rubbed her lips feverishly with her hand, trying to erase the feeling of his touch. "Never! No. No, no, no."

As Giorgieon started to rise, Aayla backed away even further until she hit the wall behind her.

"B—but I asked if we should kiss, and you said yeah?"

"I said yes as in it's something that could be done, not something that I wanted to do!" She was shaking, her voice a mixture of panic and disgust.

Realisation flickered across his face, followed by horror. "I'm so sorry, I didn't mean to—"

As he took a small step towards her, panic set in. With a sudden burst of speed, she soared into the sky, becoming a mere blur as she flew away rapidly, leaving only a gust of wind in her wake.

She wanted to fly far away until her wings ached, and she could take no more, but she circled the block and quickly returned to the roof garden, where she landed silently, unobserved. It would be incredibly idiotic to fly off on her own without a Guardian of any description. The gift of Unix blood was one she could not risk lightly. That was her burden to carry.

Tears started to fall, and she felt sick to her stomach. She was completely confused. Why was she reacting so intensely to something so minor? Why had she responded like someone already mated when she wasn't? Why did heavy tears now fall?

He had asked her and thought she had agreed. It was all just a misunderstanding, a simple mistake.

Still trembling, she paced across the roof as guilt settled over her. She felt as if she'd let someone down.

Eventually, she lay down on the ground, staring at the vast night sky, the cold air biting her skin. She felt adrift, untethered. One thing was clear, something had to change. Things had been shifting, changing in her. Was she the reason Talyn was unwell?

Time slipped by unnoticed as she wrestled with her thoughts, unable to find the strength to go inside and face what she had left behind. She wouldn't keep Talyn with her against his will, but she wasn't sure how she could live without him by her side.

Her thoughts spiralled further into confusion until her Lumina beeped, breaking through the haze. An Aldredth had been critically injured and required her immediate assistance.

Her heart froze. Which Aldredth?

Chapter Forty

Talyn finished the training session with the humans, but the physical exertion didn't ease the weight pressing on his chest. He had been thoroughly distracted throughout, unable to focus, and he couldn't bring himself to tell anyone that this would be his last session. Not yet.

"Talyn?"

He turned and saw Seth standing behind him, his brow furrowed in concern. "Is everything okay?"

"Sorry," Talyn replied, forcing a half-smile. "Just a little distracted."

Seth didn't look convinced. He took a step closer, studying Talyn's face. "Is there anything I can do to help... or anything?"

He really liked Seth.

"I appreciate your concern," he said. "I hope I wasn't too distracted during training."

"No, not at all," Seth replied, but his gaze remained sharp. "But I can tell something's... off."

Talyn exhaled deeply, running his hand through his hair in frustration. "Do you ever feel alone, even when you're surrounded by people?"

Seth's expression softened. "Yeah, I get that. We all do, sometimes." He smiled reassuringly. "You know, because you look like me, I forget that you'll live a much longer life, and you're only a child. Or is it a baby?"

His lips curved into a small smile. "Yes, I'm barely a bade out of arms. Aldredth look upon me like you would look upon a 4-year-old human child in dress up. I might be wearing the right clothes, but I still have a lot to learn. Normally, an Aldredth of my age would never be given a position of such power so early, but it is a heavy burden that every Unix carries, and I am just trying to help. Although, at the moment, I don't feel like I'm helping very much."

"You're helping me. Isn't that what matters most?" Seth gave him a wry grin. "Maybe I should stop using big words if you're only four."

Talyn laughed aloud, smiling widely at Seth. "How you're still single is a mystery to me."

Seth chuckled. "Me too!" His voice softened. "Do you miss your planet?"

Looking up at the roof, he tried to think over the question. "That's a hard one to answer. I miss Nannuval every single day. I yearn to go back there. But I feel joy visiting new worlds, being in new places, and helping people. It's why I chose to come here instead of staying on Nannuval. Just because I love being on Nannuval doesn't mean I can't also love being on other planets."

Talyn hesitated, his gaze distant. "It looks like I might be returning to Nannuval soon. Alone. I don't know when... or if I'll be back."

Seth drew in a slow, measured breath as sorrow etched in his features. "No matter what happens, I hope you'll always consider Earth a second home. One you're always welcome on, and I'm so glad to have had the opportunity to meet you and get to know you."

Talyn clasped Seth's arm warmly. "Thank you. I'm truly blessed to call you my friend."

With a nod and a small smile, they parted ways, and Talyn made his way to the Command Centre. Peaking in, he noticed a flurry of activity, but Aayla was absent, so he slowly wandered up to their private quarters in search of her, dreading the conversation to come.

Walking into their quarters, Talyn noticed Aayla wasn't there either. A frown creased his brow as he glanced at his Lumina, only to see that she appeared offline as if she had turned her tracking off. An uneasy knot tightened in his stomach.

He decided to head back to the Command Centre and check out what was going on when he noticed Giorgieon's locator was currently located outside the front entrance of Aldreth Tower.

Talyn moved quickly, his pace quickening with each step. As he entered the foyer, Giorgieon spotted him and jogged over, looking unusually tense.

"Talyn, have you seen Aayla?" Giorgieon asked, rubbing the back of his neck, worry clear on his face.

"What? Isn't she with you?" Talyn asked, his voice edged with confusion.

"No," Giorgieon hesitated, glancing around the foyer nervously. "She left, and I can't find her. I was going upstairs to check if they'd heard anything. If you'll excuse me..."

Giorgieon turned to leave, and Talyn forcefully grabbed his arm.

"What do you mean she left?" Talyn growled, his voice low and dangerous. "She wouldn't just leave. What did you do?"

Giorgieon took a step back, guilt flickering across his features. "I... I offended her, and she left."

A deep growl rumbled in Talyn's chest, and he took a few steps forward as Giorgieon continued backing up.

"It was a misunderstanding, I promise." Giorgieon insisted, his voice wavering. "I didn't mean to hurt her."

Talyn's patience snapped. "What did you do!" he bellowed, his voice a guttural roar that shook the air between them.

Giorgieon froze, his face draining of colour as he raised his hands. "It was an accident, I swear. I thought she said yes."

"Tell me!" Talyn growled, his voice dark with fury, as his hands clenched. It was then he realised he was holding his sword. He didn't remember drawing it, didn't know how long it had been in his grip. But in that moment, he was so focused on Giorgieon that the knowledge didn't concern him.

"I—I kissed her," Giorgieon stammered nervously. He continued to say something else, but Talyn didn't hear the words. He didn't hear any sounds other than a loud ringing in his ears.

All thought and logic left his mind, leaving nothing but a burning hot rage as he struck Giorgieon, knocking him to the ground.

His fury was unrelenting as he straddled Giorgieon and continued to rain down a barrage of punches. Each strike was delivered with a force that resonated through his knuckles, driven by a primal instinct he didn't understand.

His vision had gone nearly completely white, and he couldn't hear anything, but his body screamed for him to kill Giorgieon.

Despite the onslaught, Giorgieon did not fight back. Instead, he raised his arms in a futile attempt to shield his face and head from the relentless blows that now had them both covered in Giorgieon's blood.

The sound of his loud roar and the dull thud of his fists against Giorgieon's flesh filled his ears, drowning out any rational thought or mercy. It became his entire world until he felt hands grabbing at him. He fought against them, pushing them off violently until the grip tightened, pulling him back.

In a moment of blind fury, Talyn plunged his sword deep into Giorgieon's chest. The deep growl that erupted from his chest shook his entire frame.

More hands grabbed him, pulling him away from the bleeding form beneath him and shoving him into a nearby room. The door slammed shut behind him, and he turned to see several Aldredth blocking the door, their swords drawn but not raised. They stared at him—some with shock, others with wariness. But all of them were keeping their distance.

Yelling out in anger, Talyn paced the room, his chest rising and falling erratically as he breathed heavily. Every instinct in his body screamed for him to return and finish what he'd started, to kill Giorgieon. He just couldn't seem to catch his breath.

Pausing by a table in the centre of the room, he slammed his palms down, cracking the wood.

Breathing heavily, he looked at his left hand and noticed how it gleamed in the light.

Time slowly ticked by, and Talyn couldn't tear his eyes off his hand. As his breathing started to slow, his heart skipped a beat as colour returned to his vision and he saw the crimson stains smeared across his trembling hand.

His eyes widened in shock, his breath hitching as he struggled to process the sight of the blood.

Standing up, he turned his hand over and noticed how both sides were drenched in blood. Feeling a cold dread settle in the pit of his stomach, he turned to look at the sword in his right hand, and his eyes widened in horror as he noticed the warm, sticky blood smeared across the blade.

A sickening realisation hit him. He had stabbed Giorgieon.

The sword suddenly felt impossibly heavy, its weight unbearable. With a horrified gasp, he let it slip from his grasp, clattering to the ground with a metallic thud that seemed to echo in the large room.

His breath caught in his throat, and he felt a wave of nausea wash over him. His mind raced, replaying the moment in slow motion, unable to comprehend the violence that had just unfolded at his hands. His heart pounded in his ears, and nausea churned in his gut. He couldn't understand what he had done.

He lifted his eyes, meeting the gaze of the Aldredth standing in the doorway. Their faces were filled with concern, confusion, and alarm, but there was no anger.

"What have I done?" he whispered, his voice trembling as the full weight of his actions sank in.

Chapter Forty-One

Aayla descended swiftly from the balcony, landing at the building's entrance, and hurried inside. A cluster of Aldredth was gathered around someone lying on the floor. Her heart pounding, she pushed through the group, coming to an abrupt stop as she took in the scene.

Giorgieon lay on his back, blood soaking through his clothes, his face pale. Graca was pressing down on a deep chest wound while Loxian, kneeling beside him, had already begun a transfusion. But the blood was pouring out of Giorgieon as fast as it flowed in.

Aayla froze, momentarily paralysed. The harsh reality of the scene struck her, but the soft, pain-filled groan from Giorgieon snapped her into action.

"Let me help," she murmured, gently nudging Graca's hands aside. Placing her hands over the wound, she closed her eyes, ready to channel her energy to heal him. Before she could begin, however, Giorgieon's hand shakily rose to touch her cheek.

Through gurgled mouthfuls of blood, he murmured, "I'm... sorry."

"Stop talking," she urged, her voice choked. He didn't have the strength to waste on words.

Please forgive me, he rasped in her mind, his eyes pleading.

Aayla steeled herself and started to heal him when his heart rate dropped. He had lost so much blood that he didn't have enough in his body to keep his heart beating.

"I'm losing him," she cried out. "We need to shock him. Now!"

A Unix could only heal as long as the heart kept beating. With a pulse of energy precisely tuned to mimic his body's natural rhythm, they could cause a large but short-lived spike in his heart rate, buying her precious seconds to stabilise him. It was a risky, desperate manoeuvre because an Aldredth heart could only withstand a few shocks before it became too fatigued to respond.

Lifting her hands off Giorgieon while Soval shocked him, she prayed this would work.

His body jolted under the force of the shock, and she immediately placed her hands back upon him and closed her eyes whilst she continued to heal him. She barely healed a fraction of the damage before she felt his heart rate plummet again.

"Shock him again!" she shouted, her voice laced with urgency.

He was shocked again, but his heart rate was sluggish in responding. She focused her energy and slowly knitted his tissues back together, just in time before his heart stopped.

Sitting back, gasping for air, her hands trembled. Soval and Aeryn continued to monitor his vitals as Loxian resumed his blood infusion, stabilising him.

"What happened?" she asked breathless.

Graca looked down, shaking her head. "I don't know. Talyn just attacked him. We're not sure why. He's being held in there." She pointed to a nearby door.

Aayla's heart skipped. Why had Talyn attacked Giorgieon? Did he know he had kissed her? Even if he did, why would that make him mad enough to try and kill him?

Walking on autopilot to the closed doors, she paused, her hand hovering above the touchpad. A sudden wave of hesitation washed over her, a nervous knot twisting in her stomach. She wasn't sure what she would find on the other side, but with a steadying breath, she pressed her palm to the pad and stepped over the threshold.

The room was tense. Several Aldredth stood guard near the door, their expressions watchful. In the centre, Talyn sat on a lone chair, his head bowed as he stared at his hands, which were covered in blood, as were his clothes.

At the sound of her entrance, Talyn looked up and jumped to his feet, looking terrified. "Is he alive?"

"Yes," she replied softly.

Talyn's shoulders sagged as he closed his eyes, relief washing over his face. But when he opened them again, the intensity of his gaze struck her like a wave, leaving her breathless.

His eyes swept over her, worry etched in his expression. "Are you okay?"

She wanted to say yes, but the events of the last day hit her like a tidal wave. Her best friend and her Guardian were at odds. Talyn had wanted to leave her. She'd been kissed against her will, and now her best friend was barely clinging to life. Standing there, her clothes drenched with Giorgieon's blood, she felt hollow.

"No," she whispered, the word slipping out almost involuntarily.

Before he had even finished opening his arms, she slammed her body against his, hugging him tightly, her hands clenched on his clothes as if she was trying to hold him against her forever.

Talyn wrapped his arms around her tightly, his chin resting on the top of her head, pulling her close as though he, too, feared letting go. They stayed entwined in each other's embrace until she heard new footsteps entering the room behind her.

The moment shattered, and Aayla stiffened, pulling back just enough to look over her shoulder, feeling the weight of what was still to come.

"Talyn," Martok said quietly but firmly, "I'm afraid I must ask you to come with us. Giorgieon has stabilised, and it's time to discuss what happened."

Talyn gently lifted his head from atop Aayla's, nodding. "Of course."

They all walked silently toward the MedBay, the weight of what had happened hanging over them. Inside the room, Giorgieon lay on one of the beds, with Soval and Aeryn tending to him.

Filing into the room, Martok looked between Giorgieon and Talyn. "Talyn," Martok began, his voice steady. "Why did you attack Giorgieon?"

Talyn shifted uneasily, his gaze flickering to Aayla before he spoke. "I have no excuse. It was unprovoked."

"That's not true," Giorgieon rasped, his voice hoarse but resolute. "I assaulted Aayla. Talyn's response was justified."

Skyla gasped softly, and Martok's face twisted with shock and anger. His gaze fixed sharply on Giorgieon. "You assaulted her? Explain yourself."

Giorgieon tried to sit up, but Aeryn gently pushed him down, her face set in a deep frown. He was clearly in no shape to move around.

He looked hesitant, almost ashamed. "It was a mistake. I... I kissed her. I thought she had agreed. I would never have kissed her if I'd known she didn't agree to it."

Martok's face hardened, and he glanced at Aayla, his gaze intense. "Aayla, you are owed justice. As you are the one he attacked, the choice of Giorgieon's punishment is yours."

The room fell silent as every eye turned to her, and she felt the weight of their expectations pressing down on her. Shifting uncomfortably, she took a deep breath. "I don't want him punished," she said quietly. "It was a misunderstanding. I share responsibility as much as he does."

Giorgieon's face tightened with frustration. "No, Aayla. My actions were inexcusable. I crossed a line, and you can't just let this go. I need to face the consequences."

"Fine," she responded tensely, frustrated at the ridiculous situation. "My Guardian gets to stab you once."

Martok was displeased with her humour, but Giorgieon smiled. "Thank the stars you only said once. I don't think I could have handled a second time."

"Now, Giorgieon," Martok continued, ignoring them, "it's your right to determine Talyn's punishment for his attack on you."

Talyn stood motionless, his expression resigned, accepting whatever Giorgieon might decide.

Giorgieon huffed and waved his hand dismissively. "Of course, I require no punishment for him. He was doing his duty as a Guardian, defending Aayla. If anything, I should thank him for stopping short of killing me."

Talyn raised an eyebrow. "I wouldn't thank me too quickly. I was very much trying to kill you."

"Oh, please," Giorgieon replied with a half-smile. "You were standing right in front of me, and I didn't move an inch. Are you going to say you just missed? If you'd truly wanted to kill me, you would have. Instead, you stabbed me just beside my heart."

Talyn looked away, rubbing the back of his neck.

"I think that is enough for today, we can continue these conversations later once you've had a chance to recover," Aayla said as she turned towards Talyn. "Let's go and rest. We definitely all need it."

Aayla grasped his hand and tried to lead him away, but he stayed rooted in place. When she looked back, she saw the anguish in his eyes as he lowered his gaze before meeting hers.

"This doesn't change my decision to leave. If anything, it just emphasises why I need to leave," he said, his voice barely above a whisper.

Her eyes widened, shock freezing her in place. "But I need you," she pleaded, her voice shaking. "This just shows how much I need you by my side. You keep me safe."

Talyn shook his head, looking away as if her words were too painful to hear.

In desperation, she grabbed his chin and angled his face towards her. "Please, Talyn. Don't leave. Please stay with me."

"I can't!" The words erupted from him, raw and unfiltered. "There's something wrong with me, Aayla. Something broken inside of me. I am a danger to you and everyone else at the moment, and I need to leave before anyone else gets hurt."

Silence fell between them, thick and suffocating.

Finally, Talyn broke away, his voice unsteady. "I'm sorry, I need to get some fresh air. Excuse me," he mumbled, striding out of the room.

As he left, Aayla felt her world spinning, her breath coming in shallow gasps. She quickly followed him to the balcony, where he stood, gripping the railing with white-knuckled hands, his head hung low.

Approaching quietly, she stopped just behind him. She knew he sensed her presence, yet he remained utterly still, locked in his own turmoil.

She wanted to reach out, to touch him, but feared it might push him further away. "If there's something wrong... maybe I can help with it?" she asked softly.

Talyn straightened and turned to face her, looking grief-stricken. "There's nothing you can do to fix it. It's not something new. It's something I've been carrying for a long time, something I buried deep, thinking that would make it go away. But over time, that box I shoved it in has slowly started to break open."

He began pacing the length of the balcony. "I can't ignore it anymore. There's something fundamentally wrong with me. I'm broken in ways you can't fix. I don't know if anyone can, but I need to return to Nannuval until I'm not a danger to those around me."

Finally, his pacing stopped, and he drew in a shaky breath before turning back to her. The intensity of his gaze burned into her. Slowly, he stalked towards her as if he were a hunter and she was his prey. "I'm thinking things I shouldn't think. Wanting things I shouldn't want."

He reached out, his fingers brushing her cheek, sending a spark through her. Heat pooled between her legs, her breath catching as she met his gaze.

Unable to break his gaze, she tried to organise her thoughts. "You would never hurt me," she said softly.

He stepped so close that their bodies were pressed against each other. Slowly, he leaned down to press a lingering kiss against her neck. "Don't be so sure," he whispered, his breath hot against her skin.

Her voice wavered. "What if... what if I wanted it?"

Talyn straightened, releasing her with a small grimace. "You don't know what you're saying."

Anger flared at his words. "Don't treat me like a child. I know exactly what I'm saying, and there's nothing I want more than you by my side."

Her words softened his expression, and he gently reached out, cupping her face. "I'm only ever at peace when you're by my side."

She placed her hand over his, holding it against her cheek, her body instinctively gravitating toward him.

His touch was gentle and lingering. His other hand brushing against her arm conveyed warmth and intimacy. Her heartbeat quickened at his proximity, and a slight flush rose to her cheeks.

Breath hitching, Talyn's lips parted slightly as they gazed into each other's eyes. "Every time we're apart, it feels like my heart is being torn in half. Every injury you suffer torments me."

Their faces drew close, eyes half-closed, sharing a tender, intimate moment. She pressed her forehead against his and closed her eyes, her lips brushing gently against his cheek. His hand cradled the back of her head, fingers threading through her hair as their breaths mingled, warm and steady, as they nuzzled each other tenderly.

"Seeing you clinging to life the other day shattered me," he whispered, his breath hitching. "I came so close to losing you."

Their lips were so close she could feel the warmth of his breath. It stirred something primal within her.

Talyn moved closer, and their brushed together in the softest caress. It was a tentative kiss, like a question seeking an answer. The gentle sensation sent a thrill through her, her heartbeat quickening as warmth spread through her chest.

She savoured the sweetness of the moment, his hand cupping her cheek with a tenderness that made her pulse race.

As their lips continued to move together, the kiss deepened, becoming more urgent and passionate. She responded, her arms winding around his neck to pull him closer. Moaning in pleasure, he pressed his body against hers, slowly grinding in a way that sent another pulse of warmth through her. The deliberate motion, firm and unhurried, left her breathless.

The world faded away, leaving only the feeling of his mouth on hers, a dance of longing and desire that grew with each moment. The electric connection between them was undeniable and exhilarating, leaving her breathless and yearning for more. She couldn't get enough of him fast enough.

Talyn's hand slid up her back and firmly stroked along the sensitive upper edge of her wing.

A soft moan of ecstasy escaped her as she broke the kiss, gasping for breath. His lips travelled down her neck, a faint smile curving against her skin as he growled deeply until he suddenly froze.

In a heartbeat, Talyn pulled away, a look of horror flashing across his face as he stepped back, hands raised. They both stood still, breathing hard, frozen in place.

"I'm s—sorry..." Talyn stammered, his voice filled with regret.

"What was that..." Aayla asked, breathless.

Talyn backed away further, his eyes wide with fear. "I'm so sorry, I—"

"Wait—"

Twisting quickly, Talyn launched off the balcony in one powerful stroke, disappearing almost instantly. Aayla flew after him, hovering briefly before returning to the balcony after realising she had already lost sight of him.

She paced the length of the balcony, the cool night air brushing against her flushed cheeks. Her heart raced, each beat a reminder of that unexpected kiss.

Leaning against the railing, she stared at the dark skyline, her mind a storm of questions. Did he really kiss her? Who started it? What did it mean?

She hugged herself, caught between elation and confusion, the fear of what it might mean tightening her chest.

Every time she closed her eyes, she felt the warmth of his lips again, and a shiver ran down her spine. She took a deep breath, trying to steady herself, but the memory of that brief, intense moment left her trembling.

Soft footsteps startled her, and she spun around, sword in hand.

"Aayla?" Rune paused nervously with Ceeda by his side. Both glanced warily at the sword in her grip. "Is everything okay?"

"Sorry, yes, you just startled me." She lowered her sword, rubbing a hand across her face.

"Okay, that's good," Rune smiled anxiously as they continued approaching. "We're here to serve as your temporary guard detail."

A deep growl escaped her as she strode toward them, sword raised. "Where is Talyn? What did you do to him?"

"I—I don't know," Rune stammered, instinctively stepping in front of Ceeda. "He messaged to say he was on Mir'ka and wanted to ensure you had sufficient protection."

Aayla closed her eyes, taking a deep breath. "I'm sorry. I thought... never mind."

Looking around, she felt her heart pounding furiously as she ran her fingers through her hair. "Thank you," she said, her voice steadier but still tinged with the remnants of her earlier fear. "If you'll excuse me, I'm a little tired, so I think I'll retire to my quarters."

As she turned to head back inside, her eyes landed on the sleek, thin, black security camera strip along the upper edge of the wall. A cold wave of dread washed over her. She froze, her face paling as the horrifying realisation sank in. The camera had captured everything.

Her mind raced, envisioning the inevitable consequences. Glancing behind her at Rune and Ceeda, she knew she had to delete that footage.

"Actually, I just need to stop by the Command Centre quickly, but there's no need to accompany me," she said, trying to sound casual.

"If you insist," Rune answered hesitantly.

"I'll let you know if I need anything." Aayla flashed a brief smile before hurrying away, hoping they wouldn't ask more questions.

In the Command Centre, she spotted Jaxion seated by the monitors to the right. Letting out a sigh of relief, she steadied her breathing, forced a smile, and approached him slowly.

"Jaxion, how are you?"

Jaxion looked up, his face brightening. "Aayla! It's always a pleasure. What brings you here?"

"I have a favour to ask." She tucked a loose strand of hair behind her ear and glanced around before lowering her voice. "Could you please pull up the footage from balcony G5 over the last hour?"

"Of course." He typed a few quick commands, and soon, the screen in front of her filled with files. "Would you like to watch them?"

"No! No, I need them deleted."

Jaxion paused, frowning as he carefully studied her face. "Why?"

Racking her brain, she couldn't bring herself to lie, but a half-truth was easier to tell. "I had a confidential conversation that I don't want to be recorded."

Jaxion pursed his lips thoughtfully, but Aayla held his gaze with a tight smile.

"All right." He turned back to the screens, and with a few quick taps, the files vanished.

"Are these files backed up anywhere?" she asked.

"No, we only back up highlighted files, and this one wasn't."

"Perfect." Smiling broadly, she straightened and gently kissed him on the forehead. "Thank you."

"Anytime," he replied warmly as she turned to leave.

In a daze, she walked back to her room, waiting until the door closed with a soft click before sinking to the floor and hugging her knees tightly.

Why had he kissed her? Or had she kissed him against his will?

No, she was certain he'd kissed her back.

Who had started it? And why had he run? Was he afraid she'd report him and demand his execution? Where had he gone?

The questions swirled in her mind, but the loudest one of all couldn't be silenced. What does she do now?

She sat for hours before moving over to the couch by the balcony window, where she had a view of the outside in case Talyn came back.

Curling up on the couch, her eyes darted to the door every few minutes. She had opened it before moving in case Talyn returned from inside the building. Beyond the door, the familiar noises of Aldredth Tower continued. She listened to the footsteps that echoed in the hallway and the muted conversations, but these sounds, usually so comforting in their normalcy, only heightened her anxiety today.

Aayla barely noticed Becca enter the room, her mind consumed by the never-ending questions. She glanced up briefly, offering a half-hearted smile to Becca, but returned to gazing out the balcony door. Becca projected a stack of documents she wanted to discuss, and Aayla tried to listen, but she couldn't focus on what she had to say.

Sensing Aayla's distraction, Becca put her Lumina away and sat quietly beside her. Her presence was a comforting background against the swirling thoughts. Time passed in a blur of small conversations and absent-minded nods until she eventually rose and left with a soft farewell, the faint echo of her departure barely registering in Aayla's overburdened mind.

As the sun began to rise, she realised she had been awake the entire night. She had drifted off several times before being jolted awake by every distant footstep or muffled voice, hoping it was the sound of Talyn returning.

Her Lumina lay by her side, checked countless times but still empty of messages from him.

Forcing herself to face the day, Aayla drifted from one task to the next, but her mind wouldn't settle. Hours stretched as she half-listened to conversations, feeling adrift. By afternoon, her energy waning, she returned to her quarters and paced, replaying countless scenarios, each worse than the last. She opened the door to peer down the hallway, half-expecting to see Talyn coming around the corner, but only the other Aldredth passed by, smiling in polite greeting.

As evening approached, her Lumina vibrated with a new alert.

Talyn was in the Command Centre.

Chapter Forty-Two

Stupid. He was so unbelievably stupid.

How had he let this happen after burying his feelings for so long?

Talyn beat his wings hard, launching himself into the night, fleeing from the forbidden kiss he'd shared with Aayla. But he wasn't really flying away from her or the kiss. He was running from himself. He wasn't sure he could've resisted bonding with her if he'd stayed even a moment longer.

Whether she wanted it or not.

Every instinct in him screamed to go back, to complete the bond. But he knew he needed to get as far away as possible before he lost all control.

Pulling out his Lumina, he sent a quick message to Rune and Ceeda, hoping to hold on to his last shred of sanity before he was entirely lost to his emotions.

He flew for hours in the darkness of the night until he realised he was alone. Looking around, he saw that he was flying over rugged mountain ranges. Swooping down low, he landed on the peak of the closest mountain and collapsed onto the rough ground, staring at the starry night sky.

Lying motionless, he reflected on everything that had happened as the sky filled with light and the sounds of nature awakening around him filled his ears. Slowly, he tried to quiet the raging voice in his mind and push it back deep down inside of him.

Just when he thought he was beginning to get some sense of control back, he remembered the feel of Aayla's lips on his own, the press of her soft body against his, and he was overcome by a burning desire that made the edge of his vision go white.

One thing was for certain—his feelings could no longer be pushed back deep down. They would no longer be contained, and he was no longer in control of them. It was as if a dam had been broken, and there was no stopping the flood of emotions that surged through him.

Sighing, he realised the sun was getting lower in the sky. The longer he stayed away, the worse he felt. He needed to go back and accept the consequences of his actions.

Aayla had surely told everyone by now. His punishment was waiting. He deserved it for what he'd done. Did she hate him now that she'd seen what he truly was? She should, after what he'd put her through.

The bitter irony wasn't lost on him. He'd nearly killed Giorgieon for assaulting Aayla with an unwanted kiss, and now he'd done the same thing.

He stood up and soared high into the sky with a powerful beat of his wings, prepared to accept whatever awaited him.

As he neared Aldredth Tower, he didn't see any guards on patrol looking for him. Frowning, Talyn slowly circled the building before landing at the entrance.

Looking around, everyone seemed almost oblivious to his presence. Seth was standing guard by the entrance, and when he caught Talyn's eye, he smiled warmly and nodded in greeting.

Frowning deeper, Talyn slowly walked over to him.

"Good evening, Talyn. Glad to see you're back," Seth greeted him cheerfully.

Talyn hesitated, tilting his head in confusion. "You...are?"

"Of course," Seth chuckled and playfully nudged Talyn. "I'm not too proud to admit that I missed you having you around. I heard you were taking a Mir'ka, but I wasn't sure what that involved or how long you would be gone. I believe you're just in time for dinner."

Talyn glanced behind him as several humans greeted him on their way into Aldredth Tower. He couldn't understand why Seth didn't seem to know about what had happened yesterday. Maybe the humans hadn't heard what he had done yet, or perhaps he was pretending not to know. Either way, he needed to go inside and figure out what was happening.

"Thanks, Seth. Maybe I'll see you inside later."

Talyn checked his Lumina and saw that Martok was in the Command Centre. Departing quickly, he stepped into the bustling lobby, his heart pounding with a mix of nerves and anticipation.

The cacophony of voices, footsteps, and soft rustling of feathers echoed around him, amplifying his anxiety. Yet, amid the chaos, the warmth of countless smiles and friendly greetings only further increased his confusion.

When he reached the Command Centre, he found Martok focusing on a situation underway on the screens in front of him. Skyla was tucked under his wing, pointing at something on the screen. The way their wings overlapped stirred a deep feeling of envy in Talyn.

Clearing his throat, he called out tensely, "Martok?"

Martok looked up and smiled warmly. Striding over, he clasped Talyn's shoulder. "Good to see you. How are you?"

Talyn's confusion grew. Glancing around, he saw Skyla stroll over to join them. "Weren't...weren't you looking for me?"

Skyla blinked, a hint of surprise in her eyes. "Were we meant to be?" The tension in her expression was unmistakable, her gaze seeking reassurance.

"I... No, I—" Talyn thrust a hand through his hair, at a loss for words.

"Aayla did ask to be notified when you returned," Martok responded as he nodded at Skyla, clearly answering their telepathic conversation.

Skyla quickly disappeared, Lumina in hand, before Talyn could stop her.

"H—how has Aayla been doing?" Talyn asked, shuffling his feet anxiously.

Martok seemed distracted by the conversation going on at the screens behind him. His attention flicked back to the screens as Skyla returned, updating the data. "Oh, she's okay. Took a day off Mir'ka. Been missing you, I'm sure."

Talyn opened his mouth to ask another question, but he felt Aayla's presence before he heard her voice.

"Talyn!"

Freezing, he closed his eyes and tried to control his breathing before slowly turning to face her.

She looked breathless, a flush on her cheeks as if she'd rushed down here. Her wide eyes searched his face, and though Talyn tried to keep his expression neutral, the intensity of his gaze betrayed him.

"Aayla," he said, voice steady yet tense, "I believe there are a few things we need to discuss."

She nodded silently, her lips slightly parted.

"Let's go to our quarters," he suggested, then hesitated, realising she might not want to be alone with him. "Unless you'd rather talk here?"

Aayla frowned slightly and looked around the room at the other Aldredth before staring intently at him. "No, I think it's best if we discuss matters in private."

Nodding tightly, he gestured to the doorway. "After you."

They walked in silence to their quarters. Talyn walked so close behind her that her intoxicating scent filled his senses, making his pulse race. Once inside, he quickly strode onto the balcony and breathed in the fresh air, trying to clear his head.

Aayla's quiet footsteps stopped behind him, and he took one final deep breath of the cold evening air before turning to face her.

"Where did you go?" she asked softly, wrapping her arms around her body.

"I'm sorry for kissing you," he stated, watching her face closely.

She flinched as if struck. "Do you regret it?"

He exhaled hard and thrust his hand through his hair. "I'm done lying to you. And to myself. I do regret it, but not because I didn't want to kiss you. I only regret that I didn't ask your permission first."

Aayla seemed too stunned to speak.

"I'm in love with you, Aayla. And not the kind of love a Guardian should feel. I mean the kind of love I shouldn't be feeling, and I've always felt this way since the first moment I saw you. I've been pushing these feelings deep down inside of me for so long that I'm tired, and I can't do it anymore. It's like a dam has broken inside of me, and I can't push my feelings back down anymore. The box that once contained them has been torn open, and the feelings have grown too strong to be contained any longer."

Aayla stepped towards him, reaching her hand out to him.

"I—"

"Please, let me finish," he said, his voice raw.

Stepping back quickly, he looked down, the force of her gaze tearing a hole through him. "I don't know why I am this way, and I won't keep pretending everything is okay. I need to leave and get as far away from you as possible. I'll go to Nannuval and accept whatever punishment I am given. I just need you to know that I'm sorry for keeping the truth from you, and I'm sorry for kissing you against your will, and I'm sorry for... everything."

His shoulders slumped, and he turned to clutch the railing for support. The pain and longing in his voice painted a poignant picture of his grief, the intimate setting amplifying the rawness of his emotions.

"What if... what if I was in love with you too?" Her voice was barely a whisper.

Talyn whipped around, his face filled with confusion as he searched her face for answers.

Her eyes glistened under the soft evening light. "You didn't kiss me against my will. I wanted it, and I don't regret it. I love you, Talyn."

A wave of horror swept through him. "Don't say that."

"Say what?" She stepped toward him, unwavering, as he stumbled along the railing. "Say that I love you? Because I do."

"Stop!" he shouted. "Don't ever say that."

"Why?" Her gaze was fierce.

"Because you can't love me," he bellowed, his heart pounding. "I'm... I'm nothing. I'm nobody. You deserve someone better."

He paced back and forth across the balcony in anger, his hands clenched. He frowned as he searched for the right words that seemed just out of reach.

Spinning, he stalked towards her. "Worse than that, I'm broken. There is something fundamentally wrong with me, and I won't let you bind yourself to me. You don't know what you're saying."

"Don't treat me like a fool," she snapped, fists clenched in anger. "I know exactly how I feel, how I have always felt. You're not the only one who has been pretending everything was normal when it was far from the truth. I have been irrevocably in love with you from the first moment I saw you, and the only reason I haven't ever said anything about it is because you told me that you weren't my mate."

Tears rolled down her cheeks, and he thought his heart would break into two at the sight. He lifted his hand to brush them away but instead dropped his hand back down by his side, not trusting himself if he touched her.

He took a small step backward and frowned in confusion, "I never said that."

Aayla's gaze fell to the floor, her lips pressed together in a thin, trembling line, and she occasionally took deep, shaky breaths as if trying to steady herself. "When we first met, I told you that you were my mate, and you said there was nothing to stop you from acting as my Guardian."

His eyes widened, and his face turned ashen as the horrifying realisation dawned on him. His mouth fell open, but no words came out, just a silent gasp.

He took a step towards Aayla, but she quickly stepped back as if physically recoiling from him.

"I was a child," he said, his voice barely a whisper. "They told me that if I didn't agree to be your Guardian, they would take you away from me. I would have agreed to anything to keep you by my side." His gaze dropped, haunted. "I planned to tell you that, of course, I thought you were my mate. But... but then you ran off. When I finally found you in that field, you told me you'd made a mistake and that I wasn't your mate. And I..."

A cold sweat broke out across his forehead, and a tremor seized his body as the old memory tore through him, freezing him in place. The terror, the heartache, it all came rushing back, leaving him feeling as helpless as he'd been then, crushed by the weight of his own silence.

Aayla's hand flew to her mouth, her eyes wide and unmoving, as though frozen in place by the weight of his words.

"I thought..." Talyn forced out each word. "If I told you how I felt, you would have been horrified and disgusted by me. At a bare minimum, I thought you would have asked for a new Guardian. I couldn't bear losing you, not after I'd just found you."

Swallowing hard, Aayla took a tentative step toward him. "I only said I was mistaken because... because you said you'd accept the position as my Guardian, and I thought that meant you didn't... love me like that. I was ashamed of what I felt. I assumed I must have been feeling something I shouldn't have, so I tried to pretend it was just a mistake."

Talyn stepped forward and cupped Aayla's face, the anguish in her voice compelling him to move before he realised he had.

"I'm so sorry," he murmured, leaning his forehead against hers.

Her arms wrapped around him, pulling him tight against her as if she were afraid he would run away.

"So, you truly love me as only a mate should?" Her words whispered against his skin, sending a shiver of pleasure down his body.

"Every second of every day."

As Aayla's lips gently brushed against his, a surge of electricity coursed through his veins, igniting a primal fire deep within. His senses awakened, heightened to a fever pitch, as the warmth of their embrace enveloped him in a cocoon of desire.

Talyn pulled back, his chest heaving, and he shook his head. "No, we can't."

Aayla's brows knitted in confusion. "I don't understand. Why not?"

"Because what future is there for you if you mate with me!" He began pacing the balcony, a caged fury in each step. "I'll be executed the second anyone finds out, and if you are bonded with me, it will kill you as well. There is no future for us. I won't curse you to that. I won't be the cause of your death." His agitation was palpable, each step echoing his inner turmoil.

"But you would rather condemn me to a lifetime without my mate?" she challenged, her voice rising. "Leave me to wander this life with half a soul, forever aching for you?"

"What else can I do?" His plea was raw, desperate.

"You can love me! For however long that is for. I would rather have a single moment with you than a lifetime without you. Do you not want the same?" She reached towards him with outstretched arms.

He turned to the railing, gripping it so tightly his knuckles turned white as he stared out at the city's lights, glittering below. His voice was barely a whisper. "I don't want to curse you."

"Well, it's too late for that." She ran her hand through her hair and walked over to the balcony doors before turning back to face him.

"Even if you never bind with me, my heart will never stop yearning for you," she said softly, her voice thick with conviction. "Every second of every day. There will never be another I call my mate. I will be cursed by your absence."

Talyn's heart twisted as he watched her, helpless under the weight of his own emotions. Every word she spoke felt like a blade piercing the armour he had so carefully built around himself. He wanted to reach out, pull her into his arms, and tell her he felt the same ache and need. But fear held him back. Fear of the consequences. Fear of being the one to hurt her, to bring her down. His love for her was overwhelming, but so was the guilt. How could he let her tie herself to him, knowing it would kill her?

She took a few steps closer, and her gaze locked with his, challenging him, daring him to look away. "So, I need you to make a decision. Ask yourself what you really want. Forget what everyone else expects of you or what you think you should be. You need to make a decision based on what you want and what you can live with."

The depth of her words struck him like a tidal wave, washing over his doubts and his fears, exposing the raw truth beneath that he didn't want a life without her. But that same truth terrified him. He swallowed, feeling as if his entire soul was being bared before her, stripped of every layer of restraint he had held onto.

"I don't know what to do about the law," she exhaled as though releasing a burden, "but I know with you by my side, we will think of something. So here I stand, heart laid bare, asking you if you will take my hand?"

Her voice dropped to a whisper, raw and aching. "What future do you want? What can you live with? What do you want?"

The silence hung heavy between them, her question echoing in his mind. What did he want? He knew he couldn't live without her, but if he let himself go, let himself love her fully, he wouldn't be able to stop from binding with her, and she'd pay the ultimate price.

Turning, he gripped the railing, gaze locked on the blurred lights of the city, lost in his own tortured thoughts. He wanted the world for her, and he certainly wanted better for her than him.

His lips pressed into a tense line. Glancing behind him, he saw Aayla's shallow, uneven breaths, her eyes glistening with unshed tears. The cool breeze whispered around him, and he tried to will himself to fly away, but his body would not move an inch.

A long, resigned sigh escaped him. With a look of quiet defeat, he turned back toward her. "You. I will always choose you."

He closed the distance between them in three swift strides, capturing her lips in a soft, passionate kiss.

He was careful at first, holding back, afraid of hurting her soft curves with his brute strength. But as her arms wrapped around him, his restraint frayed, and he surrendered to the emotions he had tried so hard to deny.

With each gentle caress of their lips, he felt himself drowning in the intoxicating rhythm of passion, his body responding instinctively to her presence. A soft moan escaped Aayla's lips, and the sound sent a wave of exhilaration across Talyn's body, making his cock pulse.

He inhaled her rich and intoxicating scent as his hands roamed, reverently tracing the curves he had only dared to dream about. Her skin was silky soft under his touch, igniting his senses and making his body ache with need.

As their kiss deepened, he felt a surge of heat spreading like wildfire through his veins. Aayla's skin flushed, and Talyn's erection grew as he surrendered to the rush of arousal.

In that moment, time itself seemed to stand still.

Chapter Forty-Three

Aayla felt the kiss intensify, shifting from gentle to urgent, as long-suppressed feelings broke free.

Their hands roamed over each other's bodies, each touch sparking electric trails. Talyn's fingers traced the sensitive arch of her wing, and she shuddered under a wave of blinding pleasure, her head falling back as a loud moan escaped her lips.

She saw Talyn's lip curve with a small smile reeking of masculine pride, so she decided to repay the favour by stroking Talyn's wing sensually. His body tensed beneath her touch, his breath hitching before he buried his head in the crook of her neck, a deep groan slipping free as his hips thrust against her. She felt his enormous erection pressing against her, and she rubbed her thighs together in desire as heat pooled between her legs.

The intensity of their kiss continued to grow as their breaths mingled and their hearts raced in sync.

Without breaking contact, they moved as one towards the nearby bed, their movements driven by instinct and need.

Her body was yearning to feel Talyn's skin pressed up against her. Suddenly, her clothes felt restrictive and uncomfortable. She quickly pulled Talyn's clothes from his body, lifting his top over his head to reveal his sculptured chest. Without breaking their kiss, her thumbs hooked into the waistband of his pants, sliding them down over his hips in one smooth motion.

He stilled momentarily, his eyes darkening with intent before his hands shed the clothes from her body with equal fervour.

Tumbling onto the bed, their bodies entwined, every touch, every kiss was electric.

Aayla flared her wings out on the bed, and Talyn spread his wings over the top of hers. He pressed her gently onto the bed, nudging his legs between hers. His heavy arousal rubbed against her.

The weight of his body pressing down onto her felt possessive and intimate.

The feeling of their sensitive feathers gliding over each other was orgasmic, and her hands trembled on his body under the waves of pleasure that rocked her body.

His kisses were firm yet tender, filled with an undeniable urgency, as his lips explored hers with a newfound intensity. She responded in kind, her hands roaming over the contours of his back, savouring the feeling of his muscles tensing under her touch, before reaching up to stroke his wings.

Every touch, every caress seemed to ignite a deeper connection between them. As he moved above her, their eyes met, and Talyn's eyes held an intensity that stole her breath.

Chest heaving, Talyn slowed as his hungry gaze took in every inch of her. *You are so painfully beautiful. It's impossible for anyone to love someone more than I love you.*

Aayla lifted her head and grasped the back of his head, kissing him firmly. *You're forgetting about how much I love you.*

She glanced down at his muscular body hovering over her, and her breath caught as she gazed at his handsome, naked form bathed in the soft glow of moonlight. The silvery light accentuated the contours of his muscular physique, casting delicate shadows that highlighted every line and curve. His skin seemed to shimmer, and the gold edging on his wings glimmered in the low light.

Looking down, she reached out and stroked her hand along the length of his erection.

Talyn sucked in a break before thrusting his hips with a groan. He gently cupped her jaw and covered her mouth with his.

Deepening the kiss, she opened for him, drawing his tongue into her mouth.

Talyn's hands roamed all over her body, and he traced one hand along the curve of her breast before gently squeezing her nipple. The sensation made her hips rock into him, and he gave a throaty chuckle before lowering his head to take a nipple into his mouth. Sucking gently before using his teeth to gently graze her skin, a loud moan escaped her lips as her back arched off the bed, and she fisted her hands in his hair.

He lifted his head, a small smile playing on his lips. Talyn's hand travelled lower, slipping between her thighs to find her wet with desire. His name fell from her lips as he captured her mouth once more, his fingers skilfully teasing her until her hips bucked against him, her body crying out for more.

She was burning up with desire and wanted to feel him inside of her. She reached down and stroked the length of him a few times, causing him to drop his head back. Her other hand slowly moved to his wing and caressed it erotically as Talyn cried out her name in ecstasy.

He pressed the tip of his erection against her opening, and she felt like her skin was on fire from desire. Talyn paused, and a pained look crossed his face. "T—tell me to stop. I'm not strong enough to stop myself, but if you ask of it, I might be able to. It's not too late to change your mind."

Gently cupping his face, she looked into his deep green eyes, "Take me as your mate. Bond with me."

With a shudder, he kissed her deeply and eased into her, inch by inch. She gasped softly as she felt herself stretching to accommodate his enormous girth. With one final thrust, he buried himself completely inside of her. A feeling of ecstasy overwhelmed her as another orgasm rocked her body.

He withdrew slowly before plunging all the way inside of her again. Moaning in pleasure, he met her gaze. *You feel so tight. Are you sure I'm not hurting you?*

Shaking her head, she kissed him gently. *No, I'm made for you. You feel amazing.*

I love the feeling of being inside you. Slowly, he started to thrust in and out, each rocking movement triggering wave after wave of climax.

His movements were initially tentative as they explored each other's bodies, but soon, they found a harmonious sync. Each thrust brought them closer, not just physically but emotionally and spiritually, as their bond snapped into place, their two souls permanently intertwined.

As he plunged into her over and over, his primal growls hit a primitive note deep in her soul. He cried out her name as a climax hit him hard, and it sent her over the edge once more, her body arching beneath him as waves of pleasure washed over them both.

Talyn lowered his mouth over hers and curled his tongue around hers. He tasted hot and sweet, and she knew she could drink from him all night. The scent of his arousal grew, enveloping her.

"I can't seem to get enough of you."

Recovering quickly, Aayla caught her breath and pushed him onto his back, a playful gleam in her eyes as she straddled him. He was already hard for her again. His fingers gripped her hips whilst she rose onto her knees and guided him inside of her.

As she sank onto him, he groaned loudly in pleasure. His hands moved up to grasp her breasts before reaching around her back to run his fingers through her velvety soft feathers.

Wave after wave of orgasms racked their bodies as they pushed their energy into each other with every thrust.

She rocked her hips rhythmically as her movements synchronised perfectly with his. Together, they moved in a seamless, fluid motion.

When the final climax hit her, her spasms squeezed him and quickly pushed him over the edge. He drove himself into her, sheathing deep inside of her.

Aayla slumped breathless on top of Talyn and lay with her head resting on his chest, listening to the rapid beat of his heart gradually slowing to match her own. Wrapped in the warmth of his arms, she felt whole for the first time in her life.

One thing was certain. The Aldredth were right when they said you could go through life unaware of the emptiness within you, oblivious to the fact that you were only half a soul until the moment you found your mate. The missing part of you.

Talyn gently kissed her forehead, and her arousal began to grow again.

Time melted away as they became lost in pleasure, their bodies intertwined. They continued to explore each other's bodies with tender intimacy, making love throughout the night.

As dawn's light began to creep over the horizon, Aayla finally collapsed against Talyn. He tenderly draped a wing over her, encasing her in warmth.

She closed her eyes and felt Talyn brush his hand down her cheek.

I love you more than words can describe, my beautiful mate. You are the reason for my every breath, and my heart beats only for you.

She lifted her head, meeting his gaze, her eyes shimmering. With a fierce kiss, she whispered, "And my love for you knows no limits. You carry my heart with you. All that I am belongs to you."

He pulled her even closer, his arms tightening around her, pressing a gentle kiss to her forehead as she settled her head on his chest.

Trailing her fingers along his bicep, she whispered, "What do we do now?"

Talyn let out a deep sigh, his hand gliding gently along her back. "I don't know," he replied, a hint of a smile in his voice. "But I do know one thing. I'm not leaving this bed anytime soon."

Laughing, Aayla placed a soft kiss on Talyn's chest. "I think we have no choice but to stay in this bed for several reasons. Mainly because it's not safe for newly mated males to walk around, especially when the other Aldredth haven't been warned."

Talyn clicked his tongue in mock disapproval. "I think my control is better than that."

A wicked idea crossed her mind. She knew she shouldn't tease him, but she couldn't help herself. "Good. Because Rythar offered to help me with some training later. His hands are amazing at working out tension in my shoulders—"

A deep growl rumbled in Talyn's chest, so powerful it vibrated the bed beneath them.

Chuckling, she cupped his face and pressed her lips to his. "I'm kidding! Stop," she said, her voice rich with amusement.

"I'll kill anyone who so much as looks at you," he growled, his voice low and possessive.

She smiled against his lips, her tone softening. "Don't worry, I'm all yours. I always have been, and I always will be." Her kisses trailed playfully over his face as she snickered. "But this is exactly why we must stay hidden for a few days."

Talyn exhaled hard, his annoyance giving way to reluctant agreement. With a wave of his hand, his Lumina flew into his grasp. "You're right. I'll mark us on Mir'ka for the next week."

A few taps later, the device fell softly to the floor, forgotten.

Grinning wickedly, he flipped her onto her back and hovered over her, his eyes glinting with mischief. "Now, where were we?"

CHAPTER FORTY-FOUR

Aayla laughed as she captured his lips with hers. The moment his mouth met hers, a shiver travelled throughout her body, and the world narrowed to the sensation of touch, the softness of skin, and the warmth of their breath mingling.

The week seemed to blur into a single, continuous moment as they remained ensconced in the cocoon of their bed. Each day melted seamlessly into the next, marked only by the shifting patterns of sunlight and moonlight filtering through the curtains. They revelled in the closeness, their bodies entwined in a dance of intimacy and comfort.

Morning came with the soft glow of dawn, casting a warm, golden hue over their naked bodies. They stirred only to wrap themselves more tightly around each other, savouring the sensation of skin against skin, and conversations were whispered between kisses.

Afternoons stretched lazily, punctuated by gentle laughter and tender touches. They explored each other's bodies with a mix of familiarity and newfound wonder, discovering hidden pleasures in the slow, unhurried hours. The world outside faded to insignificance. All that mattered was the here and now, their shared breaths, and their synchronised heartbeats.

Evenings brought a serene stillness. The room bathed in the soft, silvery light of the moon. They held each other close, the rhythm of their breathing a soothing lullaby. Dreams intertwined as if their slumbering minds were as connected as their waking moments.

When the sunlight filtered through the curtains once more, Aayla stirred, stretching languidly as though the morning held no urgency. Opening her eyes, she saw the familiar sight of Talyn's face just inches from hers. He was sleeping peacefully, and a soft smile spread across her lips.

Reaching out, she brushed a stray lock of hair from his face, eliciting a sleepy murmur as his arms tightened instinctively around her. When his eyes fluttered open, they exchanged a slow, tender kiss, unhurried and filled with the quiet promise of forever.

Aayla rested her head on Talyn's chest, her fingers tracing lazy patterns across his warm skin. "We're going to have to leave this room at some point," she murmured softly.

"Unfortunately," he replied with a wry grin.

She bit her lip, her hand stilling against him. "What... do we say when we do?"

His gaze turned distant, his brows knitting together in deep concentration. His jaw clenched, and his lips pressed into a firm line. "We can't say anything."

Propping herself up on her elbows, she frowned. "Maybe we could explain it to them. Make them understand."

"No." His voice was firm, his tone leaving no room for debate. "I'd be dead before we even got the chance to say a word. And if I die, you..." He swallowed hard, his voice faltering. "You'd die too."

Her heart ached at the grief etched into his expression. "We have to try," she urged, her voice barely above a whisper.

"I won't take that risk," he bellowed, his voice breaking with desperation.

Aayla opened her mouth to argue but stopped. The anguish in his eyes silenced her. Instead, she leaned forward and pressed a gentle, tentative kiss to his chin.

"Okay," she relented softly. "It's too risky. But... isn't there something we can do? I don't know if I can pretend you're not my mate."

Talyn's arms tightened around her, pulling her close. He kissed the top of her head, his voice dropping to a tender murmur. "Even if this is all the time we have, I wouldn't change a thing. One second as your mate is worth more than a lifetime without you." His tone hardened with determination. "But I'm not giving up that easily. We need to learn everything we can about this law and its origins. Maybe we can find something that will help us."

Her eyes lit up with hope. "That's a good idea. Let's go now. I don't want to wait another minute."

"Wait." He caught her hand, searching her face. "Are you sure you're ready? It won't be easy lying to everyone, fighting our... urges."

Aayla shifted to sit on his lap, cupping his face in her hands. She leaned in, kissing him deeply, her passion igniting between them. When she pulled back, her voice was steady and resolute. "I want to make you mine. I've waited long enough. I can play my part a little longer."

Talyn's lips curved into a faint smile as he kissed her again, softer this time. "Okay," he whispered. "Let's do this."

Reluctantly, they dressed and began making their way to the Command Centre. The quiet of the corridor stretched before them, but halfway down, Ophelian and Rythar appeared at the other end.

"Aayla! It's good to see you. How are you?" Ophelian called out, her voice warm and cheerful.

Panic surged through Aayla. Would they notice? Could they sense the bond between her and Talyn? Had she overlooked something that might give them away?

She hesitated, glancing back, instinctively checking for an escape route when she felt Talyn's wing brush lightly against her. His touch was grounding, and she forced herself to breathe with a trembling smile.

"I'm doing well, thank you."

"That's wonderful to hear. And Talyn, how are you?" Ophelian asked, her gaze shifting.

"Better, thank you. Some downtime was exactly what we needed," Talyn said with a cheeky grin.

Aayla bumped her hip into his, giving him a pointed look, but he only chuckled, shrugging innocently.

"We're on our way to get some breakfast. Would you like to join us?" Rythar's hopeful tone lingered in the air.

We should go, Talyn's voice whispered across her mind.

No, the research is more critical.

The research will take time and, as your mate, it's my responsibility to look after you and ensure you eat properly. Talyn responded calmly. *Besides, refusing might raise suspicion.*

Sighing, she didn't want to delay, but she did want to feed Talyn. To care for him as mates do. Talyn was so devoted to her that she knew he would neglect his own needs entirely.

Smiling warmly, she turned to Ophelian and Rythar. "We'd love to. After you."

Talyn glanced at her, his approval evident in the subtle softening of his features. Together, they followed Ophelian and Rythar down the corridor.

The morning sun cast a warm glow over the bustling Dining Hall, illuminating the lively faces of their friends as they chatted and laughed. She sat among them, her heart beating a little faster than usual, acutely aware of Talyn's presence beside her.

As Aayla sipped her drink, she kept stealing glances at Talyn. Their eyes met, and his lips curved into a soft smile. For a fleeting moment, the world seemed to dissolve, leaving only the two of them connected by that look. A blush crept up her cheeks, and she quickly turned her attention back to the conversation, though the pleasant warmth of his gaze lingered.

Talyn pretended to lean forward and grab some food but used the movement to disguise his wings brushing up sensually against hers. The touch sent a shiver down her spine, and as Talyn leaned back, he kept his wing overlapped with hers.

She felt a mixture of excitement and sadness in these secret touches, longing to grab his face and kiss him openly but relishing the intimacy of their hidden love.

Each shared glance and subtle contact was a silent promise, a reminder of the bond they would cherish away from prying eyes.

The conversation and laughter of her friends surrounded her, but her focus kept drifting back to Talyn. His presence was a comforting anchor, and she smiled more and laughed more genuinely when he was near.

She leaned against him and felt a sense of contentment wash over her. The world around them bustled with energy and chatter, but in that moment, leaning against him, she felt a serene peace, knowing that she was finally complete. Whole.

Eventually, they bid farewell to the others around them and went to the Command Centre.

The rest of the day passed in a blur as they combed through every record relating to the law and the history before it.

Aayla focused her efforts on uncovering whether a Unix had ever been mated to a non-Lazuil before, while Talyn delved into the incident that had sparked the creation of the law.

Immersed in the files, Aayla lost track of time, the outside world fading as she became absorbed in Aldredth history.

Talyn finished reading and moved over to sit next to her, their wings overlapping in an intimate embrace. He stroked her back silently while she finished reading the files amassed before her.

As her eyes scanned the final page and the last sentence came into focus, a flicker of hope ignited within her. She had finally found it. Closing the file, she glanced at Talyn and saw him staring intently at her wings.

The look of love in his eyes was unmistakable. Eyes softening with warmth, he gazed intently as if capturing every detail of her. But beneath the tender gaze was a look filled with an insatiable burning hunger.

"You are so beautiful," he murmured, his voice thick with emotion.

Her heart quickened, heat surging through her at his words. *When you look at me like that, it makes me want to do very naughty things to you.*

A teasing smile curved his lips as he leaned in, his breath warm against her neck. He paused, deliberately drawing out the moment, before pressing a slow, passionate kiss just behind her ear. *I think I like the sound of that.*

A wave of longing swept over her, causing warmth to pool between her legs. She shifted slightly, her body aching for his touch.

I can smell your arousal, he groaned, his forehead dropping onto her shoulder as his restraint began to slip.

Sliding her hand up his back and along the sensitive underside of his wing. *Take me back to our room. We can discuss our findings later.*

A low growl rumbled from his chest as they stood and he rubbed his hips against her. *Anything my mate desires.*

They spent the remainder of the night entwined in each other's embrace. No matter how many times they made love, in how many ways, their hunger for one another only seemed to grow.

Hours later, as the night deepened, Aayla drifted off to sleep with her head resting on Talyn's chest. His arm held her securely, and his wing draped protectively over them, cocooning her in warmth and safety.

Chapter Forty-Five

Aayla woke slowly to the gentle sensation of fingers caressing her skin. As her eyes fluttered open, she was met with Talyn's gaze, brimming with devotion. Smiling, she cupped his face and covered his mouth with hers. Tongues entwined, they shared a passionate kiss as the morning sun filtered through the windows.

Feeling utterly content, she smiled happily.

I could stay wrapped up in you forever.

"Yes, please," he teased before pulling her into another passionate kiss. As they parted, his expression turned thoughtful. "But we should probably talk about what we found yesterday. I think I discovered some good news."

Her eyes lit up as she propped herself up on her arms. "Really? That's amazing! Why didn't you say anything sooner?"

"Well," he began with a playful smirk, "I was a little... distracted."

Blushing, she remembered the way he buried himself inside of her all the way to the hilt and the feeling of him thrusting inside as they rode wave after wave of climax.

When she met his gaze, his smug smile suggested he knew exactly what she had just been thinking about. "I think I found something, too," she said, trying to shift the focus. "But you go first."

Talyn nodded, his tone growing serious. "The incident that led to the law happened over 500 cycles ago. The Unix's name was Daesie, and the Vorax who claimed to be her mate was Gryphonar. They'd never met before, but when they did,

Daesie didn't acknowledge the bond until he touched her. The entire... incident... lasted just six hours before they both died."

"During that time, Daesie acted like a puppet—silent and obedient, without any independent thought. She never moved or said anything unless she was given direction by Gryphonar. The Aldredth noted after that her speech was unnatural, using words and phrases she'd never said before. I'm actually pretty surprised that they created a new law based on this incident because there were so many signs she was under possession. However, that's hindsight for you."

"I understand, though," she murmured. "Their hearts were shattered, drowning in the blood of their loved ones. It wasn't a time for rational decisions. Grief and anger were steering their decisions."

A heavy silence lingered between them.

Aayla drew in a shaky breath, her voice barely audible. "What about... how did they die?"

His expression darkened. "Just as we were told. The Aldredth started to suspect something was wrong. They tried to confront her, and she... she killed 56 Aldredth under Gryphonar's direction before he made her slit her own throat when he was finally cornered. Of course, they didn't realise until after that Gryphonar was also under possession."

"So many lives lost," Aayla said softly, grief heavy in her voice.

Talyn nodded, running a hand through his hair. "Yeah. It was..." his voice faltering before he cleared his throat and shook his head, refocusing. "But the good news is, there were obvious signs of possession. Not only that, but it was also a very quick incident. We have time on our side."

Aayla gently stroked the edge of his wing. His breath hitched, his eyes rolled back, and he groaned as his hips thrust against her.

"Careful," he warned, voice low. "Unless you want this conversation to end early."

Laughing softly, she kissed him. "Well, I know you're going to like what I found, too. Tell me, what do you know about how our bloodlines were organised?"

Talyn frowned in confusion. "Long ago, the heads of the six families met and agreed that we needed a ruling class bloodline. The Lazuil's were a clear choice, and the Vajjer was selected to be their guardians."

"Close," she said, excitement bubbling in her voice. "But you're missing something important. The Vajjer and Lazuil were tied to the royal bloodline. They were identical in every way. Strength, leadership qualities, everything. So, they basically flipped a coin to decide. If not for a twist of fate, you could be from the Royal bloodline. Maybe that's why you're my mate?"

Looking stunned, Talyn stared at her. "Equal? I never knew that."

"Neither did I. I don't think anyone does. It wasn't part of our education," she said, barely able to contain her excitement.

"It doesn't change what I am," he said, shaking his head.

"It changes everything!"

Getting up, she began pacing, her voice growing stronger with conviction. "Don't you see? The bloodlines haven't always been disproportionate. At one point, Vajjer and Lazuil were equals. Sure, their strongest traits have evolved over time, but one isn't inherently superior to the other. You have as much right as anyone to stand at my side. All this time, you've doubted your worth and talked about how I should be with a Lazuil because they are inherently better, but you're wrong. Nothing separates us but a twist of fate."

Talyn sat motionless, tension radiating from him. "I—I don't know…"

Kneeling beside him, she took his hands in hers. "All of this information together is undeniable. They will believe us. How could they not."

His anguished expression softened as he whispered, "But this is your life we're gambling with. I'm terrified you'll get hurt."

Aayla pressed her forehead to his. "I know. I know because I'm terrified they will hurt you, but the evidence is solid. We need to trust it and try because I won't spend the rest of my life pretending we aren't bonded."

For a moment, he said nothing. Then, determination filled his eyes, and he kissed her fiercely. "Okay. Let's do it."

"Really?" she asked, hope blooming within her.

He smiled. "Yes. Let's work to repeal the law first. Then we can announce our bond."

Beaming, she nodded. "Agreed. Let's find Martok."

They dressed swiftly, making their way to the roof garden, where they found Martok lying in the long grass beneath a brittlebush tree rimmed with rainbow snowwood. Skyla was draped across his chest, her eyes closed as if savouring the rare moment of peace.

"Martok, how are you?" Aayla called out as they approached.

"Aayla!" Martok's face lit up with a warm smile. "Always a pleasure. We're good, thanks. We spent the night helping the humans with a situation in the south, so we are just feeling a bit exhausted at the moment."

"I can imagine," she said with genuine sympathy. "Sorry to disturb you. I have a quick question."

"Of course," Martok replied, sitting up as Skyla gently shifted off his chest. "What can I do for you?"

Aayla hesitated, rubbing her hands together nervously. "I want to call a vote to repeal a law. Specifically, the one that forbids a Unix from mating with anyone but a Lazuil."

Martok's expression shifted to confusion as he exchanged a glance with Skyla. "What? I don't understand. Why would you want to repeal that?"

"Because I've uncovered evidence supporting its repeal," she said firmly.

Martok's brows furrowed, concern replacing confusion. "That law only exists to protect you and all Unix. Why would you want to repeal it?"

Talyn stood rigid beside her, his gaze fixed on the ground. Aayla could feel his anxiety radiating through their bond, a storm of worry and fear he was barely containing.

Her frustration boiled over. "Because," she snapped, her voice sharp, "I refuse to live under a law that threatens my Guardian, perpetuating the idea that one bloodline is superior to another, and most importantly, that dictates who I can or cannot call my mate."

Skyla studied Aayla carefully before turning to stare intently at Talyn.

Aayla felt a tightness in her chest as if the air had become thick and difficult to breathe. Her heart pounded relentlessly, each beat echoing in her ears like a distant drum. Her thoughts raced uncontrollably, a chaotic swirl of worries and what-ifs that made it difficult to focus. She was instantly nervous that she had made a mistake. Did Skyla see through their charade?

She couldn't keep her hands still, her fingers tapping a nervous rhythm on her leg. Every noise seemed louder, every shadow more ominous, feeding her unease. Her stomach churned, and she felt a constant sense of dread as if something terrible was about to happen at any moment. She tried to steady her breathing and maintain a calm exterior.

After what felt like an eternity, Skyla shifted her gaze back to Aayla and paused before opening her mouth. "I guess that's reasonable. It's a situation we have never found ourselves in, so we can't imagine what it must be like. For both of you."

Relief washed over Aayla, and she released a breath she hadn't realised she'd been holding. "Thank you. We'll leave for Nannuval immediately."

Turning to leave, Martok's voice stopped her. "Wait. You can't leave now. The meeting of intergalactic dignitaries is only a few weeks away. You wouldn't make it to Nannuval, debate a repeal, and return to Earth in time."

Frozen in place, Aayla closed her eyes. He was right. Approximately 36 different races were going to be arriving on Earth soon. The increased number of visitors meant there would be a significantly increased Aldredth presence on Earth for the duration of the meetings.

The sheer scale of the gathering brought a heightened risk of conflicts, making the presence of a Unix essential. Many races had also explicitly stated they would only attend if a Unix were present, valuing the additional layer of protection they provided.

Introducing a new planet to the galaxy was a rare and momentous event, drawing the attention of countless races eager to make their mark. While some arrived with noble intentions, seeking cooperation and mutual growth, others sought to exploit the naivety of the emerging race for personal gain. The Aldredth played a crucial role in these gatherings, acting as mediators to maintain peace among attendees and ensuring any agreements forged were balanced and free from manipulation.

Talyn's voice brushed softly against her mind. *We've waited this long. We can wait one more month.*

Aayla turned to him, her frustration and longing evident in her eyes. *A month of agony. Haven't we waited enough? Haven't we suffered enough already?*

He reached out to pull her into a tight embrace. *I would wait forever for you. And if everything doesn't go according to plan, then this may be the only time we have together, so I intend not to waste it.*

The light-hearted teasing made a small smile tug on her lips. Slightly heavily, she turned back to Martok. "Fine. I'll wait until after the gathering, but the moment it concludes, I'm leaving for Nannuval."

"Agreed," Martok said, his relief evident. "Thank you for understanding. I hope we don't ask too much of you?"

Aayla shook her head. "No, of course not. It brings me joy to help those around me. Truly."

Martok's face brightened at her words, and after bidding each other farewell, Aayla and Talyn retreated to the Bathing Pools.

The next few hours passed in blissful relaxation, their shared laughter and quiet moments a balm for their weary souls. But all too soon, duty called. With heavy hearts, they agreed it was time for them to separate and return to their responsibilities, leaving behind the tranquillity of Mir'ka for the demands of their roles.

However, Aayla felt a sense of relief as she returned to active duty, finding solace in the purpose and peace it brought her. Helping others offered a sense of fulfilment that nothing else could replicate. The more time she spent idle, the more guilt and anxiety crept in, reminding her of the countless people relying on her. Resting felt indulgent when she knew her efforts could make a tangible difference. The satisfaction she derived from aiding those around her had been sorely missed during her idle days.

Having just concluded an exhausting morning meeting in the Command Centre, Aayla left swiftly, her mind focused on one person. And she knew exactly where to find him.

Chapter Forty-Six

Talyn strode into the Training Centre, grinning wildly at Aayla's last joke. He felt whole. A deep sense of bliss filling every part of him.

Lost in thought, he didn't immediately notice the security force standing in the ring, all eyes on him. Most of them looked at him with open curiosity, but Seth's lips curled into a smile.

"Sorry, I'm a bit late," Talyn said, his voice steady despite the sudden awareness of being watched.

"To be honest, we weren't expecting you today," Seth replied, his grin widening before a flicker of concern crossed his face. "Are you well?"

Talyn considered the question. He had never felt better in his entire life. "I truly am."

"That would explain the glow. You're literally glowing," Mark chimed in, grinning. "Not just the happy kind, though—like, actually glowing."

Talyn unfurled his wings, letting the faint shimmer catch the light. Whatever mystery lingered could wait. Right now, he was simply enjoying the moment. Seth clapped him firmly on the shoulder, grinning. "No night hunts for you."

Talyn's lips twitched in amusement. "So, I take it you've all mastered that left-flank attack we were practising last week?"

"We're so good, you'll never need to mention it again," Mark shot back with a laugh.

Talyn chuckled and guided them through a series of exercises, joining them in combat drills. Laughter and friendly banter filled the room, camaraderie shining through.

He watched intently as the group practised. "David, your right arm is dropping too late, leaving your entire side exposed. You need to—"

Talyn's head snapped toward the door, a warmth spreading through his chest as he felt her presence. Moments later, Aayla rounded the corner, and their eyes locked, his heart swelling with love.

Aayla-mine.

Aayla gave him a crooked smile, sauntering over to him. She placed her hands on his chest as he cupped her face, their foreheads touching in a gentle, intimate nuzzle.

I love you so much, he whispered.

As I love you, my mate, she murmured, her voice heavy with longing. *I've missed you more than words can say*. She pressed soft kisses along his jaw. *Your jaw is so warm and hard... like something else I'd like to have my lips around right now.*

Talyn let out a low, guttural sound, and Aayla's laughter bubbled up, unrestrained and joyful. He pulled her close, brushing his lips against the sensitive spot behind her ear. *I'll remember this when I take my time savouring every inch of you*, he teased, scraping his teeth lightly against her skin.

She shivered, thighs clenching as a wave of desire washed over her. *I hope you do*, she purred, making him laugh in response.

Their gaze lingered, the rest of the room momentarily forgotten until Aayla glanced at the squadron, who had paused and watched them with varying degrees of amusement. Her cheeks flushed.

"I'm sorry to interrupt your training," she said sheepishly, giving Seth a weak smile. "I just wanted to stop by and say hi."

"I'm glad to see you looking so well. Breathtakingly beautiful as always." Seth replied with a broad grin.

"Stop flirting with my Charge, Seth," Talyn teased, raising an eyebrow as Seth winked.

Aayla leaned into Talyn's chest, laughing. "I'll leave you boys to it," she said, her gaze softening as she looked up at him. "Come to me when you're done."

"Always," he promised.

Biting her lip, her voice dropped to a husky whisper. *I might be deliciously naked when you return, remembering the feeling of when you thrust inside of me—*

Before she could finish, Talyn cradled the back of her head and placed a slow, smouldering kiss on her neck. *Testing my resolve? It's hanging by a thread.*

Laughing, she stretched her arms above her head, arching against him, her breasts pressed into Talyn's chest, her wings spread wide. A soft moan escaped her lips. "Sorry, I've been sitting all day. I needed a little stretch."

His hand slid down her back, pulling her even closer until her hips pressed firmly against him. He opened his mouth to speak but froze, eyes widening in disbelief. *Are you... Not wearing any underwear?*

I thought it would be a fun surprise, she replied, a wicked grin spreading across her face.

In front of all these human males? He asked, eyebrows shooting up.

Talyn was positively speechless.

You're scandalised! Aayla laughed harder this time.

He laughed along with her, shaking his head. *Go, before I swallow my tongue.*

With one final kiss on his jaw, Aayla sauntered toward the door, her hips swaying with deliberate grace. Talyn didn't move, his body frozen as his gaze followed her every step. His chest tightened with the force of his emotions, love and longing burning within him. A soft smile tugged at his lips as she glanced back, her eyes meeting his.

I love you, her voice echoed in his mind, warm and steady.

Always and forever, he whispered back, his words a tender promise, wrapping around her like an embrace.

CHAPTER FORTY-SEVEN

They returned to their usual routine of helping the humans, having meetings, undertaking media interviews, healing injured Aldredth that arrived on ships, training, and hosting nightly functions honouring various causes or people.

Every moment was intertwined with shared glances and secret kisses and touches.

That morning, they had almost been caught in an embrace by a group of humans, their lips barely parting in time as hurried footsteps echoed through the corridor. Aayla's cheeks had flushed, but Talyn had simply grinned, his confidence unshaken. So far, their moments of intimacy hadn't caused any problems.

Now, as they walked down another long corridor, Talyn's wings shifted, one sliding over her back in a quiet, protective caress. Aayla leaned into him briefly, savouring the warmth and the way his feathers brushed her skin like a lover's whisper.

When she glanced up at him, she found his gaze fixed on her, burning with an intensity that made her breath hitch. His lips curled into a soft, knowing smile, the love in his eyes unmistakable.

It's not too late to run back to our quarters and disappear for a while, she teased, her voice light with temptation.

Unfortunately, it is. Talyn replied with a low chuckle, his hand brushing hers as they reached their destination. *Because we're here.*

He opened the door to reveal the familiar studio space within Aldredth Tower. The room was a vast, sleek, open expanse filled with ambient lighting that softly reflected off high-tech surfaces and gleaming glass walls. Multiple doors lined the perimeter, leading in and out from different angles, allowing for a constant, quiet flow of people moving through the space. The layout was meticulously designed to accommodate the heightened security needs of the Aldredth, yet still felt welcoming and professional. It was a perfect blend of functionality and style.

Today, it felt more like a cozy gathering than a press event as Liz Everton welcomed Aayla back to her usual seat in front of her. The crew bustled around, making last-minute adjustments, but Liz leaned in with an easy smile, her warmth unmistakable.

"So, Aayla, thank you for speaking with me again," Liz said, her voice carrying a friendly tease. "How does it feel to be one of my regulars?"

Aayla laughed, giving a mock sigh as she settled into her seat. "I'm starting to think you just like putting me in the hot seat," she replied, her eyes sparkling with humour. "Or maybe it's my sparkling personality you find entertaining?"

"Oh, no complaints from me," Liz said with a grin. "Let's admit it, you're pure gold for ratings." She winked, and the two women shared a quick laugh.

Talyn stood behind Aayla in his usual protective stance, arms crossed and posture deceptively relaxed. A glint of amusement softened his gaze as he watched the exchange as if he'd seen this playful routine many times before.

Liz leaned in, clasping her hands together. "Let's get started, Aayla. Now, there's a lot we already know about you, but this new decision you've made regarding your desire to repeal the law made us realise how much we still don't know. Let me start with what we do know." Her smile widened. "So... you are Aayla, daughter of Sabee and Marlia?"

Aayla raised an eyebrow, playing along. "Yes, that's correct."

"The child Unix who has lived her entire life under this rule."

"Yes," Aayla answered, stifling a laugh. "Do you want my favourite colour next?"

Liz shot her a playful look. "Oh, I already know that. But out of all the Aldredth on Earth, you and Talyn stand out because neither of you has a declared mate. Which, as you've mentioned before, means that, at least by human standards, you're a virgin."

Aayla's smile faltered, a flush colouring her cheeks as she realised what Liz had asked.

Behind her, Talyn made an unmistakable choking noise, and she turned just in time to catch him stifling a laugh with a carefully cleared throat and an averted gaze. He looked down at the floor, doing his best to compose himself, but his slight grin was impossible to miss.

Definitely not after what we did this morning, Talyn's voice echoed playfully in her mind.

Not exactly helping, Aayla thought back dryly.

Talyn looked up, catching her gaze, a mischievous smile tugging at his lips. *I have complete faith that you've got this under control.*

The room was quiet as the crew waited for her response.

Aayla shot him a glare before returning her gaze to Liz. Plastering a polite smile onto her face to mask her embarrassment, she couldn't bring herself to lie, so she simply offered a subtle nod instead.

Liz, with her trademark wide grin, seemed to sense Aayla's discomfort and basked in the moment as if she had set a delightful trap.

Feeling a rush of realisation wash over her, Aayla couldn't shake the feeling that she had just fallen for her trick.

Clearing her throat, a playful gleam in her eyes, Liz leaned in closer. "So, as an unmated Aldredth…" she began, her voice dripping with cheeky wit, "you're heading back to your homeworld to tackle that Guardian Law, aren't you?"

Aayla's playful expression faded, replaced by one of unwavering focus. "Yes. We have ample evidence to support the repeal of that law. It's archaic and has no place in our modern society. Guardians and their Charges, like Talyn and me, deserve the autonomy to make choices about our own lives, free from the fear of punishment."

She glanced at Talyn, her voice softening. "We are given no more than we can bear. And this I can bear. I will not live like this any longer."

Turning her gaze back to Liz, she cleared her throat, determination etched on her face. "It's time to embrace change. In just a few short weeks, everything will be different." Aayla's voice softened as if reassuring herself. "Just a few more weeks. I can wait until then…"

Liz nodded, her tone shifting to one of gravity. "But how far are you willing to go for this? I know it's important, but it sounds like it could be a pretty serious battle."

Aayla's gaze turned steely, her voice steady and resolved. "I'll go as far as it takes. I'm not afraid to stand up to my people. This law has trapped Guardians for generations, and if I have to fight to my last breath to break it, so be it."

Liz nodded, visibly moved. "So, it's really that important to you?"

Aayla's expression softened, but her conviction remained clear. "It's the most significant thing I'll ever do. Even if it's the last thing I ever do."

Liz's expression turned serious, her gaze steady on Aayla. "So... this decision, the timing of it, does it have anything to do with everything that's happened recently? It's been quite a sequence of events. Talyn announces he's stepping down as your Guardian. Then, there was the incident with Giorgieon kissing you, Talyn attacking him, and finally, the two of you disappearing for a week 'to clear your heads.' The official statement was pretty... diplomatic. But can you tell us, in your own words, what really happened?"

Aayla took a steadying breath, glancing over at Talyn. He was staring hard at the floor, his shoulders tense. When he finally met her gaze, the weight of recent events was etched in every line of his face. The guilt of what had happened with Giorgieon lingered.

I love you, she thought, letting the warmth of that truth settle between them.

As I will always love you, my mate, Talyn's thoughts reached her, but the sadness still etched his face.

Aayla turned back to Liz, choosing her words carefully. "It comes down to an accumulation of moments—years of them—that finally hit a breaking point. I suppose, in human terms... we'd reached the end of our rope."

Liz raised an eyebrow, her confusion evident.

"We are what we are," Aayla said slowly, "and there's only so long you can convince yourself you're something else. Fighting fate doesn't make it any less inevitable."

Liz leaned forward subtly, probing further. "So, you're saying all these incidents are connected? Talyn, for instance, he only attacked Giorgieon because of that kiss?"

Aayla smirked, glancing at Talyn, who had the slightest hint of a grin tugging at his lips. "I wouldn't exactly call it a kiss. But yes, Talyn's instinct to protect me is... intense. And in Aldredth culture, uninvited touch is no small matter."

"Are there any lingering tensions between Talyn and Giorgieon?" Liz pressed, her voice laced with intrigue.

"No. Absolutely not. It was a misunderstanding that spiralled out of control." She ran a hand through her hair, her gaze sweeping the room as she reflected. "That's part of why we needed to step back. Stepping away was necessary," Aayla added, a quiet intensity in her voice.

A thick silence lingered in the air. "Sometimes, we all need to reset," she said quietly. "It gave us a moment to breathe, to be ourselves without the weight of everything else. No titles, no responsibilities. Just... us."

When she looked back at Talyn, his gaze was steady, and the depth of his love, the unspoken connection they shared, was unmistakable.

Liz paused, a small, admiring smile on her lips as she glanced between Aayla and Talyn. "Thank you, Aayla. That's very powerful, and I think a lot of people watching will understand what you're fighting for."

Aayla's cheeks flushed as she bit the inside of her cheek, suddenly aware of how much she'd let slip. She hadn't meant to reveal so much—it was easy to get lost in her thoughts.

After a heartbeat, Liz released a breath and grinned. "How about we switch gears for something a little lighter?"

Laughing, Aayla felt visibly relieved by the shift in mood. "Yes, please."

Liz pulled out her tablet, scrolling through with a mischievous look. "I asked our audience to send in some fun questions for you. Are you up for a bit of spontaneity?"

Aayla smiled warmly. "I think I'd enjoy that."

Over the next hour, they plunged into a lively stream of questions that ranged from hilariously bizarre to unexpectedly heartfelt. The conversation flowed with effortless ease, a rhythm shaped by playful banter and authentic connection. The atmosphere stayed light, warm, and unguarded, as if the cameras had disappeared and all that remained was the comfort of two old friends simply enjoying each other's company.

"And lastly," Liz said, glancing at the screen with a smirk, "what's the most unique gift you have received since arriving on Earth?"

Aayla's lips twitched, the faintest trace of amusement. "Someone gave me a broken compass," she said. "It didn't point north—actually, it didn't point anywhere. They told me it was a reminder that sometimes, you need to find your own direction."

Liz blinked, a laugh escaping her. "Are you sure they weren't just trying to offload their junk onto you?"

Aayla's eyes sparkled with warmth as she replied, "No, I think of it as a reminder. If we have the strength, we can create our own path even when nothing points the way."

Liz met her gaze, visibly moved. "That's... beautiful."

As Liz concluded the segment, she turned her attention to Talyn, acknowledging him with a smile that conveyed warmth and appreciation. "Thank you both for joining me today," she said, her voice sincere.

Then, with a more personal touch, she continued, "And Talyn, I just want to take a moment to recognise you. It's clear that you often operate in the background, and while you may sometimes be overlooked, your genuine kindness and all the good you've done haven't gone unnoticed. You are a constant source of strength. You give us something to aspire to, and I know I speak for many when I say we wish you nothing but the best."

Aayla smiled, feeling a surge of gratitude for Liz's thoughtful words. It meant a lot to her that Liz took the time to acknowledge Talyn's sacrifices and character.

Talyn seemed caught off guard by the praise, but he nodded appreciatively.

"Thank you, Liz," he replied, his voice steady but touched.

As they wrapped up, Aayla bid Liz farewell and stood to face Talyn, pulling him into a tight embrace.

The next few days passed quickly, with a significant increase in the number of requested media interviews. She wondered if it was because the humans suspected she and Talyn were mated, but no one mentioned anything to them directly in the interviews, so maybe she was wrong.

As Aayla sat beside Talyn in the bustling Dining Hall, his arm wrapped protectively around her, surrounded by friends and laughter, she stole a moment to glance at him with eyes full of love. His infectious laughter rang through the air, and she couldn't help but be captivated by the way his eyes crinkled at the corners, his smile illuminating the room.

She observed as people naturally gravitated towards him, drawn by a charm that effortlessly resonated with everyone he met, making them feel both valued and loved.

In that moment, amidst the jovial atmosphere, everything else faded away, and she was overwhelmed with a deep, unbreakable love for him. Aayla's gaze lingered on him, her heart swelling with gratitude for having him by her side, sharing these precious moments of joy and camaraderie.

He noticed her gaze and gently squeezed her hip in acknowledgment as his wings adjusted to envelop her protectively from behind.

They chatted and laughed for hours before Talyn glanced at the time and frowned. "I'm late for training."

She nuzzled into his neck and placed a soft, tentative kiss on his chin. "Go," she whispered, her voice light with affection. "I need to check on a few things at the Command Centre anyway."

He inhaled deeply, savouring her scent, before groaning softly. "I'll find you after training," he promised. *And then... I think we need a few hours. Alone.*

Warmth blossomed in her chest at his words, her cheeks heating as a knowing smile curved her lips. *You read my mind,* she replied, her voice teasing but full of anticipation.

Talyn leaned down, brushing his lips against her forehead. His hand lingered on her waist for a moment longer as if reluctant to let her go. *Until then,* he murmured, his voice an intimate caress, before finally stepping away.

Aayla watched him leave, her heart full yet yearning for the promise of their time together. She took a steadying breath and stood to make her way to the Command Centre, already counting the hours until they could steal away into their private world again.

Chapter Forty-Eight

In the expansive Training Centre, Talyn guided the security force through their regular rigorous exercises, his passion for training evident in every move he made. The room echoed with the clash of swords and the grunts of exertion, each sound a testament to the hard work and dedication of the team in front of them.

Talyn moved among them with a keen eye, observing their techniques with a mix of critical analysis and genuine pride. He loved training them, not just for their progress but for the camaraderie that had blossomed within the group since they formed.

The squad, armed with swords, practised their techniques with precision. Each swing and parry was met with encouraging nods from Talyn and occasional light-hearted banter among the squad members.

"Keep your guard up, Ethan!" Talyn called out, a smile tugging at the corners of his mouth.

Ethan, a skilled yet sometimes overzealous fighter, grinned back and adjusted his stance. Laughter and jokes often punctuated the sessions, strengthening the bond that made their teamwork seamless.

Transitioning to hand-to-hand combat, the atmosphere grew even more focused. Talyn demonstrated moves with a mix of authority and enthusiasm, and his passion for his role was evident as he sparred with his team. His movements were fluid and controlled, each demonstration an opportunity for his squad to learn and improve.

He relished these moments, where teaching and camaraderie intertwined, fostering both skill and trust.

As they grappled and countered, the squad members encouraged each other, their respect for Talyn mirrored in their dedication to the training. "Nice move, William!" one called out as a member executed a perfect takedown. Talyn watched with pride, knowing their unity and mutual support were as important as their combat skills.

Usually, a higher-ranking Aldredth would undertake training sessions. However, it had been noticed from childhood that Talyn possessed a natural ability in the training arena that could not be matched. That was how he was trusted with such an important task, for his training would be why those under him lived or died in combat. It was one of the most important positions an Aldredth could hold.

As the session ended, Talyn called the squad to gather in a loose circle and grinned at them. "Great work today, everyone. Your progress is impressive. Ethan, that guard was solid, and David, that takedown was textbook perfect."

Ethan, catching his breath, gave a thumbs-up. "Thanks, I'll keep working on my footwork."

David, stretching his sore muscles, nodded. "Appreciate it. I'm starting to feel the flow better."

Another squad member, Denzil, chimed in with a playful smirk, "Looks like we're ready for the big leagues, huh?"

Talyn chuckled. "Keep this up, and you'll be near unstoppable."

The squad members shared a few high-fives and pats on the back, their camaraderie evident. "Same time tomorrow?" asked one of them, to which Talyn responded with a firm nod.

"Absolutely. Rest up and come ready to push even harder."

As they dispersed, there were a few last comments and laughter. "Anyone up for a cool-down jog?" one suggested, while another teased, "Only if you're buying the drinks afterwards."

With one last glance at his team, pride in their progress still warming his chest, Talyn strode out of the Training Centre toward the Command Centre where Aayla awaited him. His thoughts lingered on her, her laugh, her smile, the way she softened every edge of his day.

Then, the world tilted.

A blinding pain struck him like a dagger to the heart, so sharp and sudden it almost drove him to his knees. A raw cry tore from his throat as he clutched his chest, staggering sideways into a console table. The impact sent a delicate sculpture crashing to the floor, its shatter echoing like a warning bell.

He doubled over, gasping for breath, his vision swimming. The corridor around him spun, voices rising in panic. Hands reached for him, but their words were muffled beneath the roaring white noise filling his ears.

Fumbling, he pulled down his shirt, expecting to see blood, a wound, anything to explain the agony ripping through him. But his chest was unmarked, his skin smooth and unmarred.

And yet, the pain intensified, sharp and unrelenting.

Then it hit him, a realisation colder than the void between stars. The pain wasn't his.

It was Aayla's.

"Aayla's in trouble," he choked, his voice hoarse but fierce. Shoving off helping hands, he straightened, gripping the hilt of his sword as he broke into a sprint.

He burst through the doors of the Command Centre and saw a state of mayhem as his Lumina vibrated intensely.

Aldredth were running around in a state of panic as they scrambled for answers, but Talyn barely registered the noise. His eyes locked on the central screen, and what he saw froze his blood.

Aayla. She was restrained by a hooded figure cloaked in darkness. One clawed hand clamped over her mouth, silencing her cries. The other drove an alien blade into her chest.

Talyn's heart plummeted, his breath catching in his throat. The fear momentarily paralysed him before he recognised the room on the screen. He was running in that direction before his brain registered the thought.

He reached the meeting room, its entrance crowded with Aldredth scanning every inch for evidence. Talyn shoved his way through, his eyes locking with Daxion's grim face.

"She's gone," Daxion said, his voice trembling with barely contained fury. "Someone took her."

The words hit Talyn like a blow. He staggered back, his fists clenching. "No," he whispered, the denial a fragile plea. "Who?"

Daxion shook his head. "We don't know yet, but they took her alive."

Closing his eyes, he thanked the stars that she was taken alive. The tight band around Talyn's chest loosened just enough to let him breathe.

Alive. If they wanted her dead, they wouldn't have gone to the trouble of taking her.

Turning on his heel, Talyn raced back to the Command Centre, determination blazing through the fear constricting his chest. He dropped into an empty chair, fingers flying over the console as he entered commands. The system hummed, data scrolling across the screen faster than his eyes could track.

Finally, a name appeared. The figure had been identified as a Zarkan.

Towering nearly seven feet tall, the Zarkans' skeletal frames were draped in rough, leathery skin that glistened a sickly green under any light. They had multi-faceted eyes and elongated limbs that ended in sharp, claw-like appendages that were utilised in battle. Despite their sharp claws, Zarkans used plasma blasters as their primary weapon.

The Zarkans communicated through guttural clicks and hisses through their elongated, snout-like mouths. Known for their ruthless efficiency in hunting and combat, they were relentless predators. Compared to an Aldredth, they moved slower and were weaker than a male Aldredth but slightly stronger than a female Aldredth.

Talyn's fists tightened as the security footage replayed. The Zarkan had cloaked itself with glamour, a rudimentary technology that disguised its true form. From a distance, it had perfectly mimicked the appearance of an injured Aldredth, but up close, the illusion faltered, revealing a faint, telltale shimmer that Aayla never had the chance to see.

Aayla had finished her tasks early and had been on her way to the Training Centre. To him. But when she heard cries of pain echoing through the corridor, her path diverted. She ran to the Zarkan's side.

Talyn's jaw clenched as he watched the recording. She had no idea what she was walking into.

The Zarkan moved with brutal efficiency. It used its strength to strike Aayla, knocking her down before she could see the telltale shimmer of glamour. In the blink of an eye, the Zarkan covered her mouth with one hand so she couldn't call for help and stabbed her in the chest with a blade filled with powerful sedatives that worked almost immediately. Her body went limp in seconds, and the Zarkan lifted her effortlessly.

Seconds. That was all it took.

The footage showed the creature disappearing onto a balcony, Aayla's lifeless form draped over its shoulder.

"How the hell did it get in here?" Martok roared, his voice shaking the walls as he slammed a fist onto the console.

"I don't know, but we'll find out," Rune vowed.

The Command Centre buzzed with frantic activity. Every screen lit up with data feeds, maps, and tracking attempts. Teams worked to piece together how the Zarkan had bypassed Earth's defences, infiltrated their stronghold, and, most pressingly, where it had taken Aayla.

Talyn was trying to track the direction Aayla had been taken when Daxion's voice cut through the air.

"A portal has been detected in Peru!"

Talyn's head snapped up, adrenaline flooding his veins. "Where's the nearest unit?"

"We have one in the immediate proximity and another only a few minutes away," Daxion replied quickly.

Closing his eyes, Talyn fought the urge to fly to her. Every fibre of his being screamed to act, run, fight. But he forced himself to stay rooted. He had to think. To plan. To trust.

He knew they would be long gone by the time he got there, and since Aldredth were already on the ground, he needed to trust in their ability.

"Coming on screen now."

Turning back to the screen, Talyn saw a portal opening with a dazzling display, expanding from a pinpoint of white light into a swirling vortex of electric blue and deep purple energy.

The air shimmered and distorted around it, creating rippling waves. Inside the vortex, flickering images of distant stars and galaxies hinted at a passage through space and time. The portal emitted a haunting hum, casting an ethereal glow and eerie reflections, inviting yet intimidating to all who gazed upon it.

”Zarkans don't have portal tech,” Daxion muttered, his brow furrowed. "Where did they get that?"

"It explains how they got to Earth," Martok growled.

"But not how they got in here," Talyn snapped, his frustration boiling over.

He watched the scene unfold on the screens in front of him, his anxiety a tight knot in his stomach. His heart pounded as he saw Loxian and Graca enter the fray, their swords gleaming as they engaged the large group of Zarkans surrounding the portal. The clash of battle was marked by the sickening slice of swords cutting through flesh, met with the fierce retaliation of sharp claws raking the air and the searing blasts from plasma guns.

On the screen, Loxian parried a blow aimed at his head, his sword sparking against the enemy's blade. He watched him disarm an opponent with a swift riposte, the plasma gun skidding across the ground. Graca's movements were equally fluid, easily dodging a plasma shot and slicing through an enemy's arm with precision.

As the battle intensified, Talyn's grip on the bench tightened. Ophelian and Rythar burst onto the scene, their arrival shifting the momentum even further into the Aldredth's favour. Rythar's lightning-fast reflexes were swift, disarming two enemies in quick succession, while Ophelian moved with lethal grace, her strikes efficient and deadly.

The screen captured every detail of the fight, from the coordinated efforts of the teams to the seamless transitions between offence and defence, and the growing desperation of the Zarkans. Talyn watched Rythar deliver a decisive blow while Loxian and Graca's tandem attacks left no room for the Zarkans to retaliate.

The tide shifted further as Ophelian detonated an explosive beneath the portal, severing any chance of escape. The vortex collapsed in on itself, leaving only silence in its wake.

Amidst the chaos, Talyn spotted two additional Zarkans hiding behind the battle. One of the Zarkans held a slender figure in his arms. Aayla.

His breath hitched.

"Rythar to your right!" he shouted into his Lumina, his voice cracking with urgency.

But his warning came too late. The Zarkans vanished into the shadows, taking Aayla with them before Ophelian and Rythar could reach them.

As the last Zarkan fell, the screen showed the Aldredth regrouping, their breaths heavy and faces marked with frustration. They quickly disbanded and went in different directions, searching for the two who had gotten away with Aayla.

Whilst the other Aldredth in the Command Centre set out to locate where the remaining Zarkans had fled, Talyn replayed the footage repeatedly, his stomach churning. Zooming in on Aayla, he noted every detail. A glowing band restrained her arms, legs, and wings. He noted the way her head lolled back, unconscious but alive. Relief mingled with anguish as he saw the subtle rise and fall of her chest.

Hours dragged by with no further leads. Talyn's fingers flew over the controls, searching through endless data feeds for any sign of her, and his heart ached with every second that passed.

His mind raced with a torrent of worries, each one more urgent than the last, making it impossible to focus. He could feel his stomach knotting, a wave of nausea threatening to rise. Every sound seemed amplified, every movement in the room driving his anxiety to breaking point. His hands shook, his body stiff with tension, and a crushing sense of dread settled over him, the walls of the room closing in like a trap.

Cythara had tried to offer him food several times as he had missed several meals, but he didn't dare stop for even a second. He was also so nauseous that the smell and sight of the food repulsed him.

As Cythara stopped next to him for the fourth time with a tray, he felt his pent-up fear and rage overwhelm him.

"Talyn, you need to eat something," she said softly.

In a fit of anger, Talyn shoved the tray off the bench, causing it to plummet to the floor with a deafening crash.

"I don't want any food!" he screamed, his voice filled with raw anger. His chest heaved as his fists clenched tight, every muscle in his body coiled with pent-up fury.

Cythara stumbled back, her eyes wide with shock and fear, her confusion mirrored by Daxion, who instantly materialised protectively in front of her.

Talyn squeezed his eyes shut, willing the fury to subside, but it was a tidal wave too strong to contain. He knew his anger was coming from his mating bond, but he had lost control of his emotions.

"Sorry," he muttered, the word barely a whisper, his chest tightening with regret. Without waiting for a response, he stormed out of the room, his steps heavy with frustration, desperate to escape the suffocating weight of his emotions.

He stumbled onto the balcony, gasping in the cold night air as though it could cool the fire inside him. His heart pounded, each beat a reminder that he was losing control. He was in a dangerous spot because Guardians shouldn't be emotionally affected by the separation from their Charges. If he didn't regain control of his emotions, it wouldn't be long before they realised he was responding as if only a mate would. His feelings were betraying him. The bond, the constant, maddening pull to her, clouded his every thought.

His fingers gripped the railing so tightly that the metal creaked under his strength, but it did nothing to calm the storm inside him. Every breath he drew felt like it might be his last, his body fighting against the emotions tearing through him.

"Talyn?"

The voice was quiet but full of concern. He turned slowly, bracing himself for Martok's inevitable questions.

"I'm sorry, Martok. For my outburst," Talyn said, his voice hoarse, refusing to meet Martok's gaze. His own eyes remained locked on the city lights below as if avoiding the intense worry in Martok's expression.

"We're worried for you," Martok said gently. "What's going on?"

Taking a shaky breath, he looked up to meet his eyes. "It's all my fault. I wasn't with her. I didn't protect. She got taken right under my nose, and I did nothing. And she is who knows where at this point. Every second that passes without finding her is another second they are doing who knows what to her."

His eyes brimmed with raw emotion, glistening with unshed tears as he spoke. His voice trembled with sincerity, each word a struggle to release the weight of her feelings. He knew that his face, usually composed, now displayed a vulnerability that was almost painful to witness.

Martok's expression softened, his voice steady with reassurance. "We'll find her, Talyn. We won't stop until we do."

Talyn's eyes searched Martok's face, desperately clinging to his words. "What if they're hurting her because of us? What if we made them angry when we stopped the extraction? What if they're punishing her?"

Martok stroked his chin thoughtfully, the concern deepening in his eyes. "They took her alive, Talyn. They tried to take her off-planet alive. That tells me they still need her. She's their leverage. They won't risk hurting her, not yet. Not when they need her."

Talyn turned his gaze back to the balcony, the city lights flickering below like distant stars. A quiet whisper escaped his lips. "I hope you're right."

He stood there for a long time, the weight of his emotions pressing down on him, before finally returning to the Command Centre. As the first light of dawn broke through the sky, human media was in overdrive, and countless helicopters circled the building.

Talyn replayed a security recording that was highlighted as a potential lead on her whereabouts. With a heavy sigh, he realised it was a dead-end and quickly crossed it off the list. As his finger hovered over the next potential lead, an unbearable pain shot through his chest, seizing him with a force so intense that it felt like his heart was being ripped from his body.

Crying out in agony, he clutched at his heart as the world around him blurred.

The pain was excruciating, a white-hot burst that stole his breath away. A loud ringing filled his ears, drowning out all other sounds, and his knees buckled beneath him.

Desperate to remain upright, Talyn reached for the bench to steady himself, but his vision faded to white.

Another blinding wave of pain hit him, and he cried out in agony as his legs gave out and his body collapsed forward. The world went dark, and the floor rushed up to meet him as he fell into unconsciousness.

CHAPTER FORTY-NINE

Talyn awoke with a sharp gasp, the blinding overhead lights stabbing into his eyes like daggers. His lungs burned as he sucked in air, his heart pounding erratically in his chest.

"Talyn, don't move!" Aeryn's voice rang out, urgent and commanding.

Disoriented, he blinked rapidly, his vision clearing just enough to see the cluster of Aldredth surrounding him, their faces tense with worry. The cold floor beneath him and the hum of the Command Centre brought him back to the moment.

"What... happened?" he croaked, his voice barely audible.

"You collapsed," Soval said, his tone both concerned and firm. "Your heart rate was unstable, then you stopped breathing. We thought we were losing you."

"I'm fine," Talyn muttered, struggling to push himself upright. The room swayed violently as a wave of dizziness washed over him.

Hands pressed him back down with surprising force. "No, you're not fine," Soval snapped. "Lie still."

Aeryn crouched beside him, her piercing gaze locking onto his. "Talyn, what's going on? Why did this happen?"

His chest tightened, the overwhelming weight of guilt and fear clawing at him. "Aayla," he whispered, his voice cracking under the strain. "She's in trouble... I can feel it. They're hurting her."

Aeryn's brow furrowed in confusion. "How could you know that?"

Horror flooded through him as he realised he had said too much. Guardians weren't supposed to have such connections. "She... t—told me," he lied, his voice trembling as he avoided her gaze.

Aeryn studied him, her eyes narrowing as if weighing his words. Then she gave a slight, reluctant nod. It wasn't impossible for a Unix to communicate telepathically over large distances with another Aldredth in an emergency.

"We need to get you to the MedBay," Soval interrupted, his tone leaving no room for argument.

"No, I'm fine." Talyn snapped, trying again to stand. This time, the world tilted violently, and he nearly crumpled. Soval caught him before he could hit the floor.

"No, you're not. You weren't breathing. We need to check you over. No more excuses," Soval said firmly. "We'll make it quick, but you're getting checked. Then you can come back."

Realising he couldn't win, Talyn sighed heavily. "Fine. A quick check, but that's it."

With Soval's steady grip, they guided him to the MedBay. Aeryn wasted no time running diagnostics, her sharp eyes darting between the monitors and Talyn's pale face.

Lying on the bed, a wave of exhaustion momentarily overcame him. He leaned his head back against the pillow and closed his eyes. It felt as if his mind had drifted far away.

And then he heard it. A soft whisper cut through the fog of his thoughts.

Talyn.

The voice, faint but unmistakable, grew clearer. Aayla. She was calling to him. The sound pulled him deeper into the recesses of his mind, an invisible thread connecting them across the distance.

Talyn.

His eyes shot open as he bolted upright, gasping for air. His pulse thundered in his ears, his body on high alert.

"Talyn!" Soval called out, his voice sharp with alarm. "What's wrong?"

Ignoring him, Talyn swung his legs over the side of the bed and sprinted out of the MedBay without a word. His mind was racing, every second feeling like an eternity.

Bursting into the Command Centre, he moved with single-minded determination, weaving through the startled crowd. His wings brushed against others as he forced his way to a vacant terminal. Sliding into the chair, he quickly tapped at the screen, which lit up under his fingertips.

The map on the screen spun wildly under his touch. Closing his eyes, Talyn reached for the memory of her voice. He focused on the faint trace of her presence, letting it guide him like a beacon in the dark.

His hand moved instinctively, directing the map to zoom in. When he opened his eyes, the display was locked onto a bunker deep in the shadowy expanse of the Canadian forest.

Exhaling slowly, he stared intently at the building for a long moment before the trance was broken.

"There," he breathed, his voice trembling with certainty. Then louder, he exclaimed, "She's here!"

Martok stepped forward, his face lined with doubt. "How can you be sure?"

"She told me," Talyn said, his tone resolute despite the lie. He stood abruptly, the chair scraping loudly against the floor. "I'll meet you there."

"Talyn, wait!" Martok called after him as Talyn sprinted to the balcony without another word. He would not waste one more second.

Reaching the balcony, he spread his wings and launched into the cold night sky. The wind tore at his face, but he didn't care. Every second mattered. Aayla needed him, and nothing—not protocol, not logic—would stop him from reaching her.

Flying quickly into the sunset, Talyn landed hard on the embankment opposite the shadowed structure where two Aldredth scouts crouched in concealment. Behind him, the thrum of dozens of wings announced the silent arrival of a larger Aldredth force. They landed with practised silence, their figures melding seamlessly into the encroaching darkness.

Under the cover of night, the Aldredth advanced like ghosts, their movements coordinated and deadly. Communicating through subtle hand signals and telepathic commands, they moved swiftly to neutralise the perimeter sentry, leaving no trace of their presence except the whisper of disturbed air.

Reaching the building's entrance, Daxion used his abilities to rip the door from its hinges with a muffled thud. The Aldredth poured into the building, their weapons at the ready, before spreading out to navigate the dimly lit hallways.

Talyn pushed forward, heart pounding as he scanned the halls. A burst of gunfire echoed ahead, followed by silence. His communicator buzzed as Rune's voice came through, calm but grim.

"We've encountered mercenaries. Humans that were likely hired by the Zarkans. Resistance neutralised. Proceed with caution."

Talyn moved briskly through the corridors, and any enemies encountered were swiftly taken down, the sound of silenced gunfire and brief scuffles the only evidence of their presence. His jaw clenched, frustration bubbling under the surface. Room by room, they advanced, their eyes scanning every shadow for Aayla's presence.

Talyn's heart leapt with hope when they found two Zarkans sneaking out a back entrance, but their hands were empty, and they had been killed before they could be questioned about Aayla's location.

Despite their thorough search, each empty room heightened Talyn's anxiety. They moved deeper into the building, hopes diminishing with each unchecked corner. Finally, reaching the last room, they found it devoid of any sign of her. Frustration and concern were etched on the faces of the Aldredth around him as they realised Aayla was not there.

Regrouping, the Aldredth urgently wanted to return and continue their search elsewhere.

Talyn screamed out in anger, the sound of his voice echoing off the walls around him. His hands clenched into fists, shaking as his thoughts raced. He was so sure she was here. She had to be here. The Zarkans were here, so surely, she was, too.

Unless...

The thought struck him like a blade to the chest. Were they too late? Had they moved her? Or worse?

No, she couldn't be dead. He quickly squashed the thought before it threatened to overtake him. He would have felt it. She must be alive.

Talyn's fists tightened, rage bubbling to the surface.

"She has to be here!" His voice cracked, echoing through the barren halls.

Rune placed a firm hand on his shoulder. "Talyn, I'm sorry. There's no sign of her."

"No!" Talyn snarled, shaking him off. His chest heaved, his instincts screaming that he was missing something.

"It's time to move out," Rune said quietly.

He felt like he would scream till he was horse if he opened his mouth, so he simply nodded.

Walking slowly from the building, he passed through a series of rooms he hadn't traversed before, which opened into a small wooden stairwell on a concrete base.

As he walked past the dimly lit stairwell, something made him pause mid-step. He turned his head, eyes drawn to the shadowed steps climbing up to the floor beyond. An inexplicable chill ran down his spine as he became transfixed by the sight, his breath catching in his throat. His heartbeat quickened as a sense of foreboding washed over him.

The moment stretched until Daxion's hand grasped his arm. "Talyn, I was asking if you are okay?"

"Help me move this," Talyn pleaded as his head whipped back towards the stairs.

"Move what?" Daxion responded with a confused expression.

Talyn moved without answering, crossing the space quickly to push against the staircase. He didn't know why. He just knew that he needed to.

The others hesitated, confused, but they joined him. Hands pressed against the old wooden steps, tugging and pushing with all their might. Nothing budged.

"Talyn," Daxion stated breathlessly, "this staircase doesn't move. You must be mistaken."

As everyone started lifting their hands from the staircase, he knew they were right, but he couldn't stop trying.

He turned to look at Daxion, planning to beg him to keep helping when his eyes caught the sight of Ceeda. She was standing unnaturally still, staring at the railing with frighting intensity. He watched her for a long moment before she shook her head and reached forward to grab one spindle. Twisting it slightly, a loud click echoed before the concrete pad shook and slowly started sliding backwards.

Rune swore under his breath. "How did they manage this in a day?"

Talyn leaned over the edge, his sharp gaze tracing the rickety wooden steps spiralling down into the darkness below. A cold, damp draft wafted upward, prickling his skin.

"I think it's an old panic room," he murmured, his voice low yet laced with urgency.

Without hesitation, he descended, his boots echoing faintly against the narrow, creaking stairs. The tiny cement-lined bunker at the bottom was suffocatingly small, its walls pressing in. A cracked mosaic floor sprawled beneath his feet, the intricate tiles faded with age.

Rune appeared behind him, pausing mid-step as his eyes swept the empty room. "There's nothing here," he said, his tone cautious yet doubtful.

"There has to be," Talyn muttered, his jaw tight as he prowled the room. His eyes narrowed, locking onto a specific section of the floor. He crouched, running his fingers over the worn tiles. "These patterns... they form a circle, don't they?"

Rune knelt beside him, his fingers brushing the surface. "You're right. But if it's a design, it's subtle. What are we looking for?"

"An opening," Talyn said, already prying at the edges of the design. His nails scraped the tile until they caught on a loose piece. With a grunt, he pried it up, revealing a small, rusted lock hidden underneath.

"Did any of the Zarkans have an old-fashioned key on them?" he demanded, his voice sharp with impatience.

"I'm on it," Daxion replied, vanishing back up the stairs.

Minutes felt like hours to Talyn as he stared at the lock, his heart beating so loud he was sure everyone in the room could hear it.

Finally, Daxion returned, his hand gripping a small, tarnished key. Without hesitation, Talyn snatched it and fitted it into the lock. The mechanism clicked, and the sound was loud in the tense silence.

As he flipped the hatch open, a chill swept over him. The darkness below was oppressive, swallowing the faint light from above. The hole was narrow. Far too small for an Aldredth to fit through... unless they had been broken first.

Shining a light over the hole, Talyn's heart seized. The faint metallic glint of a chain caught his eye, coiled tightly around delicate hands. Aayla's hands. His breath hitched at the sight of her bruised, lifeless fingers, hanging limp.

"Pull her up!" he roared, his voice raw with urgency. He gripped the chain with all his strength, hauling it hand over hand as the others quickly joined in to help.

Their combined strength made quick work of the distance. But when her broken form finally emerged from the depths, Talyn's blood turned to ice.

Aayla was unconscious, her head lolling against his chest as he cradled her. Dirt and blood-streaked her face, and her breath was shallow and ragged. Her wings—those beautiful wings—hung at unnatural angles.

"Aayla..." he whispered, his voice trembling. A knot of anguish twisted in his chest, and for a moment, he could only stare, paralysed by the raw depth of his grief.

Graca snapped into action, her voice sharp and commanding. "Talyn, lay her down! Let me assess her injuries."

Graca moved with swift, practised precision, kneeling beside them as she quickly assessed Aayla's injuries. Her expression was grim but focused.

"She's alive," she confirmed, "but barely."

Loxian applied pressure to Aayla's mangled wings, staunching the worst of the bleeding. Graca worked quickly, wrapping bandages tightly around her injuries and injecting Pixx to stabilise her vitals.

"We've done all we can here," Graca said firmly. "We need to get her back now."

Without a moment's hesitation, Talyn pressed Aayla closer to him, his heart pounding in his chest as he surged toward the nearest exit, desperation fuelling every stride.

His wings unfurled, and he took to the sky with a powerful thrust. The cool night air stung his face, but he barely noticed. Every beat of his wings propelled him faster, his thoughts consumed by Aayla's fragile form in his arms.

By the time they reached the MedBay at Aldredth Tower, everyone had already prepared to receive her. Soval quickly assessed the situation, nodding at Graca's report.

"The good news is that the fractures are clean," Soval said. "With stabilisation, her wings will heal quickly. I'm going to keep her sedated for two days so they can heal faster and ensure she isn't in pain."

Talyn stood frozen as they worked, his hands clenching and unclenching at his sides. When the others finally stepped back several hours later, he moved forward, sinking onto the bed beside her. His hand brushed a stray strand of hair from her face, his touch featherlight. He knew he was drawing too much attention to himself, but he couldn't stop. He couldn't force himself to sit in the chair by her bedside. The distance was too great. The thought of being separated, even by inches, felt unbearable.

Martok entered late that night, a tray of food balanced in his hands. He set it down on the bench across the room with a deliberate gentleness before walking to the foot of the bed. His eyes swept over Talyn and the motionless figure beside him. "I hear you haven't eaten anything."

Talyn didn't look up, focusing on Aayla's pale, sleeping face. "I'm not hungry."

Martok let out a slow sigh, his voice steady but edged with something sharper. "And how do you think that will make her feel?"

That cut through. Talyn lifted his head, meeting Martok's calm but unyielding stare. "What do you mean by that?"

Martok chuckled softly, though there was no humour in it, and lowered himself onto the edge of the bed. "She's going to wake up and see you like this, a shadow of your normal self, barely holding it together. Do you think she won't notice? Do you think seeing you breaking yourself for her won't hurt her?"

The words hit like a blow. "I... hadn't thought about that."

"Then think about it," Martok urged.

Talyn's jaw tightened, shame creeping in. He looked away, guilt settling heavily on his chest. "Pixx," he whispered. "I'll take Pixx, nothing more."

Martok stood, the bed shifting slightly with his motion, but he didn't leave immediately. Talyn caught the weight of his stare and saw his eyes locked on the hand Talyn had resting against Aayla's cheek.

Martok's expression darkened, his frown cutting deep lines into his face. Slowly, his gaze travelled back up to meet Talyn's.

Talyn's heart pounded, his breath caught, dread curling in his gut like a storm ready to break.

"Deal," Martok said at last, his tone curt, his steps deliberate as he walked away.

422

CHAPTER FIFTY

Aayla felt like she had been drifting in a vast, suffocating void. The Zarkans had kept her sedated for most of her captivity. Her mind has been lost in a fog so thick she could only catch fleeting slivers of reality. Fragmented voices echoed in her mind, snippets of conversations she couldn't decipher in her disoriented state.

The only time they brought her back to full consciousness was after the failed extraction. Their rage was palpable, their frustration at being trapped on the planet directed solely at her. They were convinced she knew the location of another hidden portal. When she refused to tell them anything, they retaliated with cruel precision and tortured her by breaking her wings. Their laughter rang in her ears as she mentally called out to Talyn in agony.

That was the last thing she remembered before she slipped into nothingness.

As her senses began to stir, she felt the pull of consciousness like an anchor dragging her to shore. The first word from her lips was a plea. "Talyn..."

Strong, warm arms wrapped around her immediately, and she melted into their familiar strength.

"Aayla, it's okay." His voice trembled, thick with emotion. "You're safe now."

Blinking against the blur of her surroundings, she struggled to focus, her head pounding as her memories wavered. Disoriented, she clung to him instinctively, her fingers twisting in his clothes as she buried her face into the familiar crook of his neck. His scent wrapped around her like a lifeline.

Her body trembled uncontrollably, a storm of emotions overwhelming her. Relief that they were safe, fear from the ordeal, and an unshakable terror at how close she'd come to losing him forever.

Talyn's arms tightened around her as he whispered soothing words, his lips pressing a lingering kiss to her forehead.

Under his touch, her trembling eased. For the first time in days, she felt safe.

I'm so sorry, he murmured, his heart breaking. *I wasn't there to protect you.*

She pulled back just enough to look into his eyes. *There's nothing you could have done, even if you were. I was more worried about you.*

Me? His brows furrowed in anger. *You're the one who was taken and tortured!*

They kept me unconscious most of the time, she reassured him softly. *But I knew... I knew you'd blame yourself. That you wouldn't be eating or sleeping.*

His jaw tightened, his expression a storm of guilt. *The last few days...* He exhaled sharply. *They were hell.*

Her lips brushed his neck, a whisper of comfort. *I love you, Talyn. More than words can say.*

A broken smile touched his face. *As do I, my beautiful, perfect mate.*

A quiet cough interrupted their moment, and Soval stepped forward with an apologetic smile. "I'm sorry to disturb you, but I need to check how your wings are healing. May I unwrap them?"

Aayla nodded, offering him a gentle smile. "Of course."

Soval's hands moved with care as he began to unwrap the layers of bandages. Talyn's protective presence was impossible to miss. His intense gaze followed every movement, a silent warning that he would not tolerate any misstep.

"We kept you sedated for two days to give your wings a chance to heal properly," Soval explained. "Let's see how they're progressing."

He finished unwrapping her wings, and she cautiously spread them wide. A sharp ache rippled through her muscles as they stretched, the strain a reminder of their prolonged confinement. She could also feel their weakness, the toll of being bound for so long, evident in the subtle loss of strength and tone.

Just then, Aeryn entered the room, greeting them with a polite nod before turning her attention to Soval's work. After a thorough scan, Soval offered her a warm smile. "The bones have knitted together beautifully. You're free to leave MedBay but take it slow. Gentle strengthening exercises only for now."

The next two days passed quickly, with a significant amount of time spent strengthening her wing muscles until she was confident enough to take flight and leave Aldredth Tower. Each morning began with rigorous exercises designed to build endurance and power, her muscles straining with each repetitive movement. The afternoons were dedicated to practising controlled glides and short bursts of flight within the safety of the tower's confines, her wings gradually growing steadier and more reliable.

Despite the strain, exhilaration swelled with each success. The fire in Talyn's encouraging words and the warmth of his unwavering presence fuelled her determination, carrying her through moments of exhaustion.

As dusk approached on the second day, she stood on the edge of the tower's highest platform, her wings unfurled and ready. The wind tugged at her feathers like a welcoming embrace. With a deep breath and a final nod from Talyn, she leapt off the roof, her wings catching the current as she soared away from Aldredth Tower.

The thrill of flight surged through her, electrifying every nerve. As she soared higher, the wind rushed against her face, and the powerful beat of her wings filled her with an exhilarating sense of freedom. Talyn joined her, his powerful wings beating in perfect harmony with hers as they danced erotically in the sky.

Each effortless glide and the gentle brush of their wingtips sent a spark through her that made her heart race with excitement.

Since awakening, she had spent her nights wrapped in Talyn's arms as their passion burned brighter. Each moment together was charged with an intensity that spoke of how deeply they cherished the time they had, as if every second was a gift they refused to waste.

That night, in the intimacy of their quarters, Aayla lowered herself onto Talyn's lap, her hands cupping his face as her lips claimed his in a fervent kiss. His body moved against hers, thrusting inside of her with an intensity that stole her breath, a perfect rhythm that made her cry out his name in unrestrained ecstasy.

Her arms trembled, overwhelmed by the sensations coursing through her as he plunged deeper, their connection igniting a fire that burned hotter with every movement.

His hands caressed the sensitive edges of her wings, drawing shivers that matched the tremors of pleasure building within her.

Slowly, she traced her fingers along the powerful expanse of his wings, marvelling at the strength beneath her touch. He moaned her name, and it sent a shockwave through her, tightening her chest as her heart fluttered with a mix of desire and raw emotion.

He gripped her hips firmly, guiding their rhythm as more waves of ecstasy overtook them, her body arching as she surrendered completely to the moment. Every sensation, his touch, his presence, how he filled her so completely, felt perfect, as though he had been crafted solely for her.

When their passion finally ebbed, leaving them breathless and entwined, Aayla nestled against Talyn, her body tucked securely under the protective arc of his wing. His hand moved gently over her skin, the soothing motion a quiet promise of love and devotion. As sleep claimed her, she felt the steady beat of his heart against her own, grounding her in the safety of his embrace.

The following morning, as Aayla walked into the dining hall, her wings overlapped with Talyn's, her Lumina buzzed in her pocket. Pulling it out, she read the message that made her stomach churn. Pyrion, her older brother, would arrive on Earth within an hour.

The knot in her gut tightened. This could be a problem.

They finished breakfast quickly, and Aayla's mind raced as she prepared for her next engagement, a pre-scheduled media interview with a reporter named Rachel Sinclair. The thought of Pyrion's imminent arrival had her on edge. She had hoped to avoid her family until after the law was repealed. She didn't want to lie to them, but more than that, she wasn't sure how to hide her mating bond from them. Pyrion knew her better than anyone, second only to Talyn.

A flood of questions filled her mind. Would Pyrion notice something was different about her? Would he be able to sense her bond with Talyn? The idea of facing him now made her stomach churn even more.

Aayla tried to push the anxiety aside as she and Talyn made their way to the interview. Their steps were synchronised, exuding confidence and authority despite the turmoil swirling in her mind. As they entered the brightly lit studio, Aayla's nerves flared as the blinding lights seemed to magnify her anxiety.

She sat in the lone chair across from the camera, trying to steady her nerves. Talyn stood behind her, muscles taut, silent but vigilant. His eyes scanned the room with the kind of alertness that came from years of training.

Rachel wore a bright, mismatched outfit with clashing patterns, an overly large statement necklace, and flashy, obviously fake, coloured stone rings the size of golf balls. Her attire was more suited for drawing attention to her than conveying professionalism.

Aayla glanced at the camera crew, looking for a station logo, but couldn't see any. She had undertaken so many interviews that she didn't know who she was talking to most of the time. She figured it must have been a small network currently interviewing her and one she hadn't spoken with yet.

"Welcome, Aayla! It's wonderful to have you with us today," Rachel said with an exaggerated smile, clearly relishing the moment.

"My pleasure, Rachel," Aayla replied casually.

"I have a few questions for you today, so let's jump straight into it. How do you feel knowing you are lying to everyone about Talyn being your Guardian when you two are really mates?"

The words sliced through the air, sharp and deliberate. Aayla froze. For a split second, her mind went blank, the question landing like a strike to her core. Her breath caught as her pulse hammered in her ears.

Slowly, her gaze shifted to Talyn. Behind her, his entire body had gone still, his posture rigid. His piercing eyes locked on Rachel, filled with silent warning.

Swallowing hard, Aayla turned back to Rachel, her expression hardening. "I'm not sure what you're talking about."

Rachel's smirk widened, and she pointed dramatically to the screen beside her. Images flickered across it of Aayla and Talyn walking side by side with their wings overlapped, their foreheads pressed together in a way that could easily be misconstrued as an intimate kiss from the angles shown.

"And how do you explain these, then?" Rachel asked, her tone dripping with triumph.

A fiery rage surged within Aayla, eclipsing the initial shock. She shot to her feet, her voice echoing in the room. "How dare you threaten my Guardian!"

Rachel shrank back into her chair, "I—"

"Are you trying to trick me into admitting something that would result in Talyn's death? You think you can show me videos of us standing closely together and twist it into something it's not?" Aayla's voice rose, her fury filling every corner of the room.

Rachel's confidence faltered, but she pushed on weakly. "But you're kissing in these shots—"

"No! I am not kissing Talyn in any of those clips," she bellowed, pointing to the screen. "And I'm pretty sure you know that. Tell me you didn't know that?"

Rachel's face flushed crimson, her gaze dropping to her lap. She didn't respond, and her silence answered Aayla's question.

Her rage was burning hot. "And sometimes, yes, our wings brush together, but that happens when we walk so close. This is proof of nothing. It's an empty accusation."

The anger inside Aayla surged, a low growl vibrating in her chest. Her hands clenched into tight balls as she fought the urge to grab her sword and strike Rachel down for threatening her mate.

Aayla took a menacing step forward as her voice dropped to a low, threatening whisper. "Did you think I would just sit here and let you threaten Talyn's life?"

The tension in the room crackled like lightning, and Rachel visibly trembled in her seat, not daring to meet her eyes.

With one last, seething glare, Aayla turned on her heel and stormed out of the room, Talyn following silently, his every step a mirror of hers.

The moment they stepped outside, the cool air did little to quell the storm raging inside her. Adrenaline surged through her veins as she stalked forward, her fists still clenched and her breaths sharp and shallow.

"Aayla," Talyn said softly, his voice like a lifeline in the storm.

She ignored him, her muscles coiled with tension, her mind spinning with fury. But Talyn was persistent. He moved swiftly, stepping in front of her and gently pressing her back against the cold wall, stopping her in her tracks.

"Aayla," he said again, his tone firmer this time, his eyes searching hers.

Her breath hitched, her body trembling as she fought to rein in the torrent of emotions.

"Breathe," he said softly, his deep voice pulling her attention like a lifeline. *The mating bond is amplifying everything you're feeling right now.*

Her eyes burned as she met his gaze. "They threatened your life!" she roared, her voice raw with fury.

I know. Talyn replied, his tone steady and unyielding. *You have every right to be angry, but the mating bond is exaggerating your level of anger at the moment. It's not only the males that are affected by it when it's new.*

Closing her eyes, she sucked in a deep breath, letting the scent of him—spice and warmth—ground her. Her heart thundered in her chest, but she focused on slowing its relentless pace.

"I'm sorry," she murmured, her voice quieter now. "I lost control, didn't I?"

A small smile curved his lips as his fingers brushed a stray strand of hair from her face. "She did deserve it."

She laughed, though it was tinged with guilt. "Should I go back and apologise?"

Talyn chuckled, low and rich. "Absolutely not. But," he added, his tone dipping with playful suggestion, "if you're still feeling tense, I can think of a few ways to help you relax."

His fingers brushed lightly along the sensitive underside of her wing, and a shiver rolled through her, the touch sparking a heat that curled low in her belly.

A mischievous smile teased her lips as she leaned closer, brushing her mouth along his jawline in a slow, playful kiss. "I think I'd like that."

Talyn's breath hitched, his restraint cracking momentarily before he exhaled, shaking his head. "Later," he murmured, though his voice carried a hint of regret. "We don't have time now, not if you want to greet Pyrion when he lands."

She groaned dramatically, resting her forehead against his chest for a fleeting moment before trailing one last lingering kiss along his collarbone. "Fine," she said, her tone dripping with mock reluctance. "Let's get this over with."

Their flight around Aldredth Tower was quiet. The tension between them was now replaced by a simmering energy they both knew would have to wait.

As they landed near the tower's landing zone, the sky shimmered with the telltale gleam of approaching engines. Pyrion's ship descended slowly through the clouds, its sleek frame gleaming in the sunlight as it touched down almost soundlessly.

Pyrion, a Vorax, was among the first to step off the ship. His golden-brown hair gleamed in the sunlight, complementing his azure blue eyes, which were an uncanny mirror of Aayla's. From the base of his spine, unfurled wings of shimmering silver faded into a striking cobalt blue along their length.

Standing tall with a broad, welcoming smile, Pyrion's eyes twinkled with warmth and mischief. His hearty laughter drifted across the grass, and his protective nature was unmistakable, even from a distance. Despite his jovial demeanour, there was an unmistakable readiness in his stance, always prepared to shield his loved ones from harm.

Aayla ran into his arms without hesitation. "It's so good to see you, big brother."

Pyrion hugged her tightly, his voice rich with affection. "I've missed you, little sister."

Aayla quickly turned and enveloped Haylae in an equally tight embrace. "And don't think I forgot about you, sister of mine."

Pyrion and Haylae had been mates since they were five years old. Haylae, also a Vorax, was a vision of serene beauty with white-blond hair, hazelnut eyes, and wings that transitioned from soft pink to delicate baby blue at their tips.

Her warmth was palpable, her eyes sparkling with kindness as she greeted everyone with an inviting smile. Her gentle voice and attentive nature seemed to ease those around her, fostering an instant sense of camaraderie. Though not related by blood, the terms "brother" and "sister" was a customary way to address a sibling's mate.

"Sister of mine, how are you?" Haylae laughed, her eyes crinkling with delight.

Stepping back, Aayla settled against Talyn's side as his arm instinctively wrapped around her waist. "I'm wonderful, actually. Never better."

Pyrion looked at her face carefully for a long moment before his eyes travelled from her head to toe, taking in every detail with a subtle curiosity. His eyes lingered on the way Talyn's fingers were wrapped protectively around her hip before he looked back up and tilted his head slightly. "Yes, actually, you've never looked happier."

"Talyn, it's good to see you too," Haylae said gently, her tone carrying a rare acknowledgment that caught Aayla's attention. It wasn't often that a Guardian received such recognition. Custom dictated their role as silent sentinels, detached from the conversations around them to remain fully focused on their Charges. But Haylae's kindness had always set her apart, a gentle defiance of tradition that made others feel seen and valued. Aayla couldn't help but appreciate her for it.

"Thank you, Haylae," Talyn responded with a shy smile. "That's very kind of you to say."

Biting her lip nervously, she decided to change the subject quickly. "I think you'll like the humans. Despite their tumultuous nature, they are a fledgling race brimming with raw emotion and potential, capable of forging connections through empathy and understanding. And Earth is even more beautiful in person than what you have read. It has diverse landscapes, vibrant ecosystems, shimmering oceans, lush forests, and towering mountains. Some sights that can truly take your breath away."

Pyrion's casual smile returned, "I would like that. But first, I believe you're busy building two more Aldredth Towers on Earth before the gathering, and we're here to help."

"Yes, that's right. Our relationship with this planet is flourishing. The humans approved the construction of two more bases on this planet, which will be completed tomorrow. We could definitely use your help to set up one of the towers, but since the construction side is still underway, it looks like you will be around here for a little while longer."

"Can't say I'm sad to hear that," Pyrion smirked.

Aayla's laugh rang out, light and joyful. It had been too long since she had seen her family. "Then let's go for a fly. I'd love to show you around."

"We'd love that," Pyrion replied, gently brushing a strand of her hair aside.

With a powerful beat of their wings, they took to the skies. Soaring gracefully above the bustling city, their iridescent wings cast shimmering reflections on the glass facades of skyscrapers below. The appearance of new Aldredth always created a spectacle, drawing the eyes of countless onlookers who gazed up in awe as they flew past. Their distinct wing colourings made it easy to identify different Aldredth even from a considerable distance away.

They flew with effortless grace, weaving through the urban landscape. As they glided over the city, Pyrion and Haylae took in the sights with keen interest. They were fascinated by the intricate web of streets, the vibrant murals adorning the buildings, and the ever-changing flow of human activity.

Throughout the journey, Aayla and Talyn exchanged fleeting glances and subtle touches, their bond quietly palpable. Aayla thought she noticed Pyrion watching them on more than one occasion. Each time she turned to meet his gaze, however, he looked away so quickly that she wondered if she had imagined it.

Shaking off the thought, she refocused on their surroundings. Occasionally, they descended to the ground, landing softly in bustling squares and tranquil parks. Their arrival was always met with a wave of curiosity. Crowds formed instinctively, humans drawn to them with a mix of awe and respect. Haylae's serene presence seemed to calm the onlookers as effortlessly as it did her fellow Aldredth. The humans exhibited both wonder and respect for the new visitors whilst maintaining a respectful distance.

On their way back to Aldredth Tower, they stopped to mediate a dispute and de-escalate a particularly tense situation. A heated argument had broken out in a marketplace, and a large group of people had become involved. Their intervention swiftly resolved the rapidly escalating situation, and their calm demeanour and authoritative yet gentle presence diffused the conflict.

Not long after, the tranquillity was shattered by sudden screams echoing through the streets. Without hesitation, the group diverted course, wings slicing through the air as they raced toward the commotion.

With a swift beat of her wings, Aayla descended towards the chaos unfolding on the streets, her senses sharpening as she assessed the situation.

The sound of screeching tyres and panicked shouts filled the air. With a burst of speed, Aayla intercepted one of the criminals' vehicles whilst Pyrion created a gust of wind that brought the second speeding car to a halt with a jolt.

Hovering above the now-stationary vehicle, Talyn's eyes scanned the area, his keen gaze locking onto several fleeing figures. Without hesitation, he dove towards them, his movements fluid and precise as he closed the distance with astonishing speed.

In a blur of motion, Talyn reached the criminals and disarmed them with a flick of his wrist while Pyrion landed behind them and restrained them on the ground.

The ordeal ended within moments, the criminals subdued and helpless under Pyrion's unyielding grip. The arrival of human authorities brought closure, and as the Aldredth departed, cheers and applause erupted from the crowd.

The humans looked up to all Aldredth with gratitude and admiration for their wisdom and benevolence, and they had fast become symbols of harmony and hope in the city. Their very presence reminded everyone that even in the vastness of the universe, there were beings committed to the ideals of peace and mutual understanding.

As the sun dipped below the horizon, they finally returned to Aldredth Tower. Aayla chose to land on the roof, giving Pyrion and Haylae the perfect vantage point to witness the setting sun. The sky blazed with orange, pink, and gold hues, the light bathing the city in a warm, ethereal glow.

"What a beautiful view," Haylae whispered in awe.

"It is indeed," Aayla murmured, her gaze lifting to meet Talyn's. His eyes softened, glowing with love as he reached out to cradle her face in his hand. Placing her hand over his, she pressed a soft kiss to his jaw, her touch lingering.

A subtle shift in her peripheral vision drew her attention. Turning, she caught Pyrion watching her—his expression shadowed by a faint frown.

"Pyrion? Is something wrong?" she asked, concern threading through her voice.

He blinked as if caught off guard and quickly smiled. "It's nothing," he said with a shrug, turning back toward Haylae.

But the moment lingered, and despite his reassurances, Aayla couldn't shake the nagging sense of unease.

437

CHAPTER FIFTY-ONE

"Aayla, come join us for dinner," Haylae called cheerfully.

"You too, Talyn," Pyrion remarked coldly.

The chill in his voice sent a shiver down Aayla's spine. Something was wrong. She wanted to decline, to make some excuse, but how could she? Refusing an invitation to dinner with her brother after so long would only draw suspicion.

What do you think? She asked Talyn.

His reply was calm, but his words carried weight. *What choice do we have?*

"We'd love to," Aayla said, forcing a smile she didn't feel.

Heading inside Aldredth Tower, Aayla felt Pyrion's eyes on her. She reached out to Talyn's mind. *We need to keep our distance. I think we are drawing too much attention.*

Agreed.

At the dinner table, lively chatter and laughter filled the air. Aayla left a deliberate gap between herself and Talyn as Pyrion and Haylae took seats directly across from them. Despite her efforts to focus on the conversations, she couldn't help stealing glances at Talyn. Every time their eyes met, her heart raced before she quickly looked away.

Beneath the table, Aayla's hand gently brushed against Talyn's, sending a thrill up her spine. Talyn, suppressing a smile, responded with a slight, almost imperceptible touch of his own. They exchanged fleeting, meaningful glances, each one charged with the emotions they were trying so hard to conceal.

As the food was consumed and the conversation flourished, their wings occasionally grazed, the contact brief yet heavy with passion.

Despite her best efforts to remain inconspicuous, the connection between them seemed to hum with a quiet intensity.

As she reached for a berry on the plate in front of them, her fingers brushed against Talyn's, lingering for a moment longer than necessary. She suppressed a smile, her mind buzzing with their unspoken connection. But then, she caught Pyrion's eyes on them, his gaze sharp and filled with suspicion before he slowly looked away to answer someone's question beside him.

She maintained the facade of casual interaction, joining the lively chatter and laughter with their friends while counting down the minutes until the dinner was over.

Talyn had been listening to a story, but his attention inevitably wandered back to her. When she met his gaze, the love in his eyes was so intense it made her heart skip a beat.

Gently, he lifted a hand, brushing his fingers down her cheek before leaning in to nuzzle her softly.

His breath whispered against her neck, sending warmth cascading through her. *You're so beautiful. I love you so much.*

As I will always love you, my mate.

She pressed a kiss to his cheek, her lips lingering as if savouring the moment. Their eyes met again, and for a brief instant, the rest of the room faded away, leaving only their shared connection. But as she turned back to the table, her heart still fluttering, her gaze caught Pyrion's. His sharp frown froze her in place, cutting through the warmth like ice.

Aayla's stomach churned. She forced herself to look away, feigning interest in the conversation beside her, but Pyrion's scrutiny bore into her like an oppressive weight.

Silent and motionless, Pyrion's piercing gaze never wavered for the rest of the meal.

Unable to take it any longer, Aayla stood abruptly, grabbing Talyn's hand. *We need to go. Now.*

Talyn rose without question, but as they turned to leave, Pyrion's voice cut through the air, sharp and commanding.

"Aayla, could we have a private word?"

Forcing a simile onto her face, she tried to sound casual, "Of course."

The din of conversation faded as they moved into the corridor.

"Aayla," Haylae said softly, "I could use a Unix's opinion on the latest developments on Hasfina."

Aayla blinked, her earlier tension giving way to confusion. She almost felt foolish for expecting something more ominous. "Oh, right. Of course. We can go now—"

"No." Pyrion's hollow smile cut her short. "Not Talyn. Just you, I'm afraid. But you'll only be in the Command Centre. You won't need a Guardian. You'll be perfectly safe."

Her eyes darted to Talyn, catching the concern he was trying to mask.

Talyn's voice whispered across her mind. *It's a trap.*

Her chest tightened as her breath caught. *Do we run?*

No. Not yet, at least.

Aayla turned back to Haylae, forcing warmth into her expression. "O—okay. After you."

Haylae leant over and kissed Pyrion passionately before turning to Aayla with a small smile and leading the way down the corridor.

Glancing once more at Talyn, she held his gaze for a heartbeat longer than necessary before following Haylae. Each step felt heavier than the last as the corridor stretched before her.

As Aayla walked into the Command Centre, Haylae was by her side, and the weight of the situation pressed heavily on her shoulders. The room was already bustling with key figures, maps and documents spread across the long table, and the air was thick with the urgency of impending decisions. Haylae gave her a reassuring nod, a silent reminder of their shared purpose before they took their seats to begin the meticulous dissection of their battle plans.

They discussed strategies, analysed enemy movements, and coordinated resources for hours. Aayla's mind raced with calculations and contingencies, her focus unwavering as she navigated the complex discussions. Haylae remained a steady presence by her side, offering insights and support when needed, and their teamwork was seamless.

As the meeting wound down, a flicker of unease stirred in Aayla's chest. She had braced herself for Haylae to confront her about the scene in the Dining Hall, but no mention was made. Gathering her things, she watched Haylae closely, searching for any hint of the unspoken tension. Her silence was both a relief and a puzzle.

Stepping out of the room, Aayla released a breath she didn't realise she'd been holding. She turned to Haylae, her calm demeanour offering silent comfort, and they exchanged a final glance before parting ways. With her mind still buzzing from the intense discussions, Aayla made her way through the corridors, her thoughts shifting to Talyn.

When she reached their quarters, the sight of Talyn banished the lingering tension in an instant. His face lit up as she entered, and she wasted no time closing the distance between them. She fell into his arms with a sigh of relief, grateful for the familiar comfort.

She slid her hand to the back of his head, pulling him down for a long, passionate kiss. His hands gripped her firmly, drawing her closer as he pressed against her, his growing arousal unmistakable.

The feel of his body against hers made it impossible to think. Her breath quickened, her body responding instinctively to his touch. But she stepped back, heart pounding, forcing herself to refocus. There were urgent matters to discuss before they got lost in each other's bodies.

"Haylae didn't say anything," she began, her voice steady despite the whirlwind of thoughts. "No questions. Nothing. Did anything happen with you?"

Talyn stood unnaturally still, his gaze locked on hers with an intensity that made her chest tighten.

"Talyn?" she prompted, her voice laced with worry.

He exhaled deeply, tenderly brushing the back of his hand along her cheek. "He knows," Talyn said softly, his voice heavy with certainty. "Pyrion knows."

Chapter Fifty-Two

Talyn watched as Aayla walked away with Haylae toward the Command Centre, a growing sense of unease gripping him. Every instinct screamed to follow her, but he forced himself to stay put. It was clear Pyrion was deliberately separating them. Why, he wasn't sure, but the intent was undeniable.

He turned to leave, but Pyrion's firm hand clamped down on his arm.

"Come train with me, Talyn," Pyrion said, his voice calm but edged with steel.

Talyn met his gaze, the intensity in Pyrion's eyes unnerving. He looked away, searching for an excuse. "Sorry, I was actually on my way to—"

"I wasn't asking," Pyrion interrupted, his tone cold and final.

Talyn hesitated before forcing a strained smile. "Of course."

The sun cast long shadows in the corridor as he followed Pyrion closely to the Training Centre. They walked in silence, and the air between them was thick with unspoken tension.

Talyn's heart pounded in his chest, each beat resonating with his growing anxiety. He kept his eyes forward, occasionally glancing at Pyrion's face from the corner of his eye. Pyrion's jaw was clenched, his eyes fixed forward, every muscle in his body taut with barely contained anger.

As they entered the Training Centre, Pyrion stalked to the training ring without a word, drawing his sword in one fluid motion.

Talyn hesitated at the edge of the ring before drawing his sword. The weight of the blade felt heavier than usual as he stepped into the circle.

Pyrion advanced a step, his stance aggressive, his voice low and biting. "So, when were you planning on telling me?"

Talyn's heart pounded. "I don't know what you mean."

They began circling each other, swords raised, the tension between them palpable.

"You don't know?" Pyrion's voice dripped with incredulity. "She's my baby sister. Did you really think I wouldn't notice?"

"It's not what you think," Talyn pleaded, taking a step forward.

"Don't treat me like a fool." Pyrion spat. He made the first move, a quick, precise thrust aimed at Talyn's shoulder. He parried effortlessly, the clang of metal ringing out. Without missing a beat, Pyrion countered with a sweeping arc, forcing Talyn to step back and deflect the blow.

Sensing an opening, Pyrion lunged forward with a swift, direct thrust. The force sent Talyn stumbling backward, nearly losing his balance.

"Tell me," Pyrion demanded, his voice sharp as his blade, "how is it then?"

Talyn raised a hand, trying to calm him. "There is nothing nefarious going on. I always have and always will love Aayla."

Pyrion's eyes narrowed, his grip tightening on his sword. "How long has this been going on?" He swung his blade again, and a calculated strike landed, harder this time, sending Talyn sprawling to the ground.

Talyn struggled for words, but the weight of Pyrion's accusations silenced him. He looked away, unable to meet his gaze.

Pyrion loomed over him, his breathing ragged, his fury barely contained. "Is that it? That's all you've got?" His voice cracked with emotion. "She almost died trying to protect you!"

Pacing furiously, Pyrion's anger seemed to spill into the air around them. "No. She deserves someone stronger, someone who can protect her. Not you." His words cut deeper than any blade as he turned to face Talyn. "It's time she was assigned a new Guardian."

Before Talyn could respond, Pyrion turned on his heel and strode away, leaving Talyn on the ground with the echo of their confrontation reverberating in his chest. Fury surged through him, raw and primal. His mating bond had been challenged, and the protective instinct it provoked burned like wildfire, threatening to consume him.

His muscles coiled, ready to strike, and his grip on the sword tightened. Surging up from the ground, he unleashed a sweeping strike with precision and force, catching Pyrion off guard. Pyrion barely managed to parry, his stance faltering under the sheer power of the blow.

Talyn moved like liquid fire, his movements seamless and deliberate, a perfect fusion of strength and grace. Each strike was decisive, each step purposeful. The intensity of their duel quickly exceeded Pyrion's limits. Talyn anticipated his every move, blocking with a powerful upward swing that sent vibrations through Pyrion's arm.

Talyn's speed, strength, and precision were far beyond Pyrion's abilities—a fact Pyrion was only now beginning to grasp.

The air was alive with the sharp clash of steel on steel, each impact echoing through the space like thunder. Their ragged breaths were interwoven with the relentless rhythm of their duel. Talyn's strikes were relentless, each blow calculated and unyielding. He didn't hold back, his blade cutting through the fray with brutal efficiency.

Every strike carried the force to break bones, and when his blade found flesh, it drew blood with merciless precision, leaving no doubt as to who held the upper hand.

The red haze of anger clouded his mind, forcing him to be driven by pure instinct that demanded that Pyrion suffer for threatening to take his mate from him.

Their eyes met briefly, and Talyn saw shock and confusion in his gaze. Yet Talyn didn't falter. He couldn't.

With a final, powerful strike, Talyn disarmed Pyrion, sending his sword clattering across the ground. Pyrion collapsed, winded and bloodied, as Talyn stood over him, his chest heaving, his blade poised at his chest.

"Talyn, stop!" A voice cut through the storm of his rage, distant but urgent. Yet it barely registered. He stood frozen, the raw intensity of his emotions blinding him to reason.

Pyrion's lips twisted into a slow smile, the expression cutting through Talyn's haze. He frowned, lowering his blade instinctively, confusion creeping into his fury.

"So," Pyrion rasped, wiping blood from his mouth, "you've been holding back on me?"

Talyn blinked, the weight of his actions crashing down on him. The rage evaporated, leaving guilt in its wake as he looked down at Pyrion's crumpled form.

Jaxion and Rune rushed to Pyrion's side, carefully helping him to his feet. Pyrion winced, cradling his broken arm and ribs, but his smirk remained intact.

Jaxion looked at him with suspicion. "What were you thinking, Talyn?"

"He wasn't thinking," Pyrion drawled. "Were you, Talyn?"

"I—I'm so sorry, Pyrion," Talyn stammered, his voice cracking with remorse. "I didn't mean to go that far. Are you okay?"

Pyrion quietly dismissed Jaxion and Rune, who exchanged a final wary glance at Talyn before heading off to continue their training together.

Pyrion studied Talyn for a moment, his smirk softening into something more serious. "Why have you never shown me a fraction of your true strength before?"

Talyn's cheeks burned, shame twisting in his chest. "I'm not sure what you're talking about."

"Yes, you do." Pyrion's voice was sharp but not unkind. "That was stronger than anything I've ever felt while training with you. Why have you been holding back all these years?"

Talyn thrust a hand through his hair, looking away. The temptation to lie flickered in his mind, but he couldn't bring himself to do it.

"I'm a Guardian," he said finally, his voice tight. "We're supposed to stay in the background. Unseen and unnoticed. Guardians don't stand out or lead from the front."

Pyrion stepped closer, his expression softening. He raised his uninjured hand and cupped Talyn's cheek. "You're not meant to be anything other than who you are."

The compassion in Pyrion's eyes made Talyn flinch, and he looked away, unable to meet the sincerity of his gaze.

Pyrion tilted his head, studying him. "How strong are you?"

Talyn hesitated, and the truth lodged like a stone in his throat. He knew he was stronger than most, stronger than even most Lazuil, but he had never dared to test the full extent of his abilities. The fear of being reassigned away from Aayla kept him from discovering how powerful he really was.

After a long silence, Pyrion seemed to accept that no answer was coming. He dropped his hand from Talyn's cheek with a quiet sigh.

Talyn pulled his Lumina from his pocket. "I'll ask Aayla to come down here to heal you."

"No," Pyrion said firmly, his voice tinged with protectiveness. "It'll heal quickly enough on its own. I'm not causing her pain over something this minor."

That was one of the things Talyn had always admired about Pyrion—his unwavering love for his sister. Pyrion would do anything to protect Aayla, even from herself. Unlike Talyn, who had been raised in a regimented household focused on duty and honour, Pyrion had grown up with the freedom to love fiercely and without restraint.

As a newborn, his family knew he was destined to be a Guardian to a Unix. His entire upbringing was meticulously crafted around that destiny, with every lesson, discipline, and expectation focused on preparing him for the role and upholding the family's honour.

Aayla tried to hide how much healing others hurt her, but Pyrion always saw through her facade. He never let her heal him unless it was absolutely necessary.

Talyn offered a warm smile. "Thank you."

Nodding, Pyrion extended his arm towards Talyn. "Would you mind helping me to the garden? I could use a rest."

"Of course," Talyn said softly, stepping forward to support him.

Talyn wrapped an arm around Pyrion's back, supporting him as they slowly left the Training Centre. In the quiet corridor, Pyrion glanced around, ensuring they were alone, before stopping and turning to face him.

"I owe you an apology," Pyrion said, his voice subdued. "I thought you were just overstepping boundaries. Taking advantage of her. I didn't realise you were..."

Exhaling, Talyn paused. "She's lucky to have a big brother like you."

Pyrion's gaze softened, and his voice dropped to a near whisper. "I know your upbringing wasn't built on the same kind of unconditional love I had, but know this, you will always have me... brother mine."

The words struck something deep in Talyn. His expression softened, and he inhaled shakily before managing, "Thank you." His voice was quiet, but the emotion behind it was unmistakable. "I don't know what I'd do without you."

Pyrion reached out, pulling Talyn into a firm embrace, as tight as his injuries allowed, as if to convey all the love and support words could not express. They stood there in silence, the weight of past hurts and unspoken emotions slowly lifting, replaced by the comfort of knowing they had each other.

When they pulled apart, Talyn hesitated, rubbing at his chest like it might loosen the knot of emotions tightening there. He forced himself to ask, "You... don't have any questions?"

Pyrion's face grew distant, his voice tinged with memories that clearly pained him. "Don't forget, I was there the day you met Aayla. I heard everything. I remember everything. And I am haunted every night by the sounds of Aayla's gut-wrenching sobs as I held her in my arms. I knew something was fundamentally wrong with what happened... but I was too young to truly understand. I've had many nights since then to think about it. To be tormented by it."

Pyrion fell silent for a moment, lost in thought, before returning to the present. "After today, though... there's no denying it."

Talyn's breath caught. He hadn't realised Pyrion had carried the weight of that day for so long. The shame of knowing he had added to that burden stung deeply, a reminder of the pain he seemed to bring to those around him.

Reaching out to clasp Talyn's shoulder, Pyrion gave a tentative smile. "Although tonight might be the first night that the sound does not haunt me."

Nodding, too overwhelmed by emotions to speak, Talyn turned to commence walking, but Pyrion's words stopped him.

"I know the repeal is coming up soon," Pyrion said, his tone firm. "If anything happens, before or during it, that puts either of you in danger, promise me you'll call. No matter what."

The weight of the words hung in the air, laced with more than what was spoken. "I promise," Talyn said quietly.

"Good," Pyrion said with a short nod, some tension leaving his shoulders. "Now, let's get going, shall we."

Talyn helped Pyrion to the garden, where Haylae was waiting with anxious eyes. Pyrion waved him off with a faint smile, and Talyn made his way to his quarters and waited for Aayla.

When she arrived, her presence lit up the room as it always did. His face lit up instinctively at the sight of her, a smile breaking through the shadows of his thoughts. No matter what storm raged outside, she was his anchor, his home.

As Aayla pulled his head down for a long, hard kiss, Talyn crushed her body against his and rubbed his growing erection against her.

But then, Aayla gently pulled away, her eyes searching his with a storm of unspoken questions. He felt a flicker of relief that Haylae hadn't pressed her, but the weight of his unspoken actions with Pyrion hung heavily in the air.

He froze, his thoughts lost in the depth of her gaze.

"Talyn?" she whispered, her voice laced with worry.

He exhaled deeply, tenderly brushing the back of his hand along her cheek. "He knows," Talyn said softly, his voice heavy with certainty. "Pyrion knows."

Her face drained of colour, and her voice trembled as she asked, "What do we do now?"

Talyn reached up to gently cup her face. His touch was soft but firm, grounding them both. "It's okay," he said, his voice low, almost a whisper. "He won't say anything."

Aayla's eyes searched his, uncertainty clouding her expression. "Are you sure he knows?"

Pausing, Talyn's jaw tightened as he recalled the weight of their conversation. "I never admitted anything, but he is confident in his judgment."

Her brow furrowed, confusion and concern warring on her face. "But why wouldn't he tell anyone?"

"Because..." Talyn hesitated, his gaze softening, "I think he approves."

She blinked, clearly taken aback, just as he was.

"He mentioned the day we met... and how he comforted you that night."

A shadow passed over Aayla's eyes as the memory resurfaced. "Yes," she whispered, her voice tinged with pain. "That was the night your parents took you home. They said everyone needed time to 'calm down,' as if that would fix everything. It was the worst night of my life... being separated from you like that."

A small shiver ran across her body, and he pulled her against him, their lips meeting with a fiery passion.

Their mouths moved with an urgency, exploring and demanding more. Their kiss deepened, raw and consuming.

"I'm so sorry." He whispered. "That night was agony for me all on my own, but I thought—hoped—you might have fared better with the support of your family by your side."

She placed a soft kiss on his lips. "We have each other now, and that's the only thing that matters."

Talyn deepened the kiss before pulling the clothes from Aayla's body and carrying her to their bed.

He shed his clothes, and his hands explored every inch of her wings as she writhed with pleasure under his.

Moaning his name, she begged for more as he entered her slowly. Unsatisfied with how slow he was taking it, she flipped him over on the bed and placed her hands on his chest as she lowered herself down onto him, her wings spread out behind her.

She felt so hot and tight that he closed his eyes as orgasmic waves washed over him. Opening his eyes, he feasted on the sight of her naked body as she rode him. Reaching up, he cupped her full breasts before his hands drifted behind her to stroke her soft wings. As she moaned in pleasure and moved faster, his hands drifted down to grip her hips.

She threw back her head and called out his name as another organismic wave overtook them.

They spent the next several hours wrapped in each other's arms, making love repeatedly. Each encounter was more passionate and intense than the last as they explored every inch of each other. The mating bond tied them together so profoundly that each sensation, each pulse of pleasure, flowed between them as if they were one. The connection they shared intensified every moment, creating a pleasure that was unparalleled.

Chapter Fifty-Three

The next morning, Aayla's wings twitched with suppressed emotion as she bid farewell to Pyrion and Haylae. They rose into the sky, heading off to assist with establishing the new Aldredth Tower. Talyn's arms wrapped around her, pulling her close, and he pressed a tender kiss to the top of her head.

Tears welled in her eyes as she watched them disappear into the horizon.

"Don't worry," Talyn murmured, his voice low and comforting. "He's not going too far. We'll see him again soon."

She wiped a tear from her cheek and looked up at him with a soft smile. "I know. But that doesn't mean I won't miss my big brother."

Talyn's lips curved into a cheeky grin. *Maybe I can help distract you.*

Aayla laughed, the sound lightening her heart, and she leaned up to press a quick kiss to his cheek. *What did you have in mind?*

Before Talyn could respond, Aayla's Lumina buzzed in her pocket. She glanced at the screen, her smile fading as she read the message. The Cade, the council composed of the highest-ranking Lazuil and Unix elders responsible for overseeing Aldredth operations and making their most critical decisions, had called an emergency meeting under the strictest security protocols. Her presence was required immediately.

Talyn's expression tightened, but he didn't complain. As her Guardian, he wasn't considered important enough to attend such meetings. Instead, he placed a reassuring hand on her cheek before departing. "I'll be at the Bathing Pools," he said, his tone calm, though she could sense his frustration at hiding their mating bond.

She watched him leave with a heavy heart, her mind wandering to a wistful vision of what it would feel like to walk into a room with him by her side as her mate. He was an extraordinarily strategic thinker, far superior to her or any other Aldredth she had encountered. His brilliance made him someone who belonged in the inner chambers of power, influencing decisions that shaped their world. But he couldn't afford to display the full extent of his abilities. Doing so would risk making him too indispensable to remain a Guardian, leading to his reassignment to a higher role and taking him away from her. It was a sacrifice he silently bore, all for the sake of staying by her side.

Thankfully, the meeting turned out to be shorter than expected, and only a short while later, Aayla left the Command Centre. The sun shone brightly, streaming through the tall windows as she made her way swiftly through the corridors, her thoughts already drifting to Talyn.

When she reached the entrance of the Bathing Pools, she paused, her gaze landing on him. He was seated against the edge of the shimmering water, his wings partially submerged, and his face relaxed in a rare moment of peace. Across from him, the human security team lounged in the pool, laughing and chatting in a loose circle.

The sight warmed her heart. Seeing Talyn so at ease, surrounded by people who genuinely cared for him, was a relief. She couldn't help but wonder if the humans had already planned this gathering or if they had sensed that their friend needed support. Either way, it was clear that these humans had become some of Talyn's closest and most trusted friends and allies on this planet.

A small smile tugged at her lips as she leaned against the entrance, letting herself enjoy the moment before stepping forward to join him.

As she stepped into the room, Talyn's head turned, and his face lit up with a smile that warmed her to her core. She smiled widely in return as she quickly shed her clothes and slipped into the pool. The warm water embraced her as she swam toward him. His arms opened wide, and she melted into his embrace, their faces nuzzling together as she inhaled his familiar, grounding scent.

Turning her head, Aayla glanced at the males around her. "Sorry to disturb your boys' time."

"You could never disturb us," Seth replied with a mischievous grin.

"It's called improving the situation," Ethan chimed in, drawing a chuckle from the group.

Smiling, Aayla rested her head on Talyn's chest, letting the sound of their conversations wash over her over the next hour. Her fingers absentmindedly traced patterns on his skin and circled the contours of his muscles. Talyn's arm held her tightly against him, one hand occasionally brushing down her right wing in soothing strokes. She relished the way his body thundered with laughter under her.

The contrast from weeks ago wasn't lost on her. The last time she'd been in this pool with Talyn and the others, before being mated, things had been so different. More tense, less certain. Back then, they had been sitting next to each other close enough for their wings to almost brush together, but the distance was agonising. She spent the whole-time stealing glances at Talyn and taking the time to admire his body when he wasn't looking. The blush of being caught still burned in her memory, mirrored by a similar heated look Talyn had worn when she thought she had caught him sneaking glances her way.

"We better get moving if we don't want to be late," Seth sighed, breaking the moment.

A collective groan rippled through the group, none of them eager to leave the comfort of the water for training.

Talyn pressed a kiss to the top of Aayla's head, burying his face in her hair and breathing deeply.

"Stay," Seth said, casting a pointed look at Talyn. "We'll manage without you."

Aayla shook her head, propping herself up on her arms to meet Talyn's gaze. "No, it's okay. Go. Have fun."

Leaning forward, she trailed soft kisses along Talyn's chest, stopping to linger on the spot above his heart. "But come back to me soon," she murmured, her voice a whisper only he could hear.

Talyn's breath hitched, and he lifted her face to nuzzle her, his affection spilling through their bond. The males around them suddenly found the far end of the room fascinating, awkwardly clearing their throats as they climbed out of the pool.

Talyn glanced after them before turning back to her, stealing a quick kiss as he began to stand, his wings flaring out to shield her from prying eyes.

Aayla leaned her arms on the pool's edge, watching as Talyn dried off and dressed with swift efficiency. At the door, he paused, his eyes locking onto hers with an intensity that left her breathless.

I love you, she whispered, her voice threading through his mind like a caress.

Always, he replied, the single word imbued with an unshakable promise.

The next few days passed in a blur as preparations for the intergalactic meeting consumed every available moment. The air in Aldredth Tower buzzed with a potent mix of excitement and tension, the weight of the impending event bearing heavily on everyone's shoulders.

Aayla moved swiftly through the corridors, her mind churning with a whirlwind of logistics and contingencies. In the Command Centre, everyone worked tirelessly, their faces a testament to the long hours and the gravity of their task. Becca had been handling the organisation with the human dignitaries with ease, and her calm demeanour was invaluable in the stressful environment.

Pausing just inside the room, Aayla's gaze landed on Talyn. He was seated at a console, his fingers flying across the screen as he meticulously reviewed the security protocols. Outwardly, he seemed composed, but Aayla could see the subtle tension in his posture, the furrow of his brow betraying the strain he carried.

Quietly, she walked over to him and leaned down, pressing a soft kiss to his chin. She felt the moment his shoulders eased, his body instinctively relaxing under her touch.

Looking up at her, Talyn smiled, his deep green eyes sparkling in the light. "I've reviewed the security measures again. We've reinforced the perimeter around the planet and increased the number of patrols. Still, I can't shake the feeling we might be missing something."

Aayla nodded, her eyes scanning the data on the screen. "You've done well, Talyn."

He shook his head with a thoughtful expression. "We can't afford any oversights. Every delegate attending this meeting represents a crucial alliance, and a couple less than desirable counterparts have been invited despite our best advice. This meeting could be a powder keg waiting to blow. Our security must be impenetrable."

She placed a hand on his shoulder, reassuring him. "You've done everything you can. Now, come. Martok needs us."

They found Martok and Skyla deep in discussion, a holographic projection of the conference hall floating between them. The two were debating seating arrangements with the intensity of battle strategists, their focus on fostering diplomacy while mitigating the risk of conflict.

Talyn stepped closer, studying the arrangement. A frown deepened on his face. *If the Drakari delegates sit next to the Vortans, we'll have chaos before the meeting begins. There was a border dispute last week, and I bet there will still be bad blood on both sides.*

Good catch. Aayla adjusted the hologram with a swipe of her hand. "We need to move the Vortans far from the Drakari. I don't want their recent border dispute causing any problems."

Martok sighed, his frustration evident. "Are we absolutely sure the humans can't be persuaded to uninvite the Drakari? They seem to excel at sparking trouble, no matter where they sit."

Aayla chuckled dryly, patting Martok's arm. "Believe me, we did try, but some mistakes the humans need to make for themselves. We just need to be here to help when the need arises. But you've done a great job with the arrangement so far."

Scrubbing a hand across his face, he looked back at the projection. "There's not much else we can do at this point because we've run out of options. Almost every faction has a history with another. Finding a neutral arrangement is like navigating a minefield."

Skyla placed a reassuring hand on his arm, her voice soft. "We'll figure it out. We always do. Just think of it as another puzzle."

The tension between them melted as they shared a tender kiss. Aayla glanced away, a pang of longing tightening her chest. Her heart ached to reach for Talyn in the same way, to draw him close and lose herself in his embrace. The thought burned brightly, fuelling her determination to see the meeting through without a hitch.

Later that night, Aayla found herself alone in her quarters, the silence a stark contrast to the day's frenetic activity. Talyn was out conducting a perimeter check with the junior recruits, and his absence left a void that gnawed at her. She felt hollow without him.

Allowing herself a moment of respite, she sank onto a chaise by the balcony. The stars outside seemed to twinkle with anticipation, a reminder of the vastness of the universe and the significance of the meeting ahead.

The sound of soft footsteps interrupted her reverie. The door slid open to reveal Talyn, his expression as exhausted as hers.

"Couldn't sleep?" he asked, his voice low and warm as he crossed the room. He sat beside her, pulling her into his lap, his lips finding hers in a kiss that was equal parts passion and promise.

Aayla clung to him, her words a whisper against his neck. "Without you? Not a chance. And my mind won't stop racing. Every detail feels like it could unravel into disaster. Something about this... I just have a bad feeling I can't shake."

Talyn's hand paused on her hip, his tone laced with concern. "A vision?"

"No," she murmured, shaking her head. "It's not that clear. Just... a sense."

His gaze turned contemplative, the weight of his thoughts evident. "We've done everything we can. The humans are ready. All that's left is to trust our preparations and see it through."

Aayla exhaled, his words a fragile tether to hope. She managed a faint smile, appreciating his steady presence. "You're right. Now we just have to face whatever comes next."

Chapter Fifty-Four

As the final hours before the meeting slipped away, the energy across Aldredth Tower surged like an unspoken current. Aldredth and humans moved with purpose, their excitement electric. Today would mark a turning point in Earth's history. A day poised to reshape its future forever.

Aayla stood tall on the oval beside Aldredth Tower, designated as the landing zone for visiting dignitaries. The weight of responsibility pressed heavily on her young shoulders, but the comforting presence of Talyn at her side steadied her. His wings brushed hers lightly with quiet reassurance, a touch that spoke louder than words.

She exuded composed authority, her sharp gaze cataloguing every detail, from the sleek metallic arcs of the Arcturian vessels to the organic, pulsating forms of the Zogni crafts. Talyn lingered a step behind her, blending into the background, his vigilant eyes scanning the horizon with a watchful, protective gaze.

As the alien ships descended one by one, Aayla took a deep breath and stepped forward to welcome the delegates. Her voice rang clear and steady across the expanse. "Welcome, esteemed delegates, to the first Intergalactic Meeting on Earth. I am honoured to introduce you to your hosts."

She gestured toward the human leaders assembled by her side, representatives from nations across the globe. Each stepped forward, offering brief words of greeting, their words translated instantly into every delegate's language through a variety of devices and methods. Some wore intricate earpieces or implants, while others relied on chemical or magical enhancements.

The Aldredth, however, needed no such devices. Their exceptional memory allowed them to learn the languages of countless species, rendering translation tools unnecessary. For the humans, the Aldredth had designed a discreet earpiece modelled after familiar Earth technology, enabling seamless communication.

With the formal introductions complete, the delegates were guided into a grand meeting hall in Aldredth Tower. Aayla stood at the head of the circular table, initiating the formal proceedings. Holographic displays flickered to life, projecting agendas and key topics for discussion. She navigated the initial formalities with practised ease, guiding the conversation towards common goals and shared interests.

Talyn remained at her side, ever watchful. His eyes darted across the room, cataloguing every movement, every glance, ready to act at the first sign of trouble.

The atmosphere grew tense during a heated debate between the Draconian and Arcturian representatives over a proposed resource-sharing agreement with the humans. The discussion teetered on the brink of conflict until Aayla intervened, presenting a compromise that wove elements from both sides into a balanced solution. Her deft diplomacy diffused the tension, allowing the conversation to regain its focus.

Throughout the meeting, Aayla and Talyn exchanged brief, meaningful glances. Once, she became so distracted by his presence that she lost track of the conversation entirely until Martok politely called her name.

As the sun began to set, casting a golden glow over the meeting hall, Aayla concluded the first day's session with a sense of accomplishment.

The humans had agreed ahead of time for an evening function to be hosted by a different world leader showcasing their own country's unique culture. The Australian Prime

Minister organised a grand ball for the first night, opening with an Indigenous Welcome to Country and Smoking Ceremony.

The ballroom shimmered with elegance as delegates arrived in their finest formal attire. Medals and treasures from distant worlds adorned many, while others wore ceremonial garments steeped in ancient tradition. The Aldredth didn't have formal attire, but on occasions they did adapt their clothing for events. For instance, only white shrouds were allowed to be worn on Cloyedt during their traditional blessing.

But one tradition they embraced wholeheartedly was the masquerade ball of Nannuval. For these events, the Aldredth wore silvery-white garments bearing only an Aldredth crest, without names or bloodlines. They used a shimmering silver spray to mask the colour of their hair and wings, erasing all identifying features. At the masquerade, every Aldredth was equal, a profound departure from their structured society.

Aayla hesitated at the entrance to the Grand Ball as the muffled symphony of laughter and music filled the air.

"Is everything all right?" Talyn stepped closer, his steady presence anchoring her, his voice low enough that it felt like a secret shared between them.

Her lips curved into a faint smile as she looked up at him, her fingers rising to trace the familiar line of his jaw. *I wish I could walk in there with you as my mate. As it should be.*

A flicker of something—love, devotion, pride—danced in Talyn's dark eyes. He caught her hand, his lips brushing across her knuckles before trailing up her wrist and neck, his movements slow and deliberate. *Title or not, you will always be mine. Mine alone. I can't believe I'm blessed enough to call you my mate.*

His final kiss, placed achingly close to her lips sent a shiver down her spine. The warmth of his touch lingered, sparking a fire beneath her skin.

With a final deep breath, Aayla stepped through the doorway and gracefully hosted the Grand Ball, her poise and elegance captivating the room.

The Grand Ball was a dazzling display of opulence, its vaulted ceilings adorned with cascading lights that mimicked constellations. Delegates in elaborate attire moved like galaxies in orbit, each adorned with symbols of their heritage or authority. The air hummed with energy that was a blend of awe and anticipation, with the unspoken weight of history being made.

Aayla danced with numerous dignitaries, each step a testament to her natural charm and diplomatic finesse. Her white and gold-edged iridescent wings moved fluidly with her every motion, shimmering under the chandelier's light. She kept her wings tightly folded against her back as she moved through the crowd to avoid unintentionally brushing against someone, but during dance, they flared out slightly in the joy of the moment.

Amidst the whirl of music and laughter, her eyes frequently sought out Talyn standing guard on the edge of the room. Their hidden glances of affection were a private dialogue amidst the public celebration. Each stolen look filled her with a deep yearning that grew as the evening wore on.

As the final notes of the evening drifted into silence, the Grand Ball came to a close. Delegates began to disperse, retreating to their ships or accommodations within Aldredth Tower. Aayla bid her farewells with practised elegance, but her thoughts were already elsewhere.

She allowed herself a moment of quiet reflection as she floated in the Bathing Pool, cradled in Talyn's strong arms. The warm water felt wonderful against her skin, and the tension of the evening melted away. She turned her head towards Talyn, their eyes meeting in a quiet moment of intimacy.

Reaching out, her fingers gently brushed his cheek. *How are you doing?*

Talyn's smirk was equal parts mischievous and tender. He captured her hand and pressed a kiss to her palm. *Keeping my hands off you today has been torture. But it gave me lots of ideas on how we could spend the rest of tonight.*

Aayla chuckled, her laugh light and unguarded. "You're incorrigible."

"Only for you," he whispered, his fingers trailing along the edge of her wing, sending a delightful shiver through her.

They dried off quickly and stopped past the Command Centre on the way to their quarters. During the day, there were only three unapproved incursions in the surrounding space and eight human disturbances on Earth, which was better than expected. Most importantly, the Aldredth handled all the situations without incident.

As the night sky became a dark canvas, sprinkled with countless shimmering stars and illuminated by the gentle glow of a silver crescent moon, Aayla finally walked into her private quarters.

Talyn quietly closed the door behind him. Without a word, he stepped forward, his movements deliberate and charged with intent. He pulled her into his arms, his embrace both possessive and tender.

Their lips met in a kiss that was raw, fervent, and consuming, a reflection of all the emotions they had suppressed throughout the day. But just as quickly as the intensity flared, Talyn drew back, his forehead resting lightly against hers as he caught his breath.

He gazed at her, his eyes smouldering with an emotion that sent her pulse racing. "Do you even realise," he murmured, his voice low and rough, "how completely you consume me?"

She reached up, her fingers lightly threading through his soft hair. "And you," she whispered, "are my everything."

Talyn slowly stripped the clothes from her body, kissing and tasting every inch of her skin.

Heat pooled inside of her as she watched the way his muscles flexed as he picked her up and carried her to the bed.

The world outside faded away as they got lost inside of each other. In the intimacy of the moment, they surrendered to the passion that consumed them, eventually drifting into a peaceful slumber wrapped in the warmth of their shared embrace.

Chapter Fifty-Five

Day two of the meeting dawned much like the first. It was quiet but with an undercurrent of anticipation. One by one, delegates from the farthest reaches of the galaxy entered the room, their eyes wary but tinged with hope. The soft hum of voices filled the air, and Aayla moved toward Talyn, her steps purposeful. Without a word, she drew him into a tight embrace, her arms around him like a lifeline before the session began.

I love you, she whispered, her voice a soft caress in his mind as she buried her face in the warmth of his neck.

As I love you, my mate. Talyn replied, placing a tender kiss on her hair.

As they turned toward the table, Aayla's gaze caught on Becca standing in the corridor, laughing with Seth. He leaned against the wall, his body angled toward Becca in an unspoken confession of his feelings. The chemistry between them was palpable.

Aayla glanced back at Talyn, who smirked knowingly.

He reached out and tucked a loose strand of hair behind her ear. *He's crazy about her. He thinks about her all the time. I try not to hear it, but he thinks it so loudly that it's hard to block out sometimes.*

She looks equally enamoured with him, Aayla replied, her lips curving into a small smile. *When will they stop dancing around each other and make it official?*

Talyn shrugged, his gaze shifting to Seth before returning to her. Leaning in, he pressed a gentle kiss to her neck.

Snickering softly, Aayla returned to her seat at the head of the table, signalling the start of the session.

The morning unfolded smoothly, and the afternoon concluded early to allow interested delegates to explore Earth. Aayla remained at Aldredth Tower to oversee those who stayed behind, while Martok and Skyla led the tour alongside human dignitaries.

The afternoon was also spent undertaking a large number of rapid media interviews. The world was excited to hear every detail of the meetings, and even though human cameras were recording the entire meeting, the human media still had endless questions for Aayla.

That evening, the Italian President hosted a grand Masquerade Ball, urging delegates to embrace creativity and mystery in their attire.

Talyn stretched languidly across their private lounge, a playful smirk on his face. "Shall we head down to the ball?" he asked, his voice low and teasing.

Aayla hesitated, her gaze flickering toward the door, and her lips curled into a mischievous smile. "Actually, I have a surprise," she said, her voice filled with quiet excitement.

Talyn's eyes twinkled with curiosity as he pulled her into his lap, his fingers tracing the delicate lines of her wings. "Does this surprise have anything to do with what you whispered to Becca this morning?"

Aayla's guilty smile gave her away. She had enlisted Becca for a favour, hoping to surprise him.

"Nothing gets past you, does it?"

Talyn chuckled, his hands moving to cup her face, kissing her deeply. "It's kind of my job as your mate. And as your Guardian," he said softly, his lips lingering on hers.

But as the kiss deepened, a sharp knock on the door shattered the intimacy. Reluctantly, Aayla pulled away and crossed the room to open it.

Becca strode in with a soft black bag draped over her arm, her smile wide and triumphant. "It's arrived!" she announced, her voice bubbling with excitement.

Talyn raised an eyebrow, his lips curling in a playful grin as he stood. "And what, exactly, is in that bag?"

Aayla's eyes sparkled with mystery. "A surprise," she replied, "so turn around while I get changed."

He raised an eyebrow inquisitively before slowly turning toward the balcony, his back to her.

She couldn't help but smile at the absurdity of the situation because she had never asked or wanted him to look away from her. Pulling the dress from the bag, she smiled at Becca and quickly shed her clothes and undergarments before slipping the dress on. Becca helped zip the dress up and adorned it with several pieces of diamond jewellery.

Turning, she caught her reflection in the mirror on the far wall. The white dress, with its sleek figure-hugging design, flawlessly accentuated every curve. Gold highlights shimmered in the light, weaving through the fabric like molten threads, enhancing the dress's sophisticated allure. The colour was a perfect match for her wings, the subtle interplay of hues creating a seamless harmony between her and the garment.

The tailored fit sculpted her silhouette, emphasising her natural elegance. The fabric caught the light as she moved, glistening with every movement. Intricate gold accents traced delicate patterns along the bodice and hem, catching the light and creating a dazzling, ethereal glow.

The dress featured a backless silhouette that gracefully cascaded down from the shoulders meaning no slits needed to be created for her wings. The front of the dress had a bold plunge neckline that dipped deeply, revealing the soft curve of her breasts.

The diamond jewellery accentuated the dress by adding a layer of sophistication and brilliance. The sparkling diamonds caught the light, complementing the gold highlights and drawing attention to the dress's elegant lines and figure-hugging design. Each piece enhanced the dress's overall glamour and allure.

Aayla paused, taking a slow breath. Her stomach fluttered with a mix of excitement and nervous anticipation.

"Okay, you can turn around now," she whispered.

Talyn slowly turned, and his eyes widened in awe at the sight of her in the stunning dress.

Aayla twirled, the fabric flowing around her like liquid silk, the diamonds catching the light in a kaleidoscope of radiant hues. "What do you think?" she teased, her voice playful.

His mouth opened and closed a few times, utterly speechless at her transformation. His eyes slowly swept down her body, captivated by how the dress hugged her figure as the gold highlights shimmered in the light.

For a moment, he was frozen, seemingly unable to find the words to express his emotions.

Sensing the intensity of the moment, Becca quietly excused herself from the room, leaving the two of them alone.

Talyn finally managed to whisper, his voice thick with emotion, "You look... incredible." His eyes were locked on hers, his voice barely a whisper.

Smiling shyly, she walked slowly towards him, her hips swaying sensually. "I thought it would be fun to wear a human-style dress and jewellery to the Masked Ball tonight. Becca took my measurements to a dressmaker, and they made a custom dress for me."

He swallowed hard, his gaze fixed on her. "You're breathtaking no matter what you wear, but in that dress... the way it clings to you. It's taking every ounce of my self-control to not tear it off right now and bury myself deep inside of you."

Talyn stepped forward and pulled her against his rock-hard body. His fingers traced the plunging neckline, and he dipped his head, slowly kissing his way down her chest to the edge of her breasts.

"I can see all the way down to your naval in the dress," he groaned as he rubbed his growing erection against her.

He slowly ran his hands down her back, stopping to cup her bottom, his touch sending a shiver down her.

"Are you not wearing any underwear?" He groaned, his voice thick with desire.

Laughing softly, she bit the corner of her lip, "The dress is so sheer you would be able to see underwear lines. Apparently, it's something the humans sometimes do when they wear tight-fitting dresses."

Blushing deeply, she moaned loudly in pleasure as he covered her mouth with his, his tongue slipping inside of her mouth, tasting her. Their tongues gently intertwined and moved together rhythmically, creating a sensual and intimate connection.

She felt all rational thought leave her brain as his hand drifted up her body and across her wings.

He groaned as his hands stilled. "If I don't stop now, I won't be able to stop, and you won't leave this room for the next few hours."

Sighing reluctantly, she knew he was right. "I'm pretty sure they will notice if I'm missing."

He chuckled dryly, brushing his lips over hers in a light kiss before gently guiding her toward the door. A second kiss followed, lingering for a moment longer, and she closed her eyes, savouring the brief moment of intimacy.

The door creaked open, and in that instant, she saw Talyn's hand dart toward his sword, only to release it almost immediately, as if his instincts had kicked in before he even realised it. Turning the corner, she saw Becca standing in the corridor and realised her presence had startled Talyn.

A sudden twist of unease tightened Aayla's stomach. Had Becca heard them? No, surely not. Hopefully.

Becca smiled politely, unaware of Talyn's quick movement toward his weapon.

"Becca, is everything okay?" Talyn asked cautiously.

"Yes, very much so," Becca replied, her smile widening. "I also have a suit if you would like to wear one."

Aayla watched as Talyn's eyes widened, his eyebrows shooting up in surprise. "For me?"

Aayla reached out and cupped his face tenderly. "I wasn't sure if you would want to wear something different, considering I was planning something different."

He kissed her palm with a soft smile. "Thank you for the offer, but I'd better stay on guard tonight. There's too much at stake."

"You're right," she sighed, her gaze lingering on him. "We don't want to appear too relaxed. Next time."

"Next time," Talyn agreed, his voice steady. "Now, after you, my Unix."

As she walked down the corridor, she felt the weight of Talyn's gaze on her.

I think I might kill any male who touches you tonight.

She smirked, casting a playful glance at him. *I better take enough care not to let anyone touch me then.*

Talyn raised an eyebrow, a flicker of warning in his eyes as he shot her a look that said he was clearly unimpressed by her teasing.

Pausing, she leaned in, pressing a soft, lingering kiss to his chin. *Don't worry, my mate, I am all yours.*

His eyes flashed with heat, and as she entered the ballroom, an audible gasp echoed around the hall.

The evening passed quickly, filled with laughter and lively dances as Aayla mingled with the other dignitaries. Yet, despite the celebrations, she kept a respectful distance from the crowd. Though she knew Talyn had been joking, she couldn't ignore the weight of the situation. She asked a lot of a newly mated Aldredth, especially one forced to hide their bond.

As the last of the dignitaries began to file out, Aayla made her way over to Talyn. He stood near the edge of the room, his broad shoulders and chiselled physique radiating strength and authority. The way his top clung to his muscular frame only accentuated his powerful build and the raw power he exuded. His sharp eyes scanned the room with unwavering focus.

She stopped in front of him and ran her hand down his forearm. The subtle tension in his muscles relaxed under her touch, and his gaze bore into her.

"Come dance with me," she said, her voice soft but firm.

His fingers brushed her cheek, sending a wave of warmth through her. "We shouldn't. It's not appropriate for a Guardian to dance with his Charge."

Aayla raised an eyebrow, extending her hand toward him with a playful challenge. "Well, as your Unix, I demand you dance with me."

Talyn smirked, studying her for a beat, before slowly reaching out. His hand met hers with a gentle, reassuring clasp as their fingers intertwined. "As my Unix desires."

Amidst the swirling crowd, they began to dance, their steps at first subdued, blending seamlessly with the casual movements of those around them.

The rhythm of the music pulsed through her, guiding their feet in a measured cadence, but her thoughts remained elsewhere. She focused on maintaining an air of composure, aware of the many eyes in the room. His hand rested lightly on her waist, the faint brush of his fingers against her wing sending subtle ripples of awareness through her. Their movements were graceful yet deliberately restrained, a delicate balance of coordination and control.

As the music flowed, Aayla caught Talyn's eye, and the world around them seemed to fade. She felt a shift in the air between them, a magnetic pull that drew them closer. The casual pretence slipped away. Their steps became more fluid and intimate as they moved in perfect harmony.

She felt his hand tighten slightly on her waist, drawing her nearer, and her hand rested on his shoulder, fingers lightly tracing the fabric of his shirt. The crowd around them became a blur, the music a distant hum, as they danced together, lost in each other. Her heart raced as the dance transformed into a romantic embrace, their movements a silent conversation of love and longing.

Leaning down, he pressed his face into her hair and breathed deeply as she nuzzled into his neck. Groaning slightly, he rubbed himself against her and heat pooled between her legs as a deep ache grew inside.

As they danced, completely absorbed in each other, a sudden, sharp cough from nearby shattered the spell. Aayla blinked, momentarily disoriented, and turned her head toward the sound. She spotted Seth standing just a few feet away with a concerned expression as his eyes darted between them and the surrounding crowd. As the trance was broken, the bustling noise of the crowd rushed back in, reminding her of where they were.

Blushing hard, she glanced back at Talyn, who stepped back reluctantly. His hand dropped to his side as he cleared his throat nervously, his eyes darting to the surrounding crowd.

I'm sorry, that was foolish. I've drawn too much attention to us, so I think it's best if we leave.

Sighing softly, she performed an ornamental bow to Talyn, which was traditionally performed at the end of the formal dances. *I didn't mean to get carried away. Sorry. But I do like the sound of taking you to my bed.*

A small smile tugged on his lips. *Then, by all means, please lead the way.*

They walked quickly to their private quarters, heavy silence in the air. As the door quietly shut behind her, Talyn moved swiftly, wrapping his strong arms around her waist and lifting her effortlessly off the ground. She let out a soft gasp of surprise as he pressed her back against the wall with a firm yet gentle motion. Her legs instinctively wrapped around his waist as their bodies fit together perfectly. His lips met hers in a passionate kiss, filled with intensity and longing, as their breath mingled.

Talyn's hands drifted all over her dress as he tugged at it gently.

"Can I tear it?" He groaned.

Smiling widely, she playfully pushed him back. "No, it's too beautiful!"

Chuckling, he kissed his way down her neck. "The only reason it's beautiful is because you are in it."

"Nevertheless," she laughed, "there is a zip at the back. I would very much like to see the dress not ruined."

Smirking, Talyn quickly stripped her dress, and they spent the remainder of the evening lost in each other's embrace.

CHAPTER FIFTY-SIX

On the third day, tensions flared almost immediately after the meeting began. The Arcturian ambassador had barely begun emphasising the importance of unity in the Andromeda Galaxy when a heated exchange erupted between the Kryllian and Morgulite delegates.

"Your people have always sought to undermine our trade routes!" snarled Krel, the Morgulite ambassador, his iridescent scales rippling with agitation. "This proposed deal is just another one of your ploys!"

Velas, the Kryllian representative, leaned forward sharply, his antennae quivering with outrage. "That's a baseless accusation! We have done nothing but adhere to the agreements set forth in the last treaty. Your ships are the ones that turn violent at the least provocation!"

A sudden, palpable tension gripped the room. Aayla exchanged a glance with Talyn, who subtly signalled the security teams to stay alert. The hum of charged energy in the chamber was unmistakable.

Before Aayla could interject, Krel rose from his seat, his voice rising with fury. "Do not lecture me on provocations! Your ships have violated our borders numerous times!"

Velas stood abruptly, slamming a fist on the table. "We will not be intimidated by your threats, Krel! If it's a fight you want, then so be it!"

In an instant, the room detonated into chaos. Guards from both delegations surged forward, weapons drawn, their leaders' fury fuelling their aggression.

"Enough!" Aayla shouted, but her voice was drowned out by the clamour.

The Aldredth moved swiftly to restore order. Aayla raised her hands, and a shimmering energy field emanated from her fingers, creating an ethereal barrier between the feuding factions. The room fell silent as her power demanded attention.

"Peace!" Her voice resonated with an authority that commanded respect. "This is a place of diplomacy, not warfare. Violence will not be tolerated here."

Krel and Velas glared at each other, their guards frozen on either side of the energy barrier. Slowly, grudgingly, they lowered their weapons and stepped back.

The human dignitaries cowered in their seats, surrounded by their bodyguards.

Ambassador Zarek stood, his tone steady but unrelenting. "We are here to discuss the future of a new trade agreement, not to dwell on past perceived grievances."

Aayla took a deep, steadying breath, her pulse slowing as the threat of violence ebbed. Reaching out with her senses, she scanned the thoughts of those present, ensuring no immediate danger remained. Satisfied, she nodded discreetly to Talyn, who signalled the security teams to stand down.

"This meeting is too important to let old animosities derail it," Aayla said, her voice steady but firm. "We are here to forge new alliances with the humans and secure a better future for all our worlds. Let us proceed with the dignity and respect this occasion demands."

Though still visibly agitated, Krel and Velas returned to their seats. A tense quiet settled over the room, the air still charged with the weight of the her intervention.

As Aayla lowered the energy field, Martok stood up, his eyes sweeping across the delegates. "Let us continue with the understanding that any further disruptions will be met with swift consequences.”

The meeting resumed, the gravity of Martok’s words lingering in the air. Aayla knew that while the immediate crisis had been averted, she wasn’t about to let her guard down.

The tension inside the meeting room was still palpable when, just three hours later, the piercing wail of alarms shattered the uneasy calm.

Aayla’s heart sank as she received the urgent message on her Lumina from the security team stationed outside, reporting that a portal had opened in the city centre. Unknown hostiles were pouring through.

She didn’t wait. Excusing herself from the room, she bolted toward the Command Centre, Talyn right at her side, his face a mask of determination.

The central screen displayed chaos. A swirling vortex loomed in the sky, spewing waves of warriors clad in the unmistakable Oilasct uniform. Energy blasts streaked across the scene, illuminating the skyline with bursts of destruction as they attacked without mercy. Human soldiers and Aldredth defenders scrambled to mount a defence.

“Daxion, get all available units to the city centre immediately,” Ayala ordered, her voice sharp and commanding. “We need containment now.”

Daxion nodded, already issuing orders into his Lumina.

“We need to be careful,” Talyn muttered, his voice low. “This is probably a ploy to draw us out of Aldredth Tower.”

“Yes, agreed,” Aayla replied. “But how did the portal get through our shields?”

Loxian looked solum, “I don’t know. I suspect treachery, but we’ll find out,” he promised.

Nodding in his direction, they quickly took to the sky, wings slicing through the air as they raced toward the heart of the carnage.

The battlefield was a maelstrom of destruction as the Oilascts moved with brutal efficiency. Human soldiers, though outgunned, held their ground with tenacity. Plasma rifles and traditional firearms were unleashed in a desperate bid to push back the enemy. Explosions erupted around them, sending shards of debris flying.

Amidst the chaos, Rune led a squad towards the portal. "We need to shut that thing down, or they'll keep coming!" he shouted over the commotion.

Aayla's attention snapped to the swirling vortex. "Daxion, focus fire on the generator! Take it out!"

A pulse cannon roared to life, its blast slamming into the portal's core. Sparks flew as the portal flickered and collapsed in on itself, severing the stream of invaders.

The Aldredth and human teams acted with precision, ensuring every move was calculated to minimise harm to the innocent humans caught in the midst of the battle.

"Keep them away from the civilians! Draw them South!" Aayla shouted, her voice cutting through the cacophony of battle.

As the skirmish intensified near Times Square, Aayla and Talyn found themselves at the forefront of the battle, their movements a seamless dance of offence and defence.

Aayla's telekinetic strikes hurled Oilasct warriors backward, her energy blades slicing through their ranks with deadly precision. Talyn was a force of nature beside her, his every movement a perfect blend of power and grace, shielding her while delivering devastating counterattacks.

A voice boomed across the battlefield. "The blood of the child Unix will stain the ground of this planet!"

Talyn froze, a feral growl rising from his chest. Aayla placed a calming hand on his arm, her touch steadying him.

"We will celebrate over your dead body! The Aldredth will rue the day they interfered in our business. Aldredth blood will run in the street!"

"I guess that explains why they are here. They are angry at the dealings in Frionpht, and they're here for revenge," Aayla muttered, looking at Talyn, her tone weary but sharp.

Talyn gave her a terse nod, but his eyes burned with barely restrained fury.

A sudden barrage of energy pulses erupted from a rooftop nearby, streaking toward Aayla.

"Down!" Talyn roared.

The impact was deafening, sending shockwaves rippling through the air. In a blur of motion, Talyn lunged forward, his powerful frame shielding Aayla from the deadly blasts. The pulses hit him with brutal force, propelling him several meters backward until he crashed into a parked car. Glass shards rained down around him, the sound sharp and jarring.

Aayla scrambled to her feet, the world spinning as her pulse raced with panic and fury. "Talyn!" Her voice cracked, raw with fear, as she rushed to his side, throwing up a protective shield to ward off any more attacks.

Her breath hitched as she saw dark veining creeping across his neck and face, the unmistakable mark of a Gazitha pulse. Her stomach dropped. It was a weapon designed to incapacitate Aldredth for several minutes. He was out cold.

Around them, the chaos of the battle continued as plasma fire streaked through the air, explosions rocking the city. Sirens wailed in the distance, but nothing could drown out the pounding of Aayla's heart as she fought to keep her composure. She used one hand to maintain a protective shield, and her other hand tried to roll Talyn over and assess his other injuries.

Seth had been leading two other human security team members through the city, helping to evacuate human civilians when they witnessed the attack. They reached Aayla just as another barrage of shots hit her shield. Her breath hitched, but she kept it up, her focus unwavering.

"We've got you, big guy," Seth muttered while others formed a protective perimeter around Aayla.

As another relentless barrage of shots hit her protective shield, Aayla grimaced. "I can't heal him in the open like this," she gritted, the strain on her shield nearly too much to bear. "It's too dangerous."

"What do you need us to do?" Seth asked, his voice steady despite the chaos.

"Help me move him," she said, her voice tight with urgency.

Breathing hard, she looked around and assessed the options. "I'll keep the shield up. You three carry him to that building behind us." She gestured with a quick tilt of her head. "We can take cover there."

The humans nodded, each grunting as they hoisted Talyn's heavy form between them.

Under the relentless assault of powerful blasts, Aayla's shield wavered. She gritted her teeth against the pain, every strike sending shockwaves through her body. Her shield took another hit, and the pain shot through her like fire. She gritted her teeth and held on. Just as her strength began to falter, exhaustion clawing at her, they reached the building's shattered lobby.

The building had been hit several times during the battle, and broken glass and debris were scattered everywhere. Inside, the lights flickered above, casting eerie shadows across the debris-strewn space. In the centre of the foyer, there was a large silver escalator that led up to the open second floor with a glass balustrade. Aayla's eyes darted around before spotting a small door to the right. "Over there!" she directed.

She snapped the handle off and pushed the door open, revealing a cramped storage closet filled with cleaning supplies. It was not ideal, but it was their best chance. The humans lowered Talyn to the floor, his body limp and vulnerable. Aayla knelt beside him, her hands trembling as she gently cupped his face.

She closed her eyes, focusing all her energy on healing him, mending the internal bleeding and broken bones. The effort left her gasping for air, her strength waning.

Opening her eyes, she gently caressed Talyn's face as Seth crouched beside her, his brow furrowed. "Why isn't he waking up?"

"The Gazitha pulse acts like a sedative," she explained, her voice edged with frustration. "He'll wake soon, but not before they break in here. He should be safe if we hide him and draw their attacks in the opposite direction. It's me they're after." Her voice quivered at the thought of leaving him in such a vulnerable state.

Seth hesitated, his face tight with worry. "Why don't we stay with him?"

Aayla's heart twisted, but she shook her head. "It's too risky. He's too heavy to move. If we stay here, we'll all be sitting ducks. The safest option is for me to draw them away."

A rustling sound outside caught her attention. "We have to go. Now!"

Chapter Fifty-Seven

Aayal and the security force members rushed out of the closet without saying another word, pulling the door shut behind them.

"Where to?" Seth asked urgently.

"Up the escalator." Aayla pointed toward the large silver structure in the centre of the foyer.

She watched the humans rush to the top of the escalator while she paused at the bottom.

"What are you doing?" Seth shouted down at her.

She gave a dry smile. "Making sure they take the bait."

Moments later, the Oilasct burst into the building, the glass doors shattering in a hail of debris, showering her in glass. Aayla put on her best look of surprise, selling the ruse before turning and sprinting up the escalator. The Oilascts took the bait, barrelling after her, their shouts echoing through the ravaged lobby.

The corridor was too narrow for flight, but she was fast enough to outrun the Oilasct on foot. She darted through the twisting hallway, her feet pounding against the floor.

She rounded the final corner, spotting Seth just ahead, holding open heavy double doors. As soon as she slipped inside, the doors slammed shut behind her with a force that rattled the walls. Seth backed away quickly, his face tense. Aayla moved immediately, shoving the large conference table across the room to create a defensive barrier. Her eyes scanned the space. Scattered chairs offered minimal cover but ample space for swift manoeuvres. It would have to do.

"Get to the other door," she ordered, her voice sharp, pointing to the far side of the room. "Run and hide. Now."

The humans barely had time to react before the heavy wooden doors exploded off their hinges with a deafening crack.

The echoes of the larger battle outside were muted within the confines of the stark meeting room.

Aayla's pulse quickened, her senses on high alert, as she watched three Oilasct slowly stalk into the room with predatory precision. Their heavy boots thudded against the floor as they advanced, their eyes cold and calculating as they fixed on their prey.

With sword held high, the metal glinting under the harsh fluorescent lights, Aayla took a deep breath as her eyes darted between them.

The first Oilasct raised his blaster with a snarl and fired. The searing bolt of plasma tore through the air, but Aayla was quicker. With a fluid motion, she sidestepped and swung her sword, deflecting the plasma into a nearby wall away from the humans, which scorched black upon impact.

Without hesitation, Aayla closed the distance, her movements a blur. Her sword flashed, slicing cleanly through the first Oilascts chest before he could react. He collapsed, his blaster clattering to the floor.

The remaining two Oilascts momentarily hesitated before they quickly adjusted. They raised their blasters in unison, their eyes locked onto Aayla. Twin bolts of plasma shot towards her, but she twisted and spun, evading the deadly energy with breathtaking agility. Her sword danced in her hands, reflecting the room's harsh light.

She lunged at the second Oilasct, her sword arcing upwards. He attempted to fire, but Aayla was too fast. Her blade severed his blaster arm with a swift, upward slash. He howled in pain, the weapon falling from his grasp. Before he could react further, she drove her sword into his torso, silencing him instantly as he crumpled to the ground.

The third Oilasct, now visibly shaken, took a step back, his blaster trembling in his hands. Anger and desperation etched into his features as he fired wildly, plasma bolts scorching the table and chairs. Aayla advanced with relentless determination, her movements a blur of lethal precision. She deflected another wild shot with her sword, the plasma ricocheting off her blade and striking a wall-mounted screen, which shattered in a burst of sparks.

The Oilasct's eyes focused on the humans at the back of the room and began firing at them. Aayla jumped in front of them and deflected all but one of the shots, which hit her leg.

Crying out in agony, her body jolted forward from the force of the strike. The blow had torn through her leg, the searing pain intense as the bone shattered. She collapsed to the ground, unable to put any weight on it, the world spinning as her breath came in sharp, ragged gasps.

The humans fired at the Oilasct while Seth called her name, but she stood back up, balancing on her good leg without risking a backward glance at him.

With a final, decisive leap, she soared through the air, her sword raised high. Her blade sliced through the air and, with a single, powerful stroke, cleaved through the Oilascts armour. As he crumpled to the floor, Aayla dropped to the floor, clutching her injured leg as blood pooled around her.

Seth darted to her side, his voice urgent. "Aayla, you need to heal yourself now."

Nodding, she winced as she placed her hand over her broken leg, but the faint sound of footsteps in the corridor froze her in place. Her heart skipped a beat. She didn't have enough time to heal her leg before more Oilascts would enter the room.

She grabbed Seth's arm and whispered hurriedly to him. "I can hear more Oilascts in the corridor. Quickly leave via the back door. I'll hold them off for as long as I can."

"We won't leave you unprotected and injured," he resorted angrily.

"You're no match for them, and I'm too injured to protect you. Please don't make me watch you die. Go, now."

Reluctantly, Seth nodded and signalled to the team to move out. They ran silently to the open back door and gave her one last backward glance before disappearing into the darkness beyond.

The pain in her leg was starting to burn, but she pulled upon her energy to stand up, balancing on her good leg with her sword raised high.

She took a steadying breath, her grip on her sword tightening as she prepared herself to spring forward.

The footsteps grew louder as a single assailant walked through the corridor. Her heart thumped in her ears, and she knew she had to act quickly and use the element of surprise because she couldn't win a drawn-out bargain in her current condition.

The intruder's shadow breached the doorway, and she halted mid-lunge. Her eyes widened in recognition and relief as she locked gazes with Talyn.

"Aayla!" Talyn lunged for her, and she fell into his strong arms as a wave of pain rocked her body.

Lowering her to sit on the floor, he ran his hand over her injured leg. "You need to heal yourself. Now."

Nodding, knowing she was safe in his arms, she closed her eyes and focused on knitting her broken bones and torn flesh back together one cell at a time. Although the process was quick, it was extremely painful in her drained state.

Opening her eyes with a gasp as the last piece of skin was healed, she reached up to cup Talyn's face.

"I'm so glad you're okay," Aayla whispered, her voice trembling with emotion as she cupped his face, her fingers tracing over his cheekbones as if to reassure herself he was really there. "It killed me to leave you, but it was the only way to keep you safe."

Talyn's eyes closed briefly, his forehead pressed gently against hers.

"Aayla," he said, his voice rough and unsteady, "when I woke up, and you were gone, the bond... it was like it had been ripped open. I felt frantic. I could feel your pain, your fear, and I couldn't reach you. It was like I was suffocating. I was so worried I wouldn't reach you in time."

She exhaled shakily, her fingers tightening slightly on his face. "All I could think about was you. I wondered if I'd see you again, feel your arms around me, hear your voice." Her voice cracked, and she swallowed hard as her eyes welled.

He brushed a tear from her cheek, his hand trembling. "I should have been there." His voice dropped to a whisper, filled with regret. "I'm sorry I wasn't there to protect you."

Her eyes widened, and she shook her head firmly. "No, don't say that. Don't you dare blame yourself."

Their lips crashed together with an intense, almost desperate need. Their breaths mingled as their lips met in a fervent, passionate kiss. Talyn cupped her face, his fingers threading through his hair while she wrapped her arms tightly around his neck, pulling him closer.

Their mouths moved hungrily against each other, and Aayla couldn't get enough of it. Of Talyn.

She moaned as the kiss deepened, and Talyn's hand drifted across her body to stroke her wing. Their hands gripped each other tightly as the intensity of their embrace made the world around them disappear.

A sharp, quiet gasp shattered the fragile intimacy of the moment. Talyn spun on instinct, his sword flashing as he dropped into a defensive stance.

Standing at the back door, Seth froze, his mouth slightly agape, flanked by the other two human security force members. Their eyes were wide with surprise.

Talyn's fierce battle-ready glare melted into confusion at the sight of the humans. Then, realisation struck like a thunderbolt, and horror flickered in his expression. They had seen everything. The kiss.

Aayla took a hesitant step forward, her mouth opening to explain, to plead for understanding, but before she could speak, the building shook violently as an explosion ripped through the air. The floor trembled beneath them, sending dust cascading from the ceiling.

"Quick!" Talyn ordered, the urgency in his voice cutting through the chaos. "Out the back!"

Together, they raced down the fire escape, the metal groaning under their hurried footsteps, and burst out into the open street. The city was a war zone. Smoke and fire clawed at the sky, and the sounds of battle filled the air.

Aayla scanned the scene, her mind racing. She grabbed Seth's arm and turned him toward the alley. "You take your team and head to the right. Use the alley over there to slip away from the battle. Talyn and I will go left and draw their fire."

Seth hesitated for only a moment before nodding. "Be careful," he said, his tone heavy with meaning.

With a glance over her shoulder, Aayla watched the humans disappear into the alley's shadows, her heart pounding with relief as they slipped safely out of harm's way.

"Let's go!" Talyn urged, gripping her hand as the sounds of approaching enemies grew louder.

The pair darted toward the chaos, their movements swift and precise. Together, they faced the remnants of the attacking force, their combat a deadly dance of precision and power. It didn't take long for the remaining Oilascts to be neutralised and order restored.

As the dust began to settle, a small contingent of Aldredth arrived to secure the area and begin repairs. The city centre was scarred but not broken, and with their combined efforts, the damage would be fixed by nightfall.

Aayla's thoughts, however, were far from the battlefield. She couldn't shake the image of Seth's stunned face or the implications of what he had seen.

The intergalactic meeting had been abruptly postponed during the battle, and as soon as Aayla touched down at Aldredth Tower, she rushed back to the grand meeting hall. Rythar was waiting in the corridor, his expression grim as he motioned her inside.

"We're ready to resume," he said, his tone laced with urgency.

Aayla hesitated, her gaze flickering to Talyn beside her. *We need to talk to Seth and find out what he saw.*

Talyn exhaled sharply, dragging a hand through his hair in thought. *You're right, but you need to go inside. If you don't, it'll raise questions. I'll find Seth and handle it.*

Her heart clenched, but she nodded, trusting him. *Be careful.*

Talyn's lips curved in a faint, reassuring smile as he cupped her cheek. *I will.*

Drawing a deep breath, she turned and strode into the meeting room. The atmosphere was tense, the air heavy with anticipation. Delegates from across the galaxies sat in small groups, their whispered conversations underscored by the weight of the postponed meeting.

Martok approached her immediately, his sharp eyes scanning her face. *Aayla, what happened out there?*

She quickly debriefed him and Skyla, outlining the critical points before the meeting resumed. The stakes were high. They had a traitor in their midst, someone who had already caused significant damage. Time was against them, and every second wasted could tip the balance further in the enemy's favour if more attacks were to follow.

We need to act swiftly. Her eyes scanned the room for any signs of deceit.

CHAPTER FIFTY-EIGHT

Talyn leaned casually against the wall, his sharp gaze following Aayla as she made her way toward Martok and Skyla. She would be safe with them for a moment, giving him enough time to talk with Seth.

Moments later, Seth appeared, leading his small team past the meeting room. Their animated chatter faded the instant they noticed Talyn standing in the corridor, his presence radiating quiet intensity.

"Seth," Talyn called softly, his tone calm but laced with purpose. "Do you have a moment?"

Seth hesitated, his sharp eyes flicking around the corridor before landing back on Talyn. "Ah... sure," he said cautiously.

Straightening, Talyn approached, acutely aware of how exposed this conversation was. He hated the lack of privacy, but time wasn't on his side. If Seth had told anyone about the kiss, Talyn needed to act quickly and get Aayla off-planet before the situation spiralled out of control.

He stopped just short of the group, his hand moving instinctively to rub the back of his neck. His throat was dry, and each word he needed to say weighed heavier with every passing second.

"I just wanted to thank you for your help today. We couldn't have done it without you. Truly." His voice dropped slightly, deliberate. "And I know a lot happened. So, I wanted to ask if you had any questions about... anything you might have seen today?"

Seth had looked wary at first, but at Talyn's question, his demeanour shifted, casual and unbothered. "Nope. No questions," he said with a shrug.

Talyn's jaw tightened, and his eyes darted briefly to the other team members, searching for signs of unease. Their relaxed expressions mirrored Seth's, but a seed of doubt still gnawed at him.

"Okay," Talyn said slowly, forcing himself to continue. "It's just that... in the heat of battle, things aren't always what they seem."

Seth smirked faintly. "Yeah, I know. You don't need to explain."

Talyn's fingers twitched, betraying the tension he tried to suppress. "So, there's nothing you want to talk about?" he asked, his voice lower, sharper.

Seth's dry laugh caught him off guard as he reached out, gripping Talyn's arm firmly. "Relax. We didn't learn anything we didn't already know. We protect our own. Always. You can count on us... Brother."

A faint smile tugged at his lips as he reached out, clasping Seth's arm with quiet sincerity. "Your friendship is a gift I don't take lightly. Thank you."

As he turned to leave, he stopped at the threshold, glancing back over his shoulder. His voice was quieter now, more personal. "You know I'd never hurt her, right?"

Seth's warm smile was immediate, reassuring. "I know. That's one of the many reasons we have your back."

"And I'll always have yours," Talyn said quietly. "All I ask is that if you ever have questions, give me a chance to explain before you go to anyone else."

"You have my word," Seth promised with a smile, echoed by a chorus of agreement from the other security force members. With a nod of gratitude, Talyn stepped into the meeting room. The murmur of voices washed over him as everyone settled into their seats and Martok quietly slipped from the room.

Talyn silently crossed to where Aayla sat and leaned down to press a soft kiss to the curve of her neck.

What happened? Aayla asked anxiously, her voice trembling with concern.

It's all good, Talyn reassured her. *I don't know if they saw anything, but they're not going to say anything.*

Thank the stars. She exhaled deeply, genuine relief flooding her features. *I love you so much.*

And I you, he murmured, pressing a soft, lingering kiss to her chin before stepping back to resume his guard on the edge of the room, his eyes scanning for any threats.

Aayla opened her mouth to speak when the doors swung open. Martok entered, leading a large group of Aldredth warriors, weapons in hand. The atmosphere shifted instantly, the room growing heavy with tension.

"Apologies for the intrusion, but this will only take a minute," Martok said as he stopped next to Aayla. He projected an image in the centre of the table while the other Aldredth circled Boujrn, the Drakari leader, in his seat.

"We've discovered evidence," Martok began, his voice clipped, "that this individual has been aiding the Oilascts by smuggling a portal device onto the planet and ordering another to activate it."

The projection displayed damning snippets. Boujrn pulled a small, intricate device from his clothing, handing it off to another Drakari, who was captured on camera activating it in the city centre.

The mood of the room shifted abruptly, plunging into a tense and uneasy silence. Eyes widened in shock and whispered murmurs spread like wildfire among the stunned dignitaries.

The room felt charged with an electrifying tension, as if everyone was holding their breath, waiting for the next move. Talyn was equally tense, having moved silently to Aayla's other side.

Martok looked at Aayla and nodded. As a Unix, she was the most senior Aldredth in the room, and therefore, the responsibility to address this betrayal fell squarely on her shoulders.

Drawing a steadying breath, Aayla rose from her seat and looked to Boujrn. "The evidence is indisputable. An attack on the Aldredth is a grave crime, punishable by death. Do you have anything to say for yourself?"

Boujrn shot to his feet, his face twisting with fury. "I attacked no Aldredth! I transported goods as I was paid to do. I had no knowledge of their purpose."

Aayla's gaze hardened. She knew the Drakari weren't fools, and they never agreed to anything without complete understanding. Yet without proof of intent, his claim couldn't be outright dismissed.

"Then you have been treated as a fool. The punishment for breaking the rules of this meeting by bringing an unauthorised item to the planet is immediate expulsion from the meeting and your removal from this planet. You will be escorted to your ship and leave peacefully. Any resistance will be treated as an act of aggression, and we will respond accordingly. Do I make myself clear?"

Boujrn slammed his fist against the table, baring his teeth. "Exceedingly."

Without another word, he strode from the room, flanked by his personal sentries and surrounded by Aldredth guards.

As the Drakari left, the room hummed with an undercurrent of tension. Conversations were more subdued, and everyone cast wary glances, the recent betrayal fresh in their minds.

Clearing her throat, Aayla sat back down and smiled tentatively. "Let's resume our meeting."

The silence stretched uncomfortably for a moment, but as Aayla guided the conversation back on track, the hum of discussion slowly returned. Bit by bit, the delegates relaxed, and conversations resumed with more confidence.

The third and final day ended without incident, culminating in a breathtaking ball hosted by the President of the People's Republic of China. The theme of Chinese New Year transformed the venue into a kaleidoscope of tradition and splendour, with glowing red and gold lanterns, intricate decorations, and a professional lion dance troupe that held the crowd in awe.

The celebrations stretched late into the night and a small number of dignitaries started leaving following the conclusion of the ball. The majority, however, opted to stay until morning, their departures carefully orchestrated for maximum security. The additional Aldredth, who had been on the planet for the meeting, would remain for the day to ensure the peaceful departure of the dignitaries before departing themselves in the evening.

Talyn had already arranged for him and Aayla to join the first Aldredth ship off-world tomorrow night.

In the quiet glow of morning, golden sunlight spilled across the room as Aayla snuggled into Talyn's arms, her fingers tracing lazy patterns across his chest. "One more day," she murmured, her voice soft with anticipation.

Talyn tightened his hold on her, pressing a tender kiss to her temple. "I'm equal parts ecstatic and terrified," he admitted. The light filtering through the curtains illuminated the tension in his expression, layered with hope and anxiety.

Aayla cupped his cheek gently, her reassuring smile meeting his gaze. "I feel it, too," she said softly. "It's almost paralysing, but we'll face it together. They will listen to us. I know they will. Everything's going to be okay."

She felt him calm under her touch.

"Together, forever," he vowed quietly, his voice steady with resolve. "In this life and the next."

Their lips met in a kiss that transcended the physical, their souls intertwining. Their hearts beat in unison as the world around them faded away.

Too soon, Aayla heard a soft knock on the door. With a reluctant sigh, Talyn slowly untangled himself and slipped out of bed, the cool air making her shiver slightly.

Offering a playful smile, he extended a hand. "Unfortunately, duty calls. Time to start the day."

Their fingers laced together as he helped her up, his heart fluttering at the contact.

"I'll never get enough of you," Aayla teased with a smile.

"I hope not," Talyn quipped.

CHAPTER FIFTY-NINE

The morning passed in a blur of farewells, with Aayla and Talyn bidding dignitaries goodbye. Each farewell was marked by polite exchanges and formal goodbyes as the delegates made their way to their respective transports.

Aldredth Tower buzzed with the aftermath of the intergalactic meeting, but Aayla's mind was elsewhere. She imagined the feeling of the wind beneath her wings and the freedom of the sky. Three days of meetings felt like an eternity to a winged race like the Aldredth.

Yet, she knew duty came first.

As much as Aayla was dying to go for a long fly, stretch her wings, and help the humans, a whole afternoon of back-to-back interviews had been organised. She couldn't picture anything worse.

The humans were eager to capture her final thoughts before her departure, and she steeled herself for the onslaught of questions. The prospect of flight was a tantalising distraction, but she had to focus. The media's curiosity was insatiable, and their cameras and microphones were relentless. Each journalist was eager to capture her thoughts on the success of the intergalactic meeting and to hear whether she was excited to be going home to repeal the law forbidding her mating with non-Lazuil.

They fired off questions about the implications of the agreements, the future of intergalactic relations, and her personal feelings about the impending changes. Aayla answered with grace and patience, her responses carefully crafted to convey optimism and resolve.

She sat with her wings gracefully draped over the backless chaise lounge. The lounge's open design provided ample space for her wings to drape freely, preventing discomfort or awkward positioning. Additionally, the chaise lounge offered a more elegant and relaxed seating option, suiting her graceful demeanour and allowing her to maintain a poised and comfortable posture throughout the endless interviews.

Talyn stood steadfast behind her during every interview, his presence a reassuring presence. His watchful eyes, ever alert, scanned the room as she answered question after question. His tall, imposing figure provided a stark contrast to Aayla's elegance, yet they complemented each other perfectly.

The interviews went well, though they blurred into one another with their repetitive inquiries. Aayla maintained her composure, responding with thoughtful, measured answers, but the exhaustion from the constant repetition began to weigh on her. By the time she bid farewell to the second-to-last reporter, her smile was strained, and her wings itched for the freedom she had been denied all day.

As she waited for the final interview of the day, she took a deep breath, gathering her thoughts. The anticipation of the flight she longed for was a whisper in the back of her mind, but she pushed it aside.

Talyn pressed a soft kiss to her neck, offering a reassuring nod that steadied her amid the whirlwind of the day's relentless pace. His silent encouragement was a grounding force she could always rely on.

"Please tell me we're done, Becca," Aayla teased as Becca entered the room.

"Unfortunately not," Becca smiled, "but you've only got one more to go. After that, I strongly recommend some personal time before your departure later."

Aayla opened her mouth to say that wasn't necessary when Becca cut her off with a raised hand. "And don't try to tell me that you don't need personal time because I know you must be restless after being cooped up for so long. I can literally see your wings twitching from here."

Grinning despite herself, Aayla relented. "Okay, okay. I get it."

Just then, a sharp knock interrupted them, and the door opened as Daxion entered to announce that the last journalist had arrived.

"One more to go," she murmured to herself, straightening her posture and preparing to face the next journalist. She turned her head towards the sound of sharp footsteps as Rachel Sinclair entered, followed by her cameraman.

Aayla's eyes widened, and her mouth fell slightly open. She seemed frozen in place for a moment, her mind racing to process Rachel's sudden appearance. She blinked rapidly, a flush of surprise colouring her cheeks as she struggled to find her voice.

Talyn's low growl filled the room, a soft but unmistakable warning. "Who invited her?" he snapped, his protective instinct flaring.

"Aayla," Becca implored, "you can't meet with her. You must send her away."

Rachel held her hands up in an appeasing gesture. "I owe you an apology for my previous accusations. The sources I relied on were unreliable. I want a chance to start over," she said, her tone unusually contrite.

Becca's expression darkened as she whispered in Aayla's ear, her voice tinged with distrust. "I don't like her. I think she's up to something."

She wanted to believe that Rachel had changed and truly meant to start afresh. Looking at Talyn, she saw a slight creasing in his brow.

What do you think?

Talyn's eyes never left the journalist. *I don't trust her. We should deny the meeting and send her away.*

Aayla considered it, her fingers lightly tapping the armrest. *We're trying to build positive relationships with this planet. How will it look if we refuse to offer a second chance?*

The cameraman was capturing every moment, his lens trained on them, while Rachel stood poised, her expression one of anticipation.

Talyn was silent for a beat, then gave a reluctant nod. *You're right. Humans often need to be afforded several opportunities to prove themselves.*

Then that's our decision.

With a final glance at Talyn, Aayla turned back to the journalist and offered a polite but firm response. "We would love a chance to start afresh. Please, take a seat."

Aayla braced herself for the first round of questions. She focused intently on Rachel in front of her, determined to give this last interaction the same attention and respect she had given all the others.

Rachel settled into the chair opposite her, an expression of genuine remorse softening her features. She took a deep breath, her voice quiet but earnest. "I want to start by apologising for my behaviour during our last interview. I realise I was out of line, and I deeply regret it."

Aayla, maintaining her poise, listened attentively as Rachel glanced towards Talyn standing behind her. "I'd also like to ask if Talyn could join us for this interview. I also owe him an apology, and I'd like to take this opportunity to get to know more about him and the crucial role he plays in your life."

Surprise crossed Talyn's face as he exchanged a look with Aayla. *Why would she want to talk with me?*

Rachel gestured towards the chair, inviting him to join the conversation. Her demeanour was a mix of remorse and determination.

I don't know. Aayla pondered. *Is it a trick?*

Talyn's frown deepened, his eyes narrowing. *Something doesn't feel right. It's also not very appropriate for a Guardian to sit beside his Charge during formal discussions. I shouldn't.*

Aayla's gaze flicked back to Rachel, who studied her intently, her sharp eyes dissecting every subtle movement.

I fear she will ask you questions whether you are sitting beside me or standing up. You might as well sit.

After a beat of hesitation, Talyn inclined his head slightly and stepped forward, lowering himself into the chair beside her. Their wings brushed lightly, a fleeting point of contact that anchored them both.

Any excuse to sit closer to you works for me, he said, his tone light, though the subtle tension in his shoulders betrayed his unease.

"Firstly, thank you, Talyn, for joining Aayla today to talk to us," Rachel began animatedly, her eyes gleaming with a hint of something veiled beneath her seemingly pleasant demeanour.

Talyn offered a tight smile in response, his wariness palpable as Rachel continued.

"During your short time on Earth, you have both become pivotal figures, beloved by many," she said, her tone smooth. Then she shifted slightly, her focus narrowing. "I imagine you must be excited to return to Nannuval tomorrow to repeal the law?"

Aayla glanced briefly at Talyn before answering, her smile soft but her voice steady. "Yes, it feels like a lifetime in the making. This moment will be pivotal in our history, and I'm thrilled to begin the next chapter."

Rachel beamed though the sharpness in her gaze betrayed her intentions. "And we're thrilled for you," she said before pivoting toward Talyn. "Talyn, are you looking forward to publicly announcing Aayla as your mate?"

Talyn's expression hardened as his shoulders stiffened, his eyes narrowing. "Excuse me?" he replied, his tone laced with disbelief and barely suppressed indignation.

She pointed to the small TV screen beside them with a malicious smile. "How else do you explain this?"

Turning her head towards the TV, she saw images of herself and Talyn fill the screen.

Out of the corner of her eye, she saw Talyn's jaw drop slightly.

It was a recording taken from a building opposite their private quarters. The video quality was poor, and the image occasionally shook violently because it was zoomed in so far.

Aayla's stomach clenched as a cold wave of dread washed over her. Her heart hammered in her chest, each beat louder than the last. She sat frozen, her eyes fixed on the screen as the weight of realisation crashed over her.

On the TV screen, Aayla watched herself walking to the open balcony door. She could see her mouth moving silently as if she were speaking softly to someone. Behind her, Talyn appeared, pausing to glance over his shoulder, his eyes scanning the surroundings cautiously before stepping closer.

Beside her, Talyn's jaw tightened, his eyes wide with panic. His breathing quickened, and he glanced anxiously at the door. "Aayla," he whispered urgently.

Aayla heard his voice but couldn't answer him, too transfixed by the TV screen, her eyes tracing Talyn's form. A wave of recognition washed over her. It was from five days ago, capturing one of the rare and precious evenings they had spent entirely together, free from interruptions. The details of that night came flooding back, each moment vivid and cherished.

On the screen, Talyn's form softened as he approached her, a mischievous smile spreading across his face. He slid his arms around her waist, pulling her flush against him. Aayla's breath hitched in the present as she watched the past version of herself respond to him, her body moulding instinctively to his. Their lips met in a fervent kiss, and Talyn's hands roamed over her body before slowing to stroke the curve of her wings. Aayla's head dropped back in ecstasy as a soft moan escaped her lips.

Aayla's breath hitched as the memories collided with the present. Her past self shivered visibly, her wings flaring slightly in response. Talyn leaned in closer, his lips curving into a smile against her neck as he trailed deliberate, lingering kisses along her skin. On the screen, her breath hitched as her hands gripped his wings, her fingers weaving between the soft feathers. The intimate gesture elicited a visible groan from Talyn, the intensity of the moment clear in his movements.

In the present, Aayla's hands gripped the edge of the chair as her memories collided with the vivid imagery on the screen. She barely noticed Talyn shift beside her, his breath quickening as his eyes darted nervously between the TV and her face.

On the screen, Talyn's hands slid down to her hips as he pressed against her, their kiss deepening.

Then, with effortless strength, Talyn lifted Aayla and gently set her down on a smooth, low cabinet that rested against the back of a lounge in front of the open balcony door. It was perfectly positioned to catch the evening light spilling into the room.

Her legs instinctively wrapped around his waist, pulling him closer as their lips found each other again, their kiss deep and consuming. His hands trailed up her thighs, fingers splaying across her skin as if trying to memorise every curve and line. She arched toward him, her nails grazing his back in a way that sent shivers through him.

Talyn's lips moved from her mouth to her neck, pressing soft, lingering kisses that made her tilt her head back in surrender. Her breath hitched as his lips grazed the curve of her shoulder, then dipped lower, pressing slow, deliberate kisses along her collarbone and the swell of her chest. Aayla tilted her head further back, her hands tangling in his hair as his mouth continued its exploration, his hands sliding to her hips to steady her against him.

Her hands were insistent, gripping his top in a raw, unrestrained need. Her fingers deftly sought the hidden clasps at the base of his wings. With a hard tug, she released them. He paused only long enough for her to pull his top off before leaning back in, pressing his lips again to her collarbone, trailing kisses down her neck, and eliciting another soft gasp from her.

Not to be outdone, she kissed a line from his jaw to the hollow of his throat, then lower, letting her lips skim the hard planes of his chest.

With an effortless motion, he scooped her into his arms. Aayla's arms wrapped around his neck, her finger threading through his hair while her legs instinctively encircled his waist. They kissed passionately, their movements slow and deliberate, as he carried her towards the direction of the bed.

The video faded as the two disappeared from view, leaving only the image of an empty balcony. The curtains fluttered softly in the breeze, and the serene scene was a stark contrast to the raw intensity of the moments before.

The silence in the room was deafening.

"I can fix this," Aayla whispered, her voice trembling as her heart pounded so loudly it drowned out everything else. The screen burned in her peripheral vision, each second feeling like an eternity.

Talyn's sharp voice cut through the haze like a knife. "Aayla!" he shouted, his hands gripping her shoulders firmly, pulling her from the depths of her spiralling thoughts.

Her gaze snapped to his, meeting the wild panic in his eyes, his urgency an anchor against her growing dread.

"We need to go. Now."

Chapter Sixty

Talyn called Aayla's name, his voice firm and urgent, but she remained frozen, her wide, unblinking eyes transfixed on the damning images playing on the TV screen. He didn't need to look again. The memories of that night were etched into his mind, and he already knew what secrets the footage had laid bare.

Rising quickly, he turned his head toward the hallway, his sharp senses listening for the sounds of other Aldredth nearby.

He eventually tuned into the thoughts of Daxion and Cythara, stationed down the corridor. They were watching the interview live stream on the monitors outside. The shock had given way to suspicion, and their emotions were rapidly veering into dangerous territory.

"I can fix this," Aayla whispered, her voice trembling.

Talyn clenched his jaw and grabbed Aayla's shoulders firmly as he called out her name again, louder this time. "Aayla!"

Her head snapped toward him, and the sight of her shattered his heart. Her luminous eyes shimmered with unshed tears, heavy with sorrow, her entire expression a portrait of despair and overwhelming loss.

He didn't have time to soothe her. He could already sense Daxion and Cythara moving closer to the room, their steps purposeful and brimming with intent. Every second counted now.

"We need to go. Now," he said, his voice sharp and unyielding, leaving no room for argument.

Talyn extended his hand, his gaze steady and determined. Aayla hesitated for a heartbeat before nodding shakily, her trembling fingers slipping into his. He pulled her to her feet with a firm but gentle grip, wrapping an arm around her protectively.

They sprinted toward the hallway doorway, urgency in every step, but froze mid-stride as the doors burst open. Standing in the threshold, Daxion and Cythara appeared, swords hanging loosely at their sides, their presence radiating an ominous intensity.

Talyn immediately pushed Aayla behind him, his hand moving fluidly to draw his sword. He held it at his side, the blade gleaming in the dim light.

Fear gripped him like a vice, tightening around his chest and making it hard to breathe. His heart pounded furiously, echoing in his ears with a relentless thud.

Daxion looked utterly disorientated, with deeply furrowed brows and a slight frown etched on his face. His eyes darted around as if searching for answers in the room, and he tilted his head slightly to one side, trying to make sense of what he was seeing. His mouth opened and closed as though he was about to speak but couldn't find the right words.

"T—Talyn," Daxion stammered.

He felt paralysed, caught between the urge to flee and the desperate need to lie his way out of the situation. Every shadow seems to hold a threat, and his thoughts race uncontrollably, jumping from one worst-case scenario to the next.

"Daxion," Talyn said slowly, his tone measured yet tense.

For a brief moment, their eyes locked, but then Daxion's gaze dropped to the sword in Talyn's hand. Daxion's frown deepened, and Talyn immediately recognised the subtle shift in his stance, a transition from confusion to battle-ready alertness.

The time for talk had passed.

Run, Talyn commanded Aayla, his voice sharp and unwavering.

They moved swiftly, heading for the far door that led into another meeting room. As they burst through, a volley of blasts streaked towards them. Instinctively, they deflected the searing energy with practised ease. The blasts ricocheted harmlessly off the walls, their force enough to rattle the ground beneath their feet but not enough to halt their escape.

They reached the external door of the adjacent room, but before Talyn could open it, it swung inward with a crack. Rune and Ceeda stormed in, their swords raised high, catching the faint light and reflecting it with an almost blinding intensity. Their expressions were grim, their precision deadly as they advanced with deliberate steps, their eyes locked on him.

The air in the room seemed to thicken with tension as the two opponents advanced, their swords poised to strike.

Stay behind me, he murmured, his voice low but resolute.

Without a word, the room erupted into chaos. Bolts of energy streaked across the room, colliding in mid-air with explosive force.

Talyn moved instinctively. He shielded Aayla with his body, positioning himself as a barrier against the chaotic onslaught. His movements were slow and deliberate, careful not to exacerbate the situation.

Each step back brought them closer to the window in the back of the room. His every muscle was taut, primed to act, yet he maintained a controlled presence, unwilling to escalate the violence further.

The room shook with the deafening sound of energy blasts and their impacts, reverberating in his bones before Rachel's shrill cry pierced the chaos. A stray blast had accidentally been deflected towards her, striking the floor beside her with a loud, deafening crack.

"Stop!" Aayla's voice cut through the noise like a razor, her command sharp and unwavering.

Everyone froze misstep. The sounds of battle ceased as every eye turned to her, drawn by the sheer authority in her words.

Aayla stepped forward, her posture commanding, her anger palpable. "How dare you attack your Unix! Lower your weapons immediately."

Daxion and Rune exchanged a nervous glance, their weapons still raised but their expressions faltering under the weight of Aayla's fury.

"That's an order," she bellowed, her voice echoing through the room, a reminder of her power.

Slowly, they obeyed, their swords dropping as shame clouded their faces. Daxion opened his mouth to speak, but Aayla cut him off. "You will move from my path, and we will continue our discussions in a civilised manner. How dare you raise your weapons against me."

"I'm sorry, my Unix," stammered Cythara, averting her gaze in deep shame.

Talyn knew the shock of being reprimanded by a Unix would wear off quickly, and they couldn't afford to linger. They needed to leave before the others shook off her command to stand down.

Aayla grabbed his hand firmly, and together, they moved toward the door as the others created a path for them.

A fleeting hope surged in Talyn's chest that they might actually make it out, but it was swiftly dashed by the echoing sound of footsteps in the corridor beyond.

"Stop!" Martox's booming voice rang out just as he appeared before them, sword raised, with Skyla in a fighting stance by his side.

Talyn instinctively stepped in front of Aayla, shielding her from his view.

Martox glanced over Talyn's shoulder at Aayla, his eyes momentarily filled with regret. "I'm sorry, my Unix, but I must declare you to be compromised." His tone was heavy with reluctant duty.

His gaze shifted to the others around him, who raised their swords in silent agreement before fixing on Talyn.

"Talyn," Martox said coldly, his voice devoid of warmth, "it's over. Lower your weapon."

Looking around, Talyn's stomach twisted with dread as the reality of their situation sank in. Panic gripped him, tightening his chest.

There was no escaping without blood being spilt.

His gaze flicked to Aayla behind him, and his heart clenched. She was trembling, her wide eyes full of fear, her body quivering against him. The depth of her terror was undeniable, radiating from her in waves that settled heavily on his own heart, deepening his sense of dread.

He scanned the minds around him, but all he could hear were thoughts filled with threats of violence, a cacophony of hostility and intent to harm.

Both main exits were completely blocked, leaving him with no way out except for the window at the back of the room. His pulse quickened as he weighed his options, realising that escape through the window might be their only chance for survival.

Before he could move, Aayla growled low in her throat and leapt in front of him, wings unfurling wide, creating a protective barrier between him and the others.

What are you doing? Get behind me! Talyn urged, his voice strained with urgency.

It's not me they want to kill right now, she said, her tone icy. *Stay behind me if you want to keep your head.*

Talyn's breath caught in his throat, but Aayla's resolve was unwavering. "If you want to hurt him, you'll have to go through me," she declared, her voice sharp and final.

Martok's eyes flicked to her, concern flashing in his gaze for just a moment before he turned back to Talyn, his expression a mixture of disbelief and sorrow. "Please, Talyn, don't do this. Lower your weapons."

It wasn't surprising that Martok wasn't addressing Aayla directly. He believed she was under his control, a pawn he was currently manipulating.

"Martok," Talyn implored, his voice raw with emotion. "I promise, this is not what it seems."

Martok's expression softened, a faint glimmer of hope in his eyes. "Good, good," he muttered, nodding as though the reassurance was enough. He turned toward the TV screens, which still looped the incriminating footage. "So, tell me, is that video accurate? Has it been altered in any way?"

Several more Aldredth poured into the room, crowding the space and amplifying the tension.

A heavy silence followed as Talyn struggled to find the right words. "It hasn't been altered," he admitted, his voice low. "Everything occurred as depicted."

Martok's shoulders sagged, and the light in his eyes flickered out as a heavy sigh escaped his lips. His face fell into an expression of profound disappointment, his gaze dropping to the ground.

"Then I am sorry, my brother," Martok said, his voice thick with sorrow. "Please forgive me."

Talyn's chest tightened. "Please, Martok, you don't understand."

"Then explain it to me," Martok's voice cracked with desperation, his eyes searching Talyn's for some semblance of understanding. "Please! Tell me what's going on."

He wished he could tell Martok what he wanted to hear. The words burned in his throat. "She's not under possession. I give you my word."

"I want to believe you, I really do, but you have to tell me something. Anything." Martok spread his arms wide, his voice trembling with frustration and a plea for honesty. "Just tell me the truth."

Silence stretched out, thick and oppressive, suffocating them all. The tension in the room hung in the air like a storm waiting to break.

Finally, Aayla's voice cut through the tension, clear and unwavering. "He's my mate."

The words dropped like a stone, reverberating through the room and leaving a stunned silence in their wake. Talyn closed his eyes, his chest heaving with the weight of the revelation. The bond, hidden for so long, was now exposed. There was no turning back.

Gasps of disbelief echoed around them.

Everything they had done to hide the mating bond was all for nothing now.

"That's impossible," Martok breathed, his face a mask of horror.

The others, too, looked shocked, their faces a mix of confusion and disgust.

Shame burned through him as he stood there, unable to meet their eyes. "Apparently not," he whispered, the words tasting like ash in his mouth.

He wished more than anything that Aayla had mated with someone worthy of her. Someone better than him. Someone who could offer her a future that didn't weigh her down with the burden of his inadequacy.

He knew the others were wondering what a Unix could see in him. He was nothing more than a glorified bodyguard, with nothing to offer her in return.

She was worse off for having him in her life. And now, everyone knew. The shame of it was suffocating, and he couldn't bring himself to look up, to face the disgust that was reflected in their eyes.

"Aayla," Martok said softly, his voice carrying a note of disbelief, "you don't just wake up one day and decide that an Aldredth you've known for years is your mate. It doesn't work like that. He can't be your mate."

Aayla drew in a sharp breath, struggling to find the right words. "I know, Martok. We didn't just wake up one day. Talyn has always been my mate. I knew that the moment I met him. We just... didn't complete the mating bond until recently."

Martok narrowed his eyes, pursing his lips as he scrutinised her words. The scepticism in his gaze was unmistakable, and Talyn couldn't blame him. What they were saying sounded absurd.

"It's true," Talyn added quietly, his voice firm.

Martok's eyebrows shot up, arching high on his forehead, as his eyes flickered between Talyn and Aayla. "If he's your mate, why haven't you announced it?"

"We were going to after we had the law repealed," Aayla said, her voice quivering. "It was all planned. We've waited so long and were so close."

Martok's confusion deepened. "Why would we repeal the law?"

Aayla straightened her posture as she spoke with the conviction of a natural leader. "Because we can prove when someone is under possession, and we have evidence that Unix used to mate with all the bloodlines, not just the Lazuil's. Moreover, the decision to make the Lazuil the royal bloodline was nothing more than the result of chance. The evidence is undeniable."

Martok's lips tightened into a thin line as he processed the information, his gaze moving from Aayla to Talyn, then back again. Finally, he shook his head, his tone sombre.

"Maybe so. But how could you meet your mate and not say anything? How could you walk away from him?"

All of Talyn's years of repressed emotions bubbled to the surface, and the words poured out in a rush of anger. "We did say something! I was told to either deny the bond or never see her again. I was a child! I was not strong enough to stop her from being taken from me, so I agreed to anything they said in order to keep her by my side."

The Aldredth in the room actually looked remorseful.

"But it's impossible to deny who you truly are," Talyn continued, his voice growing stronger. "And Aayla is my mate."

The faces around him hardened with distrust, their bodies shifting subtly, poised to strike.

He couldn't delay any longer. He had to reveal the final dark secret he had fought desperately to keep hidden before they attacked.

CHAPTER SIXTY-ONE

"Aayla and I are bound," Talyn confessed, his voice heavy with guilt. "If you kill me, you'll kill her too."

A chorus of horrified gasps rippled through the room, the weight of his words plunging it into stunned silence.

Martok glanced at Aayla before fixing his eyes on Talyn. "You are... mated?" he asked, his voice hesitant.

Talyn straightened his posture and met Martok's intense gaze without wavering. "Yes," he replied resolutely, his voice carrying the weight of their bond.

Aayla subtly nodded in agreement, her eyes reflecting a shared resolve.

Martok's eyes widened in horror as the weight of the news settled over him, stealing his breath. "No... please, no," he whispered, the words barely audible as if speaking them aloud might make them real. His hand scrubbed across his face in a desperate attempt to steady himself, his brow furrowing under the strain of deep, spiralling thoughts.

Around them, the others were visibly disgusted. Ceeda's eyes widened, her mouth slightly agape, as though trying to comprehend the enormity of what she had just heard.

Daxion tightened his grip on his sword, his knuckles turning white with barely contained rage.

Rune's usually composed demeanour cracked, his lips pressing into a thin line as he glanced around, seeking confirmation from the others' faces.

Whispers and murmurs broke out, everyone exchanging anxious glances, the air heavy with disbelief and unease.

"He's clearly lying!" Daxion roared, his face flushed with fury. "We have to kill him. Our law requires it."

"You'll have to go through me!" Aayla growled menacingly.

"Enough!" Martok shouted, his wings rippling in agitation. He turned to Talyn, his gaze steely. "Talyn, regardless of whether anything you've said is true, I need you to drop your sword and not make a run for the window behind you."

He couldn't stop the flicker of surprise that crossed his face. Of course, Martok knew he was eyeing the window, their only remaining escape.

Martok simply raised an eyebrow at him. "I already have a team of Aldredth circling outside and lining this entire floor inside."

Talyn felt a crushing weight settle over him as Martok's words registered. He was trapped, powerless to save Aayla. His shoulders sagged, and a profound sense of helplessness washed over him. He clenched his jaw, his eyes brimming with frustration and despair as he glanced at Aayla, who seemed so close yet impossibly out of reach.

"If you truly love her, you'll stop right now," Martok said, his voice softening. "We both know there's no way out of this. Aayla is strong enough to take us all down if she wants to. If she wants to get you out of this room, she has the strength to do it. But we won't let you just walk out. We would die to protect her from any threat. The only way out is through us, and for her to leave, she would need to severely hurt her own. Or possibly even kill her own. I can only imagine the grief a Unix would carry if they hurt an Aldredth. If you truly love her, you would never put her in that position. You would never cause her that pain."

Talyn felt the bitter taste of the truth settle in his mouth. His throat tightened, and a wave of nausea washed over him. He knew there was no way out of this situation as soon as

Martok entered the room, but now he could feel the noose tightening around his neck.

"But you already know that. It's the only reason you haven't tried to force your way out." Martok continued, his tone firm but not unkind. "So, I'll ask you one last time. Please, lower your weapon and surrender peacefully."

His heart ached with a pain so profound it felt physical at the prospect of losing Aayla. Not now, when they were so close. The enormity of the loss overwhelmed him, threatening to swallow him whole.

His wings slumped with the weight of his devastation, leaving him feeling utterly shattered and alone.

Slowly, reluctantly, he lowered his sword and met Martok's gaze, his voice filled with quiet desperation. "You need to listen to what we have to say before making any decisions."

"No!" Aayla cried, her voice raw with emotion.

"I will," Martok nodded solemnly.

Talyn hesitated, the weight of the moment heavy on him. "Okay."

Aayla whirled on Talyn, her voice quivering with emotion as Talyn stepped forward, placing himself between her and Martok. "No! I won't let you do this."

Talyn gently cupped her cheek, his touch steady despite the turmoil swirling between them. *It's going to be okay,* he said softly, his eyes brimming with both love and resignation. *There is no other choice. We have to trust that they will listen to us.*

Her hand covered his as her eyes frantically searched his face. *I can't take that risk. I won't gamble with your life.* Her mental voice cracked raw with emotion.

He sighed deeply, leaning forward to rest his forehead against hers. *We can't expect them to trust us if we don't first trust them.*

Leaning back, his eyes never leaving hers, he slowly extended his arm behind him. Gripping the sword by the hilt, the metal felt cold and unyielding in his grasp.

Finally, he turned his head and passed the sword to Martok behind him. His grip lingered for a moment before he let go. Martok accepted the sword with a slight nod before Talyn returned his focus to Aayla, seeking her forgiveness.

His heart ached at the sight of her pain, but he knew this was the only path left. Gently, he cupped her face, his thumb brushing away her tears. *I love you more than words can describe. You are the reason for my every breath. You carry my heart with you.*

Her tears spilled freely as she reached up to cover his hand with hers. *I can't live without you. You're the best part of me.*

He pressed their foreheads together again, drawing strength from their bond. Taking a deep, shuddering breath, he whispered, *It's time, my love.*

He slowly slid his hand down her arms and grasped the hilt of Aayla's sword, tugging lightly. Aayla sharply pulled the sword from his grasp.

I can't. Please don't ask it of me, she begged.

His heart broke at the sight of her tears. Gently cupping her face, he kissed her forehead. *It's the only way. I would never ask it if it wasn't the only way.*

Aayla trembled, her quiet sobs echoing in the space between them. Talyn closed his eyes, their foreheads pressed together, sharing the depth of her grief. *I don't regret anything. I would rather have one second with you than a lifetime without you. No matter what happens, they won't be able to keep us apart. We will always be bonded, always together, in this life and the next.*

She kissed his chin, her lips soft and trembling, her breath mingling with his. *I love you beyond the bounds of life itself. You are the heartbeat of my soul and my eternal reason for living. You are my everything.*

The warmth of her lips brushing his skin ignited something raw and instinctive within him, a surge of emotion so deep it seemed to resonate with his soul.

A sudden clarity washed over him. There was no longer any need to hide their love.

Overcome by the moment, Talyn leaned in, and their lips met in a fierce, desperate kiss. It was raw and urgent, a collision of passion and pain, of love and the impending loss they couldn't escape. Their hands grasped at each other as they crushed their bodies closer.

Each touch of their lips was a plea for eternity, a final, searing imprint of their love that would linger in their hearts long after they parted. It was a kiss that spoke of farewells and forever moments, a blending of passion and sorrow that seemed to stretch time itself.

Gasps echoed through the room, but Talyn barely noticed. Out of the corner of his eye, he saw the Aldredth shifting forward as if to separate them before Martok raised a hand to still them.

As their lips parted, he felt the warmth of Aayla's breath mingling with his. His heart pounded, and his hands trembled slightly as he kept her close for a moment longer, their foreheads touching.

He could feel her heartbeat against his chest, a perfect rhythm matching his own.

His eyes remained closed, savouring the electricity of the moment, the taste of her lips still vivid.

Reluctantly, he slowly opened his eyes to see her face framed by the soft glow of her light golden-brown hair.

Staring into her eyes, an intense wave of passion consumed him, drowning out everything else. He felt the familiar magnetic force pulling him closer, an irresistible draw that left him breathless and yearning. Every blink, every flicker of her gaze ignited something primal within him, making his heart race and his blood surge.

Lost in the depths of her eyes, he was overwhelmed by a fierce, all-consuming love that obliterated any sense of time or place, leaving only the raw, powerful connection between their souls.

Breathing heavily, he slid his hand gently down her arm, his fingers brushing against hers as he grasped the hilt of her sword. With a soft tug, he urged her to release it. *Please.*

Aayla let go of her sword as her tears flowed freely, the weapon slipping from her trembling hand.

Talyn stepped back, his movements slow and deliberate. He held her sword out behind him towards Martok. His gaze, however, remained locked on Aayla, unwavering and full of quiet resolve.

I love you, he whispered, his voice thick with emotion. *Forever and always.*

Her voice quivered as she responded, her trembling smile radiant through her tears. *As I love you. In this life and the next.*

Martok took Aayla's sword from Talyn's outstretched hand. His movements were measured and deliberate, the quiet shuffle of his feet barely audible.

"Hands behind your back," Martok instructed softly, his tone devoid of malice but heavy with authority.

As the cold metal of the shackles clicked shut around his wrists, he felt a sharp pang of helplessness. The weight of the situation settled heavily on his shoulders, and every click of the shackles was a brutal reminder of his powerlessness.

These shackles, designed specifically for the Aldredth, did more than bind his wrists behind his back. They also immobilised his wings and nullified his powers entirely. Their purpose was absolute. In rare instances, some female Aldredth were bound with their hands in front as a sign of respect.

He watched as several Aldredth encircled Aayla, gently taking hold of her arms. They pulled her hands forward to bind her in a rare concession, but her panic was unmistakable. Her wide eyes darted desperately around the room, her breath coming in short, ragged gasps.

The first shackle snapped onto her wrist, and she locked eyes with Talyn. For a brief, searing moment, he saw that her resolve to allow his surrender was breaking. The terror etched in her expression gutted him, a mirror of his own powerlessness.

As Rune reached for her other wrist, Aayla jerked her arm free and shoved him with a force that sent him staggering across the room.

The others reacted instantly, with Rythar and Daxion lunging to restrain her. They encircled her in a bear hug, lifting her off the ground. She swung her legs in a fierce arc, sweeping Ophelian and Ceeda to the floor in one fluid motion.

Aayla fought desperately, her movements wild and erratic as she struggled against the restraints. The Aldredth surrounded her, trying to contain her flailing limbs, but it took several of them to finally subdue her.

He watched, heart-wrenching, as they held her down, their grip firm but necessary. Aayla cried out as their arms tightened around her. Her cries of distress echoed in his ears, a haunting sound that tore at his very soul and triggered his protective instincts.

"Don't hurt her!" Talyn roared, his voice cracking with raw emotion as he thrashed against the restraints. Several Aldredth around him fought to hold him still, a sword pressed against his throat. Every muscle in his body strained against the unyielding metal and hands, each movement fuelled by a visceral need to protect her, even from a distance.

Through the chaos, Graca stepped forward, a syringe gleaming ominously in his hand. The needle caught the light, its intent unmistakable.

"No!" Talyn bellowed, his struggles renewed.

With a precise motion, Graca injected the sedative into her neck.

Her struggles grew weaker, her body slowly succumbing to the chemical influence as the sedative took effect. Her eyes fluttered and grew heavy. Slowly, they glazed over, becoming unfocused and distant, before they began to roll back into her head, dragging her into unconsciousness.

Loxian bent down, cradling her carefully. He lifted her with a sombre reverence, carrying her away as her head lolled to the side, her golden-brown hair cascading over her shoulders like a fallen halo.

Talyn sagged against his restraints, the weight of her absence crushing him. Helpless, he could only watch as they took her from the room, his heart breaking with every step.

As Aayla disappeared from sight, the Aldredth restraining Talyn forced him to his knees on the cold, unforgiving ground. His wrists, bound tightly behind his back, ached with each movement.

The weight of his helplessness was compounded by the ominous presence of a sword, its blade sharp and unforgiving, being held against his throat. The cold steel pressed so close that it cut his skin with even the slightest motion.

Talyn's gaze lingered on the doorway through which Aayla's limp body had been carried, his heart twisting with every second that passed. Finally, drawing a shaky breath, he tore his eyes away and looked up at Martok.

Martok's expression was haunted, his voice quiet and deliberate. "Please tell me you're not truly her mate. Tell me you were mistaken. Anything. Please."

Talyn lowered his head, the silence stretching painfully before he met Martok's gaze. "You know I can't do that."

Rune sneered, anger flickering in his eyes. "It can't be true."

Martok ignored the outburst, his focus unbroken as he addressed Talyn. "You said you can prove when someone is under possession. Can you prove it without a doubt?"

Exhaling heavily, Talyn shook his head. "No."

Martok frowned, his tone sharp with curiosity. "And you claimed Unix used to bond with all the bloodlines. How long ago was that?"

Talyn hesitated, the weight of the question pressing down on him, before finally admitting, "Not since the formation of the royal bloodline."

Martok's eyes swept the room as if searching for answers hidden in its shadows. His gaze finally settled back on Talyn. "Do you have any evidence, anything at all, that proves your bond is true?"

The silence that followed was suffocating. Finally, Talyn's voice came, low and firm. "No."

Martok's face fell, his devastation unmistakable. The weight of Talyn's admission seemed to crush him.

"Why are you even entertaining this, Martok?" Daxion snapped, his tone sharp with disdain. "It's clearly a ploy to stall for time. This is impossible!"

Martok's gaze didn't waver as he replied, his voice calm yet firm. "Aayla is the strongest Unix we've ever seen. Her power surpasses anything we thought possible. There is something special about her. Some even believe she's the next step in our evolution. Maybe this bond is a result of that. Nothing is impossible."

Talyn sat motionless, his head bowed low as he stared at the floor. The cold metal of the shackles bit into his wrists, but the physical pain felt distant, insignificant compared to the hollowness spreading through his chest.

His body was numb, his mind detached, and his soul felt as though a vital piece had been stripped away. The world around him blurred, the cold stares of the Aldredth piercing through him like daggers. Disgust and loathing filled their eyes, and shame burned in his throat.

He fixed his eyes on the floor, but he saw nothing. He awaited his fate with a sense of resigned hopelessness. The seconds stretched into an eternity.

Martok scrubbed his face with his hands before turning to Talyn, his voice quieter. "Are you truly bound?"

Silence stretched painfully until Talyn finally lifted his head to meet Martok's gaze. His voice was heavy, burdened with guilt. "We are. I'm sorry. I tried to fight it. I really did. I didn't want this for her any more than you do."

Martok frowned deeply, his expression clouded with conflict. He opened his mouth to speak but stopped, turning away to pace the room. After a long moment, he paused, his eyes dark with thought. "What evidence did you plan to use to repeal the law?"

Talyn sighed, his voice weary. "There was clear evidence of compulsion in the previous case. A law isn't necessary when the truth is so obvious."

Martok shook his head, frustration bleeding into his tone. "But how can we trust it? How do we know you haven't doctored the evidence?"

Talyn's shoulders slumped further as a sigh of defeat escaped him.

"This is pointless," Daxion sneered, their voice cutting through the room. "Enough of these tricks. The law is clear on the punishment required."

Martok turned to Talyn, his expression utterly heartbroken. For a moment, his hand trembled as he nodded shakily, anguish twisting his features. Slowly, he walked toward Talyn and placed his left hand on Talyn's shoulder while his right hand gripped his sword.

The blade's tip pressed against Talyn's chest, directly over his heart. Martok's voice broke as he whispered, "I'm so sorry."

Talyn took a deep breath and closed his eyes. *I'm so sorry, Aayla,* he thought. He had never wanted it to end like this, dying so soon after finding each other. He didn't want to be the reason she suffered. But at least they would be together in the next life.

CHAPTER SIXTY-TWO

Martok stood frozen, the weight of the moment etched into his face. His hand gripped the hilt of his sword, but he didn't move.

Talyn opened his eyes, his gaze meeting Martok's. The turmoil in Martok's expression was impossible to miss.

With a quick motion, Martok sheathed his sword. He dropped to his knees in front of Talyn, cupping his face in his hands. His voice cracked as he pleaded, "Please, not you. Tell me you were mistaken. Tell me it's not true."

Talyn's gaze softened. "It's okay, Martok. It's okay. We forgive you for what you need to do."

Martok's hands trembled as he searched Talyn's face. "How?" he whispered, his voice raw.

With a grim smile, Talyn held his gaze. "We've had a lot longer than you to come to terms with how this was most likely to end."

Martok pushed himself up, pacing the room with anxious steps.

Talyn's voice was soft and soothing. "I'm sorry this responsibility fell on you. You know I've always thought of you as a kind of surrogate father."

"Stop," Martok implored, his voice strained.

"Know that whatever happens here doesn't change how much I love you," Talyn said gently.

"Stop saying your goodbyes!" Martok snapped, his teeth clenched as he continued pacing.

Talyn's eyes followed him across the room. "Please, don't carry the guilt of what happens here. I don't want that for you."

Martok spun toward him, his anger flaring. "It's the law!" he shouted. "I have no choice!"

"It's okay," Talyn murmured softly, his tone calm, his weak smile a small gesture of comfort.

Martok slowly unsheathed his sword, each deliberate motion echoing in the tense silence. He stalked toward Talyn, stopping just a foot away. His heavy breaths filled the space between them as he stared down at Talyn, his hand tightening around the hilt.

Sensing the weight of Martok's hesitation, Talyn closed his eyes, making it easier for Martok to do what he must.

Several agonising moments passed before Martok roared in frustration, turning away abruptly. Talyn's eyes snapped open to see him storming toward Daxion.

"Talyn is to be taken back to Nannuval for trial by the Cade," Martok declared.

Daxion looked outraged. "You can't let him live! The law requires his immediate execution."

"To hell with the law!" Martok thundered. "The law is meant to help guide us toward the right decisions. To protect us. Not to force us into actions that feel wrong. I will not kill one of my own so lightly, not when there's even the slightest chance that what he's saying is true. Compulsion doesn't cause any pain, so Aayla will not argue with us checking all the facts before we act."

Martok glanced back at Talyn, his voice steady but heavy. "I need to check on Aayla and contact Nannuval. No one is to harm him while I'm gone." He turned to Daxion, his tone hardening. "Is that clear?"

Daxion's jaw tightened in anger, his confusion evident, but he nodded. "Yes."

Martok ran a shaky hand through his hair and muttered, "I could really use the counsel of a Unix right about now."

Talyn couldn't help himself from teasing Martok. "I know where you could find one."

"Don't you dare say it," Martok said with a reluctant chuckle.

Despite everything, Talyn's lips tugged into a faint smile at the sight of Martok's laughter.

A sharp beep from Martok's Lumina shattered the tense silence. He pulled the device from his pocket, his brow furrowing slightly as he read the message. After a brief moment, he slipped the Lumina back into his pocket and turned to Daxion, his expression hardening with focused resolve.

"Stay with Talyn," Martok instructed Daxion, his voice firm. "Make sure he doesn't move."

Daxion gave a solemn nod, resuming his vigilant stance.

Martok cast one last glance at Talyn, nodding in his direction, and left the room without another word.

As the minutes crawled by, Daxion murmured in hushed tones with the other Aldredth while keeping a vigilant eye on the room and its occupants. His gaze never strayed far from Talyn, ensuring there was no chance for trouble.

The door burst open, and Jaxion and Kythera stormed in, their expressions a mixture of fury and disbelief.

"Talyn! What is this madness I'm hearing? Tell me it's not true!" Jaxion gestured wildly toward the TV screen on the far side of the room, where the video was frozen on a damning image of the two of them locked in a passionate kiss.

Talyn's stomach twisted. They loved Amelia more than most because of the deep bonds that had been formed on Orvax-3. This revelation would cut them deeper than most.

Swallowing hard, Talyn met Jaxion's fiery gaze. "I'm sorry, Jaxion," he said quietly, the weight of his words palpable. "I can't tell you that."

The disbelief on Jaxion's face was heartbreaking. It was as though the possibility had never even crossed his mind. "It's true?" Jaxion's voice wavered, a crack in his otherwise unshakable demeanour. "No. I don't believe it."

He began pacing, his footsteps reverberating through the tense room. Abruptly, he stopped in front of Talyn, eyes blazing. "Tell me you didn't touch her," he demanded, his tone dangerously low.

Guilt surged through Talyn like a tidal wave. He wanted to deny it, to spare Jaxion and Kythera the pain, but he was done lying to his brothers. Instead, he lowered his gaze to the floor, his silence louder than any confession.

Rage consumed Jaxion. In a heartbeat, he swung a fist, connecting hard with Talyn's chin and sending him sprawling to the ground. Before Talyn could recover, Jaxion was on him, landing blow after blow in a frenzy of anger before Kythera and Daxion pulled him away.

"I'll kill you!" Jaxion bellowed, his voice shaking with fury as he struggled against their hold.

"What is going on here?" Martok thundered, his voice cutting through the chaos as he stormed in, his sword gleaming in his hand.

"Jaxion attacked Talyn for hurting Aayla," Daxion explained. "Not that I blame him."

"That's enough!" Martok thundered, his commanding voice silencing the room. He sheathed his sword with a sharp motion. "No one is permitted to harm Talyn. That's an order."

Martok knelt beside Talyn, his eyes scanning the injuries marring his face. He reached out, tilting Talyn's chin to get a better look, his expression hardening with suppressed emotion.

The room was thick with tension as Martok rose to his full height and turned to Daxion. "Escort Talyn to the holding cell immediately," he ordered. "No one is to enter without my express permission. Inform the guards, and make sure the area is secure."

As Daxion reluctantly moved to obey, Martok leaned in close to Talyn, his voice dropping to a whisper. "I'm sorry, Talyn. This is for your own protection. It's the only way to keep you safe right now. Trust me." He cupped Talyn's injured cheek, the gesture filled with unspoken support and regret.

Talyn nodded, his heart heavy but grateful for Martok's understanding in a situation without easy choices.

Daxion and Rythar hauled Talyn to his feet and guided him from the room, their grip firm but not unkind. As they rounded a corner, they came to an abrupt halt. A group of armed human security officers, led by Seth, stood blocking their path. Their weapons were raised in a silent but unmistakable threat.

"What's the meaning of this, Seth?" Daxion demanded, frustration simmering in his voice.

Seth's gaze was steady, though his expression betrayed an inner conflict. He sighed heavily, the weight of his decision evident. "I'm sorry," he said, his voice thick with regret, "but we can't let you take him away."

Daxion and Rythar exchanged tense glances, the weight of the situation settling heavily between them.

"It's clear they're mated," Seth continued, his tone resolute despite the tension in the air. "We swore to protect them. If that means standing against you, then so be it."

Chapter Sixty-Three

The corridor seemed to shrink, the tension thick enough to cut with a blade. Talyn's heart sank. He couldn't let this escalate. He couldn't bear the thought of more violence.

"Seth, stop," Talyn called out, his voice calm but firm. "Please."

Seth blinked, startled by Talyn's interjection. His mouth opened as if to argue, but Talyn's calm voice stopped him before he could speak. "Things have now been set into motion that can't be stopped. They are only doing what they must, and this is something I must see through to the end. No blood will be spilled in my name, so you must let us pass. But I am honoured by your friendship... it means more than I can ever say."

The silence that followed was heavy, charged with unspoken emotions. Seth's jaw tightened, but eventually, he nodded, stepping aside. His team followed suit, their weapons lowered in reluctant deference.

As Talyn passed, he glanced back at Seth, offering him a faint, reassuring smile before he continued down the corridor, flanked by the Aldredth.

The journey came to an end at the entrance of the holding cells beneath Aldredth Tower. The stark, oppressive atmosphere pressed in from all sides, the walls and floor lined with cold, unforgiving concrete. Above, a single row of dim lights cast an eerie glow.

The bunker housed five identical cells, each a cold, unwelcoming expanse of concrete. There were no comforts, only a solitary bench in the centre and a metal loop anchored to the floor beside it. The doors were crafted from a nearly indestructible transparent material from the Kilxiaon galaxy. The cells were designed with stark efficiency, their barren interiors ensuring no chance of escape.

As Ophelian slid the transparent door open, the sound of the mechanism echoed ominously in the confined space. Talyn hesitated momentarily before stepping forward, his footsteps muffled by the cold concrete beneath him. He stopped by the bench, the reality of his confinement sinking in.

Without a word, Rythar unbound Talyn's hands and secured his left wrist to a metal chain attached to the floor loop. The metallic click of the shackles closing resonated in the silent cell, sending a cold chill down his spine.

The Aldredth quickly exited the cell, leaving Talyn alone in the stark, cold space. He slowly sat down on the bench, draping his wings over the back of the hard surface. The dim lights overhead cast shifting shadows on the concrete walls, and the silence of the bunker was deafening, broken only by the distant, muffled sounds from the guards stationed beyond.

He glanced around the cell, taking in the sparse, unyielding environment. The cell door's transparency allowed him to view the empty corridor and the other identical cells, each as lifeless and cold as his own.

With a heavy sigh, Talyn hunched forward, his elbows resting on his knees. He stared blankly at the floor, the rough concrete blurring into a grey haze. Hours melded together, each indistinguishable from the last.

He traced the cracks in the floor with his eyes, following their jagged paths repeatedly. Fatigue weighed down his eyelids, but he resisted the urge to close them, afraid that sleep might bring only nightmares. The cell was both a cage and a sanctuary, isolating him from the world yet trapping him in his thoughts.

Time lost its meaning, and the monotony became suffocating until he heard the sound of muffled voices.

The bunker door creaked open, followed by Pyrion's enraged shout. "You will move out of my way before I move you."

"I'm sorry, Pyrion, but Talyn is not allowed any visitors—"

"This is my baby sister we're talking about!" Pyrion's voice rang out, furious. "Last warning. Move. Now!"

He heard a brief scuffle, followed by Pyrion's heavy footsteps pounding down the corridor as he stormed toward the cell.

Talyn shot to his feet, his heart pounding, as Pyrion ripped the door open, his face contorted with anger.

Backing up as far as the chain would allow, the cold metal pulling taut around his wrist, Talyn turned his head away and braced himself for the inevitable blow.

But instead of the expected violence, Pyrion's strong arms enveloped him in a tight, unexpected embrace. Stunned, Talyn froze, his mind scrambling to comprehend the sudden shift.

"Are you okay?" Pyrion's voice, once filled with anger, was now soft, laced with concern. The fury that had twisted his features had melted away, replaced with palpable worry and relief.

Talyn hesitated, still tense, before slowly turning his head to meet Pyrion's gaze. The genuine care in his eyes was a stark contrast to the rage from moments before. Talyn's breath hitched, and he swallowed, blinking away the rising emotion.

"I'm... fine," he whispered, barely able to speak.

"I'm so sorry," Pyrion murmured, cupping Talyn's face gently. "I got here as fast as I could, but they blocked me from seeing you for the longest time."

Talyn glanced at him, confused. "You're... not angry?"

"Angry?" Pyrion's shock was evident. "At you? Of course not! It's clear you and Aayla are mated. Anyone with eyes can see that."

Talyn's chest tightened, the unexpected kindness overwhelming him. "Thank you," he whispered, his voice thick.

Pyrion's face softened further, and he pressed a gentle kiss to Talyn's forehead. "I was so afraid they'd hurt you before I got here."

Talyn offered a weak smile, his heart heavy. Pyrion's fingers traced the bruises and cuts on his face, his expression darkening. "Who did this to you?" he growled, his voice low and dangerous.

Wincing, Talyn remembered just how bad his injuries must look. He was so accustomed to Aayla healing his injuries as soon as they occurred that he hadn't given a second thought to how his face might look now. With a sinking feeling, he realised it likely appeared worse than it really was. A split lip and a black eye, the aftermath of a fight he hadn't even fully registered.

"It wasn't their fault," Talyn stated, trying to reassure him. "They thought I hurt Aayla. I'd have done much worse in their place."

Pyrion's frown deepened, clearly unhappy with his response, so Talyn quickly tried to change the subject. "Thank you for the visit, but Aayla needs you more than I do right now."

"Actually, that's not true," Pyrion said with a shake of his head. "Aayla has a large family and a close-knit Aldredth community, all scrambling to support her however they can. But you..." He sighed heavily, his gaze filled with sympathy. "You're on your own, aren't you?"

Shame clawed at Talyn's chest, forcing him to avert his gaze. He didn't want to admit it, but Pyrion had hit the truth.

"Have your parents even called you yet?" Pyrion probed. "Wait, don't answer. I can guess."

Talyn's voice dropped, the shame still biting at him. "It's not their fault. They believe I've done something terrible, abhorrent. Something that's dishonoured our bloodline. They're... ashamed of me. It's probably for the best if you leave as well, for your own reputation."

"That's ridiculous," Pyrion spat, his eyes flashing with anger. "Look at me." He gently lifted Talyn's chin, forcing their eyes to meet. "There's nothing you could ever do to make me abandon you. Your parents may have taught you to sacrifice yourself for Aayla in the name of so-called honour, but you deserve more than that. You deserve support and unconditional love. Know that I'll always stand by your side. I'm not going anywhere. Haylae will watch over Aayla for us, but it's you I'm concerned about."

Talyn's breath caught in his throat, his emotions threatening to spill over. "Thank you," he whispered, his voice barely audible.

The air between them was thick with all the words left unsaid, and the gravity of the situation weighed heavily on them both.

Pyrion cleared his throat and squeezed Talyn's shoulder. "When was the last time you ate?" he asked, trying to break the tension.

Talyn shook his head, still shaken by the conversation. "I don't remember. I'm not hungry. How's Aayla? Is she okay?"

Pyrion raised an eyebrow, a slight smile tugging at his lips. "Nice try. Don't think I didn't notice you trying to change the subject. I'll have some food delivered right away because you look like shit. As for Aayla, she's okay. I saw her briefly while

I was waiting for permission to see you. She's in the MedBay and absolutely furious. She's giving them hell. They were petrified. Everyone's faces went pale, and they trembled under her gaze. It was like they forgot how to breathe in front of her."

Pyrion chuckled, shaking his head. "Honestly, I almost felt sorry for the Aldredth that were assigned to guard her. Almost."

The laughter started as a soft chuckle but quickly grew, rippling through them until tears welled in Talyn's eyes and his entire body shook with the force of it.

Chapter Sixty-Four

Aayla had awoken to the sterile chill of the MedBay, a place designed for healing but now serving as her temporary prison.

Metal shackles restrained her wrists and ankles. A wave of panic surged through her as she tugged against the restraints, but they held firm.

Her anger surged so violently that she felt as though she might shatter from the force of it. Her fists clenched tightly at her sides, nails digging into her palms as her eyes burned with a fierce intensity. She could feel her heart pounding furiously in her chest. Each beat echoed the storm of rage that threatened to consume her entirely.

A soft sound to her left broke through the storm of her thoughts. Soval approached, his eyes filled with a look of detached sympathy.

"Good, you're awake," he said, approaching her bed. "I'm sorry, but we need to run some tests."

Aayla's heart skipped. "What kind of tests?"

Soval glanced at the guards before responding. "There are concerns that you may be under some kind of spell or influence. We need to ensure you're not a threat to yourself or others."

Aayla's mind raced. "Where's Talyn?"

Soval paused, his gaze steady. "He's being held in the holding cells. He's alive."

Relief flooded through her, but it did little to quell the boiling rage that threatened to erupt.

She let her fury explode, turning on the guards and the swarm of onlookers clogging the MedBay. Her sharp gaze cut through them like a blade, making them shrink back, their faces draining of colour. Every word dripped with the full weight of her Unix authority, relentless and unforgiving. One by one, they stumbled away, fear driving them out. A part of her knew she should regret it, should feel some shred of guilt, but her rage burned too hot for second thoughts.

A short time later, Jaxion slid a tray of food onto the bed and plopped into the seat across from Aayla, his grin wide and infuriatingly smug.

"You're awfully cheerful for someone delivering prison snacks," Aayla said, arching a brow.

"It's not every day I get to see you in such trouble," he teased, unwrapping a sandwich. "I thought I'd sit here and enjoy the moment. Besides, it's hardly prison snacks. It's the finest meal this planet has to offer, prepared by its best chef. Yours truly."

Despite the circumstances, Aayla found herself grateful for Jaxion's relentless humour. It was like a lifeline, pulling her back from the edge of madness.

"Oh, laugh it up," she replied, leaning back with a soft smile. "But don't forget who saved your skin back on Orvax-3."

Jaxion froze mid-bite, then groaned. "You're not seriously bringing that up again."

"Oh, I am," Aayla said with a wicked grin. "Because it's not every day you mistake a sacred royal procession for a street parade and try to join in."

"It was an honest mistake!" Jaxion protested, setting the sandwich down. "Their uniforms looked festive!"

"They were wearing ceremonial armour," she shot back, barely able to keep the laughter out of her voice. "And you jumped in, waving and dancing!"

Jaxion pointed a finger at her. "You didn't help. You just stood there laughing while I accidentally challenged their prince to a duel!"

"That's not true," Aayla said, trying to look indignant but failing. "I was laughing and trying to come up with a plan."

"Oh, yes, a brilliant plan," Jaxion said, rolling his eyes. "You flew to the top of their sacred statue and started shouting about ancient prophecies to distract them."

"Hey, it worked!" she said, crossing her arms. "I even convinced them you were a prophesied warrior sent to bring peace to their kingdom."

"You also convinced them I had to marry the prince's cousin to fulfil the prophecy!"

Aayla burst out laughing. "Okay, that part got away from me. But at least we didn't get arrested."

Jaxion leaned back, shaking his head but smiling. "Barely. I still can't believe you talked us out of that with nothing but nonsense about celestial alignments and sacred dances."

She smirked. "What can I say? I'm a quick thinker. And besides, you pulled off the sacred dance beautifully."

"Don't remind me," he groaned, running a hand down his face.

"Well, at least we weren't executed," Aayla said, taking a sip of her tea. "And they even gave us that weird glowing fruit as a parting gift."

Jaxion snorted. "Which caused you to glow in the dark for two days."

They both dissolved into laughter that left their sides aching and their eyes watering. For a moment, the sterile walls of the MedBay felt far less suffocating.

"Next time," Jaxion said, catching his breath, "try not to promise my hand in marriage to someone."

"Deal," Aayla replied, her grin wide. "But only if you promise not to crash any more royal parades."

The next two days passed in a blur of invasive tests and exhausting interrogations. Aayla was subjected to scans that probed her mind and body, each procedure more invasive than the last. She endured countless hours of questioning, each session peeling back layers of her memories and thoughts. The Aldredth were relentless, searching for any signs of external manipulation.

Her protests of innocence fell on deaf ears.

The endless exams blurred together, and her body ached from the constant probing. Her mind grew weary from the unyielding barrage of questions. The cold, impersonal walls of the MedBay felt as if they were closing in on her, suffocating her spirit.

Finally, after what felt like an eternity, Aayla was told she would be transported to Nannuval for a trial.

The good news? She and Talyn were still alive and were being given a chance to explain their side of the story.

The bad news? No one believed them.

CHAPTER SIXTY-FIVE

Rune and Ceeda approached Talyn's holding cell with deliberate steps, their faces set in grim determination. Behind them, Ophelian and Rythar followed closely, their presence lending an air of quiet intensity to the moment. The door slid open with a low, metallic click. As they entered the cell, the harsh fluorescent light above cast stark shadows on their anxious features.

"Talyn," Rune's voice broke the silence, firm yet laced with an undercurrent of something unspoken. "You're being transported to Nannuval for trial by the Cade."

The words hit Talyn like a punch to the gut. His heart raced, his pulse pounding in his ears as the gravity of his situation sank in. He swallowed hard, but no words escaped him.

Pyrion remained by his side. "You're not alone in this," Pyrion whispered, his voice low but resolute with unwavering support.

Without another word, they moved to release the restraints holding Talyn, the clinking of the shackles breaking the tension that had settled in the air. Talyn rose slowly, his body stiff from the days of confinement, and turned so they could bind his hands behind his back.

Rythar's eyes were sympathetic, though the gravity of the situation remained clear. "We'll make sure you get there safely. It's out of our hands now."

Ceeda paused for a moment, her gaze meeting Talyn's. "I wish you all the best, Talyn."

Talyn nodded, his throat tight, unable to say anything in response. They motioned for him to move, the weight of the next step ahead pressing down on them all. With one final glance at Pyrion, Talyn allowed himself to be led out of the cell. As they moved down the cold, sterile corridor, the quiet thud of his footsteps echoed, accompanied only by the steady rhythm of Pyrion's presence beside him.

Lost in his own thoughts, Talyn barely noticed when Rune's voice broke the silence.

"Wait here," Rune instructed as he exchanged a silent look with Rythar.

Talyn glanced around the corridor, but everything seemed ordinary. Only when the sound of approaching footsteps reached him did he turn, sensing something was about to happen. As the figures turned the corner, Talyn felt her presence before he saw her.

Aayla had her hands bound in front of her, and she was surrounded by a guard led by Daxion and Cythara, but Haylae walked closely beside her, offering silent support. As their eyes met, Aayla's face broke into a wide smile, and she rushed toward him, her energy radiating as she cupped his face in her hands.

But as she looked at him closely, her smile faltered. Her gaze dropped to the unhealed bruises and cuts on his face, and her expression darkened. Without warning, she whirled around to face Daxion. "You said you wouldn't hurt him!"

Daxion's eyes flickered with regret, but Talyn's voice cut through the tension.

"It's okay," he said quickly, his voice firm despite the turmoil inside. "It was just a misunderstanding. It's nothing, really."

Aayla's eyes softened as she turned back to him, and her words whispered through his mind, *I love you so much.* Tears welled in her eyes as she gazed at him, her hands trembling as she cupped his face again.

As I will always love you, he replied, his voice full of raw emotion. Before she could respond, he leaned down and kissed her. Aayla quickly deepened the kiss, and a surge of warmth rushed through him as their energies mingled. The sensation was overwhelming, and for a moment, he forgot everything around them.

He was so lost in the sensation that he almost didn't feel the slight tingle along his lip.

Abruptly pulling away from the kiss, he looked at her with a mix of anger and disbelief. "Did you just heal me?"

Aayla dropped her hands and raised an eyebrow. "Yes. And what are you going to do about it?" she challenged.

Talyn stared at her, and before he knew it, he was laughing. He leaned forward, resting his forehead against hers. *Such stubbornness my mate has.*

He felt Aayla's soft smile. *It takes one to know one.*

Opening his eyes, he held her gaze, the weight of the moment settling between them. *Are you okay? Are they treating you well?*

Yes, she replied softly. *They've given me everything I could possibly need... except for you, of course.*

Daxion's voice interrupted the tender moment. "I'm sorry," he said to Aayla, "but we have to keep moving. You're technically not allowed to see Talyn right now. This is just... unfortunate timing."

Nodding at Daxion, Aayla turned back to Talyn. *Please be safe. I will always love you.*

In this life and the next, Talyn said, his voice thick with emotion.

Aayla cupped his face, pressing her lips to his in a quick but passionate kiss before pulling away. Talyn reluctantly lifted his head and watched her turn to leave.

"Keep him safe," she ordered Pyrion, her voice firm before she disappeared down the corridor toward the ship.

Talyn stood there for a long moment, watching after her until she was out of sight. When he finally turned back to Rune and Ceeda, his voice was low. "Thank you."

Rune smiled sheepishly. "Don't mention it."

"No, seriously," Rythar joked. "Don't mention it, or we'll get into trouble."

Despite the storm of emotions raging within him, Talyn managed a faint smile, though the weight in his chest remained.

Pyrion's voice cut through the lingering silence. "Are you okay?" he asked quietly, his eyes filled with genuine worry.

Talyn's answer was barely audible, his voice rough with unspoken anguish. "Yes. But... she's in more pain than she's letting on. I can feel it."

He exhaled sharply, the frustration of his helplessness surfacing as he turned to Pyrion. "You need to go with her. She needs you more than I do."

Pyrion took a deep breath, his gaze steady as he met Talyn's eyes. "No, Talyn. She has plenty of people by her side, but you... you have no one. You need me here." He paused, a flicker of wry humour softening his tone. "Besides, you are her heart. If I leave you, she'll kill me."

Talyn's lip curved into a slight smile at the thought. "Yeah," he said, "she probably would."

Chapter Sixty-Six

The journey was long, sombre, and isolating, with Aayla locked in a secure cell aboard an Aldredth transport ship. Haylae remained by her side the entire time, offering silent support, but Aayla was too emotionally drained to respond. The days dragged on in silence, offering her little else but space to reflect on her uncertain fate and the bleak future that lay ahead.

Upon arrival, Aayla was immediately escorted into the Grand Chamber.

The Grand Chamber was an awe-inspiring, vast and circular room with a high domed ceiling that seemed to stretch endlessly upward. The walls were lined with intricate carvings depicting the history and achievements of the Aldredth. The carvings glowed softly with a bioluminescent hue that subtly shifted colours, creating an ethereal ambience.

The expansive, circular hall was designed for communal gatherings. At the front of the chamber was an elevated platform with a striking, reflective surface made from a crystalline material that mirrored the room's radiance, creating a dynamic interplay of reflections and enhancing the platform's prominence.

Above the platform, a holographic display continuously projected detailed star maps, critical data, and vivid images relevant to the discussions taking place.

The dome-shaped ceiling displayed soft, ambient lighting that mimicked the night sky. Meanwhile, the floor beneath was polished to a mirror-like finish, reflecting the soft light from the walls. Intricate patterns, with more subtly shifting luminescent designs, were etched into its surface and gently illuminated the space.

The Aldredth did not require seating, their physiology allowing them to stand for days without fatigue, so the centre of the chamber was a vast open space.

At the far end of the chamber, a grand archway led to an observation balcony overlooking the planet's surface and the vast space above.

The design of the Grand Chamber underscored its role as a central space for important discussions and decision-making, providing a dignified and functional environment where all can gather and engage in dialogue.

Aayla was led to the raised platform at the front of the room, her restraints still firmly in place.

The Cadre, a group of the most esteemed Lazuil and Unix elders, lined the platform. Their expressions were stern and unyielding, and their eyes scrutinised her every move as if they could see through her to the very core of her being.

Behind the Cadre, the chamber was filled to capacity. Nearly every Aldredth from Nannuval, and many more from neighbouring planets, were present to witness the trial in person. Their presence was a testament to the gravity of the proceedings. Those who were unable to attend were watching the live stream from their respective bases.

The atmosphere in the Grand Chamber was one of solemnity and authority, where every decision made carries the weight of an entire civilisation's future.

Or, in this instance, several civilisations.

Aayla's gaze darted through the crowd, searching desperately for Talyn, but he was nowhere to be found. The pain of being separated from her mate was agonising, and it only intensified with time.

The strain of their separation had also begun to take a visible toll. Her once vibrant skin had faded to a pale, ashen hue. Dark circles shadowed her eyes, accentuating the weariness etched into her features. The hollows of her cheeks were more pronounced, and her posture was slightly slumped under the crushing weight of her sorrow. There was a noticeable lack of lustre in her complexion, giving her an appearance of weariness and neglect, as though the emotional toll had visibly drained her vitality. Even the natural glow that marked her as Aldredth had dimmed as if it were a physical manifestation of the bond she shared with Talyn and the agony of its separation.

The sight was unmistakable, a shared burden of all Aldredth who were separated from their mates, and an undeniable truth that no one in the room could overlook.

The room stirred slightly as the proceedings commenced, the weight of anticipation palpable in the air. A hushed silence fell over the chamber as the presiding elder, Korvian, stood and began with a solemn declaration, his voice steady and deliberate.

"The charges against Talyn, son of Sabor and Frela, are as follows..."

Each word landed heavily, the weight of the accusations hanging over the room like a gathering storm. Aayla stood silent and held her head high despite her exhaustion, prepared to face the judgement of a room that held her fate in its hands.

When her turn came, Aayla spoke with clarity and conviction. She recounted their story, her words imbued with the raw, unvarnished truth of their journey. She began with the day she met Talyn, moving through the fragile tenderness of their first kiss, and culminating in the unbreakable bond of their mating.

Her voice faltered only slightly when she described their bond, the depth of it palpable even to those who had questioned its legitimacy. Murmurs rippled through the crowd at her words, but a single raised hand from Korvian quickly brought silence.

In the days that followed, the Cade scrutinised every detail of the evidence Aayla had meticulously gathered. No argument was too small, no piece of information too insignificant to escape their notice. Aayla began her discussion with the origins of the Aldredth bloodline, weaving a compelling narrative that unravelled long-held beliefs.

She detailed the early days of the royal lineage, emphasising how, at its inception, there had been no significant distinction between the Vajjer and Lazuil factions. Her argument was clear that the supposed differences were fabrications of time and circumstance, not of true heritage. The records she presented bore testimony to a shared heritage that had been distorted by time and circumstance.

Aayla's delivery was calm but impassioned, her words resonating with those willing to confront the uncomfortable truths of their shared history.

She then discussed the heart of her case—the authenticity of her bond with Talyn. Drawing a stark comparison, she recounted the signs of compulsion that Daesie had experienced and how it was a manipulation that stripped agency and left its victim hollow. She highlighted the stark contrast with her own experience, where she only exhibited the unmistakable characteristics of a genuine mating bond, one that transcended manipulation or coercion.

Her connection to Talyn was not forged through force but through something far deeper. It was an instinctive, undeniable draw that aligned their hearts, minds, and spirits. It was a bond as ancient as the Aldredth lineage itself, untainted and immutable.

As Aayla laid out her case, numerous Aldredth stepped forward to testify about their observations and present evidence the humans had secretly compiled. Dozens of videos capturing Aayla and Talyn in moments of intimacy were viewed. Contrary to Aayla's earlier belief that she and Talyn had been careful to avoid attention, the footage revealed a different story. The humans had recorded numerous instances of them in unguarded moments of intimacy. Stolen kisses, lingering embraces, and quiet exchanges of affection. They painted a vivid picture of a bond that was undeniable in its authenticity.

The humans understood the grave implications of releasing these videos before the law had been repealed, so they had kept them hidden, aware of the potential fallout. However, with Rachel's recent disclosure of their relationship, it was decided that the videos must be immediately released so they could be used as a crucial piece of their defence.

The atmosphere in the chamber was tense as Soval took the stand to testify. He explained that he had subjected Aayla and Talyn to a battery of tests designed to detect even the slightest hint of external manipulation or coercion. Yet, time and again, the results were the same. There was no evidence of external manipulation. This testimony further reinforced the authenticity of their bond.

On alternating days, Aayla was confined to her quarters while Talyn took his turn to address the Cade. The separation was a deliberate measure to ensure they didn't inadvertently cross paths during these critical proceedings.

Despite understanding the necessity, the enforced distance was excruciating for Aayla. The physical and emotional toll of being separated from her mate weighed heavily on her, as if a vital part of her had been ripped away. Each moment spent apart felt like an eternity, amplifying the ache in her chest. The longing to be near him, to draw strength from his presence, was almost unbearable.

In the solitude of her quarters, Aayla paced relentlessly, her thoughts consumed by the void left in Talyn's absence. The pain was deep, gnawing at her resolve, but she knew she had to endure it, for both of their sakes, as the weight of the Cade's judgment loomed ever closer. The quiet moments were the hardest when the weight of uncertainty pressed down on her. And yet, she refused to crumble.

Meanwhile, Haylae defied the unspoken rules of the Aldredth, secretly sharing every detail of Talyn's meetings with Aayla. The risk was immense, but Haylae understood her need to know. Each description was vivid, as if Aayla herself were in the Grand Chamber, standing alongside him.

There, Talyn stood tall before the Cade, his figure unyielding against their piercing scrutiny. His voice, steady and sure, carried through the chamber as he recounted his journey with Aayla. Every word was a carefully chosen weapon in his fight for their bond, a blend of heartfelt truth and deliberate precision. His conviction didn't just defend their connection, it demanded belief, cutting through the scepticism that lingered in the room like a dense fog.

Aayla's gaze hardened as she processed Haylae's words, her wings shifting restlessly at her sides.

"He shouldn't have to be so careful," she said, her voice filled with frustration. "Everything we've done, everything we are, is real. Why can't they see that?"

Haylae hesitated, her expression thoughtful. "They've spent centuries entrenched in tradition, Aayla. Bonds like yours and Talyn's challenge everything they've been taught to believe. Scepticism is part of who we are."

Aayla sighed, her fingers curling into fists. "Scepticism is one thing, but they are treating him like a criminal. Holding him in a cell while I sit here, surrounded by luxury. It's wrong." The discrepancy enraged her.

"It's a tactic," Haylae replied gently. "They want to see if the pressure will make him falter. If his resolve weakens, they will claim your bond isn't genuine."

Her jaw tightened. "They underestimate him. Talyn will not break."

"I know," Haylae agreed. "But the Cade is relentless. Even if Talyn is flawless in his responses, it might not be enough to sway them. That is why your case, the evidence you've gathered, and your testimony are crucial."

Aayla nodded, her determination burning brighter despite her frustration. "I won't let them tear us apart. I'll fight for us. For him."

Haylae gave her a small, encouraging smile. "Make them see. Show them why they cannot deny what you and Talyn share."

Her resolve hardened. "I will."

As the hours dragged on, Aayla's anxiety grew. She found herself pacing, her thoughts spiralling into worst-case scenarios. She knew Talyn was strong, but the Cade was relentless in their questioning. What if they tried to twist his words? What if they didn't believe him?

Her fists clenched at the thought of him enduring their scrutiny alone. Every fibre of her being yearned to be by his side, to stand with him in solidarity. Yet she was powerless to do anything but wait.

A soft knock interrupted her racing thoughts. Aayla froze, her heart pounding as she turned toward the door.

Chapter Sixty-Seven

Aayla's heart skipped a beat at the sound of the soft knock. She rushed to the door, hope and dread twisting in her chest like a vice. Was it news from the Grand Chamber?

When she opened it, a group of Cade's aides stood before her, their faces carefully neutral.

"The Cade has summoned you," one of them said simply, their voice devoid of emotion.

Aayla's breath caught as a wave of fear and hope surged through her. She took a deep breath, steeling herself for whatever awaited. With a nod, she followed the aides down the long corridors, the sound of her footsteps drowned by the pounding of her heart.

As she entered the chamber, the room fell silent. Her gaze immediately found Talyn, who was standing shackled on a smaller platform to the left of the main platform. He was standing tall, wings held high, but she could see the tension in his posture and the exhaustion in his eyes.

The Aldredth watched her closely, their expressions unreadable. The weight of their judgment hung heavy in the air.

She stood on the platform opposite Talyn, drawing strength from his presence. His unwavering gaze anchored her as the room buzzed with unspoken tension.

Amarith, the eldest Unix and, therefore, the most senior Aldredth, nodded to Korvian and stepped onto the main platform. Her voice, clear and resonant, carried effortlessly through the vast chamber.

"We have listened to your testimonies and meticulously reviewed all the evidence. The time has now come to reach a decision. Given the significance of this matter, the Cade has unanimously determined that this decision is of such immense importance that it requires the unity of every adult Aldredth. This decision must rest not with a select few but with all. This vote transcends individual perspectives and demands the collective wisdom of our entire community."

The chamber fell into a heavy silence, the gravity of the moment sinking into every corner.

Amarith's voice cut through the stillness. "Voting will begin immediately after this meeting and will continue until every eligible vote has been cast. Each of you carries the weight of this decision, and the future of our people rests upon your judgment. Reflect deeply on what you have seen and heard. The consequences of this vote will echo through generations, shaping the course of our history. Choose with care and with wisdom."

The silence shattered as hushed whispers and uneasy murmurs swept through the chamber.

She locked her gaze with Talyn, but before she could speak, a pair of aides approached her. "You will be escorted to your quarters to await the results," one said, their tone formal and measured.

"Alone, I'm afraid," the other said as Haylae stepped towards her.

She felt a pang of anxiety at the thought of being separated from Talyn and Haylae again, especially at such a crucial time, but she knew there was no choice.

Aayla nodded, following them off the platform as Talyn's eyes traced her every step.

The corridors were long and dimly lit, illuminated only by the faint light of night. The silence magnified the echo of her footsteps against the polished floors.

When the door to her quarters clicked shut behind her, the quiet became oppressive. Alone, she paced, her mind spinning with questions and possibilities. The outcome of the vote would determine everything.

She tried to centre herself on the strength of their bond and the truth they had fought so hard to uphold. But, as the hours passed, the tension only grew. Every minute felt like an eternity.

Her breaths were shallow and erratic, each one coming quicker as the weight of her worry pressed down on her.

She paced relentlessly, her hands clenched tightly, her fingers white with tension. The silence of the room was deafening, and each tick of the clock reminded her of the precious time slipping away.

Her eyes repeatedly darted towards the door, waiting for the knock that was to signal her fate. The thought of losing Talyn forever was a crushing burden that gnawed at her resolve, threatening to undo her.

When dawn finally broke, casting pale light across the cityscape beyond her window, a soft, deliberate knock sounded at the door. The sound sent a shiver down her spine.

She moved to the door with measured steps, her heart pounding in her chest. As she opened it, a group of Cade aides stood before her, their expressions solemn.

They bowed deeply before speaking in unison.

"It's time."

Her heart pounded as she walked forward, her legs heavier with each step. The hallway stretched out before her, and the echo of her footsteps bouncing off the walls was the only reassurance that she was still moving forward.

They walked in silence, the aides leading her with a steady, unhurried pace.

As they approached the chamber, Aayla's breath hitched. The grand doors creaked open, revealing the hectic chamber within. A cacophony of voices surged before falling silent, replaced by a heavy electric tension in the air.

Swallowing hard, her mouth dry, she slowly stepped inside. The doors closed behind her with a heavy, ominous thud.

Aayla's eyes scanned the room, searching for any sign of Talyn, but he was nowhere to be seen. She scanned the sea of faces around her, but their expressions were unreadable. As the aides led her to the raised platform, Aayla scanned the crowd once more, her heart sinking further with every unanswered question.

The atmosphere was charged with anticipation as Amarith flew onto the platform.

The Grand Chamber was filled to capacity, and a nervous energy pulsed through the crowd.

As Aayla stood on the platform, a cold chill sent shivers up her spine. She could barely breathe. The tension coiled so tightly in her chest that it felt as though the air itself was too thick to inhale. Her hands, clasped in front of her, trembled ever so slightly though she willed them to be still.

"Aayla!" called Haylae, her voice cutting through the commotion as she pushed through the dense crowd, her desperation evident in every stride.

With a powerful flap of her wings, she landed beside Aayla on the platform and pulled her into a tight embrace. "I'm so sorry," she said, her voice trembling. "I tried to get to you, but they barred everyone from seeing you. Even your parents were stopped. They're terrified, Aayla. We all are."

Aayla's eyes filled with tears, her heart aching at the thought of the distress she had caused. "Where are they?" she asked, her voice choked with emotion.

Haylae hesitated, her lips tightening. "They're overwhelmed, nearly paralysed with fear. The thought of losing you is unbearable. And..."

Aayla nodded, cutting her off with a shaky breath. "I'm sorry. I never meant for this. I never wanted to put them through this."

"They know," Haylae assured her. "We all know that. But the idea that this might end at the hands of our own people... it's unthinkable." She trailed off, shaking her head in disbelief.

Aayla nodded, her heart heavy with the weight of the situation. The realisation that her parents' anguish was so profound made the ordeal feel even more overwhelming. "Do you know where Talyn is?"

Haylae's expression darkened. "He's being held in the holding cells, so if the vote goes against him, they can..." She trailed off, her voice faltering.

Aayla voiced the unspoken words. "They'll execute him immediately before I can stop it."

Haylae gently cupped her cheek, staring intently into her eyes with a reassuring gaze. "Don't worry," she said softly but firmly, "he's not alone. Pyrion is with him, watching over him."

Aayla looked at Haylae with gratitude and determination. "Thank you, both of you, for everything. If this doesn't go well, promise me you'll look after my parents."

Haylae hesitated for a fraction of a second before nodding.

The chamber fell silent as Amarith stepped forward, calling the crowd to attention.

Aayla took a breath, her gaze sweeping over the anxious faces below. The room was so quiet that the faint rustle of wings could be heard as people shifted nervously in their places.

"Fellow Aldredth," Amarith began, her voice steady but laced with the weight of what she was about to announce, "the voting has concluded, and a decision has been reached."

CHAPTER SIXTY-EIGHT

A ripple of unease passed through the crowd.

"The trial," Amarith continued, "was conducted with the utmost care, ensuring that every voice was heard and every perspective considered. Now that every Aldredth has submitted their vote, I can confirm that a decision has been reached."

Amarith turned to Korvian, who handed her a Lumina. She grasped the device and cautiously glanced at the screen as she unlocked the result. The screen glowed softly, and her brows furrowed in concentration as her eyes darted across it.

Aayla held her breath, her chest tight as she watched every flicker of emotion cross Amarith's features. Amarith's lips were pressed tightly together, a visible sign of the tension churning within her. Then her eyes widened, and a wide smile broke across her face.

"On the first count," she announced, her voice ringing with clarity, "Talyn is absolved of all charges. The evidence confirms that he did not enact a compulsion enchantment. Aayla's actions were her own."

Relief flooded through Aayla like a tidal wave, her knees nearly buckling under the weight of the moment.

"On the second count," Amarith continued, "the mating claim is validated. Aayla and Talyn are indeed true mates."

The words seemed to hang in the air, suspended in time. Aayla felt a tear slip down her cheek, the realisation of their bond being recognised washing over her like a warm embrace. For so long, she had feared that their love would be deemed forbidden, unnatural. But now, it was official, acknowledged by their highest authority in front of everyone.

The connection she felt to Talyn was undeniable, and now, so was their right to be together.

"And on the final count," Amarith said, her voice heavy with significance, "the vote to repeal the ancient law passes. The law that once forbade a Unix from bonding with any bloodline other than Lazuil is immediately dissolved. All counts were unanimous and thus legally binding."

For a moment, there was silence as the magnitude of the words sank in. Then, the hall erupted. Cheers and shouts of joy filled the air, echoing off the walls in a cacophony of celebration.

The once tense and silent assembly hall was now alive with sound and movement. People embraced, some laughing with relief, others wiping away tears. The tension that once gripped the air dissipated, replaced by a contagious energy that spread through the room like wildfire. The celebration spilled out from the hall into the surrounding areas, where more people joined the revelry.

Aayla's legs felt weak as the words hit her. The law that had once been a noose around her neck, dictating who she could love and sealing her fate in chains, was now shattered. The relief was so overwhelming that it took her a moment to realise she was smiling, a wide, unrestrained smile that broke across her face as the weight of the world lifted from her shoulders.

She exhaled a breath she hadn't realised she'd been holding, her heart pounding with a mix of joy and disbelief. It was over. The nightmare, the fear, the endless nights wondering if they would be torn apart, it was all over. The Cade had not just spared her life. They had given her a future.

Aayla looked up at Haylae, her eyes glistening with tears of gratitude and relief.

Haylae embraced her tightly, the gesture overflowing with pure joy.

As Haylae released her from the embrace, Aayla's fleeting sense of relief was swiftly overtaken by a gnawing anxiety. Talyn. Her heart pounded as she thought of him, locked away in that cold, dark cell, cut off from the world and her. Though the Cade's ruling had exonerated him, she couldn't shake the tension in her chest. She couldn't breathe freely until she saw him, touched him, and knew for certain that he was safe.

Aayla turned to the aides surrounding her, her voice steady but edged with urgency. "Please, take me to him."

They smiled while the cuffs were removed from her hands. "It would be our honour."

Without hesitation, Aayla followed, her pace quick as they guided her from the chamber. Time felt warped, each second an eternity as her mind raced with questions. Was Talyn scared? Did he know the vote had gone in their favour? Had anyone told him? Or was he trapped in silence, believing the worst?

Finally, they reached the heavy iron doors of the prison wing. Aayla's heart thundered as the guard moved to unlock the door. The hinges groaned in protest as the door swung open, revealing a dimly lit corridor lined with holding cells.

She moved swiftly, her eyes scanning each cell until she found him.

Talyn stood in the centre of his cell, his hands shackled, his expression unreadable in the flickering light. Beside him, Pyrion rested a reassuring hand on his shoulder, offering him a wide smile.

When Talyn's eyes met hers, all the fear and uncertainty melted away. Aayla could see the moment he recognised her, his tense posture softening, relief flooding his face.

"Talyn," she whispered, her voice breaking.

She surged forward as the guard hastily unlocked the cell. The moment the door swung open, she crossed the threshold and threw her arms around him, feeling the warmth of his body against hers. He was safe, solid, real.

Talyn's arms encircled her, pulling her close as though he needed to convince himself she was real. "Aayla," he murmured, his voice thick with emotion. "Are you okay?"

She nodded against his chest, gripping him tighter. "We're free," she whispered, her words trembling with relief. "It's over. The Cade ruled in our favour. The law, it's gone."

Talyn exhaled a shaky breath, his arms tightening as the weight of their victory sank in. "I heard, but I didn't dare believe it in case this was some kind of cruel dream." He pulled back just enough to meet her eyes. "We're truly free?"

"Yes," she said, her voice trembling as her own eyes brimmed with tears of relief. "We're free."

Their lips met in a deep, fiery kiss, a desperate collision of longing and relief.

As they pulled away, they remained locked in each other's embrace, their breath mingling in the dim glow of the cell. The world felt whole again for the first time in what felt like forever. Everything they had fought for, the love they had refused to give up on, had been worth it. And now, they had a future, a life they could build together, unbound by the chains of old laws and ancient grudges.

Aayla smiled up at Talyn, her heart overflowing with love and relief. "Let's get out of here."

Talyn returned her smile, his voice soft but resolute. "Together. Forever."

The guards quickly removed his shackles, and hand in hand, they left the holding cell. Aayla cast a grateful glance at Pyrion, silently thanking him for staying by Talyn's side and protecting him, but she didn't stop. Not yet. After being separated from Talyn for so long, she just needed to be alone with him. To feel him.

The moment they entered their quarters, words became unnecessary. Their kiss was fierce, a culmination of longing and relief as if they could erase every moment of separation. Clothes fell away, and in each other's arms, they found the closeness they had longed for during their separation.

In the quiet aftermath, as they lay entwined, Aayla traced her fingers along Talyn's face, memorising every line and angle as though she feared the moment might slip away.

Content, she rested her head against Talyn's chest, listening to the steady rhythm of his heartbeat. A sound she had feared she might never hear again.

For a long while, neither of them spoke. The silence was not empty but filled with unspoken gratitude, love, and the fragile hope of a future no longer overshadowed by fear.

Talyn's fingers glided softly along her back, tracing delicate patterns that extended to her wings, each touch sending a shiver through her. "To hold you like this, free at last, makes every hardship, every moment of suffering, worth it," he murmured, his voice low and reverent. "My beautiful mate."

Aayla tilted her head to look at him, her eyes shimmering with unshed tears. "I love you. Forever and always."

Talyn smiled faintly, his hand brushing a strand of hair from her face. "In this life and the next."

As Aayla opened her mouth to speak, a sharp, searing vision struck her like a physical blow, leaving her breathless. Bodies—Aldredth and human alike—lay broken across a ravaged battlefield. Everything around her was in ruins. Buildings were reduced to skeletal remains, and the air was choked with thick smoke and the acrid stench of fire. In the heart of the chaos, Aayla stood above it all, her chest tightening with horror. She turned, and her breath caught as her gaze met Seth's lifeless eyes, staring back at her, his body crumpled and still on the blood-soaked ground.

She gasped, her hand clutching Talyn's arm as her body trembled.

Talyn's eyes darkened with concern, instantly alert. "Aayla, what is it? What did you see?"

Her voice came out unsteady, laced with dread. "An attack on Earth. Not now...but it's coming. Months maybe. So many lives were lost, Talyn. So many dead."

His grip on her tightened, steadying her. "Did you see who's behind it? Or where it will begin?"

She shook her head, frustration flickering in her eyes. "No... it was all chaos. I couldn't tell."

Talyn exhaled, his gaze softening as he cupped her face, his touch grounding her. "Then it can wait," he said firmly, his voice a gentle anchor. "Tonight isn't for visions or battles. Tonight is for us."

Before she could protest, he silenced her with a kiss, slow and deliberate, pulling her away from the horrors she had seen and back into the safety of the present.

Chapter Sixty-Nine

The Aldredth celebrations stretched late into the night, a symphony of life and joy reverberating through the air. Talyn lay in bed with Aayla wrapped in his arms, the distant sounds of revelry filtering through the walls like a soothing lullaby. The night pulsed with energy, an unrelenting rhythm that promised to continue well into the early hours of the morning.

They celebrated the announcement of a new mating bond and the collective relief of avoiding harm to one of their own. Mating bond celebrations were among the most profound and joyous events in an Aldredth's life, revered as sacred milestones that often stretched across several days. When it involved a Unix, the festivities often stretched an entire week, reflecting their unparalleled depth of love and reverence for their most gifted kin.

As night fell, the city came alive with festivities. Music played from every corner, filling the air with the rhythm and melodies of musical instruments and inviting everyone to dance. Streets and skies alike were filled with jubilant Aldredth, their faces illuminated by lanterns and moonfire, casting a magical glow over the celebration.

The aroma of roasted meats, spiced breads, and sweet treats mingled with the cool night air, adding to the sensory feast. Aldredth shared meals and drinks, bonding over their shared joy as they toast to freedom and a future unburdened by the old law.

As the hours passed, the celebration showed no signs of slowing down. Laughter rang out as children raced through the streets, emberflares in hand, their joy as bright as the stars overhead.

When dawn broke, some Aldredth finally began to drift home, but the hum of celebration persisted, and the city remained alive with the buzz of excitement. By day, the public squares were filled with people recounting the historic announcement, sharing stories, and pondering the future with renewed optimism. By night, the revelry resumed, with moonfires burning late into the evening and the sound of music echoing through the streets once again.

This pattern of celebration continued throughout the week. Every evening, as the sun sets, the streets fill with people ready to pick up where they left off the night before. Artists painted murals and sculpted monuments to commemorate the historic decision, their works capturing the essence of unity and hope. The sounds of laughter, music, and cheers were a constant backdrop as the city embraced the momentous occasion.

And yet, for Aayla and Talyn, the world outside remained a distant hum. They had spent the week in their quarters, yet to venture outside. Talyn's fingers traced gently across Aayla's bare skin, which was smooth and soft under his touch. The dark circles under her eyes were already beginning to fade, replaced by the glow that warmed his heart. The sight of her brought him such profound joy that he wondered if his heart could hold it all.

As their clothes had fallen away, so did the weight of the days spent apart. They found solace in the sanctuary of each other's arms, the unspoken fears and doubts melting away in the heat of their embrace. The world outside ceased to exist as they became lost in one another, reclaiming the connection that had been so fiercely tested.

For the first time in what felt like an eternity, they were whole again. Together, safe and free. And in the quiet moments that followed, as they lay entwined in the aftermath of their reunion, Talyn felt a profound release. No guilt lingered for the thoughts or actions that had once haunted him. Only peace remained.

Aayla had remained hidden away in bed with Talyn in order to savour the closeness of their bond, while Talyn stayed because he wasn't sure if he was ready to face the world outside. The pure joy of their first night together had given way to gnawing worry. The Aldredth might have acknowledged their bond as real, but acceptance was not guaranteed. Deep down, he couldn't shake the thought that some might still believe Aayla deserved better than him.

How could he face them again, knowing that the last time they saw him, they'd been ready to end his life?

Pushing the thoughts aside, Talyn drew Aayla closer and kissed her with fervour, losing himself in her warmth. They separated breathless, hearts racing, and minds consumed by the intensity of the moment when Aayla's Lumina beeped.

With a groan, she rolled over to check the message. A sly smile tugged at her lips as she glanced back at him. "There's a surprise by our door."

Talyn raised an eyebrow in question, but Aayla only chuckled and snuggled closer.

Kissing her deeply one last time, he sighed dramatically before standing up. "This better be worth getting out of bed with my mate for."

Crossing the room swiftly, Talyn opened the door to find a small pile of Aldredth clothing folded neatly on the floor. His brow furrowed in confusion until recognition hit him like a lightning strike.

His breath hitched as he reached down, fingers brushing the intricate gold stitching on the chest. The stitching bore the unmistakable gold-embroidered Aldredth crest, but beneath it were two names woven together—his and Aayla's. His hands trembled as he picked up the garments. He had dreamed of this moment endlessly, and now he was anxious it might be nothing more than another illusion.

Clearing his throat, he turned and carried the clothes back to Aayla. She glanced at the stitching that bore their two names together and smiled warmly, her gaze soft and full of pride.

They lingered in bed a while longer, savouring the intimacy of the moment. But eventually, they agreed it was time to leave their sanctuary and join their people for a meal, rather than consuming another meal in privacy.

"Are you sure you're ready for this?" Aayla asked, her eyes searching his with quiet concern.

"Yes," Talyn replied, attempting a smile that didn't quite reach his eyes. "We can't stay hidden away forever, even if I'd love to keep you all to myself."

They stepped outside and immediately every Aldreth in the vicinity stopped to bow deeply, their unrestrained reverence filling the air with a palpable energy. Aayla responded with a small wave, her smile warm and gracious, but Talyn's hand remained frozen at his side. He convinced himself the bows were meant for Aayla, not him, clinging to the justification as a shield against the unease tightening in his chest.

They continued on and joined hundreds of Aldredth in one of the celestial gardens for an afternoon meal. Long tables stretched down the centre of the space, framed by lush foliage glowing with soft luminescence. Vibrant dragon feverfew flowers, some the size of a person's hand, released a gentle, sweet fragrance. Towering brittlebush trees shimmered with iridescent leaves, casting a soft, prismatic light over the gathering. The climate was perfect year-round, making walls and ceilings unnecessary in this open-air sanctuary.

The meal overflowed with laughter, storytelling, and an undeniable sense of unity. For a fleeting moment, Talyn allowed himself to relax, his guarded heart softening at the sight of Aayla basking in the warmth of her people. They lingered at the table, savouring the connection and joy shared across generations of Aldredth, before quietly passing word of Aayla's vision to Amarith and retiring for the night.

By the time the celebrations drew to a close that evening, many Aldredth had already begun returning to their stations off-world. But the spirit of the celebration, the camaraderie, and the shared joy remained. It marked the beginning of a brighter, freer chapter for all. A promise of unity and renewal that would echo far beyond that single day.

Early the next morning, before the sun had fully risen, Aayla's Lumina alerted, the noise echoing in the room.

"What's happening?" Talyn asked, reaching for his own Lumina as the same alert flashed across its screen.

"The Drakari are attacking Vyron," Aayla said, her tone sharpening. "I need to get to the Command Centre and check the developments."

Talyn nodded, and they quickly dressed before flying to the Command Centre. Upon arrival, Korvian greeted them with urgency. "I'm sorry to wake you, but this requires everyone's input."

Aayla strode purposefully to the centre console, her focus unwavering, while Talyn lingered near the door, leaning casually against the wall. He crossed his arms, his gaze drawn to Aayla as his thoughts turned to Drakari's recent actions. Lost in reflection, he almost didn't notice the shift in the room's energy until the silence hit him. Glancing up, he found every eye fixed on him.

"Talyn," Korvian said gently, "your place is at this table, beside your mate."

For a moment, he hesitated, the words catching him off guard. "Of course," he nodded. Then, with deliberate steps, he moved to Aayla's side, her hand already extended toward him. He took it, her touch grounding him as he fought to steady his nerves.

"I'm sorry you weren't allowed to stand by her side before," Korvian continued, his voice heavy with regret. "We wronged you in ways I am only beginning to understand. I hope, in time, you can forgive us."

Talyn's throat tightened, and all he could manage was a nod. Aayla squeezed his hand gently, her silent reassurance guiding him as they turned their focus to the glowing screens.

At the centre console, Aayla and Talyn stood shoulder to shoulder. Their movements were synchronised as they poured over the holographic map of the besieged planet. Fragments of enemy ships flared across the display, their routes intersecting with defence lines barely holding steady.

"Shift focus to the eastern quadrant," Aayla directed, her tone calm but edged with urgency. "The resistance forces there are vulnerable to being flanked. We need to deploy the secondary fleet to reinforce their position."

Korvian nodded in agreement. "And if we reroute energy reserves from the orbital satellites to power their shielding, we can buy them more time to regroup."

Their strategy fell into place, every move calculated, every risk weighed. Yet, as Talyn studied the display, something gnawed at the edge of his mind. His sharp gaze traced a faint shift in the enemy's movement, a subtle, almost imperceptible deviation.

It didn't belong.

CHAPTER SEVENTY

Aayla.

Talyn's voice brushed against her mind, low and urgent. *There's a problem. Look at the western corridor. If they push through here, it'll leave the capital entirely exposed. It's a perfect blind spot, and no one's noticed.*

Aayla's jaw tightened as her eyes flicked to the area he indicated. *You're right, but you should be the one to raise it. Your voice carries as much weight as mine now. No more hiding. Not anymore.*

His response was immediate, his frustration breaking through their bond. *This isn't about hiding. We're running out of time, and they need to hear it from you. They trust you—*

And they'll trust you, too. Speak, Talyn. I won't take credit for your genius anymore.

Her words left no room for argument, and Talyn released a breath he hadn't realised he was holding. Straightening, he raised his voice, cutting through the command centre's controlled chaos. "There's a vulnerability in the western corridor. If we don't address it, the enemy will breach the capital within hours."

The room fell silent, everyone turning their attention to the console as Talyn highlighted the weak point. He continued, his tone steady and confident. "We can redirect reinforcements from the northern sector. It's risky, but their line is more secure and can hold without additional support for the next phase. If we concentrate firepower here,"—he gestured at the highlighted path—"we'll cut off the enemy's advance before they can capitalise on the opening."

A ripple of acknowledgment moved through the room. Korvian and Amarith exchanged glances, nodding as understanding dawned.

"That's brilliant," Korvian murmured. "We would've walked straight into a disaster if you hadn't caught that."

"How did we even manage without your mind, Talyn?" another added, shaking their head in admiration. "It's like you see the battlefield before it even unfolds. You always have."

Talyn glanced at Aayla, and she met his gaze with a mixture of pride and something softer, a flicker of vulnerability in her otherwise unyielding demeanour. Her thoughts brushed against his. *See? I told you. This is your place now, too.*

His lips twitched in a faint smile, and he turned back to the console, his focus sharpening. "Let's move quickly. We don't have time to waste."

The following hours passed in a blur of tense coordination, each decision carrying the weight of countless lives. Together, Aayla and Talyn navigated the chaos, their combined strength anchoring the others around them as the battle tilted slowly in their favour. When the immediate crisis finally eased, the two stepped out of the Command Centre, the weight of responsibility slowly lifting from their shoulders.

"Late breakfast?" Aayla asked, her tone lighter now, though the edge of exhaustion lingered.

Talyn smirked, the corner of his mouth lifting in that familiar way she found infuriatingly endearing. "On you?"

She laughed, a sound freer than it had been all morning. "I was thinking on the table in the celestial gardens, actually."

Talyn chuckled, his eyes glinting with amusement. "Not quite the indulgence I imagined, but I suppose it'll do." He spread his wings, the motion fluid and practised, readying himself for flight. "Let's go before something else falls apart."

Aayla rolled her eyes but couldn't suppress her grin. With a shared, charged glance that lingered for a long moment, they launched into the air, their connection crackling like a spark in the wind.

As they flew, Talyn's keen eyes spotted Pyrion and Haylae walking below. Landing silently, Aayla quickly rushed into Pyrion's arms.

"Thank you, big brother," she said, her voice trembling with emotion. "For everything you've done for us."

"I would gladly give my life to protect you," Pyrion replied, his voice low but steady. "You never need to thank me for that."

Talyn watched the raw emotion on Aayla's face and felt a pang of longing. He envied the bond they shared, wishing he had a sibling with whom he shared such a deep bond. "I'll give you three a moment," he said softly, stepping back.

"No, Talyn," Pyrion said earnestly, turning to him. "You're as much a part of this conversation as anyone."

Talyn hesitated, then shook his head gently. "You were by my side during the trial when it mattered most, Pyrion, but Aayla missed you terribly. You both deserve this moment together. I'll go arrange some food for her. I'll see you in a minute."

Pyrion's expression softened, and Haylae leaned over to kiss his cheek affectionately before Talyn walked away, leaving them to share the moment they so deeply deserved.

Talyn walked towards the garden, his steps quiet on the soft earth. As he entered, the gentle murmur of conversation faded, and all eyes turned toward him. He felt the weight of their stares and paused, uncertainty creeping into his heart.

Just as he was about to turn and leave, the gathering rose as one before silently bowing deeply towards him.

Their faces were solemn, their movements deliberate, and Talyn realised they were offering him a profound sign of respect.

The air was thick with unspoken recognition, a deep acknowledgment of all he had endured. He stood rooted to the spot, the significance of the moment settling over him like a heavy cloak as the crowd continued to bow around him in reverent silence.

Talyn nodded in quiet acknowledgment, the gesture small but deeply significant. The tension that had gripped Talyn's chest began to ease, the weight of years of alienation and lies slowly lifting. For the first time in his life, he felt something new, something unexpected. He felt acceptance.

The crowd began to straighten, and the quiet murmur of conversation slowly returned. Talyn moved toward the nearest table, where a space had been eagerly made for him. The others around him resumed their places as the garden returned to its serene state. As he sat down, he could feel the eyes still on him, but this time, they weren't filled with judgment or curiosity. They were filled with genuine and unwavering respect.

For the first time, he felt a sense of belonging that had always eluded him.

He glanced around the table, his gaze meeting Aayla's as she walked in. Her eyes were filled with pride and reassurance, a silent reminder that he had always been worthy of this moment. He smiled at her, feeling their connection strengthen with each passing second.

"So," Ophelian asked, curiosity in her voice, "will you be staying on Nannuval for long?"

Aayla cuddled into Talyn's side and tilted her head in thought. "We haven't decided yet. I've missed being home, but... I can't shake the guilt of leaving those who still need me. Still, I think we could use some rest for a while..." Her gaze flickered to Talyn, her expression thoughtful.

Talyn reached out, his hand brushing against her cheek as he tucked a loose strand of hair behind her ear. "I've rested long enough. It's time to go where your heart tells you we need to be."

Aayla's lips tugged into a small smile, the warmth in her eyes softening as she bit her lip in thought. "I do miss helping the humans," she admitted, her voice quiet but resolute. "And I feel like we're not done there yet. There's something big coming... something we're meant to stop. I could feel it in the vision."

"Then it's settled," Talyn said with a decisive nod. "We'll return to Earth soon. There are many friends who will be very glad to see you again."

Aayla's smile deepened, and her heart lightened by his words. "And you too," she whispered, her voice thick with affection.

They exchanged smiles as the warmth of their decision settled over them.

Talyn's thoughts drifted to Seth, wondering if his friend had faced any repercussions for trying to help him. A sense of relief washed over him, knowing they'd soon be back to support him and set things right.

Talyn cupped Aayla's face, his gaze softening as he leaned down to kiss her. The kiss was slow, infused with the weight of everything they had endured and everything still to come. In that moment, their energies intertwined, and he felt the weight of years of secrecy, fear, and distance fall away. For the first time, they were free to love openly, without hesitation.

A deep, unfamiliar sensation stirred within him, something he couldn't quite place, a feeling both new and old.

Aayla nestled against his chest, her eyes shimmering with affection as she gazed up at him. "I think my eyes are betraying me, but you almost look like you're glowing." Her voice was teasing yet full of warmth.

Talyn chuckled softly. It wasn't the first time someone told him he was glowing. Seth had said something similar back on Earth, though Talyn had dismissed it at the time. He extended a wing and glanced at it briefly, noticing a faint glow emanating from it. But in that moment, he was too content to give it much thought. That was a mystery for another day.

"So," he teased, curling his wing protectively around her, "when does the next ship leave?"

ABOUT THE AUTHOR

578

Faye Larkspur is a passionate storyteller who lives with her husband, two young children, and a happily chaotic household of beloved pets.

When she's not writing about women who fight hard, love harder, and defy impossible odds, she can be found hidden in the garden, chasing adventures on snowy mountains, or exploring new corners of the world. She believes in the power of soul-deep love, family, and the bravery it takes to claim your own fate.

Between Blood and Desire is her debut novel, born from a dream and written for all who believe in the power of love.